P

"Non-stop action makes Smits' novel a fulfilling read."
—*RT Book Reviews* on *The Marine Finds His Family*

"Compelling and beautifully written...honest and unflinching."
—*Goodreads* on *A Family for Tyler*

Praise for *New York Times* bestselling author Kathleen Eagle

"A good man is hard to find, but a romance by Eagle is a good place to start."
—*Kirkus Reviews* on *The Last Good Man*

"Beautiful writing coupled with endearing, genuine characters in need of healing makes this one story that will touch the heart deeply."
—*RT Book Reviews* on *One Brave Cowboy*

"Eagle...delivers her signature energy."
—*Publishers Weekly*

"Eagle's smooth, sweet storytelling works magic on the emotions of the reader who expects slightly larger-than-life fantasy along with her romance reading."
—*WNBC.com*

HOME ON THE RANCH:
TRUSTING A HERO

—————— ⚒ ——————

ANGEL SMITS
New York Times Bestselling Author
KATHLEEN EAGLE

HARLEQUIN® HOME ON THE RANCH
™

ISBN-13: 978-1-335-50711-2

First published as A Family for Tyler by Harlequin Books in 2014 and The Prodigal Cowboy by Harlequin Books in 2012.

Home on the Ranch: Trusting a Hero Copyright © 2018 by Harlequin Books S.A.

The publisher acknowledges the copyright holders of the individual works as follows:

A Family for Tyler Copyright © 2014 by Angel Smits

The Prodigal Cowboy Copyright © 2012 by Kathleen Eagle

Recycling programs for this product may not exist in your area.

This edition published by arrangement with Harlequin Books S.A.

For questions and comments about the quality of this book, please contact us at CustomerService@Harlequin.com.

® and TM are trademarks of Harlequin Enterprises Limited or its corporate affiliates. Trademarks indicated with ® are registered in the United States Patent and Trademark Office, the Canadian Intellectual Property Office and in other countries.

Printed in U.S.A.

CONTENTS

Angel Smits shares a big yellow house, complete with gingerbread and a porch swing, in Colorado with her husband, daughter and Maggie, their border collie mix. Winning the Romance Writers of America's Golden Heart® Award was the highlight of her writing career, until her first Harlequin book hit the shelves. Her social work background inspires her characters while improv writing allows her to torture them. It's a rough job, but someone's got to do it.

Books by Angel Smits

Harlequin Superromance

A Chair at the Hawkins Table

Last Chance at the Someday Café
The Ballerina's Stand
The Marine Finds His Family
A Family for Tyler
Seeking Shelter
A Message for Julia

Visit the Author Profile page at Harlequin.com for more titles.

A FAMILY FOR TYLER

ANGEL SMITS

I've been blessed in my life to have grown up in a close family, and to have built one of my own with my husband, Ron. But there are two people who complete our home. Jennifer and Joseph, you are, without a doubt, the best kids I could ever ask for. Thanks for putting up with all that goes with having a writer for a mom—and for not thinking I'm too crazy. I love you both.

when they'd barreled through as children. Nor did the hinges squeal to remind Dad it was time to oil them.

It simply opened to a dark, musty room. A house full of stuff but empty of people.

Just then, a red convertible parked across the street. Both Wyatt and Addie turned to watch their younger sister Mandy climb out, her long blond hair shining in the sun. Her sky-high heels tapped across the paved street as she headed toward them.

Right behind her, the bumper of Tara's Jeep almost kissed the chrome of the convertible. The engine rattled a moment after she turned it off. There was no door on the side of the vehicle to slam. She simply swung her legs out and landed on sneaker-clad feet and trotted up the walk.

The shiny gray Lexus that pulled into the drive next would normally turn heads, but they were all used to Jason's flash. Even his black suit looked polished to a glow.

Last, as always, DJ arrived on his monstrous motorcycle, gliding up to the curb and just barely stopping from parking on Mom's pristine lawn. After removing his dark helmet, he cut the rough engine and silence returned to the quiet neighborhood.

They were all here.

No one spoke a word. Wyatt watched his brothers and sisters traipse in one by one. His family. Three of the six wore sunglasses, even as they entered the dim interior of the house.

Oddly enough, they passed the living room, the front hall and, in a long-honed habit, settled around the kitchen table. Six chairs. Six kids. No need to pull out the spare ones in the hall closet. They hadn't used them

CHAPTER ONE

WYATT HAWKINS PULLED his black 4x4 pickup into the familiar drive and killed the engine. The huge truck was well suited for the wide Texas plains of his ranch, but here in Austin, at Mom's house with all these close-knit homes, it seemed out of place. He stayed in the cab and stared through the dirt-streaked windshield at the place he still considered home.

But without Mom, it would never be the same.

The faint sound of footsteps made him glance in the rearview mirror. His sister Addie headed up the walk. Her shoulder-length blond hair and flowing black skirt rippled in the breeze. She stopped at the truck door and rapped, unnecessarily, on the window. He rolled the glass down and peered into her tired, sad face.

"You ready for this?" he whispered, hoping she'd say no and let them all off the hook. Being Addie, she didn't, of course.

"As ready as I'll ever be," she said on a deep sigh.

She hesitated a moment, then kept walking to the front door as if she knew by stopping she might never get started again. Wyatt climbed out of the truck and silently followed.

She unlocked the front door and pushed the heavy wood open.

The door didn't smack against the wall like it had

that often anyway, since they'd seldom all been home at the same time.

"Looks like we're all here." DJ spoke first, rubbing his hand over his military buzz cut as if even after two years, he still wasn't used to it.

"I guess we should have brought lunch." Tara's voice sounded too much like Mom's. They all smiled, missing the woman they'd said a permanent goodbye to only a few hours ago.

The laughter and tears mingled. The sunglasses came off and the healing began.

"Mom loved this room." Tara stood and went to the cupboard. The coffee, sugar and creamer were just where Mom had always kept them. She started a pot and plunked the containers on the table.

"We all did," Wyatt agreed, walking to the silverware drawer where he pulled out five spoons. Wyatt didn't need one. He took his coffee black.

As the coffee brewed and they fixed their cups, they talked. Voices overlapped and memories entwined. Even Jason relaxed, pulling off his jacket and rolling up his pristine shirtsleeves. Mandy's heels fell to the floor in a mangled heap of leather. "This feels right," she said as she rubbed her toes.

Addie smiled sadly. "Mom would have liked this— us all here together."

Wyatt silently leaned on the counter as Addie's words jabbed at his heart. She was right. If only they'd taken more time when Mom was alive. Sipping his coffee, he took in the view. Normally this group was a rowdy, teasing, rambunctious bunch. Today, rightfully so, they were quiet. He missed them all, missed who they were. Not just because Mom was gone, and they'd just come

from the cemetery…but because they were all scattered
across the country and he didn't see them often. Who
knew when, or if, they'd ever be together again.

Addie was the only one who still lived in Austin. But
the wear and tear of caring for Mom as she'd battled can-
cer showed on Addie's face. He set his cup down and
reached out to rub her shoulders.

She'd filled her coffee cup first yet it was the fullest.
Not because she'd been doing most of the talking, either.
He watched her, feeling the tension in her shoulders,
noting the circles beneath her eyes. She'd been Mom's
caregiver clear up until the end. He'd helped when he
could, driving in every weekend to give her a break,
but the ranch was a full-time operation two hours away,
never mind that he hadn't known what to do. The toll
that the past few months had taken showed in the lines
around Addie's eyes.

She turned her cup around, the ceramic making a
soft grinding sound against the old wood. She turned
it again. And yet a third time. He knew, without being
told, that she was formulating what to say. He almost
held his breath waiting for her.

"Those last couple days," she began.

Wyatt reached out, as if subconsciously thinking he
could stop her. Then he had to stop *himself.* She needed
to say this.

She took a deep breath and started again. "The social
worker at the hospice called it life review," she whispered. "Mom talked about her childhood. I learned a
lot about her family. Stories I'd never heard before." She
didn't go into those stories, but he saw everyone perk
up, hoping, like him, that she would.

The silence grew and for a minute Wyatt thought

maybe Addie had decided not to go on. Tara spoke up first. "What kinds of things did she talk about?"

Tara looked ready to break. The youngest, she'd always been coddled by them. While that babying hadn't necessarily been the best for encouraging Tara to grow up, the old habits helped Addie regroup. She shook off the trance and faintly smiled at Tara.

"Lots of things. I… I started writing them down. I'll get them together for you all. But I think there's one story you should hear now." Addie took a deep breath. "About a week ago, we were sitting out on that big old porch. The orderly, William, you all met him?" She looked around and they all nodded. He was a big man with a gentle touch. "He carried her out there, all wrapped up in that quilt Aunt Bess gave her. We sat out on the swing."

Addie cleared her throat and took a deep swallow of her obviously cooled coffee. Everyone waited. "She told me about when she met Daddy."

Wyatt smiled. He'd always thought it was strange that his sisters, well into their adult years, still referred to their father as Daddy. Now he appreciated the affection that went with the moniker.

"I'd never heard her talk about that," Addie continued. "Did you know he used to drive a cattle truck out to her dad's ranch? Out where you live, Wyatt. He'd come out every week, just about the time she was getting off school. He'd pick her up and drive her the rest of the way home."

Jason chuckled, the lawyer in him coming out. "Nowadays he'd get arrested, not marry her."

Mandy laughed and swatted Jason's arm. "You are so

not a romantic. He was what, two years older than her? He had to have been only eighteen."

Jason had the smarts to laugh at himself. "Go on, Add, tell us the rest."

"Seems Gramps didn't like him much. But Daddy's father paid the best for the stock. Daddy was actually bribing him to let him see Mom." Addie genuinely smiled. "I had no idea they snuck off and eloped the day after she graduated."

"No, they didn't," Mandy protested. "What about all those wedding pictures?" The book was still upstairs, Wyatt knew. Addie was taking it with her. He'd helped her find it and wrap it up just this morning.

"They had the formal wedding the next summer, once Gramps cooled off."

"Wow." DJ got up to refill his cup. Shaking his head, he turned his back on them, looking out the kitchen window over the yard. "There's so much we'll never know about her." His sadness filled the room.

"Maybe." Addie turned in her chair and met Wyatt's gaze. He nodded and moved closer to their youngest brother. The man was a soldier to the rest of the world, but here, he was the little boy they'd all patched up a million times.

"We all have our secrets, Deej. It's not a bad thing," Addie said.

DJ met Wyatt's gaze. The soldier was back and Wyatt immediately missed the boy. "Yeah, I suppose."

Addie stood, too, dumping her cold coffee down the drain. "Mom had a wonderful life, and she gave us all an amazing home."

Addie took her gaze from him and looked over her shoulder at the others. Finally, Addie's composure fled.

Her shoulders drooped and Wyatt did as he always did; he tried to fix things by pulling her into a reassuring hug.

"I only hope I can be as good of a mom if I have kids someday," she said.

Silence, punctuated by only a few soft sniffles, filled the room. Finally, Addie moved away and Wyatt felt cast adrift. He vaguely wondered who'd been comforting whom. As he settled back in his seat, Addie reached into her purse and took out several folded sheets of paper. She slowly handed them out.

"Mom divided everything. Here are your lists. All we have to decide on is this." She ran a loving hand along the edge of the huge, old table.

They each looked down at the chair they were sitting in. Not a single eye was dry. Wyatt found himself caressing the chair's arms, just as their father used to do so long ago. Mandy turned and ran a finger over the curved wooden back.

"Can… Do we have to… I mean…" Tara hiccuped and her words faded. Silence reigned for an entire moment. Then pandemonium broke loose.

"I want it."

"Me, too. But I don't have room right now."

"I can't imagine being without it."

Wyatt listened as their voices mingled and no one seemed to fully hear what the others said. Finally, he stood, an idea forming. He whistled to get their attention. "I know what we can do."

"What?" Addie looked at him, hope and a bit of panic in her eyes.

"None of us needs this whole set or this huge table. Let's each take our chair. I know it sounds silly, but it's the one thing that will always remind us of Mom and Dad."

Again, silence. Then they looked around and everyone nodded. "What about the table?" Addie asked.

"Let's leave it with the house. It's too monstrous to move, anyway." The real estate agent was scheduled to come tomorrow and put it on the market. Maybe a new family would love it, as well.

Again, they all agreed—an unusual occurrence. After they'd taken their lists and made plans to move their things out of the house, the chairs were lined up in the front hall. No one wanted to leave them behind today.

Wyatt and Jason helped DJ find bungee cords in the garage to strap his chair on the big bike. Then they worked to fit Jason's in the backseat of the Lexus.

Mandy looked odd driving away in the red convertible with the four legs of her chair sticking up in the air, but no less strange than Tara's Jeep with her chair strapped in the back with the remaining bungee cords.

Addie had walked over, her house being only a few blocks away. Wyatt put her chair in the truck's bed with his and gave her a ride home.

She climbed into the big truck, not bothering to look back. Wyatt glanced in the rearview mirror and then quickly away. "Goodbyes suck." He reached out and squeezed her hand.

"The decision about the chairs was good. Thank you," she whispered.

"Yeah."

They drove in silence until they reached her equally small drive. She didn't open the door right away, then just as she curled her fingers around the handle, she looked over at him. The sorrow in her eyes nearly broke his heart.

But for the first time since he'd learned he had a baby

sister and took on the unspoken responsibility for her, there was nothing he could do to fix her hurt.

THREE MONTHS LATER, to the day, Wyatt sat in his truck again and stared at another empty house. This one was clapboard with narrow windows. On the front porch that ran downhill, a small boy sat on the uneven steps.

The boy looked as if he'd lost his best friend. Which—if he was who Wyatt thought he was—he probably had. The world the boy had always known was about to change, irreversibly. Forever. Wyatt swallowed the lump in his throat, dreading the role he had to play in this mess.

The boy rested his chin in the palm of his hand and smacked a stick against the sidewalk in an uneven beat. Wyatt reached into his jacket pocket and pulled out the letter he'd received nearly a week ago. The paper looked small and white against his suntanned hand, but what snagged his attention was the picture. Damn, the kid looked so much like DJ had at that age. It was spooky. He refolded the letter and slipped it back into his pocket.

He stared at the boy as his thoughts spun. How had this happened? How could DJ have had a child he'd never known about? And why the hell had the woman decided *now* to contact him? No answers came to Wyatt, which frustrated him even further.

It wasn't the boy's fault who his parents were, or how they'd behaved. But Wyatt knew he'd probably be the one to pay the heaviest price.

The hot Texas sun beat down on Wyatt's shoulders as he climbed out of the truck. A warm wind slipped past, seemingly unnoticed by the glum boy.

The kid did, however, look up as Wyatt crossed the

broken walk. The old metal gate creaked when he pushed it open. The boy's eyes narrowed with distrust. "Who are you?" His words sounded more like an accusation than a question.

Wyatt stopped. "I'm your uncle, Wyatt Hawkins. You're Tyler?" Silence. For a second Wyatt wasn't sure if he'd get an answer.

"Tyler Easton, yes, sir," the boy whispered, and continued smacking his stick on the sidewalk.

"Is your mother around?" The woman he'd talked to on the phone yesterday had assured him she'd be here. She had a lot to answer for.

The boy looked up again, and Wyatt swallowed the sucker punch that hit him. No child's eyes should hold that much hurt.

"She left."

"Left? When?"

"S'morning. Said someone from my dad's family was comin' and I was s'posed to go with 'em. Is that you?"

Wyatt didn't know how to answer. He pulled the paper out of his shirt pocket and unfolded it. "I suppose I am."

"I was 'fraid so." The boy looked back at the ground, slowly drawing circles with the stick.

Wyatt read the letter again. How did you tell a child that his mother didn't want him anymore? That she'd waited until his dad, a man he'd never met, shipped overseas? A man who couldn't speak for himself from a thousand miles away.

Men didn't deny their flesh and blood. Wyatt and DJ might have their differences, but at the core, he knew DJ took his responsibilities seriously. His brother would claim the boy, but until he could, Wyatt was all he had.

"You ready to go?" He didn't think twice about his role in this boy's life. Responsibility had always been something Wyatt easily shouldered, and he didn't hesitate now.

He'd already gotten Jason's legal advice, and his brother was working to contact DJ. Just looking at the kid, there was little doubt Tyler was DJ's son. And Addie would be thrilled to have someone to take care of once Wyatt told her about him. But right now his sister needed the vacation he'd finally convinced her to take.

"I packed my stuff." Tyler used the stick to point at two plastic grocery bags beside the door.

"That's all of it?"

"Yep. Mama took the rest. She told me to be ready and not tick you off."

"Is that so?" Wyatt's chest hurt, for himself, for the boy and mostly for the man who didn't even know he had a son. DJ was in for one heck of a surprise when, and if, he ever got back home.

Slowly, Wyatt stepped toward Tyler and sat on the step beside him. He figured he could take a few minutes to start to get to know his nephew, an apparently angry little boy of eight years old, who'd been totally unknown to him—to anyone in the family—until last week. If only Mom had gotten to meet him. She'd have loved Tyler, but would have killed DJ. Wyatt smiled and refocused on the boy.

Where did he start the conversation? But before he could say anything, Tyler jumped up. "Guess we'd better get goin'." He grabbed a grocery bag in each hand and returned to stand next to Wyatt.

Wyatt stood. "Guess so. Need any help with those?"

"Nope." The boy marched down the steps and was

halfway across the bare yard before Wyatt moved. The wind had died down and the only sign of life in the battered neighborhood was a flutter of curtains in the house across the street.

Wyatt hurried to catch up and open the gate for Tyler. The sooner they got out of here and left this mess behind, the better. He helped settle the bags on the truck's floorboards and buckled Tyler in before either of them said another word.

"Ready?" Wyatt met the boy's stare.

"Yep." Tyler looked straight ahead, not even glancing toward the old house as they pulled away from the curb. Wyatt glanced in the rearview mirror and thought perhaps Tyler was wiser than his years. It wasn't much to look back on. With nowhere else to go, and not much else to say, they headed through Austin and on west to the ranch where Wyatt lived…and where Tyler would be living, too.

The hot Texas wind followed them, reaching in the window and ruffling the boy's blond hair just as Wyatt used to ruffle DJ's hair. DJ had always hated anyone touching his hair. Now he was in some godforsaken corner of the world with all his blond hair long gone to the barber's razor.

Wyatt leaned back and returned his gaze to the two-lane blacktop.

What in the world were they going to do now?

CHAPTER TWO

EMILY JANE IVERS liked—no, demanded—predictability in her world. Unfortunately, few people or events lived up to her expectations.

Just like every other morning, she headed to her office. She checked with the clerk, scanned the docket and arranged her day's schedule. She loved the consistency of her calendar. It shook up her whole day if there were cross outs or Wite-Out on it.

Today, she could only stare at the normally orderly page on her desk. The bright yellow sticky notes were not expected and she felt herself tense at the events spelled out on them.

"I don't do juvenile cases." She ripped one sticky from the page and headed to Dianne's desk. "I don't do juvenile cases," she repeated to her clerk's face.

The tiny, bespectacled woman behind the counter peered over her dark frames. "You do this week. Judge Ramsey is out sick and we're covering any emergency situations."

"Emergencies?" No one really had emergencies; they just thought they needed something done *now* and called it an emergency. She and Dianne had had that conversation often enough.

"There are already two cases scheduled." Dianne

rounded the desk, her arms loaded with files. She moved from desk to desk, delivering a few to each clean blotter.

"Can't they be *re*scheduled?" Emily picked up the datebook that served as the department's master calendar, needing something to hold on to.

"No." Dianne grabbed the datebook and slapped it back on her desk. "It'll be good for you." Dianne's blue eyes sparkled behind those infernal glasses.

"No. It won't." Emily knew there was no way this was going to end well.

No case was simple, not in family court, and certainly not in the juvenile arena. Emily didn't like messy cases, and it drove her crazy whenever she had to preside over one. That was why she'd left that division. Well, part of the reason, anyway. "Do I even have any of the reports?"

"Nope." Dianne glanced up at the old clock on the wall. "You'd better hustle if you're going to get over to Ramsey's courtroom in time."

How did Dianne take control like that? Who was in charge around here, anyway? Emily resisted the urge to smile. Dianne, of course. Magistrates and judges came and went over the years, but good law clerks were priceless and Dianne was the best. She'd been in the building for nearly twenty-five years.

As Emily hurried through the familiar dim halls of the courthouse, her mind worked. She'd never had second thoughts about her job. Heck, she'd never been one to look back or second-guess her actions, period. Right now, though, she was tempted.

Reminding herself that she knew how to do this, she headed to the second floor. Still, as she climbed the steps, her hand curled tightly around the cool bar of the handrail, her heart raced.

To save time, she cut through the common area. She wasn't supposed to mingle with the public on court days, just in case she ran into one of the case participants. But she didn't have time to go all the way around to the back stairs.

Still, all the people crowding around her set her on edge. By the time she reached Judge Ramsey's chambers, her palms were damp and her heart had hit a painful pace.

She barely had time to catch her breath before Rita, the judge's clerk descended. The distraction shook Emily out of her impending panic.

"Oh, thank goodness." The older woman jumped up. "I've tried to get hold of you, but didn't have your cell number."

Emily refrained from telling her that no one had her cell number.

"The first case begins in ten minutes."

"But I haven't reviewed the files yet," Emily protested.

"That's okay. There aren't any. Just listen. The first is a pretty obvious bad situation we need to get the kids out of ASAP. The one this afternoon is pretty cut and dried. You can look at those files over lunch."

The woman grabbed the file and put it into Emily's hands, then guided Emily toward the inner door. Was *People Moving 101* a class in law clerk school?

"Then why is it an emergency?" Was that her blood pressure going through the roof? Rita looked over her glasses, much as Dianne always did. Emily frowned, reminding herself she was the magistrate, but they both knew she abhorred situations where a child was at risk.

"Mother's missing. Dad's overseas with special

forces. The uncle's requesting temporary custody until Dad's back."

Emily's entire body tensed. Her heart froze in place. No she could not, would not do this. Images of William Dean's face came to mind.

"Not permanent?" Her mind worked even if the rest of her seemed frozen in place.

"No. He's convinced his brother is coming home and will take over full parental responsibility. He just wants it temporarily."

Shadows from her last juvenile case stretched out to her and she shivered.

Cut and dried, indeed.

"The first participants will be here any minute." Rita's voice pulled Emily out of her thoughts.

Opening a small closet, Rita grabbed a thick black robe and helped Emily slip it on. Before she could ask, Rita explained. "Dianne sent it over first thing this morning."

She'd always loved her judicial robe, and today it felt like the shield she often envisioned it to be. A shield that could protect her from all the hurt and pain that entered her courtroom each day. A shield that kept her emotions hidden from the people sitting in the seats below her bench.

The ritual complete, Emily met her reflection in the door's glass. Gears in her mind shifted, and she left behind Emily Ivers and became E. J. Ivers, magistrate.

WYATT DRESSED EACH morning in jeans, a button-down shirt and his hat. Black Stetson in the winter. White straw in the summer. He was a traditional cowboy.

Over the past two weeks, he'd struggled to understand

his nephew's enchantment with T-shirts. Seldom-white T-shirts with words, pictures and at times, sayings that could be taken more than one way. Every day, Tyler pulled the T-shirt down over his worn jeans and slipped on battered tennis shoes that he never tied.

In the kitchen, filling his morning's first cup, Wyatt leaned against the counter. He had to admit he looked forward to each day's billboard or insult.

Today, Tyler didn't disappoint. He came barreling into the kitchen at breakneck speed. Across his thin chest was a tabby cat, ears perked, fangs exposed and claws extended. Wyatt took a deep swallow of his coffee as he read the bold orange words: Stressed out! He smiled. It wasn't typical for most eight-year-olds. But then, Tyler wasn't a typical eight-year-old.

Tyler wasn't exactly stressed, but he was definitely in training to lead a type-A-personality life. The pockets of his jeans bulged and Wyatt wondered what he'd stuffed inside.

"That what you're wearing to court?" Wyatt asked softly, trying to sound as if it didn't matter to him. He'd learned that pushing Tyler was like pushing DJ at that age. A waste.

"S'all I got." Tyler didn't look at Wyatt. He busied himself dragging a box of cereal out of the cupboard and grabbing the milk carton from the fridge.

"We could stop at the store and pick up a button-down shirt for you. We have time."

Tyler stilled. "I ain't got no money."

"You know, your dad does. We'll use his." Wyatt had learned early on that Tyler didn't like taking money from him. He'd sworn he "wasn't no charity case." That backbone would serve Tyler well, later. Wyatt had circumvented the boy by telling him it was DJ's job to support him. Tyler liked that idea. Wyatt used it all the time now.

"Well, I s'pose I should look businessy."

The kid seriously needed grammar lessons, but Wyatt knew that was the least of their problems at this point. "Then it's settled. Hurry and finish breakfast so we can get going."

"I can wear my jeans, right?" Tyler looked up, panicked, from his cereal.

"Yeah, those are fine." Wyatt wondered what was important about those particular jeans.

Another thing he'd learned was that Tyler's emotions weren't hidden, they just didn't always make adult sense. Settling in the kitchen chair, Wyatt finished his coffee as Tyler worked out the games on the back of the cereal box.

Again, Wyatt cursed DJ as he reminded himself that DJ didn't even know he had a son.

Taking care of Tyler until DJ came home was all Wyatt could do right now, and this afternoon's court date would get that ball rolling. As he looked down at the boy, Wyatt realized it wasn't enough. But it was all he had.

Tyler was silent the entire trip into town but by the time they reached the courthouse, the new white shirt already had a dirt smudge on one elbow. Wyatt could only shake his head and smile.

Despite the quiet trip, the whole process of getting into the courthouse fascinated Tyler. His eyes grew wide with wonder as they went through security. The guards smiled at his questions, and Wyatt felt an innate sense of pride for his new nephew.

Now both of them stared at the double doors leading into the courtroom. "Well, here we are." Wyatt spoke with as much reassurance as he could.

"Yep," Tyler whispered.

"Come on. Let's get this over with." The sound of Wyatt's boots and the scuff of Tyler's tennis shoes seemed loud as they pushed open the doors and walked across the marble floor.

The courtroom didn't look at all like the intimidating rooms he'd seen on TV. This room was smaller with only two tables, a desk that sat up on a dais and a high chair, which he presumed was a witness chair. A brass tag on the desk read, E. J. Ivers, magistrate.

"That desk is big." Tyler's eyes were still wide with wonder.

"Sure is." Just then, the young attorney Wyatt had met with a few days ago arrived. She smiled distractedly and guided them to the table on the left.

Soon a woman came in and sat down at a small side desk and a man in a uniform opened a door at the back of the room. The judge entered and the entire mood of the room became formal.

Wyatt saw Tyler swallow, and he resisted the urge himself. He put his hand on Tyler's shoulder and squeezed.

"YOUR HONOR." THE attorney finally spoke. Emily forced herself to concentrate on the young woman's words instead of on the faces of the man and boy seated at the big table. They weren't the ghosts in her mind, she reminded herself.

"We're asking that Mr. Hawkins be given temporary custody of Tyler Easton until his father, David James Hawkins, returns from overseas."

"Temporary?" Emily looked over at the boy, Tyler.

"What about the mother?" The sadness that filled the child's eyes was quickly blinked away.

"She's abandoned him." The attorney lifted a thin sheet of paper. "I've labeled her letter Exhibit A."

"Could you bring that to me?"

The woman's heels were a sharp staccato on the tile floor as she approached the bench.

Emily read the letter and frowned. "Is this correct?" She faced the man sitting beside the boy. "Your brother doesn't even know he has a son?" Mr. Hawkins looked surprised at being addressed.

"Uh, yes. We're trying to reach him. He's special forces, so it's tough. He hasn't been informed yet, as far as I know."

"What makes you believe he's going to be willing to take on a child, when and if, he returns?"

"My brother will accept his responsibilities." The man's voice was hard, telling Emily that even if his brother didn't want Tyler, this man would do everything in his power to make him accept the boy.

She leaned back in her chair, the swivel giving her a better view of the man. Her stomach did a strange little flip-flop and she struggled to ignore it. "Who's the caseworker?"

"Elizabeth Morgan is assigned to this case. Unfortunately, she just went out on maternity leave," the attorney said.

Messy, Emily reminded herself. Juvenile cases were always messy. She knew the answer to her next question, but needed it in the record. "Can't we get another caseworker on it?"

"The county is already overloaded. With the recent budget cuts, all caseworkers are carrying double loads."

Emily sighed. They didn't need a caseworker *today*, but she would prefer one. If she'd just gone on leave, there should be a preliminary report here somewhere. Damn. She wished she'd had time to review the whole file thoroughly.

"I'm not comfortable with the state of this case," she said directly to the attorney. "What did the caseworker recommend?"

"There are no recommendations in place yet," the attorney explained.

"What about provisions in case something happens to the father?" Emily nailed the attorney with a direct stare. "The military requires that."

"Yes, ma'am. But the father left without knowing the boy existed. That's not been set up."

Emily looked over at the man. His jaw moved and he seemed to want to speak. She held up a hand. She needed to think without being interrupted. "Temporary custody isn't an option here." She met both the attorney's and the man's stares, daring them to disagree. "I'll only grant permanent custody." There needed to be someone there for the long haul, someone who'd be there when the parents didn't show up or take on their responsibilities.

"No!" Tyler spoke for the first time.

Emily looked down at the boy, who seemed unable to remain in control any longer. "Don't you want to have your uncle as your guardian?" Images of The Boys Home flashed in her mind and she cringed. Families needed to stay together.

"I don't want it to be forever."

"Why not?"

"Mama's coming back. She promised."

Emily's heart broke and hurt for the boy. This was

part of why she hated juvenile cases. People didn't keep promises, and unless she forced them to, this boy would end up a ward of the court like so many before him. No, this man needed to be held accountable and not just for the short-term.

She drummed her fingers on the desktop and leaned forward in her chair. "Young man, why don't you come up here so you and I can talk?"

Tyler glanced up at his uncle, the apprehension strong in his eyes.

"Go on, Tyler. It's okay," the man urged, his big hands patting the boy's shoulder.

"Right here." Emily tore her gaze away from the poignant sight and walked down the two steps to stand beside the witness chair. Tyler walked slowly toward her, and she helped him climb up into the high seat.

"There, now I can see you better." She smiled to reassure him.

"I can see you better, too." He grinned and her heart caught. He was going to be a looker someday, and the resemblance to his uncle was all too close. She cleared her throat and her mind. "So, Tyler. Do you know why your mom left?"

He shrugged. "Nope. She just said I'd be better off and safer with my dad."

"Not your uncle?"

"We didn't know my dad was gone."

Emily nodded, not pleased with the lack of family connections.

"Does your mom have family?"

Tyler nodded. "Grandpa and Grandma Easton are old. Too old, Mama said, for a boy like me. My aunt Nancy has two kids. Mama said they caused enough headaches since Uncle Willie left last year."

This story just got better. Emily realized his mother—Tammie, was that her name?—would have no secrets if Tyler knew them. She could pump him for information, but didn't think she needed to. Not yet, anyway. The knowledge did give her a higher level of comfort.

She looked back at Wyatt Hawkins. "Do you know any of these people?"

He shook his head. "I'm in the process of trying to find them. No luck yet."

"Keep looking," she instructed then turned back to Tyler. "So you've never met your dad?"

"Nope. But Mom told me lots of things. And I have stuff that proves I'm his kid." The boy's chin notched up.

"You do?"

"Uh-huh." Slowly, Tyler stood and reached into the bulging pockets of his jeans. He pulled out a couple plastic lizards, an old playing card and a key that had been wound with neon-green yarn. "This is stuff Mama said my dad gave her."

She couldn't wait to hear this one. "What are they?"

"These two lizards are like the ones on the beach where they met. In Florida." He handed Emily each one very carefully. "This is a card from when they played stip poker."

"Stip?" She nearly bit her tongue. She shouldn't have asked but the question just came out.

"Yeah. When you bet your clothes."

Emily was proud of herself for not reacting, though she heard a stifled groan come from his uncle. "And the key?"

"She said it went to somethin' he had back home where he kept his really special stuff."

Emily took the key and held it up. "Do you recognize this, Mr. Hawkins?"

He was looking at them both, his gaze intense, and he squinted at the key. She walked over to the table where he sat and handed him the key. He turned it over a couple times.

"Yeah." His voice broke. "It goes to Dad's old shop."

His voice sounded sad and wistful. For a long minute, she looked down at the seated man, realizing that she had possibly misjudged him. He tilted his head back and their gazes clashed.

There was no angry glare, no macho attitude. Just emotions she couldn't quite identify, and a pleading question. Her gut told her he was a good man. She swallowed, uncomfortable with the idea. To give herself a moment to think, she walked slowly back up to the judge's seat.

"I'll make you a deal." She faced Tyler, hoping she wouldn't regret this, and made an offer. "I'll make it provisional. If at any time, either of your parents returns, we can meet again. Okay?"

Tyler responded, "What's 'probisional' mean?"

"It means it can be changed," she explained. "But until they come back, your uncle's responsible for you."

"It'll work out, Ty," the man mumbled as if he didn't want her to hear. She appreciated his reassurances to the boy, but she couldn't quite let herself believe him. The expression on the boy's face told her that he wasn't buying it, either.

"And—" she said.

The man stared at her.

"Until the caseworker is back to work, I want you to meet with me. I'll be your caseworker for now."

"Your Honor, that's rather irregular," the counselor objected.

"I don't much care. This case doesn't make me comfortable. Until it does, I'll keep an eye on things. Write up the orders, counselor, and I'll sign them. Anything else?"

"No, Your Honor."

"We're adjourned." Emily stood and didn't bother to look back at the man or the boy. She needed to keep a clear head in her work and that small face and those reassuring hands were already tugging at something she never allowed in her courtroom.

Her heart.

CHAPTER THREE

A WEEK LATER, Wyatt found himself headed toward the county court offices. The building was old. Not ancient old as to be pretty, but built-in-the-1970s old, with harvest-gold siding. Wyatt stared at the ugly-as-sin building and frowned. Why had the judge asked to see him without Tyler? What was she up to?

Not knowing the answer made him uncomfortable. Very uncomfortable. He'd climbed out of his truck into the late-spring heat and headed for the glass doors. By the time he entered the cool air-conditioned inside, he was irritated.

He hadn't dealt much with the legal system—that was his brother Jason's arena—but he'd been in the cattle industry a long time, so he had plenty of experience with government agencies. This felt very similar.

Hat in hand, the brim cupped in his wide palm, he took a calming breath and approached the desk. The brunette sitting there looked up at him over a pair of half glasses that seemed to practically glow in the dark. What color were those supposed to be?

"Can I help you?"

"I have an appointment with Magistrate Ivers." Wyatt didn't even recognize his own voice. So formal. So distant.

"I'll let her know." The woman stood and walked down the short hall to disappear behind a thick wooden door.

He sat down on one of the chairs lined up neatly along the far wall. He was the only person here and the room was quiet. Where the outside of the building had hurt his eyes, this office was polished and modern. He liked the marble and glass.

A rack of brochures on how to be a guardian caught his eye. He'd just read the titles on the third row when the woman returned. "She'll be right out."

Wyatt nodded and stared at the sign beside the door. E. J. Ivers. He leaned closer to read her full name printed in smaller letters beneath. His frown deepened.

In Wyatt's book, E. J. Ivers, magistrate, was *not* supposed to be Emily Ivers of the soft, feminine variety. Before last week, he'd had a vision of a graying older man with a booming voice. Or maybe one of those polished judges like on TV. Showed what he knew.

All through court, Wyatt had been stunned by the much younger, much prettier, definitely female judge. The long, black robes had hidden everything except the collar of the vibrant pink blouse that had set off her dark hair.

On the bench she'd been thorough and direct, and intelligence had snapped in her dark eyes. He ran his fingers through his hair in frustration. Now here he sat outside her office wondering what the hell to expect next.

EMILY GLARED AT the stacks of papers and files lined up on the conference table that took up nearly half her official chambers.

Even if she wanted to have a meeting here, she couldn't. The piles never really seemed to shrink, though she knew Dianne frequently shuffled them around.

Emily stalked past the stacks and flopped down into

her desk chair. She arranged the current file neatly on the blotter, reluctant to add more to the table.

She was tired. Court had been exhausting this week, covering for Judge Ramsey as well as her own responsibilities. And then there'd been Wyatt Hawkins and his nephew.

Emily leaned her head back and closed her eyes. Half of last night she'd tossed and turned, seeing Wyatt's handsome face and feeling his reassuring hand on *her* own shoulder. She'd awoken before dawn this morning from a particularly vivid dream so clear she'd known there was no sleep left.

Now here she sat, waiting for the man to arrive at her office, barely able to keep her eyelids open. Shaking herself out of the stupor, she sat forward and opened the file.

Tyler Easton was an adorable kid. Instead of seeing the brown folder, she pictured his earnest young face. He wanted so badly to believe his mom was coming back for him and that his dad would want him. He'd pulled every worldly possession from his pockets to prove to her how important he was, to prove he belonged.

She smiled, wondering at the depth of those pockets. How could a boy carry so much around with him?

Once again, Wyatt Hawkins's face came to mind. He cared for the boy—it showed in the softening of his eyes as he watched Tyler, in the protective hand he kept on the boy's shoulder as they sat together and the reluctant smile that tugged at his lips. By granting provisional custody, she'd preserved Tyler's hopes and given the uncle an out, if necessary.

Emily flipped through the file and reread her notes. Next she pulled out the preliminary caseworker's notes that had been in the file, but which she hadn't had time to review until afterward. She frowned as she reread the tightly typed paragraphs.

Wyatt Hawkins lived in the country in an aged ranch house. He'd owned it for just over five years. He was single and his family lived in Austin, a two-hour drive away. No one here to help him raise a child. No wife. No mother. No sisters. Not even a girlfriend?

That thought lingered just a moment too long.

The caseworker had managed to visit the house before going on maternity leave, billing for eighteen point seven miles from town. The house had been clean, uncluttered and drafty. It sat just yards away from the barn and outbuildings. *An environment fraught with potential for risk and danger.*

Emily almost smiled. She'd grown up on a farm far from the safety of city streets with their gang shootings and drug deals.

The woman's final remarks were short and to the point. The caseworker didn't believe Wyatt Hawkins could provide a safe family environment for a little boy.

Emily sighed. Why did she feel as if he was the enemy? She'd never felt like this before about a case or a man. It totally unnerved her. *He* unnerved her.

One last look at the caseworker's notes and she moved them to the back of the file. Something about all this didn't feel right. She needed to figure out what that something was.

Dianne didn't bother knocking when she came in. She never did if Emily was alone. She grinned broadly and winked at Emily. "A hunky cowboy is here, right on time. Whew." Dianne fanned herself. "That man's sure got somethin' goin' on." She grabbed half a dozen files off the table. "And if you don't want some, I'm ready for a hefty helpin'."

The clerk left the room before Emily could respond. She never should have asked him to come here. She should have kept it all in the courtroom where she had distance and her robes to protect her. And where Dianne couldn't add her two cents' worth. Standing, she took a deep breath and smoothed her skirt. This was just a case. He was just a man.

Just a man. If only.

WYATT LEARNED THAT "right out" meant at least another five minutes. Finally, the woman he'd last seen in the courtroom stepped through the doorway. Instead of the dark robes, she wore a pale blue blouse and narrow black skirt. There were the curves he'd suspected.

Her hair hung loose around her face instead of being pulled back. For an instant, he simply stared. She was pretty. Very pretty.

"Mr. Hawkins. Welcome. Won't you come in?" She smiled stiffly and extended her hand.

She sounded so distant and formal. He frowned, trying to chase the worry away as he followed her down a narrow hall.

The walls of her office were lined with shelves of thick legal books. She led him past a conference table stacked high with files to a pair of wing-backed chairs that faced a Chippendale desk. Not a thing was out of place on the desk, but she straightened the blotter before sitting down behind it, anyway.

He got the impression she was trying to intimidate him for some strange reason. She didn't know him, he reasoned, or she'd have realized she was wasting her time. Wyatt Hawkins wasn't easily intimidated.

"I know you're wondering why I asked you to come here without Tyler."

"Yeah, it's crossed my mind."

"I need to know the truth." She scooted back in her chair. "Please be honest with me—do you really want to take on the responsibility of being Tyler's guardian?"

There was no hesitation in her stare. He knew she hadn't become a judge by being a wilting flower, but the distance in her eyes sent a shiver through him. He knew a smokescreen when he saw one.

And this lady had more than smoke around her. She'd put up full, solid walls. What the hell had he done to piss her off? Taken aback, he shifted into negotiation mode and met her gaze with a stubborn one of his own.

EMILY STARED AT the man from across her desk. She'd purposefully put the desk between them. Originally, she'd thought to sit in the other chair, beside him, seeking a friendly, nonthreatening meeting.

That plan had flown out the window the minute she'd seen him sitting there in the lobby. He'd taken up all the space in the narrow chairs. Now he seemed to inhabit her entire office, stealing all the oxygen from the room.

She took a deep breath, waiting to hear him admit that he really didn't want the boy. That he had a life, and a nephew he'd never met before had no place in it. It was what she expected. His words startled her.

"Ms. Ivers," he said through clenched teeth. "You don't know me, I get that." He turned the brim of his cowboy hat along his palm. "That's why I'm not totally ticked off by your question. That, and I know you want what's best for Tyler. But let me explain."

He leaned forward, his elbows on his knees, hat in hand. He looked up and that deep blue stare held an intensity that made her flinch.

"I'm the oldest of six kids. My dad died when I was fifteen and ever since then I've been taking care of my brothers and sisters. And my mom." His eyes grew distant for an instant. "A man doesn't turn his back on responsibility. Right now, until DJ comes home, Tyler is my responsibility." He waited a long beat, letting his words soak in.

She analyzed them as her gaze roamed over him. His gaze intensified, if that were possible, and the lines around his eyes and lips indicated he smiled often. He wasn't smiling now. She didn't expect him to, but suddenly she wanted to see him smile. Wanted to experience his strength. He was a strong man.

"Mr. Hawkins."

"Please, call me Wyatt. This feels too danged formal for me."

She tried to smile. "Wyatt." She cleared her throat. "I've been a magistrate for too long to trust the initial impression. I have to ask the hard questions. If I don't, someone, and that someone is usually the child, gets hurt." She couldn't let her mind go any further. If she thought about the abuse she'd seen…that she'd experienced…

Stop. She put her thoughts on hold, refusing to go there. Not now.

"I understand," he said, saving her from the threatening morass in her mind.

"Actually, I don't know that you do." She couldn't sit across from him any longer. Even with the desk between them, he was too close, too real. "You said you cared for your siblings. Who took care of you?"

"I took care of myself." He didn't seem to think that was odd. "My mom worked and supported us. She was always there for me, but I didn't need her to take care of me." His voice broke, and he cleared his throat. "She passed away a few months back. She'd have loved Tyler." His voice cracked hard.

"I'm sorry." Emily paced to the window to look out over the lawn that stretched across nearly a city block. She didn't look back, but she could see him in her mind's eye. Tall. Intense. Strong.

Everything she expected. That was what worried her most. He couldn't really be that good. There had to be some flaw. She had to find it, had to expose it. Then she'd know if this was really going to work. For Tyler's sake. "Your sisters don't live nearby, do they?" she asked. "Do you have any family here?"

"At the ranch? No."

"And you're not married, are you, Mr. Hawkins?"

He laughed, but the sound held little humor. "No."

She glanced over her shoulder at him. "Is something funny?"

"Well," he drawled, "either you're channeling my mother—she always bemoaned the fact that her kids had yet to marry—or you're making a pass at me."

She glared at him and spun around to fully face him. "I am most certainly not."

He laughed again, this time warmly. "At least now you're looking at me." He stood and moved around the desk toward her. "I realize you have your concerns, but don't judge me before you know me. I've been taking care of Tyler just fine these past weeks."

His laughter was gone, and she realized she'd squandered her opportunity to see the smile she'd wondered about earlier. He'd moved into her space, and she wanted desperately to move away. The cool glass of the window at her back stopped her. She looked up and noticed how tall he was. And how close.

"I'm only trying—"

"To do your job? I know." His voice softened. Could he actually have moved closer? "Don't be the judge right now. Save that for the actual courtroom. You said you'd be the caseworker. Be that now. Let me show you I can do this."

She stuck to her guns. "Words are easy to hear, not necessarily to believe."

His eyes narrowed and he clenched his jaw. She'd hit a button somewhere.

"Then come see the world I live in, the one I'm sharing with Tyler." He reached into his back pocket and pulled out a worn wallet. "Here's my business card. Come out to the ranch and then we'll start this conversation over again."

He tossed the card onto the desk and turned on his heel. He reached the door before he spoke again. "Afternoons are best, and no, I'm not trying to hide anything." He frowned at her over one broad shoulder. "Tyler starts school tomorrow, and I refuse to have him miss any more class than he has already."

And with that, he left.

WYATT STALKED TO the elevator, resisting the urge to slam his fist into the lit button beside the double metal doors. The woman was a pain. She'd practically called him a liar, which grated on his nerves.

She obviously thought a woman made a better care-giver than a man. He'd done just fine with his brothers and sisters, thank you very much. Granted, he'd had his mother around part of the time, and Addie. He cursed. He should have told her about Addie.

No. That would be admitting defeat. He wanted her to realize he was perfectly capable of taking care of Tyler.

"Mr. Hawkins."

He turned around and saw the judge walking toward him. He tried, unsuccessfully, to ignore the sway of her hips and how her hair rippled with her movement. She looked as ticked as he felt. Good. That meant they were in the same boat. "Yes?"

"I'll be there tomorrow. At three. Does that work with your schedule?" She crossed her arms over her chest and glared at him.

Wyatt would have laughed if he weren't so ticked. She'd be on his turf. He felt much more comfortable with that. "Perfect."

The tiny ding of the elevator announced the car's arrival. The doors swished open, and he stepped inside. He lifted his hat and settled it on his head before tapping the brim just as the doors closed.

He figured she'd be there right at three. He'd be ready at two-thirty, since Tyler got off the bus at two forty-five.

Suddenly, Wyatt felt all of his thirty-two years. He couldn't let Tyler down, but for the first time since he'd picked up his nephew at that godforsaken house, he didn't want to go home. He couldn't reassure Tyler that things were going to be okay, when one wrong thing to-morrow could end it all.

Once Wyatt reached his truck, he sat in the cab and stared at the uglier-than-sin building. How long he sat there, he didn't know, but the West Texas heat had permeated the very air he breathed before he turned the ignition. The air-conditioning kicked on but did little to alleviate the scorcher of an afternoon. "Damned infuriating woman," he mumbled as he pulled out of the parking lot.

All the questions she'd asked him rang through the air in time with the whine of the tires on the highway. No, he didn't have a wife. No, his sisters didn't live nearby. No, he had no intention of taking Tyler to Mars anytime this week.

He growled at his own stupidity and frustration. He knew what he had to do. He didn't want to admit that he couldn't do this by himself. He'd always been the one to take care of things. The one in charge. The one who needed no one.

This time he needed help.

He wasn't a fool. His pride might get in the way, but keeping Tyler was far more important than his ego. He'd learned that a long time ago, when he'd been young and stubborn.

He thumbed open his cell and pushed the speed dial for his sister. Addie had gotten back from vacation last night. When he'd first received the letter from Tyler's mom, he'd toyed with the idea of calling Addie, but she would have cut her trip short, and he hadn't wanted that.

He'd almost given in a couple times, especially that first night Tyler had come to stay at the house. But they'd gotten along well, and while the boy had been sad when he'd gone to bed, he hadn't made any fuss. Only later when he'd peeked in on the boy had Wyatt seen the tear tracks on the boy's cheeks.

Now he had no choice. And if he thought the judge

had given him a rough time, it would be nothing like the tongue-lashing he knew Addie would give him for keeping this a secret.

Part of him hoped it would roll over to voice mail. It didn't. "Hi!" Addie's voice sounded like the girl he remembered instead of the tired woman he'd come to know since Mom's diagnosis.

"Hi, yourself. How was the trip?"

"Awesome. Stupendous. I'm exhausted." She laughed and Wyatt knew it wasn't the bone-weary kind she'd lived with for years. This was a happy tired.

"That's great. It wasn't the same without you." They usually talked several times a week, and her absence reminded him of all that was missing in his life. "I have something to tell you."

"Uh-oh."

"It's not bad. Not really."

"Double uh-oh."

He laughed, thinking that maybe he'd avoid the tongue-lashing after all.

"Spill it, brother dear."

Okay, maybe he'd been thinking too positively. *Here goes*. "Right after you left, a registered letter arrived." He paused and sucked in a couple lungfuls of hot Texas air. "Apparently, DJ has a son."

The silence on the other end of the call grew heavy and thick. Was that a storm brewing or just shock?

"I… Tyler is with me. He has been for almost three weeks." There, he'd said it.

"Tyler?" she whispered.

"That's his name. He's eight. God, Addie, he looks just like DJ at that age." Wyatt's voice broke. He missed his brother and worried where the special forces soldier was in the world. And if he still *was*.

"How... I don't understand."

"His mother abandoned him. She sent a letter and just left the boy."

"He's with you, there?" He heard her moving around and hoped it meant she was heading to her car.

"Not right here. He's back at the ranch with Chet and the crew." He knew his foreman, a father of four, was well acquainted with little boys. "I'm just leaving the judge's office. I'm trying to get custody."

"Good." More rummaging. "I'll be there in a couple hours."

"Thank God."

"What?" She was silent a long minute. "Who are you and what have you done with Wyatt?"

Her comment did as he knew she intended and he laughed. "I... The judge keeps asking me about a woman in my life to help take care of Tyler."

Addie laughed this time. "Oh, this is gonna be fun. I'm on my way. 'Bye. Oh, and we'll discuss your failure to tell me about this later." She hung up.

Wyatt groaned. Addie's ire was legendary, but at this point he couldn't let DJ or Tyler down.

CHAPTER FOUR

EMILY DIDN'T MIND COFFEE. She actually enjoyed a cup, heavily laced with cream and sugar on a bitterly cold, winter day. Otherwise, she'd rather drink pretty much anything else.

There was, however, something comforting about its scent that reminded her of the mornings before she left for school, back when it had been just her and her mother. Mom would make a pot while she fixed Emily's breakfast, then halfway through the second cup, she'd scoot Emily out the door to the bus.

It wasn't until just this instant that Emily wondered what her mother had done with the rest of the pot…or even what her mother had done the rest of the day. Helen had never worked outside the house. And to Emily as a child, it was as if either her mother vanished while she was at school, or just sat there, in a holding pattern, waiting.

Emily sat outside Sunset Haven, the assisted living that had been her mother's home for a couple months now, staring through the windshield, the scent of the coffee wafting around her.

It felt good to sit. Emily leaned her head back and closed her eyes, though she couldn't do that for long for fear of falling asleep. She was *so* tired.

With Judge Ramsey still out on medical leave and

Judge Helton announcing his retirement yesterday, Emily was swamped.

And to top it off, she'd barely slept last night. Why couldn't she get Wyatt Hawkins and his nephew out of her mind? At the most inopportune moments yesterday, his words had echoed back at her. She'd tossed and turned all night, seeing his face, hearing his accusations.

And why the uncle? Why not the little boy? That was whom she really cared about, wasn't it?

Maybe it had something to do with where he lived. She sighed, knowing that she'd started thinking about Wyatt Hawkins again the instant she'd looked up his address online.

He and Tyler lived out in ranch country. The same part of the county she'd grown up in.

Emily knew she was stalling. She wasn't in the mood for Mom today, and no one, except a few staff members at the facility, would ever know if she didn't visit. No one would begrudge her. But Emily would know she'd let her mom down. Again.

For Emily, her mother had been gone a long time already. All that was left was the shell of a woman whose mind, as well as her body, had faded.

Slowly, she reached for the door handle and climbed out into the hot Texas sun. She grabbed the two cups from the holders and closed the door with her hip. Her heels sank in the soft black pavement, and she hurried to the concrete walk. If she slowed down or stopped now, she might not make it. Luckily, the air-conditioning was on in full force today and the small lobby felt blessedly cool inside.

"Hello, Ms. Ivers." The bouncy little receptionist

greeted Emily. She was always there, always chipper. Emily hadn't a clue how the woman could be so happy.

"Hello." Emily nodded and headed down the hallway. It seemed eternally long today, though she only had to pass four doorways before she reached her mother's.

The large bundle of yellow silk roses attached to the door were just as she'd last seen them. They were from the house, something the staff here had encouraged Emily to bring in to help Helen find her own room more easily. It worked sometimes, though Emily had received several reports about her mother being found in other people's rooms. It saddened her. The mother she remembered would have been mortified by such behavior.

"Mom?" she called from the open doorway, knowing that startling her mother was a bad thing. It only increased Helen's confusion. "Mom, are you here?"

"Oh, yes, deary."

Uh-oh. *Deary.* Emily's heart sank. That meant her mother didn't remember who she was today. Deary was her catchall name for everyone. Her mother stuck her head around the divider curtain and smiled blankly at Emily.

"Well, hello." Helen stepped around the curtain. "Can I help you?"

Emily's heart hurt. She missed the long-ago days when she'd come home from school and her mother would open her arms to give her a big hug.

"It's me, Emily." She often had to remind her mother who she was, but just because she was used to it didn't mean she liked it. "I brought you some coffee." She lifted the cup marked decaf. She'd learned that trick a long time ago, too. No caffeine for Mom. Not if the staff here ever wanted her to go to bed at night.

"Oh, how lovely. You shouldn't have." Helen frowned, but gladly took the cup. "Won't you come in?" She led the way to the sitting area just inches away. The two chairs that had been in Helen's front room all Emily's life were situated just as they had been at the house. Yet another clue for Helen as to who and where she was that the staff had suggested. Sitting in the chairs was a comfort to Emily as well, and she smiled. They were worn and comfortable. Home.

"How are you today, Mom?" She sipped her own cinnamon-laced, caffeine-enriched chai. She needed to stay alert so she had no qualms about a fully leaded drink for herself.

"Oh, Emily!" Helen shook her head. "When did you get here?"

Emily smiled. "Just a minute ago. How's your coffee?" she asked, reminding her mother of the drink in her hand.

Helen looked down at it with a frown that quickly vanished. She took a tentative sip then smiled. "Very good."

Emily knew not to let the conversation stop or she'd lose the connection with her mother, but she couldn't think of anything to say. Work filled most of her waking hours, and she couldn't tell Mom about the cases she was working…though it wasn't as if Mom would remember.

God, this sucked. Emily wished she had someone to talk to, someone whose advice she could trust…. She missed her mom even more right now, though the woman sat right in front of her.

The sudden wave of sadness took Emily by surprise and made her quickly change her train of thought. She immediately slammed into the image of Wyatt Hawkins.

Cursing under her breath, she stood and paced the tiny confines of her mother's room.

"What's the matter, hon?" Helen's voice broke into her thoughts.

"Oh, nothing." What a lie.

"Now, you can't hide from me, you know."

Emily laughed. Mom might be disconnected, but she was still Mom. "No, I never could. It's just work stuff."

"Are you in trouble?" Helen frowned over her coffee cup.

Emily laughed again. "No." The fern in Mom's window looked healthy, but Emily busied herself cleaning dead leaves and rearranging the tiny branches. "Hey, Mom? When we lived out at Grandpa's place, did you know anyone named Hawkins?" She could have bitten her tongue.

"Hawkins. Hawkins." Helen repeated the name several times before looking up with a smile. "I do remember them. Lots of kids in that family. Five or six, I think."

Emily wasn't sure if her mom meant her generation or the current one. She knew there were six in the current one.

"Nice family." Helen took a sip of her coffee, the cup hiding her face for an instant. Once the cup was back down, Emily felt a little hitch. The distance was back. She wasn't going to learn any more from Mom about Wyatt and his family. Maybe that was a good thing. It wasn't appropriate to combine her personal life with business.

"Have you heard from your father?" Helen asked. "I haven't seen him."

"Me, either," Emily whispered. It always hurt when Mom asked about Dad. She never asked about Earl, which Emily was thankful for—she couldn't discuss that jerk. But it was also hard to discuss the father she missed so much.

"Helen?" A man's voice came from the hallway, and Emily looked up to see an elderly gentleman leaning on his walker, standing in the open doorway.

Helen frowned for just an instant, then smiled. "Hello." She didn't say the man's name, so Emily knew she didn't remember it. But she did recognize the man, if the warmth of her smile was any indication.

"Oh, I'm sorry," he said. "I didn't know you had company." He started to move away, but Emily knew an escape when she saw one.

"I was just getting ready to leave." Emily stood.

"Oh." He smiled. "I came to see if Helen was ready to head down to dinner. They're having a round of bingo beforehand, and I thought we could play."

"I think Mom would like that." Emily smiled at Helen and stood, hoping her mother would get the hint. Thankfully, she did. Setting her coffee on the table, Helen headed to the door.

"I love bingo." Helen fell into step as the man led the way down the hall, Emily once again forgotten.

Emily stood there, a half-empty cup in her hand. Suddenly she didn't want any more. She just wanted to get out of here and go back to the office. She could think there. She knew what to expect from the stack of files that needed to be read.

"Did Helen already go to dinner?" A nurse's aide entered the room.

Emily recognized her as Rose from her earlier visits. She liked Rose. "A gentleman with a walker came by and is going down with her."

Rose laughed. "That describes most of the men here. I'll bet it was Hal. He's taken a shine to your mom. Keeps her out of other people's rooms by getting her back here after every meal."

Relief that Mom had someone watching over her slid through Emily. She grabbed her mother's barely touched coffee and took it to the sink to pour it out. She emptied her own as well then tossed the cups into the trash.

"She really is doing well." Rose came to stand beside Emily. "She's going to activities, she cooperates with care most of the time and she even joined in yesterday's sing-along."

Such simple progress...and yet it was very big news. Helen was different now from the skin-and-bones, withdrawn and frightened woman who'd been brought here just a couple months ago. She was still thin, but she was clean, neat and eating regularly. Though it didn't help ease Emily's guilt.

"I'm glad." She smiled at Rose. "And I appreciate everything you all do for her, really I do." She gathered her purse and headed to the door.

"She talks a lot about you, you know."

That stopped Emily. She slowly turned back to look at the aide.

"When I help her get ready for bed, we talk." Rose stepped close. "She's so proud of you. She talks about you and your horse, Sugar. She told me how hard you worked to get into law school."

"She remembers all that?"

"Yeah." Rose took a deep breath. "The best part of this job is that I get to see that. She's still in there, she just doesn't show up often. Usually at night, after the sun sets, she's more..." Rose seemed to struggle with the words. "More aware? I don't know how to describe it. But she seems to wake up, just for a little bit."

Emily was surprised. "I wish—"

Rose interrupted her. "Don't do that. Just accept her for who she's been and who she is. She's a very sweet lady."

Emily nodded, fighting the tears that were tight in her throat. "I know. You should have known her when I was a kid." She laughed as a myriad of images flashed through her mind. Happy times, not the painful memories from after Dad's death, or when Earl had entered their lives. She recalled sitting on the couch reading storybooks, putting together puzzles and watching soap operas on school holidays.

"You keep those memories." Rose patted her arm. "I think she'd like you to."

Emily watched Rose leave the room and head to the dining room. She'd needed that today. Needed to be reminded that she was still important to someone. She didn't even cringe when she went past the dining room and saw her mother struggling to read the bingo cards. Emily just smiled, waved at Hal, at Rose and the other dozen people seated at the square dining room tables.

The sun was low in the afternoon sky as she reached her car, though the heat hadn't lessened any. The door handle was still hot and she cursed as she gingerly opened it. She dreaded getting inside the scorching car.

She was just a block away when her cell phone rang. She pulled to the side of the road to dig it out of her purse. She'd never paid attention to the thing before, but now, with Mom where she was, she tried to keep it handy. It would help if she had a smaller purse. Her heart pounding, she breathed a sigh of relief when she saw the number was her office. She glanced at the clock. What was Dianne still doing at work?

"Hello?"

"Emily? It's Dianne. Are you coming back to the office?"

"I'd planned to. Why?"

"I, um… There's a man here." Dianne's voice lowered. "He says his name is Drew Walker? He says he knows you?"

Emily's heart sank. Drew? She hadn't seen her stepbrother in five years, and then only for a few hours—which was fine with her. What did he want? "I'm on my way. Is he willing to wait—" she glanced at her watch "—fifteen minutes?" She heard Dianne ask someone the same question.

"Yeah, he'll wait. See you soon." Dianne hung up.

Emily sat there for a long minute. She closed her eyes, forcing her mind to shift gears. She was no longer the heartbroken daughter. Now she was back in legal mode. *Much better. Much easier.*

WYATT WATCHED AS Addie stared down at the little boy lying in the huge double bed. He could almost hear her thoughts, he knew his sister so well. They'd been together all but a few years of their lives, the first two before she was born and then the four years she'd been away at college. They were close, and he realized he should let Tyler go live with her. She'd make a great mom.

He turned his focus to the sleeping boy. It was eerie, really. He looked so much like DJ. Wyatt swallowed. The worry about DJ that had taken up residence since he'd gone overseas leaped into his throat.

"I want to reach out and hug him," Addie whispered. "It's almost like I'd be holding DJ. I wish I knew where he was." No one in the family had heard from him in nearly three months. This wasn't the first time since he'd joined the military that he'd essentially disappeared off the face of the earth. No news was good news, Wyatt kept telling himself.

"I'm not sure we really want to know." Wyatt turned away from the door and headed to the kitchen. There was no escaping the nightly news or the daily headlines. Wyatt had a pretty good idea that whatever DJ was doing would scare the hell out of Addie.

Grief and worry shone in her eyes and she stepped away from the door, leaving it ajar.

"What if he never gets to see Tyler?" She followed Wyatt to the kitchen.

Wyatt poured himself a cup of coffee and sat in the chair he'd brought from Mom's house after the funeral. Dad had sat like this, at the head of the table, hundreds of times when they were kids. Now Wyatt took that spot. It felt right. Maybe some of Dad's wisdom would seep out of the worn wood.

"We'll cross that bridge when, and if, we get to it." He took a sip of his coffee.

Addie headed to the stove. "How can you drink that stuff this late and not bounce off the walls until dawn?" She made herself a cup of the chamomile tea he kept at the ranch especially for her before sitting down to face him. "Have you learned anything about the mother? How could anyone just abandon him? He's such a sweet kid."

Wyatt laughed. "You've only been here a few hours. Give him a chance. He's a boy, remember? *And* he's

DJ's son." Amazingly, Mom hadn't died of a heart attack from some of DJ's antics.

"The letter didn't say much. No one seems to know a thing about his mother except Tyler, and he isn't saying much. I'm not pushing him."

"Where's the letter?" Addie asked.

"The judge has it. I've hired a private detective to look for his mother, but he hasn't come up with anything."

"I'm still confused as to how she found you."

He sighed. *Might as well get the tongue-lashing over with.*

"She didn't. She sent the letter, registered, to Mom's place. As executor, all the mail's being forwarded to me, so it came here."

"Gotcha." Addie sipped her tea thoughtfully. He was surprised when she didn't say more, like "Why didn't you call me?" or "Don't you think I should take care of him?" The thought of Addie taking Tyler home with her twisted something inside him. Wyatt didn't like admitting it, but he was getting attached to the kid.

"So tell me about this judge." Addie interrupted his thoughts.

"What's there to tell?"

"What's she like? I need a little preparation. She's going to be here tomorrow to scrutinize everything about us, about this place. We have to be ready."

"I know that." He set his cup down and stared at it for a long minute. "She's younger than I expected. I pictured some crotchety old goat of a judge, like half the other judges in the county. But she's probably our age. Dark hair. Dark eyes. Smart. She listened to everything Tyler had to say. She's got a way with kids."

Silence permeated the room. And then Addie laughed. "What?" Wyatt frowned at her.

"You're attracted to her."

"I— What are you talking about?" Wyatt felt the heat rise up his neck. "You asked what she's like," he accused.

"I asked about her as a judge. You just described her as a woman."

"I—" This time he didn't even bother to deny or say anything. What was the use? It'd be a lie. He *was* attracted to her. Damn it.

"Oh, this is good." Addie leaned back, obviously enjoying the moment. Her grin widened.

"Stop it, Addie. This is serious."

"Oh, I'm definitely serious. You know, big brother—" She'd always loved reminding him of that relationship at times like this. "You could make this work. Is she attracted to you?"

"Addie!"

"What? I'm only looking at the realities. Come on, Wyatt. You're single. Good-looking. *Available*. Wine and dine her, for God's sake. Win her over."

"I can't believe my sister actually paid me a compliment." He turned away and shook his head, but not before he felt a flash of guilt. He'd already thought about and discarded the idea Addie was suggesting.

The silence grew long before Addie spoke again, and her words came out soft. "What if she comes back?" Addie sat quietly sipping her tea, not meeting Wyatt's eyes.

"Who?" he asked, knowing full well who Addie meant. "The judge?"

"Don't be obtuse." Addie suddenly shot to her feet

and moved to the fridge. She opened the door and stared inside.

"What are you looking for?" They'd just finished dinner. Addie wasn't hungry. She was anxious despite the usually relaxing tea. Wyatt sat for a moment watching her.

"Nothing." She closed the door and sat back down, only to squirm in her chair.

Something about all this was bugging Addie, something more than the judge's impending visit. Something about Tyler had set Addie on edge, had turned his normally calm and together sister into someone he barely recognized. "You gonna tell me what you're thinking?"

"I—" Finally, she looked up. Wyatt was shocked to see a flash of deep pain run through her eyes. "What if DJ doesn't make it home?"

"Is that what all this fidgeting is about? Don't think about that. He'll come home safe." Even Wyatt doubted his own words.

Addie curled her fingers around the mug, not lifting it to her lips, just staring into the cooling contents. "His mother could come back at any time and take him."

"Yes, she could," Wyatt admitted, reaching across the table to cover Addie's hand with his. "But legally, she can't. She abandoned him, and the judge wants this custody to be permanent. I agree."

She sighed, breathing deeply, before looking at him again. That look struck a note inside Wyatt. This was *his* family, and while Tammie Easton had given birth to DJ's child, he didn't see where she had any place here. She'd given up that right.

The protective instinct that was so ingrained in Wyatt surged to the surface. "She shows up here and she'll have one hell of a fight on her hands." He spoke the words loud and strong, ignoring the doubt they covered.

He could fight her, legally, but what would that do to Tyler? What would DJ do? He'd obviously felt something for the woman at some point. What would he feel once he learned she'd kept his son a secret for eight years?

With a curse, Wyatt rose to his feet and dumped the rest of his coffee down the drain. "I'll be back later. Don't wait up."

He shoved the screen door open, letting it slap shut behind him. The night engulfed him within only a few feet, but he didn't have to see where he was going. He knew the path to the barn well.

His eyes easily adjusted, and he soon could make out the forms of the barn, the stable, the corral, the garage. Movement caught his eye and a sense of relief washed over him. His feet made their own way to the corral fence. Prism waited for him. The beautiful white horse shook its big shaggy head, greeting Wyatt as it always did. A friend saying hello.

"I should've brought you a treat, huh, boy?" Wyatt whispered and rubbed the smooth brow. Long minutes passed. The horse's breathing, the distant croaks of the frogs down at the pond, the faint whisper of something—probably a rabbit in the grasses—soothed him. He closed his eyes and took it all in, letting home comfort him.

Addie's question haunted him. What if Tyler's mom did come back? What would he do?

"You up for a ride, boy?" He patted Prism's neck and the horse seemed to nod his agreement. "Come on." Wyatt opened the gate and just as he had dozens of times before, he climbed up on the horse's bare back, hanging on to the thick mane. "Let's go."

This was no orderly canter; they both knew this. Prism knew him. Prism understood. And Prism ran. As if the troubles of the world were on *his* tail. Just as Wyatt wanted and needed.

FROM HIS PERCH on the dresser by the windowsill, where he'd climbed after Aunt Addie and Uncle Wyatt had gone to the kitchen, Tyler stared out across the yard at the starry sky. He'd waited until they'd walked down the hall to open his eyes. Playing possum, as Mama called it, had let him learn lots of things grown-ups didn't tell him.

He could still hear Uncle Wyatt talking. Aunt Addie seemed nice enough, but her questions worried him. Especially the ones about Mama.

Tyler liked Wyatt. Liked him a lot. For an instant, his view wavered, and he rubbed the heel of his hand against his right eye, then his left.

He refused to cry. Big boys didn't cry, Mama had always said. Then she would describe how Tyler's dad was big and tough and strong. He was a soldier, and Tyler didn't think soldiers ever cried.

Was his dad like Wyatt? Tyler wondered. They were brothers. Tyler wondered what it would be like to have a brother. He thought he might like it. Sisters, he wasn't so sure about. Sometimes, he thought, he'd just like to have someone around when he was lonely.

He hadn't felt lonely since Uncle Wyatt had come and gotten him, though. But the lady judge scared him. He didn't want to be alone again. He'd tried really hard to make her understand that he wanted to stay with Uncle Wyatt, that he wanted to get to know his dad when he got home. And that Mama wasn't bad; she just had stuff to take care of.

That word, *abandoned,* didn't sound good. Uncle Wyatt's frown had told Tyler he agreed with the lady judge. But Mama hadn't left him forever. *No,* his heart cried. She'd be back. He knew she'd come back. She'd promised him.

But would she even know where he was? Panic made him hiccup and his eyes watered again. Aunt Addie had asked Uncle Wyatt about Mama's letter and he'd said it had been delivered someplace else. Was that where Mama would go to get him? But he wasn't there—what if she couldn't find him?

Tyler scrambled off the ledge and reached for his jeans. In the right front pocket he pulled out the one thing he hadn't shown anyone.

Mama had called it a locket. She had shown him how to open it, but he couldn't remember how she'd done it. Instead, he curled his small fist around the locket and its chain before stuffing it back into his pocket.

When she'd given it to him, she'd promised she'd come back for it and for him as soon as she could.

He believed her.

He had to.

She was Mama.

His eyes burned and he curled his arms around his knees and rested his face on the patches of his jeans.

She'd be back.

She would.

Wouldn't she?

CHAPTER FIVE

"I DIDN'T GO to kin-de-garden." Tyler answered Wyatt's question without turning from the video game on the television screen.

Exasperated, Wyatt sat at the kitchen table, trying to fill out the school paperwork. Since Tyler wasn't his kid, and without any records to guide him, the forms weren't easy. Luckily, Tyler's mother had managed to pack his shot records or they'd be in a whole different mess.

"What do you mean you didn't go to kindergarten? I thought you had to?" Why was he asking an eight-year-old about this? He hadn't a clue. Too much time in said eight-year-old's company, he guessed.

"That's rule stuff. Maybe you could ask that lady judge 'bout it."

"I don't think so." Lady judge. An image of Emily Ivers flashed through Wyatt's mind. Those long black robes and that tiny pink collar peeking out…

"I went to Walt Whitman Elementary for part of first grade then some other place till the end of the year." Three more monsters disintegrated before Tyler spoke again. "Second grade was some place named after a tree. I was supposed to start at Wilson something for third—"

"Slow down." Wyatt scribbled as the boy once again listed off the schools, then looked over at him. "How many times have you moved?"

"Lots." Tyler focused on the screen, zapping more monsters with two swift finger blasts.

None of those school names rang a bell with Wyatt. "All in Texas?"

"Nope. Florida and Louisiana." The monsters fought back and Tyler didn't say anything else.

Wyatt leaned back in Dad's captain's chair and wished it were the man instead of a piece of wood. Dad's death when Wyatt was fifteen had made him grow up damned fast. Since that time, though, Wyatt had called on a lot of his dad's lessons and wisdom—at least what he'd managed to absorb in those short fifteen years. But nothing seemed to fit this situation.

He'd give anything to have his dad's input now.

"Okay, buddy. Let's get moving. I'll drive you to school today since I have to turn in these papers."

Tyler shut down the game, meticulously saving his play then grabbed his backpack. He struggled under the weight for an instant.

"What've you got in there?"

"Stuff." Tyler glared up at him and Wyatt backed off.

He'd approach that issue later. Tyler still didn't trust him completely. *One step at a time.* He heard his father's memory and smiled.

Yep, one step at a time.

EMILY SHOULD HAVE KNOWN. Drew lied. Again. Last night he'd told Dianne that he'd stay until she got there. It took her longer than the fifteen minutes she'd said—it had taken her seventeen, thanks to one obstinate stoplight—and he'd been gone when she got to the office.

So here Emily sat at her desk today, waiting. She'd

spent all last night awake, dreading the confrontation, because it *would* be a confrontation.

Now as she read through the legal briefs for Monday's cases, her mind was only half focused on the words in front of her. He'd show up when he was ready, not when it was convenient for her.

Just like Earl.

Her phone rang and she nearly jumped a foot. As it was, she knocked the file to the floor, pages scattering across the polished wood. "Yes," she answered.

"He's here," was all Dianne said before disconnecting. Emily knew she wasn't going to escort Drew back. Dianne would happily let him cool his heels in the lobby for hours, except Emily didn't want her clerk to have to put up with him any longer than necessary. Dianne was too good for that.

Emily straightened her desk, readjusted her skirt a couple times then grumbled at herself as she walked to the lobby.

Drew was a big man, just like his father. If anything he'd grown bigger, and not in a good way. He scowled at her, but as she looked back, she wasn't sure if she'd ever seen him without a scowl on his face. She'd first met him when their parents had married. She'd been thirteen. He'd been fifteen...and trouble.

His father had forced him to wear a buzz cut back then; now his chin-length hair was slicked back from his forehead with something that looked a lot like... Vaseline.

"Drew. Nice to see you again."

For an instant he looked taken aback and then the scowl deepened. "This isn't a social visit, Emily. I'm here on business." His voice came out deep and coated with impatience.

What kind of business could Drew have with a family court judge? "Let's step into my office." She didn't wait for him to follow, knowing that he would.

Much as she had yesterday with the tall cowboy, she sought protection behind the wooden desk. Where Wyatt had completely ignored the barrier, Drew settled uneasily in the spindly wing-backed chair facing her. She resisted the urge to gloat.

"So, Drew, what can I do for you?"

"I want Dad's stuff." He leaned forward, apparently trying to look menacing.

"What stuff?" She had no idea what he was talking about. Mom had given away all of Earl's clothes when he died and had tossed most everything else. Drew hadn't asked for anything then. What was this about?

"I know your mom has moved out of the trailer. I was out there yesterday. I want the keys so I can get my half."

The idea that he'd been out there made Emily shiver. What if Mom had still been out there alone?

"Your half?" she repeated. "Of what?"

"The ranch."

Ranch? The single-wide trailer out in the middle of the desert, a ranch? Last she'd seen, the barn, what was left of it, was falling over. The small corral was long gone. The only thing of value might—*might*—be the desert land it all sat on. But she doubted it.

"That land was my mom's before she married Earl. Besides, she's still alive, Drew." Even though the dump her mother had lived in was *a dump* it was hers as long as she was living.

"It became half his when they got married. I know,

he showed me the paperwork. Anyway, it's not like she's using it." His voice rose and he leaned even farther forward.

"Using what? The land or the trailer?"

"I want my half of the estate. Now."

Emily stared across the small office. She wasn't up to explaining that there was nothing for him. One second she wanted to laugh, the next she had to bite her tongue to keep from letting loose nearly twenty years of pent-up anger.

Estate? The man was delusional. "We don't know that she won't go back. Besides, there's nothing there, Drew. Just a pile of junk."

She forced her mind not to see the hellhole she'd moved her mother out of. The hovel she'd had to live in until she'd been old enough to escape.

"There has to be." Drew shot to his feet, leaning over her. His eyes practically glowed with rage and he wiped away spittle from his lips with the back of his arm. "That bastard had to leave me something."

Emily refused to be afraid of Drew anymore. She had been once. One night in the barn, she'd been hiding from Earl—again. Drew had found her, at first friendly, cajoling and soothing. Then when he'd tried to pin her down to the hard wooden floor, she did what her real dad had taught her. And the well-placed kick had kept him away from her for the rest of that summer. Months later, after Earl had belted Drew one too many times, the boy had run back to his mom's house. He'd never returned for any extended stays.

"If you won't tell me where it is, I'll get the answer out of your mother." Drew headed toward the door. Emily resisted the urge to run after him and grab him. She couldn't let him see her fear, but she wasn't letting him near her mother.

"Where what is, Drew? You're not making sense." He didn't stop walking. "You go near Mom and I'll have you arrested." She didn't move, but the tone of her voice stopped him.

"What the hell for?" He rounded on her, his hands curling into big meaty fists. Just like Earl. She refused to let memories scare her. She was a judge, a grown woman with power, not a young girl scared of her own shadow and getting hurt. And she was all that stood between Drew and her mother.

"Well, menacing an at-risk adult to start. You take anything from her and I'll have you arrested so fast your head will spin." The flare in his eyes told her she might have gone too far. He took a step toward her, but stopped.

"You think you're so smart, don't you?"

Suddenly, Dianne appeared at the office door, breaking the tension in the room. "Your Honor?"

Your Honor? Oh, how official Dianne sounded. Emily swallowed back her thankful smile. "Yes?"

"You need to leave if you're going to make your appointment."

"We're not finished." Drew ground out the words.

Oh, yes, they were. "Well, we'll have to finish later. It's court business." She didn't elaborate. Emily stood and walked to the coatrack by the door, effectively shutting off anything Drew had to say. "I'll walk you out." The last thing she'd do was leave him in her office unattended.

He beat her to it, stomping down the hall and slamming the outer door. His last words of "I'll be back" were nearly cut off by the sound of the wood hitting its frame.

"Well, isn't he a charmer," Dianne drawled from behind her desk. "Your family reunions must be a real joy."

Despite her nearly flippant words, Emily could
see the concern in Dianne's eyes. Emily leaned back
against the wall, closing her eyes and taking several
deep breaths. "Lord. I need to call the facility. He can't
see Mom." She didn't have to explain anything to Dianne. She'd heard every word.

"He seems like the kind who will, no matter what
you do. Just be prepared."

Emily's heart sank. Dianne was right. Earl had never
listened to anyone and Drew seemed much the same. He
was after something and wouldn't give up until he got
it, or was satisfied with the results. Thinking of the pathetic balance of their parents' combined lives, she realized he'd never be satisfied.

Slowly, Emily peeled herself away from the wall to
dial the all-too-familiar number, and spoke with the administrator. She explained the bare minimum. Being a
judge, she didn't have to elaborate and she took advantage of that. She was afraid that if she said too much,
she'd lose it.

Finally, with the administrator's empty promises that
Drew wouldn't be allowed to see her mother without her
permission, Emily sank into the nearest chair.

Why couldn't things have been different? Why had
her father died? Why had her mother had to meet Earl?
If only…

With a determined shake of her head, Emily once
again prepared to leave.

The look on Dianne's face, however, told Emily there
was more than the appointment on her clerk's mind. She
knew Dianne wouldn't volunteer.

"Okay, what's up?" she prodded.

Dianne tried to pretend surprise. "Why? Nothing."

"I can see the wheels turning in your head."

"Oh, fine." Dianne paused. "You sure you know what you're doing?"

"With Drew? No."

"No. With this court case."

"Of course I do." Emily grabbed her purse and the briefcase she'd stuffed with the case files she thought she might need, plus files to read at home tonight.

"Mmm-hmm." Dianne looked over those infernal glasses. "The caseworker has done most of the required work. Just because it's not in the final form doesn't mean you have to double-check it." That look—over the glasses—said there was no escaping her questioning.

"Look." Emily leaned against Dianne's desk. "I'll feel better seeing things for myself." She really did appreciate Dianne's concern. "Besides, you're always after me to get out of the office."

"I meant to do something fun. Not more work."

"Hey, maybe this will be fun." Emily smiled and hustled out the door before Dianne's words could totally catch up to her.

"Someday you're going to have to learn to trust someone." Dianne's words slipped through the door right behind Emily and kept bouncing around in Emily's mind as she drove through the desert.

Warm midday sunshine poured in the sunroof and landed squarely on Emily's shoulders. The car's air-conditioning made the West Texas heat bearable—but she still felt the damp sweat drench her body.

She *was* nervous doing something she really shouldn't, something totally out of her routine. Out of her element.

But as she'd told Dianne, she needed to do this. It couldn't hurt, and if the little boy was at risk, as Emily feared, she'd save herself and the system a great deal of pain—not to mention Tyler.

And so she drove through the backcountry, through places that reminded her of so much hurt, risking her impartiality in a case simply to give herself peace of mind for a while.

Emily hadn't driven out here in ages. The grasslands and desert of Southwestern Texas was a place she barely acknowledged, much less thought about. She stayed in town, lived her life, ignored where she'd come from.

The two-lane highway wound through the hills, dissecting the desert along with dozens of dirt roads and driveways that led deep into the ranches. Ten miles to the north her grandfather's ranch sat, abandoned, its pastures rented out to another rancher up the road. The plot of land her mother had recently left sat another ten miles beyond that.

The Hawkins ranch was closer to town than Emily had ever lived. She'd looked at it on the county map. He might live modestly, but he was land rich, with a large spread that ran along one of the large rivers that bisected the area.

Her hands sweaty around the steering wheel, she tried to focus on the pavement reaching out in front of her, staring at the yellow stripes. All she had to do was get there, take a look around and head back to town.

Breathing in deep, she swallowed the panic rising in her throat. Maybe she should just turn her car around and trust in the system she'd always believed in. She slowed again, this time her eyes on the road ahead instead of the potholes in her past.

A movement at the edge of the road ahead startled her. She hadn't passed anyone in nearly a quarter of an hour. Surely no one was out walking in this heat. It must be the shimmering illusion on the horizon.

Whatever or whoever it was ahead kept moving. She braked to slow down even more. It *was* someone walking. A child. She pushed the brake again.

Tyler.

Her heart sank. What had happened? Why had his uncle let him come out here alone? She envisioned the tall, handsome man who'd been in her office yesterday. He'd been very clear that he wasn't the type to abandon anyone, but the evidence was right before her. Then another thought came to mind. What if something had happened to Wyatt?

She slammed on the brakes this time, pulling off the two-lane road and onto the soft dirt at the shoulder. Dust settled around the tires as she opened the door. Hot air slammed into her, and she wanted more than anything to crawl back into the air-conditioned interior.

But the sight of the little boy trudging along beside the road stopped her. "Tyler?" she called, not wanting to scare him.

He stilled then looked up at her. His eyes widened and rather than stopping, he broke into a run. The backpack he'd been carrying tumbled to the ground and he dragged it through the dust. The scrape of the cheap plastic on the rough rocks was loud.

"Tyler, wait!" She jogged after him. She was wearing a suit with a knee-length skirt and matching pumps. Definitely not running clothes.

But Tyler's eight-year-old legs were short and the backpack was obviously heavy. She was out of breath and soaked with sweat when she finally caught up to him. He yelped and tried to kick her as she grabbed him.

"No," he squealed.

"Tyler. Stop that." Guilt almost made her let him go. Common sense told her he'd perish out here in the heat. She trudged back to the car, struggling to hold on to him. She'd have dozens of bruises, but at least he'd be alive.

The backpack scraped loudly beside them. "I'm not going to hurt you," she tried to reassure him.

"I know that," he yelled back, and she realized he was angry, not scared. The little rat. Her guilt faded a little.

Finally getting him to the car, she pulled open the passenger door and felt the last of the cooled air wash over them. She grabbed her water bottle and after plopping him on the seat, she handed it to him. "Here."

He let go of the backpack, and she grabbed it and tossed it into the backseat. She pulled on the seat belt and awkwardly buckled him in. If she ran around the car, she might get in before he was loose. Maybe.

With a wary eye, she closed the door and hustled around the front of the car. He had his belt unbuckled but hadn't gotten the door unlocked or open before she was inside. She wrestled him for the belt and finally got it back in place.

"Sit," she commanded, and it was enough to take the steam out of the boy. She thought for an instant that he was going to cry. But he didn't. Instead, he crossed his arms over his chest and stuck his bottom lip out in a huge pout.

"Thank you." She leaned back against the seat. "What are you doing out here?"

At first she wasn't sure he'd answer. "Goin' back to town."

Emily's heart sank. What had happened? All her fears leaped out of the hot desert. She'd been right to come out here.

The click of the seat belt brought her out of her thoughts. "Hold it." She clicked the buckle back in place again. "Start talking." She leaned back in the seat and cranked the ignition. After a second, cool air blasted from the vents. She aimed two of them at the boy. Tyler's face was flushed but he nearly emptied the water bottle, so she thought he'd be okay.

"You can't take me back."

"Why not? Tell me why. I promise I'll listen. Is your uncle so bad?"

"N-no. He's okay. Even lets me ride horses." The sound of longing was thick in his voice. "And pet a baby cow."

"You like baby cows…er…calves?" He didn't say anything, but the way his eyes lit up told her he did. "Then—did he hurt you?"

"No!" He glared at her. "He's not bad."

"Then what's wrong?" Only the blow of the air conditioner broke the heavy silence.

"Mama won't be able to find me out here," he finally whispered.

Emily's chest tightened. She wanted to pull him close and ease the uncertainty cloaking those words, but she knew he'd never allow that. His mother wasn't coming back for him, but Emily didn't have any desire to tell him that right now.

Instead, she put the car into gear and pulled back onto the road, heading to the ranch. She heard him sniff and forced herself to ignore it. She was a judge. An officer of the court, sworn to protect children, not put them at further risk. Even if her heart hurt as she made the decision.

Emily's eyes darted back and forth from the road to the boy. Tyler slouched in the seat beside her, his legs in constant motion.

"Sit still, Tyler."

"Why?" Tyler increased the rhythm of his legs.

"I just need to concentrate, okay?" Emily muttered.

They didn't have far to go, but it seemed to take forever. Finally, she saw the turn-in to Wyatt's land. The metal reflectors at each side of the drive winked at her as she slowed and steered in between them.

She'd read the initial caseworker's notes, but the neatly kept house with its yard and large trees was a bit of a surprise. It was homier than any place she herself had ever lived. The wraparound porch stole her heart.

She didn't look over at Tyler, but saw out of the corner of her eye that his eyes were large and damp.

"It'll be fine. Don't worry." She knew her promise was empty but she had to say something.

She was surprised at what she saw once she faced the big ranch house. It had to be a hundred years old, judging by the style, but it was immaculate. Old-fashioned metal fencing stretched between posts to surround the big white house with a lush green lawn. She pulled up to the fence, just a few yards from the gate.

A gate that stood wide-open and for some reason, Emily knew that Tyler had left it that way. She hoped Wyatt didn't have a dog or other pet that could now be loose in the wilderness. She laughed. Wilderness. Ranch land was *not* wilderness, not really.

A woman came out of the door, the wooden screen slapping loud against the frame. "Tyler?" The woman's blond hair fell in long ringlets. Was this a friend—a girlfriend of Wyatt's? Emily frowned. Had he been distracted by the woman, thereby allowing the boy to run away?

Tyler reached for the door handle and turned to climb out of the car. Before he could move, though, Emily clamped her hand around his thin little wrist. "Hold on."

He frowned but slowly turned his head to look at her through the mop of hair hanging in his face. "What?"

Wow! Plenty of attitude in that half-hidden glare. But that attitude made something in her shift. Her anger evaporated, drifting around for an instant to land somewhere near her heart.

"Are you sure you're okay here?" She tried to see Tyler's face, see what he was thinking. Was he afraid? Was he comfortable here? Was there something here that had caused him to run away?

None of those answers stared back at her.

"She's waiting for me," he informed Emily and finally pulled his arm free. He shoved the door open with his tennis shoe and bounded out. "I'm here," he called just before he slammed the door closed.

Emily took a deep breath, wishing desperately that she'd never decided to do this. She should have kept it all in her courtroom, where she was safe behind her robes, behind the bench, across the room from any of the participants.

Her palms grew damp, and she rubbed them around the warm steering wheel once, twice, then before she could shove the car into Reverse and turn tail and run, she opened the door and climbed out. She refrained from slamming it as Tyler had done, though barely.

The hot Texas sun beat down on her head, but she

stood up straighter and shoved her purse over her shoulder. She curled her hands around the strap as if it were a lifeline and stepped forward.

The woman knelt in front of Tyler, her hands on his shoulders. She was speaking, but for some reason, Emily couldn't hear her words. Maybe it was the roaring in her ears. She took a deep breath, noting the relaxing scents of the fields and heat. She could do this.

She stepped forward, moving through the open gate. She extended her hand just as the woman started to speak to Tyler again.

"He was walking into town," Emily interrupted.

The blonde's jaw dropped open. "That's over ten miles."

"He didn't get there." Anger and a dose of panic rippled through Emily. She should have trusted her gut. She should have sent this boy to social services. She should have—

"Tyler, you scared us half to death." The woman had none of Emily's hesitation in grabbing him and hugging him tight.

"Sorry," he mumbled from inside her tight embrace.

She finally let him go and took his hand in hers. "Let's go call Wyatt."

"He's not here?" Emily felt her brow rise.

"No." The woman turned back with her own frown. "He's been out searching for this one. I hope his cell works in the gullies and canyons he's checking."

"Oh." Emily felt silly. Her suspicious nature always made her feel like a shrew. "I'll… I'll get his backpack from the car."

"Oh, thank you. Please. Where are my manners? I'm

Addie Hawkins. Wyatt's my brother. Guessing by the time, you're Judge Ivers."

Relief slid through Emily and she forced herself to ignore it. This was his sister…not—she forced her mind to focus on her steps and the task of getting the backpack—not a girlfriend.

The beaten backpack was heavy in Emily's hand. What had he packed? She pulled it out and walked around the car.

A thundering roar grew in the distance, freezing Emily in place, stealing the words she was about to say. She'd heard that sound before, a long time ago—a lifetime ago. She shook her head, looking up at the sky, hoping to see a building thunderhead somewhere, anywhere. Clear blue skies stared back at her.

Her heart pounded in her chest. The damp that had been in her palms spread throughout her body. Her breath froze.

Emily watched the solitary rider appear on the horizon. Wyatt sat atop a wide-shouldered horse whose mane and tail were silhouetted in the afternoon light. He was riding quickly toward the house, and she nearly expected his hat to fly off like in all those old cowboy movies she'd watched as a kid.

He drew closer, the shadows let go and she could see the details of him. He was dressed the part of a cowboy, unlike the man who had appeared in her courtroom just days ago wearing an expensive tailored suit. No, this cowboy wore a blue shirt that contrasted with his worn Levi's. Costly but worn Ropers were snug in the stirrups.

She'd just turned her head, catching a glimpse of white, when the great white horse rumbled into the yard, clearing the low fence with ease. He landed with a heavy thud just inches from her.

Wyatt jumped down from the horse's back, landing with a similar thud.

"Where is he?" Wyatt barked out the words as he swung out of the saddle.

She looked up at him. Sweat glistened on his face and he yanked the Stetson off and swiped his brow with his sleeve.

"In the house."

Before she could say or ask anything more, he tossed the reins to her and loped across the lawn.

She caught the reins—a habit she'd thought long forgotten. He'd made the assumption, like everyone did, that people who lived in Texas knew horses. She did, of course, but she hated his assumption.

She stood there a long, silent moment.

Big. Huge. Brown eyes stared at her. She could see the horse's long lashes as it blinked at her. It—she glanced around and amended—he.

The horse tossed his head and whickered before taking a step forward. Emily froze and dropped the reins. The well-trained horse didn't move, but Emily saw a whole new set of images. Of another horse. One not as big, but whose eyes were just as beautiful and soulful. Whose coat was just as pure white.

"Sugar," she whispered. But Sugar was gone. Long gone.

The horse's big chocolate eyes stared at her, slowly batting its big eyelashes. The horse took a step toward her, and Emily crumbled into the darkness.

CHAPTER SIX

"AH, HELL." WYATT realized his mistake the instant he let go of the reins. He spun around just in time to keep the judge from landing on her pretty little butt in the grass.

He'd been in such a hurry to check on Tyler that he'd barely registered that she had arrived. Great timing. Maybe she didn't realize Tyler had been missing for the better part of the afternoon. He could hope.

He curled his arms in, pulling her up against his chest. Her softness, and the scent of something sweet wafting in the air, registered along with Prism's shadow falling over them. Wyatt whistled and his foreman, Chet, stuck his head out of the barn.

"Come get Prism, will you?" Wyatt yelled.

The wiry old man hustled across the drive and through the gate to take the horse. "Gracious, who you got there?" Chet peered past Prism's shoulders.

"The judge," Wyatt explained, knowing Chet knew the situation with Tyler. "Seems she's scared of horses." Her eyelids fluttered and Wyatt hastened to the steps to get her inside and away from the horse.

"Come on, boy. Just my luck. He gets to catch the girl and I'm stuck with you." Chet's words followed Wyatt toward the house as the old man led Prism out through the gate.

"Addie," Wyatt yelled as he stepped inside the foyer.

He headed to the living room, and was halfway to the couch when the judge's eyes opened. Wyatt found himself staring into a very startled pair of deep brown eyes. Her panic surprised him.

"Put me down!" She wiggled and Wyatt struggled to keep from dropping her. She managed, with his help, to land on her feet—barely. She wobbled and he wasn't sure if it was her condition or those ridiculous heels.

"Sit down," he commanded and guided her to the couch. "Better yet, lie down until we figure out if you're okay."

"I'm fine." She did, however, sit down.

"Uh-huh."

Her color was returning and she closed her eyes while she took several deep breaths.

Lame horses, banged-up cowboys and even flash storms, Wyatt knew how to handle. Women didn't normally swoon at his feet, so he was at a loss of what to do. Where the hell was Addie? "Can I get you anything?"

The judge looked at him then, and the shimmer in her eyes startled him.

"Maybe some water. I…must have been out in the heat too long." She rubbed her forehead with a trembling hand.

"Sure. Add—" he yelled then stopped himself when he saw his sister appear in the doorway. Tyler was behind her, munching on a cookie that was bigger than his hand.

"Tyler, where have you been? Are you okay?" Wyatt hunkered down beside the boy, the judge left to Addie's care.

"I'm okay," Tyler said around a mouth full of chocolate.

"What are you yelling for?" Addie stepped forward,

seeing the judge sitting on the couch. "What happened? She was fine a minute ago."

"You knew she was here?" Wyatt frowned at Tyler.

Addie frowned back. "Yeah. She's the one who brought him home."

Wyatt's heart sank. There went that hope. "I carried her in."

"What?" Addie simply stared back at him then hastily moved to the couch. "He carried you?"

"I...uh...fainted. Must be the heat. I'm fine now."

Wyatt took a deep breath and turned his focus back to the boy, who wouldn't meet his eyes. "You got something you want to tell us?"

"No." Tyler turned toward the kitchen and climbed back up onto the chair he'd obviously been sitting in. He grabbed the half-full glass of milk and took a drink.

"Are you sure about that?"

Tyler didn't say anything, and to keep from grabbing the kid, Wyatt slid over into Dad's chair. "So where have you been?"

"I don't know." Tyler swung his legs and stared at the ground, reminding Wyatt of the day he'd first met the boy at that abandoned house. He needed to tread carefully here.

"I can answer that."

Wyatt turned back to see the judge standing in the doorway. She was no longer pale and her eyes were a stormy brown. The vulnerable woman he'd glimpsed was gone and the no-nonsense judge was back. Addie was right behind her.

"Please, have a seat. I made coffee," Addie said.

"I'd prefer something cooler, if you have it. Water would be great."

"Of course." As Addie got busy, the judge—Emily, he reminded himself—headed toward the table. He hastily pulled out a chair and noticed her hands still trembled as she sat.

"I'm sorry Prism scared you. I—I was focused on Tyler." The soft perfume he'd noticed earlier mingled with the sweet scent of the fresh cookies. Temptation.

"Understandable."

Addie took a seat after setting a glass of ice water in front of the judge.

Then the silence descended.

LONG, PAINFUL MINUTES ticked by. Finally, Emily couldn't stand it any longer. "Do you want to tell your aunt and uncle what's up, or shall I?" She pinned Tyler with her best courtroom stare.

He hung his head and it took everything in her not to reach across the table and fold him in her arms. She saw the same struggle on Addie's face but couldn't see Wyatt's features from this angle.

Tyler simply shrugged.

She cleared her throat. "I was on my way out here when I saw him, about five miles from here, walking beside the road."

"How'd you get so far?" Addie's alarm came out loud and clear. Tyler didn't answer.

Wyatt did. "You got off the bus down by the Richardson's spread, didn't you?"

Tyler looked up and met his uncle's eyes. Emily saw the boy swallow then nod.

"Where were you going?" Addie asked.

Again, Tyler remained silent. Emily wanted him to step up, but he was only eight, she reminded herself.

"Apparently, from what he told me, he overheard you two talking and realized his mother wouldn't be able to find him out here. He was going to town to where his mom's letter was originally sent."

"I was just gonna put a note on the house. Then come back," Tyler defended himself, and if it weren't so foolish, Emily would have applauded his loyalty and determination.

"Oh, Tyler." Addie reached for the boy, but Wyatt beat her to it, putting his hand up to stop her.

"So rather than asking us about it, you just took off?" Wyatt's voice was soft, but the anger in it was strong.

Tyler simply stared.

"Here's the deal." Wyatt leaned forward, resting his forearms on his knees so he and Tyler were nearly eye to eye. "In this house, we have a few rules. I realize you're new here, so you're going to get a break this time."

Wyatt leaned back in his chair, looking relaxed, but Emily sensed the tension in his body. "We don't eavesdrop. We talk and ask questions if we don't know what's going on. And last—" he looked over his shoulder at Emily then back again "—the Hawkins men face up to their issues. We speak up and admit when we do wrong."

"Yes, sir." Tyler's voice trembled, but he straightened his shoulders.

Emily guessed it had something to do with the notion that he was one of the Hawkins "men." She resisted the urge to roll her eyes, but had to give Wyatt credit for how he was handling this.

"If you'd asked me, I'd have explained. The post office forwarded the letter here. I get all the mail. And, Tyler, you know I'd have found a way to help you leave that note."

Emily appreciated that he didn't belittle the boy's plans.

"Am I…" Tyler cleared his throat. "Am I gonna get punished?"

Wyatt seemed to ponder that and Emily waited, curious. "Well, what do you think? Does running away deserve punishment?"

Emily held her breath. What would Tyler say and what would be Wyatt's reaction?

"Yeah. Mama would think so."

Tyler's voice came out so pathetic and sad, Emily had to bite her lip to keep from smiling. He was just too danged cute. She glanced at Wyatt, who'd leaned his chin in his palm, his finger curled over his lips, but she could still see the hint of a smile.

He nodded. "Well, then, for once I agree with your mom. So let's see." He paused for pure drama; she could see that. "Whatcha think it should be?"

Emily could tell Wyatt already had a plan, but he wanted Tyler to be part of it.

"You aren't gonna spank me, are you?"

"No!" Addie erupted. "Who spanked you before? Your mother?"

"No." Tyler vehemently shook his head. "Dom did, though."

"Dom? Who's Dom?" Emily asked.

"Mama's boyfriend. He was mean."

Emily put that little note in the back of her brain, wondering if Dom had anything to do with his mother's decision to leave Tyler behind. "Did Dom do anything else to you?" She opened the door but wouldn't lead him.

"No. Just spanked me with his belt."

Outrage and something akin to understanding had

Emily wanting to take Tyler home with her and keep him safe.

"Well, we don't do that here," Wyatt said. "Anyone tries that, you come see me, okay? I don't tolerate abuse of people or animals. Understood?"

Anger cloaked Wyatt's voice and the red flags on his cheeks told Emily Dom had better not cross paths with Wyatt anytime soon—if ever.

"Well, then, what?" Tyler was totally perplexed.

After a minute, Wyatt's anger had faded and he glanced at Emily, then Addie, before focusing on the boy. "I think a week of mucking out stalls with Chet should do. Every day after school, you come straight home and head to the barn."

"Is that all?" Tyler's face lit up at the mention of the barn.

"You want more?"

"Oh, no. No, sir." Tyler was fighting a grin.

"Now go upstairs and unpack that backpack, then go see if Chet needs any help today. He might be almost done."

Tyler reached for his glass of milk and finished it in nearly one swallow, then grabbed the backpack and lugged it out of the room. His footsteps were fast and loud up the stairs, as was the thud of the backpack he dragged behind him.

As soon as they heard him reach the top of the stairs, Wyatt turned to face Emily. "So, Judge. How'd I do? You going to take him away?"

She heard Addie gasp, but Emily looked at Wyatt instead. His blue eyes said so much. In the past few minutes, she'd seen them wide with concern, spark with anger, bracketed by a smile and now direct and challenging. She felt herself falling deep into them.

"I…" She cleared her throat. "And rob him of a whole week of barn time? I don't think so."

Addie audibly released her breath.

"You agree with what I did?"

"As opposed to smacking him with a belt? Absolutely."

Wyatt settled back in his seat, and she realized he, too, had been on edge. The tension oozed out of him. "Hell," he whispered. "That boy took ten years off my life today."

Addie stood up and poured coffee into thick earthenware mugs. "Like father, like son. Do you drink coffee… Judge?"

"Please, call me Emily." Emily relaxed a little. "And no. No, thank you. I'm much more of a tea fan. I'll stick with the water for now, thanks."

"See?" Addie pointed at Wyatt. "Not everyone drinks coffee. I've been trying to tell him that for years."

"I realize there are other drinks in the world." Wyatt grinned, not bothering to defend himself. He lifted his cup and took a deep swallow of the pure black brew.

"Beer doesn't count," Addie mumbled.

Wyatt slid the cookie plate toward Emily. "Better get one now. Once Tyler and the boys remember they're here, they won't last long." He took two for himself.

"Was Tyler's father a handful?" Emily ventured as she bit into a cookie. It melted in her mouth. No wonder everyone wanted them.

"And a half. I'm surprised Mom didn't have a heart attack—multiple times," Addie said.

Wyatt chuckled. The sound was warm and filled the

room. Emily glanced at him over her newly replenished glass of water.

"He wasn't the only one," Addie continued, causing Wyatt to scowl at her. Emily wondered at that story but left it for another day.

"Our father died, what was it, almost twenty years ago?" Addie asked Wyatt. He nodded.

"Mom had six of us to raise. Wyatt's the oldest. DJ's second youngest. Wyatt was as much father to DJ as Dad was."

"As if he listened to a fifteen-year-old." Wyatt took a big bite of cookie. "I'm shocked he's managed so well in the marines. You'd think they'd have thrown him in the brig by now."

"What exactly does he do?" Emily asked.

Wyatt shrugged. "He says if he tells us he has to kill us." He smiled.

Emily couldn't help but respond to the warmth in Wyatt's voice. He obviously cared about his family, if the relationship with Addie was any indication. Some of her doubts began to fade away. "Do you know anything about Tyler's mother?"

"Didn't even know she existed. I've got to admit I'm curious as hell. DJ never stays with a girl very long. Always looking for greener pastures."

"Now that makes him sound like a...a philanderer," Addie admonished. She turned to face Emily with a frown to Wyatt. "He's always been a good-lookin' kid who just never found the right girl."

"Not for lack of trying," Wyatt mumbled.

So Addie was the romantic. What about Wyatt? Emily found herself wondering more than she thought she should. She turned her focus to Addie. She wasn't much older than Emily, if at all, and yet there was a mature, motherly air to her. Emily liked her, and for an instant, wondered why she wasn't the sibling taking care of Tyler. She almost asked when thundering footsteps down the stairs broke the silence.

Tyler raced across the kitchen and yanked open the refrigerator door.

"What are you doing?" Wyatt asked.

"Gettin' carrots for Prism and Dancer." He raced out of the kitchen, a carrot in each hand, as quickly as he'd entered.

"P… Prism? Dancer?" Emily swallowed hard, surprised at the way her heart raced as images of the big horse filled her mind.

"Some of our horses. Don't worry. He's safe. Chet won't let him do anything stupid."

Emily took several deep breaths, then shot to her feet before her mind could kick into overdrive. Wyatt and his men were competent, she knew that. She had to shift back into her professional mind-set, and ignore her personal hang-ups. Easier said than done.

She gripped the edge of the table to keep from tripping over her own feet and making a fool of herself in front of this man—again. "Well, why don't we get to the rest of this visit," she said.

Wyatt watched her, his eyes not giving away anything. "Sounds good." His chair scraped loud on the linoleum.

Emily hadn't brought her briefcase in, but there was no way she was going outside to retrieve it and possibly come face-to-face with any animals. She would just have to rely on her memory to write up her report later. "Why don't you give me a tour of the house?"

"Sure."

Wyatt headed to the living room, stopping in the doorway to wait for her. "This way."

She'd already seen the living room, but now she took time to really look around. Sparse, yet clean. The heavy leather furniture definitely announced this was a man's home. No throw pillows, and only the braided rug that filled nearly the whole room served as decor. The walls, though, were a soft tan.

Stairs split the house in two. As they headed to them, she noticed a set of old-fashioned double doors that stood closed across the hall. Wyatt didn't offer to show her that room. "What's in here?"

He stopped midway up and looked down at her. "Tyler's room is upstairs."

"But Tyler lives in the entire house, doesn't he?"

She didn't think he was hiding anything in there, but his reluctance made her want to see. "If he'll be exposed to anything, I need to see it."

The scowl on Wyatt's face told her he didn't think much of her nosiness. Good. She didn't like it, either, but saw it as part of her job.

He came down, boots thudding on the worn tread of the stairs. "Fine." He opened the doors and let the light from the hall into the darkened room. She could make out the shapes of a big wooden desk, file cabinets and a few scattered chairs. His hand hit the light switch, and an overhead light splashed gold throughout the room.

She knew instinctively that this was his space. His office. His domain. She stepped farther into the room, stopping only when she stood in the middle.

The room was beautiful. Absolutely beautiful. Mahogany, if she had to guess. Real mahogany.

"My grandfather built it. It's the heart of the business." Wyatt hadn't moved, but his casual stance, leaning against the doorjamb, didn't fool her. He didn't like her being in here and she wasn't sure why.

Looking around, hoping to find a reason to stay here for a minute longer, her gaze landed on the huge carved bar at the far end. It was beautiful—and very well stocked.

"That's quite an impressive collection of liquor." She met his gaze with an inquiring one of her own. "Do you think that's appropriate with an eight-year-old boy in the house?" She hadn't seen anything in the previous caseworker's notes about the bar, or this room, actually. She doubted she'd even noticed.

"I think it's appropriate for my lifestyle."

"As the guardian of a child?" She knew she was hitting all the right buttons. He was trying, quite admirably she had to admit, to control his temper.

"As the owner of a ranch several miles from town." He strolled into the room and stopped beside her. "My men and I work hard. We earn the chance to relax at times. And it's safer to offer them the opportunity here. Cowboys driving into town to get drunk is dangerous. I'd rather they had a couple drinks here."

No one in Texas would dispute the picture he painted. "Well, then." She stepped away from him. "I can understand that." She headed to the door, ignoring the incredulous look he sent her. "Please plan to keep that bar, and this room, locked whenever it's unattended." She left the room and headed up the stairs.

As Emily climbed, she fought the urge to look back over her shoulder to see if Wyatt was following. She was fairly certain she could find Tyler's room on her own, but she didn't think he was up to letting her have free rein of his house. When his footsteps sounded behind her, she bit back a grin. She was right. She was proud of herself; figuring this man out was proving interesting.

"Second door on the right," he instructed. When she reached it, his arm shot past her and he opened the old wooden door for her. Startled, she jumped and bumped her shoulder against his chest. Her recoil nearly shot her into the room. She glared at him when he chuckled.

Fighting the urge to watch him, she turned and once again focused on the room. "Good-size room." It wasn't much, actually. A bed, dresser and in the corner was a pile of things that were obviously Tyler's. She frowned at them. "Why are his belongings in the corner?" She turned an accusing glare at Wyatt.

"He wants them that way. I had them all in the dresser. I've actually put them away twice. He keeps putting them back on the chair."

She looked closer, realizing there was an old, scarred wooden chair beneath the pile. She frowned. It looked familiar.

As if reading her mind, Wyatt answered. "That's DJ's chair." At her confused glance, he explained. "When Mom passed away, we split up the dining room set. Each of us took one of the chairs. Mine's the captain's chair downstairs."

Emily walked over to the pile and saw the organization to it all. Shirts folded neatly. Jeans stacked beneath. The backpack leaning against the rungs. In the center of the seat, she saw the assortment of items Tyler had pulled from his pockets in her courtroom. The plastic lizard and the playing card were tangled in the links of an old chain. She didn't even know what to say, or think, or do. "I— Does he know it's his dad's chair?"

"Yeah. I told him the first night he came here. I thought it might help him feel welcome."

Emily turned to look back at the man she'd foolishly thought she'd figured out. He stood in the doorway, his hands wedged into the pockets of his jeans. It wasn't a casual stance. And somehow it made her confident that she—and Tyler—were totally safe with him.

WYATT DIDN'T DARE move farther into the room. He wasn't sure he could trust himself that close to her.

She was trying hard to maintain the professional, observant caseworker facade. Trying and failing. Her heart was too visible in her eyes, her emotions too strong to hide. The realization that Tyler kept all his worldly goods tucked into DJ's old, battered chair tore at her. He could see her trying to figure out a way to shut off her reaction.

It wasn't working. And he was having a tough time fighting the urge to ease her concerns. Why was this woman so reluctant to face her emotions, and why did he feel the need to protect her? He barely knew her— she was technically the enemy—and yet he knew she had Tyler's best interests at heart.

"He's—" She backed away from the chair, and before Wyatt could step away, she headed for the door. She tried to move past him, but the doorway wasn't big enough for them both. He touched her arm, making her stop.

"He's what? A hurt little boy? Yeah." Wyatt said it softly, wanting to soothe her at the same time he wanted to make danged sure she didn't take Tyler away from here.

"How could she do that?"

"His mother? Do what? Leave him?" He didn't let

go of her arm despite the warnings running through his brain. He let her perfume wrap around him, ignoring the fact that she could destroy his entire family with one signature. "Now you know why I'll do everything in my power to make sure no one takes him or leaves him again. He's staying here." The last came out through clenched teeth no matter how hard he tried to relax his jaw.

Emily stared up at him then and not for the first time he noticed how frail she looked. He nearly laughed. Frail, yet tough as nails. She'd fight him with everything she had if she thought this was the wrong place for the boy.

He knew the instant she'd made her decision, the instant he'd won. Her shoulders didn't sag, not really, but her rigid battle stance faded.

"Are you okay?" he asked, concerned about the pallor of her skin.

Her head snapped up. "I'm fine. Why do you keep asking me that?" Anger tinged her voice. Anger and something else he couldn't place. "My fainting earlier was simply because I got too much sun, running through the hills retrieving the boy who, might I remind you, you're responsible for."

That dagger landed a little close to home, and Wyatt winced at her accuracy. His anger rose in reaction. "I'm not saying I won't make mistakes. But I'll do as good, if not better than his mother has."

"Very well." She stepped away from him, dragging her arm from his grasp. "He can stay." She took another step backward. "But if anything happens…"

"Like him running away again?" Wyatt taunted her. He knew she wanted to get past him and into the hall. Away, her body language screamed.

He let her go and moved out of the doorway to give

her room to pass. She was no fool. She took the escape and hurried down the stairs, her back ramrod straight. She might want to run, but she clung to that damned stiff persona. She bid Addie farewell and disappeared out the front door.

From Tyler's window, Wyatt could see her pull out of the drive. The taillights glowed in the dust cloud that rose up behind her.

"What the heck did you do to her?" Addie yelled up the stairs. "Are you crazy?"

Not yet, he thought. Not yet.

CHAPTER SEVEN

EVERY TIME EMILY entered the small coffee shop in the basement of the courthouse, she wished she could learn to like coffee. It smelled so heavenly.

But what she really craved was a nice warm cup of tea. Lack of sleep lately made for frequent caffeine runs. Half the time now, they had her favorite drink ready and waiting before she got to the head of the line to order. She didn't even have to think. Today was no exception. "Thanks, Meg." She smiled at the girl who seemed to always be behind the counter as she paid for her drink.

She didn't often sit down in the coffee shop, either, but today it wasn't as crowded, and her brain was nearer to mush than normal. She slid into a chair. She seriously needed a good night's sleep.

In the past week, she'd managed to sleep only one night through. She kept dreaming about things her mind refused to remember. She probably should be glad, but she wasn't. She was tired and frustrated.

The tea helped. Taking a slow sip, she curled her hands around the warm, sturdy cup and closed her eyes. She barely bit back the sigh of pleasure.

"I'll take a large black coffee. Plain. No frills." The familiar deep voice broke into her thoughts and her sigh morphed into a frown.

Wyatt Hawkins stood at the counter, a worn wallet in

his hand as he extracted a couple bills. Meg set a large, steaming to-go cup in front of him and smiled brightly at him. He didn't even seem to notice her interest.

He took the cup and came to stand beside Emily's table. From her vantage point, he looked tall. Too tall, but somehow his size didn't intimidate her.

The cowboy hat he wore shaded his eyes, but his smile was clearly visible. She felt herself respond. "H-hello."

"Hi." He set the cup down, shaking his hand to dispel the heat. "I wasn't planning on getting a coffee, but I saw you in here and thought I'd join you."

"What? Of course." She waved to the seat across from her. She couldn't exactly tell him to go away. "Uh, what brings you into town?"

"The endless battle of licenses that comes with owning a ranch." He shrugged but didn't elaborate.

It had been nearly a week since she'd been out to the ranch. Emily had come back from that last visit, filled out the caseworker report and signed off on the final custody papers. She hadn't taken time to think about it. She'd just…finished. If only it were that simple—she still had to continue the court- visitor visits that she'd ordered.

He settled in the small bistro chair across from her. The scent of his strong coffee overpowered her softer tea. Much like the man himself.

"Thank you," he finally said.

"Wh-what?" She stared at him. She sounded like a fool, repeating herself. She needed to get her focus back. He wasn't smiling, and she realized he was serious. Sitting up straighter, she wondered what was going through his head. "What for?"

"The paperwork. Thank you. I wasn't sure you were going to approve."

Oh. That. She was just doing her job, she told herself. Mentally, she tried to shift gears, tried to go back to being the judge. "You're welcome. It's the best thing for Tyler. How is he doing?"

"Fine. I think he's settling into school. Though he still seems to be having a tough time, missing his mom."

"Of course." The silence stretched out. "Have you heard anything from your brother?"

He shook his head, and she saw the lines deepen around his eyes. His worry was as strong as his sense of obligation.

"Can I interest either of you in a piece of pie?" Meg brought out a plate and displayed it in front of them.

Wyatt smiled politely at the young girl. "No, thanks." Then he turned his attention back to Emily. With what sounded like a grumble, the girl went back behind the counter.

The scent of pumpkin wafted in the air between them. Emily simply shook her head and fought to breathe as a memory slammed into her like her stepfather's fist. She tried to swallow back the bile rising in her throat. *No. Not here. Not now.* Not in front of this man. He had to see her as the competent judge. He had to—

Mom had been teaching her how to make a pumpkin pie. It was a family tradition from her mother's side. Mom had promised that this year Emily was old enough to do more than watch.

Except that was also the same day that Earl had lost his job...again. She couldn't escape the memories that flooded her mind. She heard the screams—hers and her mother's—echo out of the past. She wanted to cover her ears and block it out as she had then. But she knew it wouldn't do any good. The sounds and smells were trapped inside her memories.

Emily shot to her feet, nearly tipping her chair over. "Excuse me. I need to get back to work." She backed away from the table, leaving her tea and walking quickly to the door. She didn't stop until she reached the bank of elevators. She pounded on the dimly lit button with the worn black arrow pointing up, smacking it several times. She had to get out of here. Had to escape the pain and memory swirling around in her head.

"Emily?" Wyatt's deep, warm voice broke through, luring her away from the pain.

Looking over her shoulder, she saw him striding toward her. Comfort washed over her, confusing her because she'd never felt that way before. Wyatt's image came clearly into focus, the past receding just a bit. The elevator dinged and the doors slid open with their usual swish. She tried to move, but couldn't. The doors closed.

"Emily." His voice was softer now.

Reality slowly returned, and heat swamped her cheeks as she realized what had happened and where she was. And who she was with. She closed her eyes and mumbled a curse. How could this man possibly think she was competent when she didn't? Not at the moment, anyway.

"I'm sorry. Excuse me. I really need to go." She headed for the stairs. Her office was only three flights up. Her heels snapped against the thick steel stairs, echoing up the entire shaft, her only indication she was actually moving.

But her mind couldn't escape that kitchen and her mom's screams. The stairs blurred as tears filled her eyes. She stumbled, feeling hard metal bite into her shin.

Gravity reached out for her and in that instant she wondered if she'd die—and escape the memories—if she fell all the way down the long flight of steps.

She didn't think she'd mind. But the option was taken out of her control when strong arms caught her. Slowly, Wyatt lowered them both to the steps.

The metal was cold against her backside, but thankfully solid as he sat down beside her. The only warmth she felt came from him as the steps were narrow, and he had to sit close. For a long moment she simply focused on catching her breath, but there was no ignoring him, or what had happened.

"You going to tell me what's going on, or just deny it like you did the last time?"

Emily closed her eyes, wondering what to tell him. It wasn't as if she knew why things were falling apart around her. She couldn't pinpoint a specific cause. Maybe she was losing her mind. "I've had a lot going on. I guess I'm overtired, or something." She looked up at him then, because even seated, he was taller than she was.

"That's all you've got?"

She tried to smile. "At the moment, yes." Reaching out, she curled her hand around the cold metal handrail and pulled herself to her feet. She took a minute to steady herself and smooth her skirt, then turned and continued up the stairs.

"Where are you going?" He fell into step behind her.

"To my office."

"There's a perfectly good elevator down there."

"I know." And a dozen pair of eyes in the coffee shop that had seen her bolt. No, thanks. "It's only three floors up. The exercise is good for me."

"And Addie thinks *I'm* crazy," he mumbled and continued to follow her up the stairs. They'd just reached the next flight when the heavy fire door to the hall below slammed open, hitting the concrete wall like a gunshot. Emily gasped and stumbled. Before either of them could think, his arms were around her again, warm and strong.

Two kids jogged up past them. "Get a room," one of them commented as their footsteps headed up. Emily cringed at the kid's crude comment. Just because they were standing close didn't mean...although she was all too aware of Wyatt's arm around her back, his big hand splayed across her side, his thumb just brushing the edge of her breast.

She froze. His fingers curled against her ribs, holding her tight. She didn't try to move away. His warmth felt so good. His eyes looked so earnest. "I..." she whispered.

Time vanished as Wyatt's gaze met hers, and just when she thought she'd gotten lost in them, his eyes moved, sweeping down her face to rest on her lips. She couldn't remember the last time she'd been this close to a man.

The shadow of the whiskers on his jaw tempted her to reach up and touch, and the warm, sunbaked scent of cowboy lured her to lift her chin....

Sanity returned with the click of a set of high heels on the stairs above. Emily jumped away from Wyatt. She didn't look at him again, and with the determination that she kept forgetting she had whenever in this man's presence, she set her jaw and her resolve in place and went up the rest of the way without incident. She didn't stop until she was back inside her office, leaning against the locked door.

What was wrong with her? She berated herself. This

was not okay. He was a participant in a case where she was the judge. She could lose everything. She'd worked too hard to lose all she'd worked for because her hormones were in overdrive.

How much time passed she didn't know, but the soft knock on the door surprised her. For an instant, she thought maybe he'd followed her, then realized there was no way Wyatt would ever timidly knock on any door. And why she thought he'd bother to follow her was beyond her.

"Emily?" Dianne's voice came through the door to accompany another soft knock. "Are you okay?"

Emily took a deep breath. This was not acceptable, she told herself. Straightening her shoulders, she breathed in one more time and opened the door.

Worry lined Dianne's face and Emily immediately felt guilty. "I'm sorry—"

Dianne shook her head to dismiss the apology. "I tried to call down to the coffee shop but they said you'd already left. Mr. Watson called. Your mother's fallen. He wants you to contact him immediately." She handed over a yellow sticky note with the assisted living's number scrawled on it.

All the air rushed from Emily's lungs and for an instant she froze. Then she ran to her desk and had to dial the number three times before she got it right. Her heart beat so loudly in her ears that she hardly heard the phone ring. When the receptionist put her on hold to transfer her, she nearly screamed in frustration. But Dianne's hands on her shoulders gently guided her, and she reluctantly sat in the chair.

"Hello? Ms. Ivers?" The man's voice sounded calm. Too calm.

"Yes."

"I'm sorry to tell you this, but your mother took a rather nasty fall."

Emily's heart sank. "What happened? Is she hurt?"

"We're not sure yet. Rose found her on the floor of her room when she went to get her for lunch. Her face is badly bruised. While I don't think her arm is seriously injured, she's cradling it, and she won't let us look at it."

The past shivered over Emily's shoulders. "Her right arm?"

"Yes. How did you know?"

"She hurt it years ago," Emily whispered, fighting the images crowding her mind, images she'd nearly banished while in Wyatt's arms. Oh, why did she have to think of him now? "It never healed properly." It might have, if Earl had taken her to the doctor.

"She won't let us treat her." The man's frustration was loud and clear even if his words were soft. "We thought if you could come down, maybe she'd cooperate."

Emily wasn't so sure about that, but at least they were trying. "I'll be right there." A sigh of relief came through the line and without saying goodbye, Emily hung up.

"Oh, God, Dianne." Emily's voice broke and the older woman put a comforting arm around her shoulder. Emily almost let herself lean into the comfort. Almost.

"I'll take care of your appointments. You just go."

Emily nodded, not sure where she'd left her keys. Or her purse. Or anything. She realized her purse was where she always put it, in the bottom drawer of her desk. She was halfway to the door when she spun around again. Keys. She needed keys.

"Are you okay to drive?" Dianne's voice came from so far away.

"Yes. Sure." Emily headed to the door again, her mind filled with images of her mother, cradling her broken arm, crying with the pain. She never should have taken her mother to that place. She should have found a way to keep her at the house, or move her into her own apartment.

How many times had she had this same argument with herself, and how many times had she realized this was the best option?

"I'll take you." A voice cut through all the chaos raging in Emily's mind. She spun around. Wyatt stood in the open doorway, his hands at his hips like some Western lawman taking control.

"I'm fine."

"No, you're not. Come on. My truck's just out front."

"I'm perfectly capable of taking care of myself and my mother." Emily knew she sounded ungrateful, but she'd already shown too much of herself to this man. She had to keep her distance. It was hard enough to appear professional and competent around him.

"I think it's a good idea," Dianne chimed in.

Emily glared at her. Traitor.

Slowly, Wyatt walked into the room, not the stalking gait of the powerful man he was, but gently, as if he were approaching a spooked horse. "I'm not trying to force you," he crooned, but belied the softness with a frown. "Look, I know what you're dealing with. I lost my mom just a few months ago."

Their gazes met and she saw pain in his eyes. Saw the understanding and empathy there, and felt that same calmness she'd felt when he'd caught her on the stairs. Knowing he and Dianne were right, and not wanting to admit it, Emily simply nodded and moved past him and out the door.

FOLLOWING EMILY'S DIRECTIONS, it only took ten minutes for Wyatt to make the trip to Sunset Haven. And all ten of them were silent. It wasn't until Wyatt pulled into visitor parking that Emily turned and faced him.

"I can handle it from here." Emily reached for the handle of the door, effectively dismissing him.

"Yeah, but how will you get back home?" He didn't wait for her answer. Instead, he climbed out and led the way to the entrance.

She was angry, he knew that. He also knew that she wasn't really angry with him. She was angry at the situation, at herself and just maybe a little at life. He remembered those days, before Mom passed away, when he couldn't do a thing to help her. He hated that useless feeling.

Emily stalked past him, her hair flying behind her. If he weren't so concerned about her state of mind, he'd definitely let himself enjoy the view.

He didn't like the fact that he was attracted to her. In that stairwell, he'd wanted nothing more than to pull her close and taste her. For an instant, he'd seen her soften, felt the gentle pull of her attraction.

An older woman in a bright blue uniform met Emily at the door and surprisingly gave her a hug, which Emily accepted. Something he doubted she normally did. Together, the women entered a room down the hall.

Not sure what to do, Wyatt stopped outside the door. He'd hung around outside Mom's room a lot during those last few days. Addie had always been the one in with her.

He leaned against the wall, wondering and waiting. Despite his best efforts, he couldn't ignore the conversation going on in the room, but no matter how much he wanted to, he knew better than to go inside.

"Mom, it's okay," Emily said, a thick veil of tears in her voice.

"No. I can't. He'll find out."

"Who's he?" an unfamiliar voice asked, probably the nurse.

"My stepfather, I think." He could barely hear Emily's whisper. "Mom, Earl's not here anymore. It's okay."

"He'll come back. He always comes back." Her mother's voice broke with panic.

"No, Mom, he's—"

"It's okay." There was a shuffling sound as the nurse spoke, interrupting Emily. "Helen, we'll make sure he's aware of what's going on."

"No. He won't like it," her mother sobbed.

"Okay, Helen. We'll wait."

"But—" Emily's words abruptly stopped again. He heard footsteps, but they stopped on the other side of the door.

"Arguing with her will only upset her more," the nurse said.

"But Earl's dead. Shouldn't that make her feel better?"

"Maybe. But let's let the medication relax her, and then we'll see how she does. She's already much calmer since you got here. Wait here, sit by her. Think of good things to talk about. I'll be back in a minute."

"All right."

Wyatt didn't move, not even sure if Emily remembered he was here. It didn't matter—he wasn't leaving. The nurse came out and looked at him with open curiosity. She nodded then headed down the hall. What should he do?

He was saved from making a decision by the sound of a shuffled step and a rattling noise. An old cowboy pushing a metal walker with bright yellow tennis balls instead of rubber feet headed toward him. He wore a dark brown Stetson and a pearl snap shirt. Other than the walker, this guy could be him someday.

The man stopped in front of Wyatt. "Family?" He tilted his head toward Helen's room.

"Nah. Just a friend."

The old man grinned. "Must be a mighty good friend."

"Why do you say that?"

"People don't often come to places like this voluntarily. Mostly obligation."

"Ah."

"How's Helen doing?"

Wyatt was surprised the old man knew what was going on and that surprise must have shown on his face as the old man chuckled.

"We all know what's goin' on around here. The grapevine is alive and well in this place, even if nothin' else is."

Wyatt had to smile at the old man's twisted sense of humor.

"No sense coolin' your heels out here. It could be a while." The old man extended his hand while he carefully balanced and held on to the walker with his other hand. "I'm Hal Cooper."

"Wyatt Hawkins." Wyatt hastily shook his hand then let go so Hal could balance better. "Pleased to meet you."

"I'll buy you a cup of coffee. Come on." Hal started moving noisily down the hall. "I'll let Rosie know where we're headed."

With the racket the walker made, Wyatt doubted Rosie, whoever she was, would have any trouble tracking them, but he fell in step beside the man as they headed to the large dining room.

"They just put in the new crappachino machine," Hal explained.

"I don't think there's an *R* in that word," Wyatt suggested as he settled in a chair where he could see Helen's door.

"Don't be too sure. You haven't tasted it yet."

CHAPTER EIGHT

WITH THE CURTAINS DRAWN, her mother's room was dim. Emily turned on a small bedside lamp, casting long shadows over the tiny figure in the bed. Emily's heart hurt, missing the woman who'd raised her, the woman she'd come home to after school each day, who'd been her shoulder to lean on.

"Mom?" She didn't want to startle her mother if she was sleeping, but she didn't want to leave her mother alone in her worry, either.

"Emily?" Helen turned her head to smile weakly at her. Emily smiled back. "You're here. I missed you."

Helen tried to sit up, but Emily gently pressed a hand to her shoulder. "Go ahead and rest. I'll just sit here. We can chat if you want."

"I'd love to, but I'm so sleepy, sweetheart."

"Then rest. I'm not going anywhere."

"You're such a good girl." Helen smiled and closed her eyes. "I don't know what I did to deserve you."

Emily's heart constricted at the unaccustomed praise. "We're both lucky, I guess."

Helen winced. "My arm aches today." Her voice sounded distant, as if the notion surprised her.

Emily wasn't sure what to say to the sudden change of topic and was saved by her mother continuing, "Make sure and answer the phone, will you? He said he'd call back."

The blood in Emily's veins froze. "Who?"

"Earl." Helen's eyes drifted closed, a frown creasing her brow.

Earl wasn't calling anyone, Emily knew, but still she glanced over at the phone on the table. Every room in the assisted living came wired for them. She'd debated about paying for the extra expense when she'd moved her mother here. But it had been a good way for the two of them to talk. Her mother still understood an "old-fashioned" phone, whereas cell phones were foreign to her.

Now Emily wasn't sure it was worth it.

"Did…did you get a call earlier, Mom?" Had someone really called or had Helen imagined it? Helen didn't answer as she'd fallen asleep.

Getting up quietly, Emily lifted the receiver, and with trembling fingers, dialed to call back the last number.

"Hello?" Drew's voice was painfully familiar.

Emily bit her tongue and barely resisted the urge to slam the receiver down on the plastic cradle. Damn him. She yanked the cord out of the wall and wound it around the phone. She'd visit Helen more often if that was what it took to keep in touch, but she wasn't giving that man a way to get to her mother.

With the phone in her hand, she stalked out of the room and headed toward the director's office. Two steps into the hall, she froze. Wyatt sat casually in the dining room with one of the residents. She'd seen the older man before, but didn't remember his name. Wyatt was smiling and the old man was talking, his gnarled hands waving in the air. Like old friends.

She'd expected Wyatt to be gone. He didn't have to stay. She'd call a cab to take her home. She wasn't helpless.

He laughed at something the old man said and it warmed his face, brightened his eyes. As if he felt her gaze, he turned his head and her breath caught in her throat.

He stood and walked toward her, his smile fading with each step. "What's the matter?"

She couldn't even begin to explain Drew to Wyatt. The very idea sent ripples of fear through her.

"I...need to talk to the director. I'm fairly certain this is why Mom fell." She held up the phone, wishing she could throw the thing. Instead, she calmly walked to the director's office.

WYATT SAT BEHIND the wheel of the truck, the glow of the dash the only light as Emily settled into the passenger seat. Night had fallen sometime between their walking in the front door and Helen finally falling asleep, her arm bandaged and pain meds in her system. Emily looked completely exhausted.

"Thank you," she said softly, staring out the windshield. She didn't glance his way. He wasn't sure she even moved.

"No problem." The engine roared and he put it into gear. It wouldn't take long to get back to where her car was parked. He wasn't sure she was safe to drive, but he'd learned that questioning her abilities was the fastest way to a disagreement. Neither of them had the energy for that tonight.

The parking garage at the courthouse was deserted. A small sedan was the only car left. It had to be hers.

All the calm vanished as the headlights glistened off the pavement. Broken glass. He cursed and pulled to a stop several feet away. "Stay here," he told her.

"Why?"

Instead of answering, he climbed out of the truck and headed toward her car.

"What happened?" Her voice echoed around the empty concrete structure.

"Looks like someone broke into your car." Wyatt peered in the now permanently open window. "They went through the glove box. Did you have anything valuable in there?"

He was surprised she wasn't standing right there beside him. He looked back and found her leaning against the side of the truck, her head thrown back so she could stare at the garage's ceiling. "What else can go wrong today? I should have stayed in bed."

Wyatt laughed despite knowing she probably wouldn't appreciate it. "Is there any security here?" he asked, already knowing the answer. Maybe if they were in a big city, or over at city hall. But here in the county offices… even he knew there wasn't money for that. He still waited until she shook her head before he pulled out his phone and dialed 9-1-1.

Apparently, being a magistrate had its perks. The police cruiser pulled into the parking lot, lights flashing, quicker than he'd expected. Still, it was late before the tow truck finally left with her car, after the man had told them that the thief had tried to hotwire the car and had fried the electrical system.

"Even I know you can't hotwire a newer model car." She was sitting in his truck again, staring unseeingly through the windshield.

Wyatt didn't start the truck right away. Instead, he turned to look at Emily. Her hair fell down around her face and soft shadows settled beneath her eyes. The fluorescent lights of the garage weren't flattering to anyone on a good day, but something about her drew him and he enjoyed just watching her. "You okay?"

"I'm fine. Tired and really ticked, but fine."

"Let's get you home."

"All right." She reluctantly gave in and fumbled with the seat belt.

Downtown vanished quickly, morphing into side streets and neighborhoods of houses, apartment buildings and strip malls. She directed him to turn onto a tree-lined street that held rows of pretty, little, well-kept townhouses. All exactly the same on the outside.

Light splashed out nearly every window, but when Emily directed him to turn into a narrow drive, he saw that hers was void of any illumination. He pulled in and turned to face her again. She simply sat there, staring out at the darkness. In the glow from the neighbor's window, he saw a trail of tears on her cheeks.

He cursed, got out and walked around the truck.

He didn't think twice. Instead, he opened her door. "Hey," he said softly, not wanting to startle her.

She turned her head slowly as if she was just waking up. She didn't say anything, simply let her gaze move up until their eyes met.

"Come on." He reached into the car and unbuckled her seat belt, then curled his hand around her elbow. "Let's get you inside."

She didn't say a word, just turned and planted her feet on the pavement. He helped her stand, and they both froze when the movement brought her close to him. The faded whisper of perfume startled and pleased him. He stepped back reluctantly, fighting the urge to pull her close and swing her up into his arms. She was too independent for that, but he was tempted.

Instead, he cleared his throat and guided her up the sidewalk to the front door. "You're exhausted. So don't give me any of that crap about being strong enough to stand on your own two feet. I don't want to hear about how you can take care of yourself, your mother and the rest of the world. You've already proved that."

At the door, she stopped. Not to unlock the door as he expected, but to face him. Her keys were in her hand and he almost smiled at the tight grip. She'd taken a self-defense class somewhere along the way. Another point in her favor.

"You going to open the door or gouge my eyes out with those?" He chuckled.

She didn't laugh. She didn't put a key in the lock, and she didn't aim them at him. Win-win, he thought.

"Are you always so…bossy?" she asked.

"Not always. But if the situation warrants it—" He shrugged. "I'm not leaving until I'm sure everything inside is okay." He paused and waited. "Open the door, Emily," he commanded softly when she didn't move.

"Don't you need to get home to Tyler?"

"Nope. My foreman and his wife are at the house tonight. You know, the longer we argue about this, the later I leave."

"Fine," she huffed and turned the knob with the loud clatter of keys against wood. "But only to keep you happy and get this over with. *Not* because I'm afraid."

Finally, she stepped inside a small foyer, her heels loud against the wooden floor.

There were no lights on, but Wyatt got the sense of stark emptiness. He reached for the light switch beside the door. It slid, rather than flipped, telling him it was a dimmer.

Slowly, the lights came up. A ceiling lamp cast gold over cream walls, a small table to the right and a narrow set of stairs that led up.

There were no pictures on the wall, though a square mirror in a golden frame hung above the table. A darkened room lay to the right and straight ahead, shadows blocking his view. Pretty, he thought, but cold. Like a show home.

He looked at Emily and saw more clearly the tear tracks on her face and the exhaustion in her eyes. She didn't look at him, but silently walked past. She tossed her purse onto the small table and stabbed the button on the blinking answering machine. A mechanical voice broke the silence, telling her there was one message, but no message sounded. It beeped as she deleted the note.

"I'll be just a second." She passed through the living room, to a far door. He saw the end of a bed in the flash of light before she closed the door. "If you're going to look around, go ahead and get it done with."

Odds were the car break-in had been random, but Wyatt wanted to make sure. He set his Stetson on the table near her purse and headed into the living room.

There was little in the townhouse that told Wyatt much about who lived here. Certainly this room full of rented-with-the-place furniture gave no indication of who she was.

The curtains were still drawn as she'd been gone all day. The townhouse was as silent as the proverbial tomb. No cat came out of the shadows to twist around his ankles. No dog came yapping out of its kennel to greet him or provide any warning. Just quiet, dark, silence.

Was this what she came home to every night? Wyatt compared the insanity of the ranch house to this. The hands coming in, stomping their feet and heading to the kitchen. Tyler giggling and laughing as one of the cowboys teased him. Addie or Chet's wife, Yolanda, slapping huge platters of food on the table. Noise, light and life everywhere.

He turned on a lamp and was surprised when the dim light reflected off the rough edges of a picture frame. It was the only knickknack in the room.

A hodgepodge of metal flowers rimmed the frame, their hearts painted with yellow and gold. A butterfly sat frozen in silver in the corner.

He picked it up, surprised to find it was heavy. He tilted the frame toward the light, wondering whose picture she displayed. Two young girls had their arms wrapped around each other, hugging tight, their lips turned up in a frozen giggle. The picture was too old to be Emily.

"My mother." Emily's voice came from behind him. "That's her and her younger sister, my aunt Judy."

He thought it a bit odd that she kept a picture of her mother from a time when she hadn't known her. Why not something more recent?

He gave in and asked, "Why this picture?"

She was silent so long he wasn't sure she intended to answer. "That's how I always wanted her to be. I don't remember her ever happy like that."

Wyatt's mind flooded with memories of all the laughter in his mom's house—even on the afternoon of her funeral when they'd gathered around the kitchen table.

He felt a stab of sadness go through him at all that Emily must have missed.

He looked back at the picture again, seeing the resemblance and knowing that there were no pictures of Emily
as a child that held such joy. There were a couple times
tonight, as the nurses had taken care of her mother, that
the older woman had said things that seemed to stir up
painful memories for Emily. He'd wondered, but hadn't
said anything. She'd grown more and more withdrawn,
more and more distant.

Suddenly, he wanted to give her a reason to smile like
the girls in the photo were.

He swallowed to ease his dry throat. Forcing himself
to step away, Wyatt continued his inspection of the place.

He headed to the kitchen, and the back door, and she
followed him. Fluorescent light shattered the mood as
it overwhelmed the quiet light and showed him a wide
kitchen. The back door was locked solid and the outside
lights flooded an empty backyard.

Stepping back into the kitchen, he realized that, if
there was a heart to this place, this room was it. Filled
with modern appliances and new counters and cabinets,
it was welcoming, with bright flowers and butterfly decorations.

"When was the last time you ate?" he asked.

"Does the tea I had count? Um, breakfast, I think."

The fact that she was actually answering his questions
told him more than anything how exhausted she was.
She wasn't fighting him. "Where are the frying pans?"

"Uh, over there." She pointed to a large cabinet beside the stove, a frown on her face. As he headed toward
it, she seemed to revive a bit. "Wait a minute. What are
you doing?"

He smiled over his shoulder at her, not stopping. He
opened the wide wooden door and chose a pan. "I'm not

the best cook in the world, but I can make a decent omelet. You have eggs, right?" At her nod, he pointed at the tall chairs against the island. "Have a seat."

"Wyatt, I'm really tired. I just want to go to bed—"

"No, not yet." He almost laughed when she bristled. He needed to shake her out of the slump she was in. Feed her, then send her off to bed. He paused in midstride and pulled his mind back from that little cliff.

She did as he asked and climbed up on the chair, her compliance surprising him. She rested her chin in her palm and watched as he tried to find his way around her kitchen. Her eyes drooped. If he didn't make conversation, she'd fall asleep right there.

"So, as a judge, you ever officiate over a wedding?" What the hell had made him think of that?

"A few." She sat up a little straighter, trying to stay awake. "Most of them haven't gone well."

"Why not? Someone say something when you get to that part where anyone objects?"

She actually laughed. "Courthouse ceremonies are usually pretty small. But recently I did have one that was interesting."

"Really?" He focused on melting the butter in the pan and cracking the eggs instead of on the smile that was waking up her face.

"Yeah. A couple months ago. We used Skype with the parents."

"Really?"

"Yeah. I think the bride and groom thought they were safer with distance."

"I'm guessing they weren't."

"Uh, no. We actually had to turn Dad off."

Wyatt laughed, imagining the usually prim and

proper judge E. J. Ivers in such a situation. He liked her flustered, and that would definitely fluster her.

Letting the eggs cook, he turned around and looked at her. She was more awake now; the tears had faded. She'd scrubbed all evidence of them from her cheeks. Their eyes met. He took a few steps and without warning, leaned down and put his lips on hers.

The kiss lasted only an instant, so when he stepped away to check on the eggs, Emily blinked several times, her confusion apparent.

"WHAT WAS THAT FOR?"

"You just looked like you needed it." He grinned over his shoulder as he added ham and cheese to the omelet, along with other goodies he'd found in her fridge.

"Well, I didn't *need* it." She looked away. "But thank you," she whispered.

What exactly did needing a kiss look like? Emily wanted to ask, but didn't dare. She was already way out of bounds with this guy. But somehow, the line she'd crossed had vanished and she didn't know how to get back.

Wyatt set the full plate in front of her and suddenly she was starving. And after just one bite she had to admit that he was right—he did make a great omelet.

Once she was full from the delicious food and more awake than she'd been all day, Emily sat at the counter, watching Wyatt move around her kitchen as if he lived here. She thought over every encounter she'd had with the man. In her courtroom. Out at the ranch. In the coffee shop. In the dining room of the assisted living facility. And now in her kitchen. Was there any place he wasn't totally comfortable? Any place that shook up that cool exterior?

He noticed everything around him, noticed the people and stepped up to take care. He was a caretaker, not a caregiver, she amended. Making sure everyone and everything was handled, put in place and fixed.

It was who he was.

What she didn't know, and what concerned her was his motivation. "Why are you doing this?"

He paused and frowned. "Doing what?"

"Being so nice. Helpful. Taking care of me."

He looked confused, but she just couldn't believe that anyone took care of someone without personal motivation. She didn't trust easily, if at all, and that distrust was sending out bright warning signals.

Slowly, he set aside the dishes he'd been stacking in the sink. He leaned back against the counter, crossing his arms over his chest. He looked down at her, and she barely resisted the urge to stand. Not that it would put them at eye level, but she'd feel stronger.

He shrugged. "It's what I've always done."

"You don't even know me."

"So?"

Was he really that oblivious? Could he possibly be that altruistic? She thought of all the people she knew. No one had a clean slate. Her father had been the best man she'd known, but even he'd made mistakes, done desperate things. Her stepfather was the worst. His fist had done most of the talking and her stepbrother, Drew, seemed to be following in his father's footsteps. Even her mother kept secrets and lied. Emily's heart hurt at all the deceptions her mother held. All the lies she'd told to protect Emily from Earl, but also to keep her from hating Earl too much.

"No one does anything without an ul—agenda." She'd almost said ulterior motive but knew that would probably tick him off.

Slowly, he walked toward her, his boots loud against the wood floor. "You've been in the courtroom too long," he whispered, never breaking eye contact. "You've seen too much of the bad in this world."

He was in her space, his body heat reaching out to nearly overwhelm her. Emily wished she'd given in and stood, as then she'd be able to back away from him. She shuddered, fear of what she didn't understand sliding through her.

He lifted his hand, and even though all he did was run a rough finger along the edge of her chin, she flinched. He frowned at her reaction and the questions in his eyes surprised her.

So why was her disappointment so strong this time? She wasn't foolish enough to think he was different. She'd stopped being foolish a long time ago. "You already have Tyler's custody paperwork. You don't need to butter me up."

His eyes flashed, this time with anger. Ah, she had hit a nerve.

Before she could analyze why, Emily jumped from the chair and hustled away from him. Wyatt stared at her, deep furrows in his brow, no words coming out of his mouth. She tore her gaze away from those lips. *Not going there.* Definitely not going there, she reminded herself, though the memory of his earlier touch was too fresh to totally dismiss.

"Thank you for making me eat." She grabbed her

used dishes and headed to the sink. "That helped. I'll take care of the rest of the dishes," she told him.

Silence cloaked them. Heavy, nerve-racking silence. "I'm sure you'll need to get home." She quickly led the way to the front hall and he slowly followed. There was no reason for him to stay any longer. Except she didn't want him to go and didn't know why. Which meant she needed to send him on his way even more quickly.

He took the hint, though without any smile. "You okay to stay by yourself?" he asked.

"I do it all the time," she reminded him.

"Yes, you do." The air grew thick and he stepped closer. His palm cupped the side of her face. "I'm not even going to apologize for this." He leaned in and kissed her again.

This time, it wasn't the comforting kiss he'd given her before. This was deeper, harder and definitely the kiss of a man wanting a woman. His arms closed around her, melding her against the solid planes of his chest.

Emily sighed, all her reserves to resist the flood of emotion gone. Want. Need. Longing. Desire. All pulsed through her.

She hastily pulled away from him and marched to the door, mentally cursing the fact that she'd kicked off her shoes. Her bare feet made barely a sound and she stood even shorter. She reached the front door and yanked it open. Damn. Her hand trembled on the knob.

He stood there for a long minute, then with a deliberately slow pace, he walked toward her. She felt his anger, and something else vibrate across the room. He took his time grabbing his Stetson off the front table and settling it on his head. He stopped for a minute, and she saw his reflection in the mirror. His broad shoulders filled the glass. As he approached the open doorway, she saw him clench his jaw as if resisting the urge to say something. Probably curse.

"Thank you again for making dinner." She half hid behind the door. Then forced herself to step forward and lift her chin.

He stopped, filling the doorway, the night behind him. "That question you asked earlier about why I did all this? If anyone else had said that to me…"

"You'd do what?" She brought her own anger out to hide her uncertainty. She'd never cringed from Earl's fist, and she refused to cringe from this man's. But she'd danged well take action against him. She was not her mother.

"I don't know what's wrong with you, Emily. I don't know what you've been through or seen to make you this way. But in my world, we take care of each other. You ever want to see what real life is like, come out and spend more than an hour at the ranch. Then maybe you'll get it." He readjusted that damned hat and stepped out into the night. His footfalls were hard on the pavement and his truck roared in the night. She stood there, her chin high until the bright red taillights vanished around the corner.

Emily slammed the door and turned the lock with more force than necessary. "Damn you," she whispered to the empty house. "Damn you for making me want to care."

She leaned back on the door, her eyes automatically drawn to the now-empty glass of the mirror. She wanted *so* badly to believe him, to believe *in* him. But she couldn't. He was right; she was damaged. Too damaged to let anyone in. He might not know what was wrong with her, but she did. Fear.

That fear—fear of trusting, fear of letting someone in too close to hurt her—snaked through her now, insidious and cold. She pretended she was tough, putting on the facade each day. But she was exhausted.

Her eyes burned and she slid down the door, her legs no longer able to support her. She curled her arms around her raised knees and let the tears she'd been fighting for days have their way. Her shoulders shook as the last barrier fell.

CHAPTER NINE

IN EMILY'S OFFICE, files tended to get stored away in chunks, sometimes sitting on the table for weeks, sometimes vanishing into the great-gray-drawer wasteland in a matter of hours. It all hinged on Dianne's mood.

Emily started riffling through the stacks, hoping she'd locate Tyler's file before Dianne got in.

"What are you looking for?" Dianne stepped into the office.

Too late. She knew better than to lie to Dianne. The woman remembered everything. "The file for Tyler Easton."

Dianne's eyebrows rose in surprise, but she didn't say anything. Instead, she sorted through a different stack and quickly extracted a thick folder. "It's right here."

Emily took it and headed to her desk. "Thanks."

Dianne, never one to let things be, followed her. "Is something wrong?"

"No. Just checking on a couple things."

Dianne frowned. "How'd it go with your mom? She okay?"

"Yeah. Bruises mostly. Thank goodness." Emily looked up for only an instant then turned back to determinedly flipping open the file.

The woman had more questions, Emily saw it in her eyes. She did not want to get into the details of last night with Dianne, but knew she'd have to soon. The rental car her insurance company had provided should be dropped off before lunch.

Emily slowly read through the pages, trying to find something, anything, that might tell her what motivated Wyatt Hawkins. Some secret she'd missed before. Ignoring Dianne, she didn't stop until a shadow fell across the file.

"What are you doing?" Dianne stood, arms crossed tapping her fingers on her forearm.

"Just reviewing the file."

"Uh-huh." Dianne wasn't buying it. "For what? You've already finished it. I was getting ready to put it away."

"Well, I remembered a couple things last night—"

"What'd he do that put a burr under your saddle?"

"No-nothing." Flashes of stolen kisses and delicious omelets came to mind. Emily felt her cheeks warm and dropped her gaze.

"Just as I thought." Dianne reached for the file and before Emily could react, she'd swiped it, hugging it close. "I know you, Emily Ivers. He was nice to you. He helped you and now you think he has ulterior motives."

"All people do."

"No, they don't. You just don't trust anyone." Dianne walked away, the file tight in her hands. She stopped in the doorway. "Emily, he's a good man. Give him a chance. Both as Tyler's guardian and maybe, just maybe, as something more than a case."

"That's not appropriate."

Dianne sighed and came back to the desk. "Why not? The case is closed. It's signed off, and you can always transfer the caseworker responsibilities to someone else."

She glanced back at the overflowing conference table. "It isn't as if they don't dump on you plenty."

Emily looked at the table, too. She always prided herself on sticking to her commitments. But right now, it all seemed overwhelming. "That's not how it works. Plus, it could take weeks to get a new caseworker." She couldn't risk any questions. Besides, it was already too late.

"So? The boy's in good hands." Dianne paused. "Wait… What did you do or say to tick him off?"

"Nothing!"

"I'm not buying it." Dianne headed out of the office, stopping again when she reached the doorway. "Whatever it was, you should think about apologizing. Especially since you've scheduled a caseworker visit this afternoon."

With that, Dianne finally left her alone.

Emily groaned, glancing at her Day-Timer. Sure enough, there in bold ink, in her handwriting, was the very appointment Dianne mentioned.

The first thing Emily always did when she came into the office was check her calendar. Every morning, that was her routine.

This man had her completely befuddled and she didn't like it. Not one bit.

WYATT HAD TO get back to the house. The court visitor was scheduled to be here this afternoon—first one since Addie had gone back to Austin. He was fairly certain it wouldn't be Emily. She'd find someone, anyone else after last night's fiasco. But Wyatt knew he wasn't going to make it. Right now, the men needed him out here.

Chet had called him on his cell fifteen minutes ago

and it hadn't sounded good. "Where's Chet?" Wyatt asked as he climbed out of the truck.

"Follow me." Walt, who'd worked for the ranch since Wyatt's grandfather's day, waved toward the group of men standing at the edge of a ravine. The ugly scent gave Wyatt his first clue. The buzz of flies in the heat confirmed it. He knew he wasn't going to like what he'd see down there.

"It's Dancer," Walt whispered, the man's pain apparent. None of the other men would meet Wyatt's eyes. Wyatt peered down the hill and then looked away. Chet was on his knees, huddled beside the big horse lying mired in thick, black mud. Looked like he'd been there a while.

The wild look in Dancer's eyes told Wyatt he was more than stuck. He was hurt. Wyatt's heart sank. The big, beautiful horse couldn't die like this. Wyatt skidded down the side of the sandy hill, joining Chet in the dirt.

Dancer loved Chet and didn't seem to mind the man's poking and prodding. With Wyatt's arrival, the horse cried in panic. Wyatt spoke softly, trying not to alarm the animal any more. "Easy, boy. What's the verdict?" He looked over at his foreman.

"I'm not sure, boss." Chet kept moving his hands gently over and, as best he could, under the fallen horse. "I don't think anything's broken, but I don't know why he's not fighting to get up. It's like—" Dancer screamed, flailing in the mud. Chet cursed and both men scrambled away from the deadly hooves. Blood coated Chet's hands.

"What?" Wyatt asked.

"He's been cut. Felt clean, like wire."

Wyatt joined his cursing. Barbed wire had long been the bane of a cattleman's existence. A necessity thanks to none-too-bright cattle, but a danger that threatened all other beasts.

Wyatt glanced around. There wasn't any fencing near here. He spotted a dark trail that looked like blood coming down the far side of the ravine. "Josh," he called. The cowboy stepped forward. "See if you can follow that trail and see where he was hurt." A nod and the sound of receding hoofbeats was the only answer.

He turned back to Chet and Dancer. "Bad?"

"I don't know. It'd be easier if I could see." The horse had calmed and they stepped closer again. "Easy, boy," Chet whispered, smoothing his hand over the horse's ears.

Wyatt knew the horse wouldn't lay so still for anyone but Chet. If the man could save this horse, he deserved a raise. "Can we get him up?" A horse on the ground was dangerous. Too dangerous.

Chet frowned, then nodded once. "I think we can try, but it won't be easy on any of us." He looked up the hill at the rest of the men ringing the edge above. To a man, they nodded. Slowly, hoping not to spook Dancer, each man walked or slid down the hill, just as Wyatt had done moments before. It would take every one of them to get the horse back on his feet and up that hill. *If* they could stand him up.

"You think we can get a sling under him?" Wyatt thought of the vet's rig. "Can we wait until Max gets here?"

Chet shook his head. "Without knowing how bad he's hurt or where, I think that could be dangerous."

Wyatt nodded. "Okay, your call. You're in charge."

Chet took a deep breath. "I'll take his head. Keep him calm best I can."

Wyatt looked around at the others. They didn't always get along, but they were all good men. Again, they all nodded. Chet continued to soothe the horse, but Wyatt saw a plan forming behind his eyes. Chet started giving directions, a natural leader—his strategy keen and well planned.

He put each man exactly where he would be at the best advantage. Ryan at the back as he was the smallest and could move out of the way fastest. Chet held the reins and guided Dancer's head. Wyatt and Paulo at each shoulder. The other two, Walt and Manny, stood at each flank, hands gently rubbing the smooth coat to soothe Dancer, ready to do whatever Chet asked of them.

Slowly, they moved in unison. Wyatt's pride and pleasure at his crew filled his throat with a lump.

An hour later, after sweat had drenched them all and dirt had been ground into nearly every pore, Dancer wobbled on his hooves, breathing hard and angry. His eyes were wild and yet he held Chet's gaze, apparently ignoring his own pain to please the man he loved.

Wyatt rubbed at his own eyes, sure it was only the dust that brought the dampness to them. Dancer had never really belonged to him, and he surely didn't now. Chet was this horse's master.

"He needs the doc," Walt said. The older man shook his head in displeasure. "And soon." Not only was Dancer's side covered in blood, but the sand and half the men had soaked up a good portion. At least the bleeding had slowed and from what Wyatt could see through the dirt, it didn't appear as deep as they'd thought. But it was still bad.

"Can we get him up the hill, or do you think Max can get out here soon enough?" Wyatt asked. The trailer seemed a million miles away, and the vet was coming from halfway across the county.

As if knowing what they were asking of him, Dancer took a step. Tossing his head and flinging dust and damp over them all, he took another step. Toward the hill.

"He's gonna try, boss." Chet's smile covered most of his face. And so the slow progression began. Two hours after Wyatt had driven to the spot, Dancer crested the hill and whinnied into the wind, as if to taunt the elements with the fact that he'd survived.

He made it to the trailer on wobbly legs, letting Chet slip into the compartment with him.

The trip over the prairie was just as tedious. Wyatt drove as fast as he dared, but not nearly fast enough, with Walt riding shotgun. Chet held on to the back of the trailer door as he crooned to the animal and made sure the wound was protected.

When Wyatt finally crested the last ridge and saw the house, he breathed a sigh of relief. He was fairly sure Dancer would make it, if for nothing else than because of his love for Chet, but Wyatt was glad all the same that they were back home with the vet on his way.

Driving into the yard, Wyatt's stomach dropped. Well, damn. Miracles were all over today. Emily, not some other caseworker, sat on the front porch. The fact that she was here gave him a smidgen of hope. The fact that she was sitting there talking to Tyler, who'd been home from school for—he glanced at the dash clock—forty-five minutes extinguished most of that hope.

The only saving grace was Yolanda's truck parked in the drive, a clue that she was here making dinner and keeping an eye on the boy.

Wyatt pulled the truck up to the barn doors, angling the back gate of the trailer as close as he could to the opening. The rest of the crew pulled in behind him, a cloud of dust announcing their arrival, turning his mind back to Dancer.

"Dancer!" Tyler came barreling down the walk, his concern at seeing the horse in the trailer apparent on his face. Emily didn't follow. If anything, her complexion paled and she grasped her bag tighter. He lifted a hand, wishing he could reassure her, but knew this was as good as he could do.

He had to focus on Dancer. Tyler tried to run past him but Wyatt reached out to stop him.

"Stay back, buddy. He's hurt. Let Chet set the pace." He kept his arm across Tyler's chest, letting his men guide the horse out of the trailer. They were all competent, knowledgeable men and he hated holding back. He should be helping them, but keeping Tyler at bay was just as important. Everyone held their breath until the horse's big shoulders cleared the edge of the metal gate.

BREATHE IN. BREATHE OUT. And again. Emily forced herself to focus inward, trying to ignore the events in the yard. If only she could wipe away the images she'd seen in that first instant. If only she could tear her gaze away.

Men poured out of the truck or rode up on horses they quickly dismounted. The older man, who she knew was Chet, opened the horse trailer. Slow hoofbeats on wood and then on hard-packed dirt filled the late-day air. She saw blood. Bright red, glistening on the horse's light brown coat.

Flashes of a memory stabbed her mind. Emily shut it down nearly as quickly as it appeared. *Not here. Not now. No.* She focused on the men, staying in the present. Barely. She noted the copper smears on the men's clothing. More deep breaths.

As if in slow motion, she turned to look at Wyatt, seeing the same stains on his shirt and jeans. And the strain of concern on his face as he held on to Tyler and watched his men closely.

She swallowed hard, knowing it was the horse's blood, not Wyatt's, but still the idea he could be hurt leaped into her mind and twisted around. Ranching was dangerous work. Emily knew that more intimately than most. Memories of her father's death strobed through her mind.

She focused on the men guiding the horse into the barn. Carefully, reverently almost. Wyatt's deep, calm voice carried over the yard as he explained to Tyler what had happened and what was going on. The boy's eyes lit with interest and concern.

A white-when-clean pickup truck roared into the yard, announcing in big bold letters on its side that the vet had arrived. A collective sigh rippled through the group as a tall, gangly man climbed out.

"Do me a favor," Wyatt said, resting his hand on Tyler's arm. "Go back with Ms. Ivers until we get him in. I'll call you as soon as Dancer's settled."

Tyler didn't move, looking up at his uncle, pleadingly, then he nodded and trudged back to Emily's side.

"Doc." Wyatt met the man with a brief handshake, then hustled him into the barn.

Having Tyler there with her flipped a switch inside Emily. Her panic faded and she concentrated on the boy's emotions. As he sat down beside her, she slipped an arm around his shoulders. He leaned into her, and she felt an unfamiliar warmth inside her. Her own tension eased and drained away.

She needed to stay strong for him—a strange, yet wonderful feeling.

No one had ever really depended on her before. Even her mother was the responsibility of the staff at the facility.

It was pleasant.

Just then, Wyatt stuck his head out of the barn door and waved for Tyler to join them. He took off at a dead run, leaving Emily alone.

Last night she'd practically bragged to Wyatt that she was used to being alone. So why didn't she feel comfortable? Why did she nearly stand and follow them?

EMILY HADN'T PLANNED to stay for dinner. But Wyatt's challenge last night, to spend more than an hour here, rang loudly in her mind. When the housekeeper, Yolanda, made it clear she expected Emily to join them, she didn't argue. Standing in the big country kitchen, Emily watched, enthralled.

Though Addie had gone back to Austin, to her job and her life, Emily could still see her influence. The rough and tumble troop of cowboys that filed into the kitchen looked the worse for wear, but they'd changed into fresh clothes, each of their faces was washed and their hands were clean. When they sat down at the table, they each unfolded their napkin and covered their laps.

From there on, Addie's influence, however, vanished. Everyone talked, ate and generally enjoyed being together all at once.

Wyatt sat at the head of the table, with Tyler on his left, and a seat had been set for Emily on his right. "You sit there." Yolanda smiled and gave Emily a nudge. She settled gingerly in the seat.

Emily couldn't remember ever seeing so much food on one table. She hadn't taken time to notice it on her previous trip, but thank goodness it was also the sturdiest table she'd ever seen, the top a huge, thick slab of wood. Yolanda should be exhausted, but the woman drifted and flitted around the table and the men like a mother hen with her flock of chicks, clucking all the while.

Emily thought about last night's quiet dinner at her place. Just the two of them. She glanced over at Wyatt from under her lashes. What a difference in their worlds.

He finished putting a heavy pile of mashed potatoes on his plate and offered her the serving dish. She took it. The bowl hovered in the air between them as their eyes met and held over the fluffy white potatoes. Finally, she saw him swallow and let go of the dish. He looked down at his plate and then at the next platter. She forced herself to focus on not spilling anything as she passed the potatoes on to Walt.

Since she'd arrived, Wyatt had been very polite to her, but she could feel the distance. She didn't like it, though she knew it was appropriate. He was doing a better job than she was of keeping this relationship professional.

Admittedly, there hadn't been any time for her to grab even a moment alone with him since she'd arrived. Between the crew bringing in Dancer, the vet's arrival and now dinner for this huge group, he'd been busy.

Too busy, she realized, if the lines of strain around his eyes were any indication.

Heavy footsteps announced more arrivals. Chet and another man came in the door, stomping the dirt from their boots. While Chet hovered near his wife, the other man settled in a seat at the far end of the table.

"Dancer's all bedded down," Chet said. "Doc thinks

he'll be fine." His grin spread across his face. He looked over at Yolanda, pleading and apology in his eyes. "I thought I might just make a plate and go back over to keep him company."

"Is Doc with him now?" Wyatt asked.

"Yeah, he's cleaning up. Said he'll send you the bill."

"You take this." Yolanda was already piling potatoes and chicken onto a large plate. She ladled gravy on top. Chet grinned at her and licked his lips.

"Thanks." He took the plate and, leaning in, smacked a kiss on her cheek. Then he was gone.

"Can I go and take my dinner to the barn, too?" Tyler's high-pitched voice cut through the din of all the men.

"Uh, no." Wyatt's smile had returned.

"But why not? Chet gets to."

"Chet's taking care of Dancer. We don't need a whole bunch of people out there riling him up."

Tyler's shoulders slumped but it didn't stop him from biting into the chicken leg he held.

"Not with your mouth full," Wyatt said, anticipating the next request as Tyler opened his mouth.

Tyler chewed furiously as if the thought might evaporate before he could say it. He swallowed. "Can I go check after dinner?"

"We'll see."

"I can take him, boss," Walt offered. "If you've got—uh—business to take care of."

"Sure, thanks."

Emily's cheeks warmed as several pairs of eyes turned to her. "What we need to do won't take long." She had to force herself to look Wyatt in the eye, not because she was fearful or intimidated—no, she was afraid of getting lost in them.

"You learn anything, Josh?" Wyatt interrupted all the interested stares turned her way.

"Yeah. Followed the blood trail. Sorry, ma'am," he apologized, apparently seeing Emily's face pale.

She felt the heat in her cheeks drain away and let him think the blood was all that bothered her.

"And?" Wyatt prompted the cowboy.

"The fence 'tween here and Haymaker's is stained."

Walt's whispered curse told Emily there was more to this than a horse simply getting too close to the fence.

"There were tracks on both sides of the fence."

"Do you think he jumped it?" Wyatt clenched his jaw.

"No, sir. They weren't the same shoe. And Dancer's our best jumper. He'd have never missed."

"Another horse?" Emily asked, her curiosity getting the better of her.

Wyatt recovered first and focused his gaze on his dinner rather than her.

"Yeah. Probably a pretty little filly batting her eyelashes at Dancer," one of the cowboys across the table said.

Walt and several of the other cowboys chuckled, but Walt explained. "Our neighbor wants to breed his mares with our best stock, but doesn't want to pay the stud fees."

"What's a stud?" Tyler asked and all the men laughed.

Emily couldn't hide her own smile. Wyatt said he'd explain later. She almost wanted to be around for that conversation.

In the end, Wyatt took Tyler down to see the injured horse once dinner was done. Returning to her perch on the front steps, Emily waited for their return. She still needed to talk to Wyatt, to apologize, but she couldn't bring herself to go with them. The adrenaline of earlier was gone and the shadows of her past were too dark.

The cool night air felt good, but her pounding heart echoed in her ears. To relax, she focused on the immediate area, looking out over the valley below.

The evening had finally fallen quiet. Not silent, as in the distance Emily could hear the men talking down in the bunkhouse. And fainter still, she heard the animals, in the barn and the wild, moving and chattering to each other. A patch of bright light spilled from the open barn door.

Footsteps finally came out of the dark and Wyatt, with Tyler at his side, materialized from the shadows. Tyler's shoulders slumped, but Wyatt's voice was familiar and comforting. "Don't worry, buddy. It's just the medicine. He'll eat it tomorrow." They reached the steps and stopped in front of Emily. "Go on and put it in the fridge for him for tomorrow."

"Okay."

"Then get ready for bed," Wyatt further instructed.

When Tyler didn't argue, Emily frowned up at Wyatt. What was going on?

"He'll be better tomorrow, you promise?" Tyler stopped at the screen.

"Promise."

When Emily saw the uneaten carrot in Tyler's hand, she understood.

"'Night, Uncle Wyatt. 'Night, Ms. Ivers." The boy disappeared inside, the screen door smacking wood on wood in his wake.

Wyatt settled down on the step beside Emily, leaning back on the top step. Casual and comfortable, at home. The pose accentuated his long legs and broad shoulders. Her mouth went dry and she looked across the yard again to hide her reaction to him. "Will... Dancer really be okay?"

"Yeah, it'll take time for him to heal, but he's from pretty tough stock."

The silence grew long and heavy.

"I—"

"Can—"

They both spoke at once, then laughed. "Ladies first," he offered.

She nodded and spent a long second wringing her hands, struggling to find the right words. "First, I owe you an apology."

Wyatt didn't move, but out of the corner of her eye, she saw him turn his head toward her. She knew she couldn't say what she had to say if she looked at him. "This morning, my clerk, Dianne, gave me an earful. She knows me too well."

Emily laughed softly, clasping her hands again. "I jumped to conclusions and I accused you of something that's not...appropriate." She clasped her hands yet again. She finally looked up at him but couldn't read his expression. He was listening at least, so she took a deep breath.

"Tonight, the way you helped with Dancer. The care you showed Tyler." She licked her lips. "It says a lot."

"Thank you. But why do I get the feeling there's more?"

She laughed softly. "Because there is?" She cleared her throat. "Normally, when I'm working in family court, I don't help out with the children's division. I used to. It used to be my primary job."

"Used to be?"

"Yeah." Her mind was filled suddenly with images of William Dean. "But I had a case. A bad one." She fought for air as the guilt swamped her. Guilt she knew she'd never escape, though she went long stretches where she forgot. Wyatt and Tyler brought it back, front and center.

It must have shown on her face. "Shh." Wyatt leaned in close to her. "You don't have to explain."

"Yes, I do." She looked away; she couldn't get through this if she looked at him. "The mother was killed in a car accident. The father was active duty and scheduled to ship out overseas. The boy wanted to finish school here, then join his dad later. They'd agreed to give temporary custody to the boy's uncle."

"Wow. A little close to home."

"Yeah," she whispered and dared to look over at Wyatt. "That decision was a mistake. A *big* mistake." Her voice cracked and she swallowed to put it back in place. "The boy, William, never had a chance. His father died when an IED destroyed his convoy. The boy died after his uncle hit him one time too many."

Carefully, Wyatt reached over and curled his big hand around her fist. She hadn't even realized she'd squeezed her hand so tight. He slowly uncurled her fingers and wove them with his.

"I'm sorry," he whispered.

"Me, too. I try not to let it influence my judgment."

"But?"

"But it does. At least it did in this case."

"Are you sure?" He leaned close. "Or did it just make you more cautious? I can appreciate that."

Wyatt's understanding words touched her and surprised her. She couldn't speak. He was close, so close she could see the details of his face even in the dim light.

The lashes that rimmed his blue eyes, the dark whiskers that covered his strong jaw and cheeks, his lips. Lips that hovered so close.

"Why did you kiss me last night?" She hadn't really meant to bring that up, but since it was out there, she wanted to know.

"I told you, you looked like you needed it."

She pinned him with a glare. "That was the first time. You told me that. What about the second one?"

He didn't move, but met her glare. "That one, *I* needed." He leaned closer and while she knew she should back away, the longing to lean in was stronger. Somewhere in the back of her mind, warning bells were going off. They faded into nothing as he reached up and cupped her chin with his big, rough hand.

Emily closed her eyes, taking in the faded scent of him, the barn and the night. Her mind turned off. All the thoughts she could never escape vanished.

The strength of his shoulders under her hands comforted and drew her. She could easily lean on him, trust him.

A noise inside the house, distant but real, made Emily start. Suddenly, she felt a million eyes on them. Tyler? Chet? Every hand in the bunkhouse?

What was wrong with her? Her cheeks flushed. This wasn't why she'd come out here, was it? She refused to answer herself on that one.

She jumped away, nearly stumbling as she hurried across the night-blanketed yard toward her car. Toward escape. What was she thinking! Wyatt probably thought she was nuts. But what else was new? The man had seen her at her worst over the past couple weeks. Heck, other than in the courtroom, he'd never seen her at her best.

Away from the lights of the house, the night air, thick with early-summer humidity and the sound of the night bugs closed around her. She couldn't remember the last time she'd been outside like this. She usually headed home after work, made a quick dinner then climbed into bed, exhausted. She'd forgotten how much she liked evenings.

Voices drifted up from the barn. Chet and Walt she vaguely identified. Other voices, muted and less recognizable, wafted up from the bunkhouse. She knew life on a ranch. She knew the men wouldn't be up late. Dawn would get them out of their beds. She remembered the days before her mother had remarried, when they'd stayed out at Granddad's.

"You running from me? Or yourself?"

She hadn't heard Wyatt follow her, but she wasn't surprised. He wouldn't let her go without some type of explanation. What could she say? The broad arms of the oak gave her an artificial escape and she slowed her steps. She ducked under the shadow-making branches. She wasn't hiding, not really. Was she?

He waited outside the shadows, the white yard light falling over him. She moved slowly, finally leaning back against the rough bark, watching him, enjoying the view. Knowing this was a one-of-a-kind night.

She shouldn't even be here. She knew that. But for some reason, she didn't care.

"You going to answer me?" he prodded, still not moving.

She took a deep breath. "I don't know the answer," she whispered, letting the soft breeze take her nonanswer to him. He didn't move at first, but then he started walking—slowly—toward her. She'd recognize that loose-hipped gait forever. She could barely see him once he stepped inside the shadows, but she didn't have to. She felt him next to her. Warm. Alive. Waiting.

CHAPTER TEN

EMILY STARTED TO SPEAK, but Wyatt's lips silenced her. Surprised, she froze, but only for an instant. Whatever she'd been about to say disappeared. She could lie to the world all she wanted, but she knew she wanted this, wanted him.

The tree bark dug into her back, but that soon vanished as Wyatt pulled her into his arms. The solidness of him seemed nearly as strong as the tree.

Beneath her palms, she felt the contours of his chest. Sliding her arms up, heat engulfed her as she dug her fingers into the soft hair at the nape of his neck.

Emily had dated sporadically, even seriously once in college, but none of those experiences had prepared her for this. This kiss was strong and deep and overwhelming. She couldn't get enough.

When the kiss ended, Wyatt didn't move away. His hold tightened.

"Just so we're clear." His voice was deep, raspy with desire. "This is about you and me. Not Tyler. Not your job. There's no hidden agenda here."

Emily tried to see his eyes through the shadows, tried to read his thoughts. "I—"

"Nope." He ran a work-roughened finger over her lips and all coherent thought flew away. "You think too much." Wyatt leaned in closer, his hands cupping her face. "Don't think." His lips brushed hers. "Just feel."

This kiss went deeper, his tongue gently prodding until she opened for him. She sighed, the sound never reaching the night air.

She felt the rough calluses as his hand slid down the column of her neck, then down her spine to the small of her back. With a little pressure, he guided her hips tight up against the hard evidence of his arousal. Another groan, this one louder, filled the night air.

Emily ached to curl into him. His strength was something she coveted, his determination something she admired. He sent emotions rolling through her, wonderful, good emotions. Like nothing she'd ever felt before.

Under the cover of the branches and the blanketing shadows that wrapped around them, she felt safe.

She stopped thinking, letting his touch guide her. Her breath came in quick bursts, and he breathed harder, too. He moved his mouth away from hers, tracing the line of her jaw and neck. The rush of his hot breath on her bare skin sent shivers of anticipation along her spine.

"Wyatt," she whispered.

"Don't tell me, I know." He took a final taste of the soft curve of her shoulder before pushing the fabric of her blouse back into place. She hadn't even realized he'd released the top button to give him better access. The air was cool on her skin as he leaned back and tried to button it up with trembling fingers.

She wanted to scream, "No, don't stop." The words nearly tumbled loose. She caught herself leaning toward him instead of away. She couldn't stop from resting her forehead against his shoulder, gathering her courage to face him again.

He didn't give her much chance, as his hand gently nudged her chin. "Don't hide from me."

She accepted his challenge and fought from falling into the sparkle in his eyes. "I'm not," she denied.

He laughed and gently kissed her forehead. He pulled her back into his arms, her open blouse forgotten as he simply held her. He rested his chin on top of her head, taking in a deep breath before he spoke. "There's no such thing as privacy around here." He didn't exactly apologize, which she was grateful for.

"That's not what I came out here looking for." She needed to regain control. But the pounding of her heart and the flush of heat racing through her entire body told her that wasn't happening anytime soon.

"Why *did* you come out here? I know it wasn't just to apologize—you could have just called."

She tried to make her brain think. "You said to come and stay for more than an hour." She'd always secretly wondered what other families were like, knowing hers wasn't normal. And he had offered her a glimpse into his world, a world so different from what she'd known growing up.

Wyatt was the first to step away, though she could tell it wasn't easy. He shoved his fingers—the fingers that had just been caressing her—through his hair. He paced to the edge of the shadows, looking back at the house, ablaze with light.

"You're not even going to ask me why I kissed you?" His fingers made another pass through his already ruffled hair.

"No."

"Good. 'Cause I haven't a clue."

He sounded as disturbed by the lack of control as

she was. She smiled. Good. It was nice to know she wasn't alone.

She followed him to the edge of the darkness, silently agreeing with the message he was sending. This was, as he'd said, just between the two of them.

WYATT LET HER move in close before he turned back to face her. He couldn't read her expression, but the faint light still glinted in her eyes. He expected her to turn and run. Every inch of her body screamed that she was ready to take off.

The urge to reach out and grab her was strong, but he forced his arms to remain at his sides. If he touched her now, there'd be no turning back.

She looked up, her bottom lip between her teeth. He swallowed hard, remembering the taste of that lip.

"I…" She started to speak, then stopped and took a step backward. He couldn't let her go now. His hand shot out and he tried to gently curl his fingers around her wrist. She looked down at his hand, shaking her head. "I really should get going."

"Come with me," he whispered, giving her arm a gentle tug. Maybe if they got out of these shadows, he'd stop wanting to pull her back into his arms. She didn't resist, though he had to slow his steps to keep from dragging her. He led her toward the corral, away from prying eyes.

He doubted she wanted him to see the way her eyes darted toward the corral. "This isn't the place for me."

Prism wasn't asleep. Wyatt wondered sometimes if the big horse ever slept. He was always awake, waiting and ready when Wyatt wanted to ride. The horse sauntered over to the rail. Out of habit, Wyatt reached out and rubbed the soft ears. "Hey, buddy. Be nice to the lady."

Prism tossed his head and nickered softly as if agreeing to Wyatt's request.

Emily held back, though she'd followed him without saying anything.

"Come on. He's waiting for us." The horse stood there, patiently, his head leaning past the rail.

"I can't," she whispered.

Wyatt turned and looked at Emily. The moonlight caressed her features, revealing fear and pain. Her wide-eyed gaze never left Prism. Slowly, he stepped back and wrapped his arms around her. She trembled against him. "Don't be afraid. He'll never hurt you."

His words seemed to break the panic that had engulfed her. She shook her head and looked up at Wyatt as if just realizing he was holding her. "I'm not...afraid." Her words croaked out, making Wyatt frown.

"Then what?"

The night and the silence stretched out thick and heavy between them, despite there not being even an inch of space separating their bodies. Emily shook her head, her long curls whispering across his arms.

"When I was a girl," she whispered, "my father bought me a horse. His name was Sugar."

Her eyes filled with distance, and though he held her tight, he sensed her moving away. "What happened?" he prompted, softly, gently.

Her head snapped up then and the anger in her eyes shocked him. She pitched backward, ripping herself away from him. She'd gone nearly ten feet away, back toward the house before she turned around.

"What happened?" she cried, shattering the smooth night. "What happened? I killed him, that's what happened."

"Uncle Wyatt?" Tyler's voice made them both look toward the front porch where Tyler stood, wearing his pajamas. He'd put a hand over his eyes, trying to see through the darkness.

"Over here, buddy," Wyatt called, but didn't move. When Tyler started down the steps, Wyatt told him to stay put. "I'll be right there," he called and turned back to Emily. "Look—"

"No, go on. Take care of him." Emily headed to her car, and just as she reached the driver's door, she looked back over the roof. "Don't worry. This never happened."

"'Bye, Ms. Ivers," Tyler called and waved from the steps. Emily looked back and then hurriedly ducked into her car, but not before Wyatt saw the yearning in her eyes. It took in the house, the horse and for a long minute, him.

He wanted to run after her, but couldn't leave Tyler. "Ah, Emily. What happened to make you so afraid?" he whispered, though she couldn't hear him as her car door was already tightly closed.

LUNCHTIME AT SUNSET HAVEN was early, so by the time Emily arrived during her own lunch hour, Helen had already returned to her room. Hearing voices, Emily slowed her steps as she neared the doorway. Her mother laughed and Emily smiled. She hated to interrupt a happy time.

"Ah, and here's your lovely daughter now," Hal's voice boomed, and Emily realized she couldn't hide.

"Hi, Mom." She went in and gave her mom a brief hug. It felt so good, she almost didn't want to let go.

"Hello, sweetheart." Helen returned her hug one-handed, still favoring her injured arm. The bruises on her cheek and eye were ghastly green and purple but looked as if they were healing.

"We're having a good day." Hal pulled himself up by grasping his walker and winked at Emily. Good days were code words for Mom being more alert. She'd learned early on in Mom's diagnosis that those times were precious and rare.

Hal headed to the door slowly. "You ladies enjoy your visit." He stopped next to Emily and touched her arm. "My late wife had a similar condition." He nodded at Helen. "I learned to relish days like this. See you at dinner, Helen." With the rattling sound of his metal walker, he headed down the hall.

"You've made a friend, Mom." Emily settled into his seat.

"Oh, it's nothing serious." But she blushed, anyway. They both laughed.

"What brings you here? I'm sure you're busy," Helen said.

"Never too busy for you, Mom." Emily knew her mom wouldn't be around forever and just thinking about it hurt. She flashed back on Wyatt's admission the other day that he'd recently lost his mother. She experienced a twinge of sadness but let it slip away. She didn't need to be thinking about him right now.

Last night had shaken Emily—but it wasn't just the kiss or Wyatt. The whole setup intrigued her—the loud raucous group of cowboys and the laughter that permeated the house fascinated her.

"What's the matter, hon?" Helen leaned forward and patted Emily's knee.

"I don't know." She should have brought coffee or something. It would've given them something to do.

A voice came from the doorway. "Oh, what perfect timing." Rose stood there, smiling. "I was just thinking I should give you a call."

"Is there something wrong?" Emily's heart sped up. She knew she should trust these people, knew they cared for her mother, but the anxiety never quite faded.

"No, no problems. We're doing great, aren't we, Helen?"

Helen nodded, though Emily could tell she didn't really connect with who Rose was.

"I was just about to call and ask if you could go out to the house and get a few more things for your mother."

"Like what?" Emily watched as her mother looked down, picking at imaginary lint on her pants, avoiding having to pay attention. Emily turned to the nurse. "How about I come find you after our visit?"

Rose looked at Helen and nodded. "That would be perfect. Have a nice chat." The woman left as quickly as she'd appeared. Once Rose was gone, Helen stopped picking at her clothes. She looked at Emily and smiled as if Rose hadn't ever been there.

"Don't you like her, Mom?"

"Oh, yes." Helen wasn't especially anxious, but she leaned forward. "But I don't know who she is."

Emily smiled. She could fix this. An echo of the feeling she'd felt last night when Tyler had leaned against her rippled through her. Something warm settled in her chest. "Her name is Rose." An idea that Rose had suggested when they'd brought Mom here made Emily look up at her own picture on the wall. The one she'd labeled "Emily." "She helps take care of things here. Why don't we take her picture and I'll put her name on it so you'll know? Like we did with mine."

Helen brightened, almost relieved. "That would be nice. You're so smart."

"I'll take her picture when I leave and get it printed."

"Did you bring a camera?"

Emily wasn't even going to try to explain how her phone had a camera in it. She'd learned that little fibs hurt no one. "I have it in the car." Technically, it was in her purse, which she'd stowed in the trunk.

Helen smiled. Simple solutions.

For the first time since she'd moved her mother here, the visit went well and time flew. Emily didn't want to leave, but she had to get back to work. It made it harder, knowing that everything would be different next time she came to visit. Helen might not even recognize her. Emily refused to think about that right now.

"I enjoyed today, Emily." Her mother met her gaze with a clear one of her own. Emily could almost believe the dementia was gone.

"Me, too." Emily's throat tightened. "I love you, Mom," she whispered as they hugged goodbye.

Helen leaned back, a frown on her brow. "You sound like you're going somewhere."

Emily almost laughed. "Not far. Just to work."

"Don't be gone long. Dad should be home soon and I'll start supper."

Emily's heart sank. The randomness of her mother's illness was the hardest part sometimes. "Okay," was all she said before heading to the door.

At the door, she stopped and looked back at Helen, who stood staring out the window. "Mom?"

She glanced back, her eyes distant. "Uh, yes?"

"Do you want me to bring a picture of Dad, too?"

Helen paused. The blankness seemed to recede, at

least Emily hoped so, for a moment. "That would be nice."

She refused to even bring up Earl, or believe that her mother could have ever felt something that strong for such a monster. She knew Mom and Dad had loved each other. As Emily walked down the hall, she wondered if the dementia was as much defense mechanism for Helen as it was illness. Maybe it was a blessing that Earl had been wiped from her mind.

She stopped at the front desk and the receptionist called Rose for her. "What exactly did you need me to get?" she asked as soon as Rose appeared from the dining room.

"Nothing major. Summer's coming and some of her outfits are too warm. Also…" Rose hesitated.

"It's okay." Emily had learned that Rose hated giving her bad news. "I know Mom has…issues."

Rose smiled and put her hand on Emily's arm, reassuring and friendly. "We seem to have trouble getting your mom to wear more than a couple of her outfits. She says they aren't hers. We thought maybe if you brought some of her more familiar clothes, she'd like those better. Maybe she'll cooperate more."

Emily's stomach tightened and reality slammed back in place. All of Mom's clothes were out at the trailer. She gulped. "I'll see what I can do." She wasn't committing to anything. Not if it involved going back there. Rose nodded and moved to turn away.

"Uh, she keeps forgetting who you are," Emily said. Emily explained about the photo idea, which Rose enthusiastically agreed to. After retrieving her purse, Emily took the picture, promising to bring it on her next visit.

Reaching her car, Emily stopped and looked back at

the building. Mom needed her—and Emily liked being needed. Liked feeling a sense of purpose helping someone else.

For the first time, Emily understood why the people here did what they did.

She lifted her chin with resolve. All they gave and they still thought of ways to help her mom. The least she could do was go to the trailer and retrieve a few pieces of clothing.

THE NEXT AFTERNOON, Emily drove across the abandoned pasture, past the fallen barbed-wire fence and up the hill to park in the old drive. The battered trailer house sat where it always had—on the edge of the knoll, protected from the hot sun and blasting wind, but from little else.

Emily half expected to see her mother come out the door carrying a small Tupperware bowl or unfolding a dish towel to gather a few vegetables for the coming meal from the garden. The garden, of course, was now choked over with weeds and was as dry as a bone, but still a straggly plant here and there poked out of the dirt. Mom would cringe to see the garden she'd loved in its current state.

But Mom wasn't going to see the garden anytime soon, if ever.

Emily knew she should clean out the trailer, but she just couldn't face the idea of that task. Too much stuff, too many memories and not enough reason to dig any of it up. Other than her mother's clothes, she didn't care if the Texas prairie swallowed the place whole.

The front door wasn't locked. No shock there. Earl had kicked in the door in a drunken rage so many times, she was surprised it even stayed latched. She didn't bother to close it behind her, hoping that maybe some of the fresh air outside would slip in.

Oddly enough, a sense of familiarity fell over her when she stepped into her mother's broken-down kitchen. Nothing worked, as the power had been off since two weeks *before* she'd moved Mom to town. The unseasonably icy wind had been horrid that day, cutting through the tin-can house. How Mom had stood it for those two weeks, Emily hadn't a clue.

She'd never know, because Mom couldn't remember, just like she hadn't remembered to pay the utility bills. She'd barely recognized Emily that day.

The worn linoleum and faded green carpeting made her cringe. She hated this place. Really hated this place. Hated the ancient decorations. Hated the smell of time, heat and leftover lifetimes. Hated the harsh words that still echoed in the stale air.

Hurrying down the hall, she tried to dodge the memories, with little success.

Emily went past the closed door to her old bedroom. She hadn't opened that door since she'd left all those years ago. Even when she'd stayed for holidays, she'd slept on the couch or on the narrow bed beside her mother.

She knew what was in that room and didn't ever want to remember being the girl who had lived there.

She didn't want to see the trophy that Earl had told her she deserved, right before he threw it across the room, breaking the horse from its blue base. The collection of tiny horse figurines was still stored on the dainty shelf behind the door. He hadn't seen those, so they were about the only things that had survived his angry tirades.

She immediately thought of Sugar and winced as she

recalled telling Wyatt about him last night. The white horse had been a gift from her father. A gift Emily had instantly fallen in love with. He'd never been intended as a weapon.

In her mother's room, she pulled open the closet door to face a wall of clothes, crammed together on bent wire hangers. How had Mom ever found anything? Struggling to sort the mess and find some summer clothes, Emily finally gave up and grabbed an armload and dumped it on the bed. A cloud of dust rose up in the dim air. Emily didn't even care. She batted the dust motes out of her face, then turned back for another load. By the third batch, she'd picked out a week's worth. That was enough.

What was the point in putting them back? She laughed at herself. Mom wasn't coming back, and when and if she had to sort through all this, the pile would make it easier.

Heading toward the door with the clothes for Mom, she glanced at the half-empty closet and stopped. Why was there a square of the wall cut out and taped back in place? How strange. If it had been one of the other walls, she might not have noticed it. Earl had put plenty of holes in walls with his fist. But in the back of the closet?

No, this was different. At first she thought it was an access panel to pipes or something, but that wasn't possible. This wall backed up to the hallway. She stuck her head outside the bedroom door, just to make sure.

Placing the clothes on the nearby dresser, she went back to the closet and peered at the square.

Clear packing tape held the patch in place. Caution had her staring at it longer than necessary. Finally, she pulled the tape, the ripping sound loud in the empty trailer house.

The piece, with the tape still attached, came away

in her hand and Emily stared at the hole it left. A hole that wasn't empty. An old wooden box was wedged in between the studs.

Surprised and confused, she simply stood there. Why was Mom hiding this and where had it come from? It took her several minutes of wrestling with the box to finally pull it free.

The thick layer of dust made her shudder. The wood had been varnished once, and the leather straps that held it closed were dry and stiff. It wasn't heavy. She wondered if there was anything in it.

The room was dark, with the curtains drawn and no electricity for the lamps. She added the box to the pile of clothing and headed out into the front room. The only place where there was any light was the kitchen, and that came through the window over the sink. She set the box on the counter and unlatched it.

A familiar photo in an old metal frame lay on top. *Daddy*.

She remembered this picture, though couldn't remember when she'd seen it last. He wore his military uniform. And that smile, so alive. Her eyes burned, and she looked away from the image before she lost it completely.

Dad would have never let them live like this. When Emily had been little, and her dad had been alive, he and Helen had dreamed of a horse ranch, of a big house to raise a big family. Probably a lot like Wyatt's house.

The yearning was painful now, throbbing in her chest. What would it have been like to be part of a real family?

Her dad had died under the hooves of a horse while trying to make their dreams come true. A wild stallion they'd wanted to breed with McPherson's stock over in

Harrisburg. All her mother's dreams, and Emily's future, had died in that barn with her father that day.

Suddenly, she wanted—*needed*—to get out of here. She opened the front door and stopped. A light rain was beginning to fall. Just like back then. The memories she'd been outrunning swept full force into her mind.

She was back to that night all over again. The rain had come down in a torrent, splattering against the thin windowpanes and turning the semblance of a yard into a huge mud hole. The lights of Earl's truck created twin beams of gold that swept the side of the trailer. He slammed on the brakes, barely missing the front of the house. An old horse trailer was hitched to the back bumper.

He shoved the driver's door open, slipping on the clay mud and cursing loud enough to be heard above the storm. He didn't head to the house, but instead to the small shelter several yards away. Sugar stood under the enclosure, trying to avoid the drips of rain falling through the holes in the roof.

Emily stood at her bedroom window, watching. "No!" Without thinking, she ran through the house and out the door. The metal door on the side of the trailer made a wicked whacking sound.

She ran through the mud. "Earl!" she screamed. By the time she reached the barn, Earl had the halter on Sugar and was trying to pull the reluctant horse out of the stall.

"Get your ass back in that house, girl," he yelled.

"No."

She thought he might come after her, but he never had before. Sugar shuffled around in the small space, whinnying loudly over the roar of the storm. His confusion shone in his wide eyes. "Let Sugar go."

"I said get," Earl yelled. "He's not yours anymore. I sold him."

"He's mine. You can't do that."

"I already did." He yanked on the halter and Sugar reared back, his hooves pawing the air. He thumped back to the ground just inches from Earl. Anger flared in Earl's eyes as the reins slipped from his fingers. "I'll show you."

Earl reached for the nearest thing to him, a pitchfork that Emily had used earlier to clean the stall. Sugar's scream of pain broke through the night, echoing forever in Emily's brain.

"No!" Emily ran toward Sugar, but not before another scream finished breaking her heart. Risking everything and knowing she'd regret it later, she slapped Sugar's flank and gave the command to run.

The horse bolted through the yard, nearly trampling Emily in his haste to get away. Thunder roared across the sky, drowning out the sound of Sugar's hoofbeats as he ran into the storm.

A flash of lightning lit up the fields and Emily saw the horse racing toward the horizon, his white coat stained with streaks of night-blackened blood. She'd never see her beloved Sugar again. She hurt all over, inside and out, but it was worth it. At least out in the hills, on his own, he'd have a fighting chance.

"You little brat." Earl grabbed her hard, his big hand fisting in the neck of her shirt, making it impossible to breathe. The cloying scent of his whiskey-soaked breath made her gag. She struggled, but she was only a kid, just fifteen. He was well over six feet tall and a good two hundred plus pounds. For the first time, she thought he would hit her.

"Earl. No. Stop." Her mother's voice came out of the fog that had filled her brain.

"What the hell are you going to do about it, woman?"

At last, his grip loosened and Emily could breathe. She fell to her knees, struggling to pull air into her lungs. Her throat hurt from the pressure of her shirt collar. She couldn't stop coughing long enough to catch her breath.

"Please, Earl. Don't hurt her."

"Do you know how much money she just cost us? Making me damage the horse that way? That damned horse is more trouble than it's worth."

That wouldn't be a problem any longer, Emily thought, though she couldn't yet speak.

"It's not her fault, nor the horse's," Mom tried to explain.

"Then whose is it?" He stalked toward Mom. "Must be yours."

The crack of his fist against her mother's cheek was loud, and Emily screamed as her mother fell. Earl had never hit Helen in front of Emily before. He'd pushed her, like the time she'd hurt her arm on the oven door, or waited until later when Emily could only hear, not see. Something had changed. Emily searched her mind for something she had done that would have caused all this. . . .

Mom didn't move.

"That'll teach you both," Earl growled as he stalked to the truck. Emily heard the door slam, and the rev of the engine as he backed out of the drive.

He left. Thank God he left, she thought, and then she

panicked. Mom wasn't moving. Her eyes were closed, and her skin was as white as the lightning that split the sky.

"Mom?" Emily crawled across the rough mud. "Mom?" She heard her mother breathing and relaxed a little. Still, she didn't move. Emily had to get help.

Emily stood, stumbling and nearly falling over the pitchfork. She looked down at it and realized it was blurry. She wiped the tears from her eyes and struggled through the muddy yard to the trailer. She dialed 9-1-1 and soon the blue-and-red strobe lights broke through the storm.

Mom's going to be okay, she kept repeating to herself as the paramedics checked her out and helped Helen wake up. Even as they loaded Mom into the ambulance, those words kept echoing in Emily's head. The police officer who put her in his car said very little that interrupted the words.

Mom had brought Emily home a few weeks later, after struggling with social services to get her back from the foster home where she'd been living.

But Emily didn't want to go back to the trailer. She'd liked the Wilkerson family. They were good to her. The house was cozy and they'd actually sat down to dinner at the table every night, together. And the TV wasn't even on. The other girls who lived there were nice, too, and everyone was quiet. No one yelled.

And while she'd missed Mom, Emily missed Sugar more. After Mom stopped the car, Emily quickly looked over at the meager stable before tearing her gaze away.

Life and Mom were never the same after that. Thankfully, Earl never came back. But he didn't send a single dime of money, either. They survived on welfare checks, food stamps and the few vegetables Mom grew in the garden. By the time Emily was sixteen, she was working full-time at the Dairy Barn and going to school. She had straight As and a burning desire to get even.

Too bad Earl was already dead by that time. His own stupid drunk driving had gotten to him before Emily could get him through the legal system. She'd have enjoyed putting his backside behind bars. Now he was lying on one side of the cemetery next to an eternally empty plot. Helen Walker was getting a fresh new plot clear across the green pasture. On the side with the pretty trees, and no assholes to torment her for eternity. A place near Dad.

Grabbing the box and the pile of clothes, Emily headed to her car. She popped the trunk and settled everything inside before slamming it shut.

She had a long drive back into town. When she reached the gate at the main road, she stopped and looked left, then right. She didn't bother to glance back in the rearview mirror.

There was nothing else she wanted there.

CHAPTER ELEVEN

TOSSING AND TURNING most of the past two nights had left Wyatt in a foul mood. He'd considered the idea of a cold shower twice, but with the bathroom right next to Tyler's room, he'd refrained. It was bad enough trying to explain to a kid who'd grown up in the city what a "stud" meant in regards to horses. Explaining a cold shower was not even on the list.

By noon, Wyatt was exhausted. He'd had way too much coffee and his stomach made sure he knew that. He stood at Dancer's stall, beside Chet. Neither of them spoke as the horse moved around, apparently feeling much better already.

"You look like hell, boss," Chet said, breaking the silence.

"Why, thank you," Wyatt snarled. "You're lookin' particularly lovely yourself today."

Chet threw his head back and laughed. "Now I know why I like working here so much." Dancer came over to them and Chet rubbed the horse's broad nose. "Hey, boy. You come to see what's eatin' the boss, too?"

"Nothing's eatin' me," Wyatt denied, though the image and lingering feel of Emily in his arms flashed bright and clear in his mind. *Yeah, nothing.*

"Man, you can't lie worth a damn." Chet chuckled again without even pausing in his gentle rub of the horse's ears.

Wyatt half expected the horse to roll over and start purring. "What do I have to lie about?"

"You think every man in that room the other night didn't feel the tension between you and that judge? Hell, Yolanda didn't even have to fire up the stove." He shook his head in amusement. "She sure has her opinions about you two."

"What's that supposed to mean?"

"She's already planning what to make for a wedding feast."

Wyatt cursed, and even Dancer gave him a wide-eyed, surprised stare.

"It's not like that." Yet Wyatt didn't know what it *was* like. Nothing he'd ever experienced before.

"She know that?"

"Yeah." That she did. She'd been the one who couldn't get away fast enough that night. The one who'd told him to pretend it never happened. He should be relieved. So why was he wrestling with disappointment?

"Why don't you get the hell out of here?" Chet turned away from the horse, who nickered in protest.

"What?"

"Take some time off. There's nothing me and the boys can't handle this afternoon. You've been running hell-bent for leather ever since the boy arrived. When was the last time you did anything besides work?"

The idea held way too much appeal. Wyatt glanced at his watch. Tyler would be home soon. He remembered times like this when he and DJ had been kids. They'd take their poles and go fishing. He glanced around the big barn. "Fishing poles still where we left them?"

" Wyatt looked back at his nephew, who was
ing out the driver's window. The little rat.
ould come with us, Ms. Ivers." Tyler looked
 forth between the two adults, not looking
nnocent as an eight-year-old should.
ouldn't."

hen, we'll be off." Wyatt pulled open the cab
ried to guide Tyler back across the seat.
"

urned around slowly and peered back at Emily.
humped. She was actually considering it.
ou can't wear your good clothes. Uncle Wyatt
yler volunteered.

at disappointment he saw flash in her eyes?
ve anything else with me. I do have a pair of
es in the trunk." She looked down at herself
ed. Wyatt's eyes followed hers.

age of her in nothing but cute little running
n by the lake nearly gave him a heart attack.
 have his head examined.

tty sure there's some of your dad's old clothes
closet. They'd probably fit Ms. Ivers," he told
ad been a scrawny kid until he'd joined the

Come on, Ms. Ivers." Tyler, with a kid's en-
nd no clue about the tension between adults,
wn, grabbed Emily's hand and started to-
ouse. She had no choice but to follow or get

 guess I'm going." She shrugged, but didn't

man who came out of the house a few mo-
 stole what was left of Wyatt's breath. The

"Yep."

"Tell Yolanda not to plan on Tyler and me for dinner.
I'll take us some sandwiches." Anticipation brought a
smile to his lips. Dancer tossed his head and whinnied.
"You agree, too, huh?" He gave the horse a nice rub between the ears and headed toward the shed.

WYATT DUMPED THE bag of ice into the cooler, the clatter
loud. He grabbed the six-pack of soda and a couple beers
and shoved them into the mound of frozen water. Yeah, it
was going to be a good afternoon. There was just enough
room left to ice down the lunches he'd made for them.

Tyler was upstairs, changing out of his school clothes.
Wyatt had told him that he couldn't wear his good
clothes to the pond. He needed his rattiest, dirtiest jeans.
That should keep him busy long enough for Wyatt to
get things packed up.

No boy, city or not, should grow up without learning how to fish properly. The fact that Tyler was DJ's
son made it even more imperative that Wyatt teach him.
DJ had always said it was a great way to waste a Friday afternoon.

"I'm ready." Tyler bounded down the steps and ran
to the passenger door. Wyatt peered around the truck.
Yep, he'd found a very disreputable pair of jeans. Wyatt
chuckled. And he wore a T-shirt with a huge fish em-
blazoned across the front. Where had he gotten that?

Wyatt slid the cooler into the truck bed, right beside
the poles and tackle box. Two of the poles were Wyatt's
and the small one had been DJ's when he was a kid. He
didn't think DJ would mind Tyler using it. Wyatt had
filled the time until Tyler got home from school cleaning it and getting the pole back in shape. Still, it looked

as if it hadn't been used in years. If it didn't work, he had the backup.

He tried to recall the last time he and DJ had gone fishing. He couldn't remember. A couple years, at least. Too long. He shut his thoughts down and slammed the tailgate into place.

"All right, buddy, let's get going." He ambled over to the driver's door. The handle was hot against his palm, and just as he yanked the door open, a tail of dirt rose up on the road. Wyatt cursed, wondering if he could get in the truck and gun the engine fast enough to outrun whoever was headed this way.

It was a wayward thought and instead of racing away, he sighed and waited. Whatever it was would probably involve him, anyway.

"Who's that?" Tyler asked, leaning out the driver's window and looking over Wyatt's shoulder.

"Don't know. Guess we'll wait and see."

"Do we have to?" Tyler was fast stealing Wyatt's heart. He forced himself to think like an adult.

"Yes, we do. This shouldn't take long."

Wyatt regretted those words as soon as they came out of his mouth. When Emily's rental car turned into the yard, he groaned, part of him dreading what lay ahead. The other part he completely ignored.

"Uh-oh. She's back." Tyler slipped back into the cab.

"Now, don't you abandon me." Wyatt tried to lighten the mood. "Let's say hello and be nice. Then maybe she'll go away soon."

"Okay." Wyatt could tell Tyler's heart wasn't in it. Still, Tyler dutifully stayed put.

Emily pulled her car to a halt a few feet away. She climbed out, her pretty high heels and skirt totally out

of place. She forced a smil

gled across the rough dirt d

an ankle, but he knew bett

leaned back on the cab doo

chest and waited.

"Hello, Wyatt, Tyler." She

you getting ready to leave?"

"Yeah," Tyler piped up. "V

"Oh." She looked at Wyatt,

like she always did when she

something.

"Uncle Wyatt says no cowl

up without learnin' fishin'," Ty

Wyatt didn't say a word. He

grew too heavy. He couldn't sta

a reason you came out here tod

"Actually, I was just…" She

and he saw her swallow hard. "

"Just in the neighborhood?

Judge?" He failed to keep the sa

He knew it would get a reactic

He almost laughed at the way h

eyes narrowed. He recognized

ters. She wanted to hit him. Sh

He was impressed.

"Of course not." Emily lifte

needed more information, and

week my schedule is open."

"Uh-huh." He almost believe

"Uncle Wyatt?" Tyler interru

"Uh, yeah?"

"Do judges need to learn to f

worn jeans were cut for a boy, but her girl curves filled
them out way too well. The navy T-shirt she wore was
knotted at her hip, most likely to keep it from hanging
clear to her knees. Her dark hair hung loose, whispering against the dark clothing. Wyatt rubbed his hands
down the sides of his jeans, trying to get rid of the itch
to touch every inch of her.

"Let's go!" Tyler leaped off the steps and was up on
the running boards, pulling open the passenger door
of the truck before Wyatt could blink. Emily followed
more slowly.

That gave Wyatt time to get around the truck and
boost the boy in. "Sit in the middle," he instructed. It
was probably totally illegal, or at least immoral, to use
a kid as a shield, but in this case, it was all Wyatt had. If
she sat next to him on that wide bench seat, they might
not make it off the property.

HICKSON'S POND WAS a whole lot more than a pond.
Climbing out of the truck, Emily could barely see the
opposite shore. She knew from growing up around here
that it had been much smaller back in the day.

"Wow!" Tyler's eyes were wide as he jumped down
behind her. "It's huge."

Wyatt laughed as he reached into the truck bed to retrieve their gear. "Here, buddy. Take this." He handed
Tyler a blanket and a small lawn chair. He met Emily's
gaze. "You want the poles or the cooler?"

She looked at the huge cooler and caught the glint
in his eye. If she could get away with it, she'd take the
cooler, but there was no way she could even get it out of
the bed, much less to the shore. "Smarty." She held out
her arms to take the poles and tackle box.

Wyatt laughed again, the sound warm in the afternoon air, and pulled the cooler across the metal truck bed with a loud crunch of shifting ice cubes inside. He lifted the thing as if it weighed nothing and Emily had to make a concerted effort to not stare at the muscles in his arms.

It was bad enough that he led the way down the trail and she had to pretend not to watch his tight backside.

Wyatt had picked the perfect spot. She emerged from the line of trees to find a flat stretch of beach where waves gently lapped at the shore. Tyler should be safe enough here.

Tyler dropped the blanket and the chair in the sand then ran over to the water's edge.

"Don't go too close yet." Wyatt set the cooler down and Emily froze as she watched the muscles of his back and shoulders flex. The other night, under the trees, those strong arms had held her so gently. She ripped her mind away from that train of thought.

This could be a *really* long afternoon.

What had she been thinking? He turned around just then and their eyes met. She blinked and hastily handed over the poles. "Here you go." She turned away and started spreading out the blanket and setting up the chairs.

"You're gonna fish, right, Ms. Ivers?" Tyler stood next to her. How did the kid move so fast?

"Yeah, you're gonna fish, right?" Wyatt mimicked Tyler's voice. He was laughing at her. Well, she sort of deserved it for agreeing to come along. She couldn't blame an eight-year-old for this—she was the adult here.

But the idea of going back home to her lonely town-

house with the memories of Sugar so fresh and painful…
It wasn't an option.

"I hadn't really thought about it." She'd left her office this afternoon in a skirt and heels—fishing hadn't been on her agenda.

"Have you fished before?" Wyatt asked.

"A few times. When my dad was alive. And with Granddad a couple times." She hadn't thought about those trips in years. She didn't remember actually fishing. She remembered being a child, just like Tyler, thrilled to be included, happy to run wild in the woods and in the water. "I haven't fished since."

Wyatt frowned and looked more closely at her. The laughter was gone. Time stretched out, filled with a multitude of unspoken words and feelings. "Come on," he said softly. He extended a pole toward her. "Take this one." Then he handed a smaller one to Tyler. "Let's go." Wyatt headed to the water with the remaining pole in one hand and tackle box in the other.

Even when he wasn't trying, his swagger caught her attention. She swallowed. Why hadn't she just said no? She could sit here on the blanket, watch and relax. Why was she agreeing to do anything that would put her in close contact with him?

"What now?" Tyler looked up earnestly at Wyatt. Her heart skipped a beat. He was such a good kid.

And Wyatt, ever patient, knelt down beside the boy. "Well, that's what we're here to figure out."

Moments passed as Wyatt taught Tyler the basics of baiting the hook and casting a line. She remembered her dad doing the same with her. Her eyes burned with the memory. She missed him.

Time passed quickly and soon the sunset on the water

painted the horizon red. Emily remembered why she hated fishing right about the time Wyatt put the worm on the hook. She returned to the blanket to watch the red fade to gold, then dark.

Tyler, on the other hand, had discovered his latest passion and had no intention of leaving anytime soon. Within five minutes of casting out into the waves he'd caught a small sunfish.

"Too small to keep," Wyatt had proclaimed and Tyler reluctantly agreed to put the little thing back in the water. It had, however, cemented the boy's desire to catch another one.

"Don't go any farther out," Wyatt warned him and headed back up the beach.

Watching him approach set Emily's nerves on edge. He hadn't yet said anything, hadn't made any reference to the other night. Not that they'd had even a minute alone. Until now.

He reached into the cooler and pulled out a longneck. He offered her one but she shook her head. Like that would be a good idea? Not. He twisted off the top and she watched, all too aware of the man just feet away. Forcing herself to stop acting like a fool, she looked back at Tyler.

"So why the hell *did* you come by today?" Wyatt didn't move, but the way he stood over her put her on guard. It didn't help that she didn't have much clue of what had made her turn left instead of right out of Mom's driveway. Oh, she'd come up with several great tales—lies, if she was being honest with herself—as she'd driven the all-too-familiar country road.

Emily didn't meet Wyatt's gaze. "I…had to go out to

Mom's old place today to pick up a few things. It's just a few miles east." She waved in that general direction.

This wasn't anything like what she'd rehearsed. "They need a few of her summer clothes at the facility." Yesterday's visit with Mom came to mind and she let herself smile.

Wyatt settled down on the blanket beside her and she nearly yelped. He was so close. Almost as close as he'd been the other night. She glanced from him to Tyler. Tyler wasn't paying them any attention, his full concentration on the water.

She kept her focus on the boy as she spoke. She cleared her throat. "I've closed the file."

Wyatt didn't react, but she knew she'd surprised him. He didn't move. She glanced at him. She wasn't even sure he breathed.

"Tyler's custody file? I thought we were done. I have the paperwork. What do you mean?" he asked softly.

How did she explain? Sitting here next to him muddled her thoughts. She needed to put space between them.

When she started to get up, he caught her wrist. "Don't," was all he said.

She stared down at his hand curled around her arm. Big and strong, he could… She swallowed hard. Normally, she'd yank her hand away and loudly declare her independence if a man grabbed her. But the kiss under the trees had changed all that.

She took a deep breath. "I signed the orders. It's final, but the file is still open. Remember we made it provisional? Besides, I never should have put so many visits in the court orders. I was being paranoid. He's in a great place." She spoke softly and realized her mistake when Wyatt leaned closer to hear.

She tried to focus on what she needed to say. "We, uh, can open it if—when—his dad or mom comes back. But until then, he's all yours. No more visits."

Inches, mere inches, separated them. Stumbling through the words wasn't what Emily had planned. Wyatt apparently didn't care as his hand slipped around the nape of her neck and urged her closer.

His lips were warm and his hand solid as he leaned in. She should have felt overwhelmed but she didn't. It was more a feeling of coming home. She sighed and leaned in toward him, wanting so much more.

"Uncle Wyatt!" Tyler's screams tore them apart, and Wyatt was halfway to his feet before either of them realized the boy was standing just inches away. "Look!"

A bright, wet sunfish, not much bigger than the last, thrashed around in the air as it dangled from the line of Tyler's fishing pole. "Look, Ms. Ivers."

"Uh…how nice." Emily tried not to laugh as she wiped the drops of water that had flown off the fish and onto her face.

Wyatt did laugh. "Come on, kiddo. Let's get him back to the water."

"Aw, do I have to?"

"Yeah. He needs to grow a little more." The two had reached the water when an idea struck.

"Let's at least take a picture," Emily suggested.

"Can we?"

Wyatt smiled. "Yeah. Use my phone." He pulled it out of his pocket and tossed it to Emily. After he gave her instructions, she'd taken the photo of them both with the poor, hapless fish.

"Lemme see." Tyler jumped in the sand as Wyatt knelt to release the fish.

The photo filled the phone's screen and Emily compared the grinning man in the picture with the one at the water's edge. Her heart sped up as she remembered what Tyler had interrupted.

Just then, Wyatt looked up and smiled at them both. Their eyes met. He didn't look away. Emily's breath caught and her heart seemed to drop to her knees.

The heat in his gaze told her they were far from done.

DRIVING INTO THE YARD, Emily noticed the bunkhouse was dark. A lone security light was all that lit the barn, and the yard light cast a wide circle. Inside, the house was dark.

Tyler remained asleep, leaning against Emily's shoulder as Wyatt steered the truck in next to her car and killed the engine.

"Thank you," she whispered.

"Uh, what for?"

Loaded question. She laughed. "A lovely afternoon." Their eyes met and held in the dim light over Tyler's head.

"Uh, let me get him." Wyatt got out and came around to help Tyler. "Hey, buddy. Time to go to bed."

"Don't wanna," Tyler mumbled, snuggling tighter to Emily. They both laughed.

"Come on, kiddo."

"Let me scoot out," Emily offered, though the doorway wasn't wide enough for them both. She nearly groaned when her body slid almost the entire length of his.

She hurried to hold the screen door as he carried the boy inside.

"Be right back," Wyatt said. "Come on in and make yourself at home."

She should leave. It was late. She had to get up early to go to the office tomorrow. But...it *was* Saturday, so she could justify sleeping in.

"Stop thinking." Wyatt's voice came back to her from halfway up the stairs. She laughed and walked into the house.

He took the steps quickly, and she could hear him moving around upstairs. Walking into the living room, Emily fought the urge to run. She didn't turn on any lights, as the porch light fell in chunks through the big picture window. No sense announcing to the whole world that she was still here. It was bad enough that her car sat out front.

Emily heard Wyatt come back down, heard him walk over to her, felt his body heat against her back. She tried focusing on a picture frame that sat atop an antique hutch.

Strong, work-roughened fingers brushed the hair away from her neck, and Emily closed her eyes. His lips found the soft skin of her nape as his arm snaked around her waist. He pulled her back against his chest and her breath left her in a whoosh of anticipation.

Slowly, he slid his hands down her hips and over her thighs, then back up her arms to her shoulders and down her sides again. "I've wanted to do that all afternoon," he whispered.

She leaned her head back against his shoulder, burying her face in the crook of his neck. The soft stubble of his chin felt wonderful against her cheek and nose. She didn't even try to resist the urge to put her lips against the strong ridge of his jaw.

His hands splayed across her belly and she felt the shudder of his restraint. "Wyatt," she whispered, every inch of her aching for more. "Touch me."

Slowly, as if expecting her to change her mind, Wyatt inched his hands up to her breasts. When he cupped both in his palms, she couldn't hold back the sigh, nor the instinctual way her body melted into his.

"You're making me crazy," he whispered, nuzzling her neck as his fingers gently squeezed.

She gasped, words lost as she spun around in his arms and found his lips with hers. Her entire body throbbed and she wanted, needed, to taste him.

He was happy to oblige. His hands anchored her hips to his then moved up again to slip between them, back to where her breasts pressed against his chest. Dear God, he knew every *on* switch that her body had.

"Not here," he croaked.

"What?" When had he remembered how to talk?

Wyatt pulled slightly away, though his fingers stayed right where they were, making coherent thought on her part impossible. She pushed her hips up against his, not letting him off the hook.

"I'd gladly take you right here. Right now." As if to accent his words, he pushed his hips forward, and they both groaned. "Upstairs. Now," he growled.

She felt his hesitation as he struggled to wait for her agreement. "Yes." That one word was all it took.

She barely remembered hitting a single stair tread. But as they passed Tyler's closed door, she hesitated. "What if…"

"That kid could sleep through a train speeding through his room." Wyatt stopped and gently but firmly pushed her up against the wall. His lips found hers and she wasn't thinking about Tyler, or the wall, or anything except Wyatt and how alive she felt.

WYATT REMINDED HIMSELF he wasn't a bumbling, randy teenager, though he sure as hell felt like one. He had enough experience to make this good for both of them. He would do this right.

"Come on." Moving away was nearly painful. He took her hand and led her away from the wall and two doors down to his room.

He didn't hit the light switch—the windows were open and the white glow from the yard light showed her clearly enough. It fell over her, shining in her hair and outlining all those curves that had made concentration impossible for the past four hours.

"Beautiful." Complete sentences were beyond him. The T-shirt she wore made him wish for the buttoned-up blouse she'd had on last night. He wanted to unwrap her like a Christmas present.

Slowly, he untied the knot at her hip, slipping his hands up beneath the soft fabric. She helped, grabbing the hem and pulling the whole thing over her head. The lace and cotton wisps of her bra that greeted him hiked up his pulse.

He didn't even have to ask. She reached behind and popped the hook. And there she was, just for him.

Wyatt swore as his patience snapped. He ducked his head and took the first taste. Sweet heaven. She trembled in his hands, and scooping her up, he strode to the bed.

He didn't move away, but with one hand slid open the fly of her jeans, shucking the pants down her legs as fast as his shaking hands could manage. The tiny slip of lace between her thighs put cardiac arrest on the menu.

He leaned over and planted a soft kiss right there on the sweet lace, claiming her and surrendering in the same instant.

Emily leaned up on an elbow, her breath coming in short pants. "Now you."

She reached for his shirt collar and he backed away. If she touched him right now, he was pretty sure he'd lose control. He stepped back and did it himself, all under her watchful eye.

"Damn boots," he cursed as the last one thudded on the wood floor. And then he was there beside her, fitting her curves. His groan of relief filled the room when his lips finally found hers again.

EVERYTHING ABOUT THIS MAN was different. Emily had been kissed before, but nothing like this. Never had she trusted so completely. Never had she wanted so badly. Never had she felt so treasured.

"Wyatt," she whispered his name, claiming him as much as caressing him with her voice.

"Mmm?" His lips traveled down her neck, across her shoulder and over her breast. His tongue on her nipple made her arch into the intimate kiss. He took her into the warmth of his mouth, and she buried her fingers in his hair, holding him there.

His fingers feathered down her belly to nudge her legs apart. Carefully, almost reverently, he touched her. Each pass of his thumb sent her desire rocketing higher. She knew what lay ahead, and while she yearned for it, she didn't want to rush it.

"Let go, babe," he whispered.

"You. Want you."

"Not yet."

"Now!"

Wyatt laughed and groped in the nightstand for protection before finally aligning his body perfectly with hers, and with a single thrust, settled inside her.

Neither of them moved for an instant, their gazes locked, his holding that same promise she'd seen beside the lake. She tried to hold back, but she wanted him, all of him, moving inside her. She nudged him on, until finally he gave in and pulled her tight.

Wyatt was so attuned to her body, to her reactions. And when her cries of pleasure tore loose from her throat, his lips came down hard on hers. He swallowed the sound as he thrust one last time, and his body shuddered against her, sending them both over the edge.

CHAPTER TWELVE

THE WINDOWS STOOD WIDE-OPEN. In town, Emily *never* left her windows open. In the dead of summer, she kept them closed tight and cranked the air-conditioning.

It was the antithesis of her childhood, where they'd had no A/C—the old single-wide had probably been built before it was invented. So they'd sweltered all summer, pretending that open windows let in cool air.

That was why she'd awoken with such a start at the horse's whinny.

For a brief moment, she'd thought she was back at the trailer. And Sugar was waiting in his stall for her, expecting to be fed, combed and ridden like hell across the hills.

But when she opened her eyes to the strange room, to the warmth of Wyatt's body, she knew she wasn't back there. Relief warred with the renewed grief that Sugar was gone.

Instead of waiting for the panic to creep in, Emily looked at the man asleep beside her. The sheets slipped low enough to entice her. Memories—new memories—cascaded into her mind. She tried to tell herself that last night had been a mistake. A wonderful, amazing mistake, but a mistake. She should have never come out to the ranch. She should have stayed in town, safe in her apartment. Should have never...

But if she hadn't come out here, she'd have missed out on the laughter and the fun. And this strange sense of belonging that had settled around her.

Last night, Wyatt had made such sweet love to her. She wanted—desperately wanted—more.

But the past had too strong a hold on her. The panic attack she was fighting off told her she was too messed up.

If things progressed between them, would she be able to live with the anxiety and pain? Would he?

Caretaker. That word came back to her. It was who he was. He'd want answers and he'd do his damnedest to fix it—fix her.

But he couldn't—could he?

When he held her, when the house buffered her, she felt safe and at home. But the ranch was more than Wyatt and a house. It was animals, people and constant reminders.

She wanted more than that. She wanted to be part of his life. All of it. But those reminders too often triggered the anxiety attacks. That wasn't fair to him.

Dare she try? The very idea scared her to death.

The sounds of the horses drew her attention again, and for the first time, she felt the yearning stir inside her. Carefully, Emily crawled out of bed. Maybe from here she could peer at the horses. They were far enough away…and Wyatt was here. The longing was too strong to resist. She swallowed and moved ever so slowly.

The T-shirt she'd worn last night was nowhere to be found, but Wyatt's shirt was draped over the end of the bed. She grabbed it and hastily pulled it on.

Only part of the corral was visible through the trees' thick branches. But she saw movement and flashes of white here and there through the leaves.

She glanced over her shoulder at Wyatt again. She was a fool to think anything could come of this. He lived here—she looked back at the corral just as Prism stepped into the open—with *them*.

The only way she could look forward was if she dealt with her past. Trepidation and anticipation warred within her. She hadn't a clue where to begin.

WYATT STOPPED AT the screen door. A coffee cup in each hand, he looked down the long length of the veranda. There in the early-morning light, curled up on the porch swing, a blanket from his bed wrapped around her, sat Emily, staring across the yard and south meadow.

He'd awoken to find her no longer beside him, but the fact that her clothes remained scattered around the room, where they'd landed last night, told him she hadn't gone far.

Still, he was surprised to see her out here, her eyes glued to Prism as he pranced and played.

He leaned on the doorjamb, just watching at first. She had that scared-doe look about her again, and the last thing he wanted was to scare her away.

"It was all misty on that ridge until the sun burned it off," she said softly.

So she was aware of him. She seemed disappointed that the mist was gone.

"It does that this time of year." Slowly, Wyatt pushed through the screen, and when he reached her, offered her one of the cups. He wasn't a tea drinker, so he hoped he'd made it right. The strong scent of his coffee wafted around them, right and warm.

She didn't grimace at the first swallow—good sign. She looked beautiful this morning. Her hair was still mussed from his hands, and was that *his* shirt collar peeking out of the blanket? He swallowed, knowing he'd enjoy taking it off her. The sunrise-tinged light painted itself all over her. Just like he wanted to do.

His heart picked up the pace as he breathed in her early-morning scent. "When was the last time you rode?"

Blushing, she glanced over her shoulder at him. "That's an interesting morning-after line."

He smiled back, thankful the spell that had held her was broken.

She shook her head and laughed. She leaned back and sipped the tea. "I'd forgotten how quiet the country is—no sirens or blaring engines." She looked past him, her eyes glazing over again. "I could hear the horses."

As if on cue, a horse's whinny cut through the cool morning air. A playful sound meant to wake the world, yet somehow brought on god-awful pain in Emily's eyes.

He leaned down and placed a kiss on top of her head before sitting beside her. Though she curled her legs up and made room for him, her fingers tightened around her cup.

"You should have woken me," he said.

"Why?"

He looked away and she chuckled. She playfully kicked at him with her bare feet, setting the swing in motion again. He nearly spilled his coffee and this time, she laughed outright. Wyatt didn't think he'd ever seen her so carefree. These glimpses of her sense of humor intrigued him.

The waking-up sounds of the ranch settled around them and they drank in silence for a long time. Half a dozen conversation starters ran through his head, but there was only one thing he wanted to talk about. He just didn't know how to ask.

"I want you to know that you don't have to worry, Wyatt." She took a deep breath before continuing. "You're doing a great job with Tyler. He's happy and healthy here. This—" she waved her hand in the air between them "—doesn't affect my decision to close the file."

"I'm not worried about that."

"Then what's on your mind?"

He didn't answer right away. Instead, he set his cup on the railing, reached over and plucked her cup from her hands, setting it beside his, and took her hand. "What's next for us? Without the court-ordered visits, you don't have to come out here every week."

She curled her other hand tight into the soft blanket. "Do…" She swallowed. "Do you want me to visit?" Her dread was thick in the air.

Before he spoke, Wyatt reached over and dragged her across his lap. "After last night, you have to ask?" With his arms around her, he could tell the only thing she wore was his shirt—and the blanket. He swallowed hard.

And then there weren't any other sounds in the morning, as he slowly kissed her.

"I—I NEED TO go home," Emily whispered against Wyatt's lips.

He didn't say a thing, just pulled back and lifted an inquiring eyebrow. "You move even an inch and everyone will see more than you want them to."

Her whole body blushed. Ranch hands and little kids were notorious for getting up early. Surreptitiously, she glanced around, hoping there wasn't anyone watching.

It wasn't as if Wyatt hadn't seen her...but she'd had the shadows to wear last night.

She felt the blanket slip and the slight morning breeze stole in, whispering over her skin. His palm was hot against her back. Gently he urged her to him. Looking up, she saw her indecision reflected in *his* eyes. It *almost* hid his desire.

"Don't go, Emily," he whispered. She heard him this time, loud and clear, and saw his lips moving. Closer. Caressing the softly spoken words just as they had kissed her lips, her body.

She told herself to pull away. "I can't stay here. It's... It's..." How could she tell him it was too painful to be here when it wasn't his arms or touch that hurt her? She couldn't, *wouldn't* burden him with her pain.

It was *her* pain, damn it. She had to figure it out before she let this go any further.

She wasn't stupid. She knew herself well enough to know that she desperately wanted a hero, a man to come into her life and fix everything.

But this was life, not a fairy tale. There would be no knight riding into her life bringing all the privileges of contentment with him. Even if he did own the requisite white horse.

She stood, but found he'd wrapped the blanket around his powerful fist. Shocked, she glared at him. "Let me go, Wyatt."

"Not yet." The smile was gone. The resolve in his eyes caused her heart to race, and surprisingly, not in fear.

She'd never liked forceful men. Force reminded her too much of the jerk she'd called stepfather.

But this was the kind of strength and power that encompassed, not engulfed.

"What are you afraid of?" he demanded.

"It's not you—"

"I know that. But after what we shared last night, I deserve your honesty."

His offer, given in words, with his protective instincts firmly in place, was nearly irresistible. She knew she could lean on him, trust him. So why was she so hesitant? Why did the very thought send a cold shiver through her?

Because all it took was one mistake and he'd see her faults, her failures. Her pain.

And then would he look at her differently? Would he grow weary of her? She couldn't bear that. He mattered too much. She'd stayed last night because... Her thoughts stumbled, and yanking the blanket from his grasp, winding it around her own hand, she hurried inside and up the stairs.

She didn't look back at him. She didn't dare. He might see her heart. Dread rippled through her, and she hastily gathered her clothes from his room before stepping into the bathroom.

She had to go. Needed to return to the way things had been before she'd fallen in love with him. Emily froze. Love? Did she even know how to do that? Her heart pounding, she quickened her pace.

She dressed and pulled the bathroom door open to find him leaning against the opposite wall, his arms crossed over his chest, glaring at her. She'd hurt him.

He didn't speak—which she was thankful for. She didn't think she'd be able to resist if he pushed her up against that wall again. If he touched her... Kissed her...

She also knew that if she left now, like this, she'd forever damage what they'd created. She couldn't hurt him anymore when he'd given her so much. He was right. She at least owed him honesty.

"I'll try to explain," she whispered, her eyes darting to the open bedroom door to the jumbled covers on his bed. "But not here."

She headed down the stairs.

WYATT WASN'T LETTING her leave. She was right about not having the conversation in his bedroom—he knew there would be no talking done. But she might never come back if he let her go.

Breakfast seemed like the safest suggestion. He was pleasantly surprised when she agreed to stay.

"You've asked about Mom's arm." She jumped right in, which told Wyatt how much she didn't want to do this.

He almost stopped her, but decided it was best if she set the pace.

"And I told you about Sugar dying." She stirred her tea for the third time, though she hadn't touched the food he'd set in front of her.

"My stepfather, Earl, was abusive. He often hit Mom. The time she hurt her arm... Mom was teaching me how to make pumpkin pie. Like Grandma's." Emily's voice was soft and singsongy, like a little girl. It was as if she simply wanted to recite it. Get it over with.

"How old were you?" he whispered.

"Thirteen."

The silence stretched again. He waited.

"We were almost done when Earl came home. He'd been fired. Again. Mom was putting the pie in the oven when he came in." Her voice grew weak. "He startled her and she spilled it on the oven door. To this day I can't bear the smell of pumpkin pie."

She shuddered, her eyes distant.

Gently, Wyatt placed a hand on her knee. She was trembling. Rather than push his hand away, she reached for him and curled her shaking fingers around his hand as if grasping a lifeline.

"He pushed her." Tears cloaked Emily's voice. "I can still hear her screaming when she hit that hot door. The pain was a living thing in her voice."

"The pie at the coffee shop. That's what upset you that day?"

She nodded.

"Did he hit you?" The anger at even the possibility had Wyatt seeing red. He clenched his jaw to keep from fisting his hand around hers.

She shook her head. "Not often. Mom usually stepped in and stopped him."

She didn't have to elaborate. He could guess that Helen had taken the blows for her.

"After a while, he realized there was a better way to hurt me." Her voice was barely a whisper now and her gaze turned toward the barn where one of the horses neighed.

"My horse, Sugar." Even she heard the wistfulness in her voice. "My dad bought him for me just before he died." She didn't speak for a long time and Wyatt waited. "Earl hurt Sugar instead of me."

"Emily, I'm sorry."

Almost as if he'd never spoken, she went on. "When I was about fifteen, Earl came home one night. Drunk again. He headed to the barn and I noticed a horse trailer hitched to the back of his truck. I ran out into the rain to stop him. He said he'd sold Sugar."

Part of Wyatt thought that was probably a good thing,

at least for the horse. Emily's anguish told him it was horrible for her.

"He picked up a pitchfork… Oh, Sugar." Tears streamed down her face. "I let him go. I made that poor, frightened horse run out into the rain, into the desert."

Wyatt pulled her into his arms and held tight. Every nerve in his body ached to shush her, to tell her he didn't need to know any more. But he couldn't leave her to face the memories alone.

"There was blood all over Sugar's coat. I saw it in the rain. That bastard cut him at least three times."

How many times over the years had she relived this memory? Once was too much.

"I never saw Sugar again." She hiccuped. "I'm sure he died out in the desert, all alone, in pain."

And then she cried. Wyatt let her. Let her tears fall all over his chest. He ignored all the thoughts and questions in his mind. Finally, when her tears were spent, he took her upstairs again. This time to sleep.

NORMALLY ON SATURDAY, Emily spent the morning at her office before visiting her mother in the afternoon. Instead, yesterday she'd slept most of the day away—in Wyatt's bed. He hadn't pushed her to talk anymore, and she still felt the strength of his arms when he'd let her cry. She didn't even want to know how he'd explained her presence to everyone. Thankfully, Tyler had been so excited to spend the day with Chet in the barn, he hadn't commented.

"Mom?" Emily called from the doorway Sunday afternoon.

"Yes?" Helen sat unmoving in the big old wing-backed chair. Mom seemed to be in that chair a lot these days, especially late in the day, like now.

Emily slowly walked into her mother's room, not quite sure of the reception she'd receive. She brought with her the photo frame, cleaned and polished, with a color copy of Dad's old picture. The staff had told her not to bring the original old photo—it was back at her townhouse, safely tucked away. This one looked nearly as good. She hoped Mom couldn't tell the difference.

Helen looked up at her, not saying a word as Emily settled in the facing chair. "How are you today, Mom?"

"What's that?" Helen's voice was soft and apprehensive. "I didn't ask for anything."

Emily frowned, half-afraid to show Mom the photo. But the last time she'd been here, Helen had talked about Dad and she'd liked the idea of having his picture. Had her emotions changed? Maybe the picture would help.

"I brought you a present."

"It doesn't look like a present. Presents are pretty."

Emily had to agree, the brown paper wrapping wasn't exactly *pretty*. "I think you'll like what's inside." She extended the package to Helen with trembling fingers.

Helen grabbed it, and Emily wondered when her mother's hands had gotten so thin. All of her was thin, she realized. Emily's eyes misted. She missed her mother's strong, warm hands. The ones that had bandaged scraped knees, wiped pain-filled tears—and had fought off Earl's blows.

These clawlike hands ripped the paper, the sound loud in the tiny room. Helen tossed the sheet of paper onto the floor as if it would fade away all by itself. And stared. Her eyes wide, her fingers curled around the frame, her knuckles white.

"It's Dad, Mom," Emily whispered.

Helen looked at Emily then, a deep frown on her brow. For the longest time, that stare bore through Emily. She swallowed the hurt that bubbled up from somewhere. From the past? Was this Mom?

The loud crash startled Emily as Helen dropped the picture. Emily shot to her feet. Helen was standing, too, and there they were. Face-to-face.

"No," Helen mumbled. "No," she said louder. She started to pace, the pieces of the broken frame crunching under her feet. "No!" she screamed.

At a loss, Emily was saved by Rose appearing in the doorway.

The aide breathed a sigh, her hand on her chest. She slowly stepped into the room. "Helen?"

She walked right past Emily, and Emily knew she wasn't being rude. Her first concern was Helen.

"Emily," Rose asked softly. "Can you grab a broom from the janitor's closet down the hall?"

Glad for something to do, Emily hurried to the small door near the front desk. When Mom had first moved in they'd shown her around and explained all the various locks on the top of the doors in case she ever needed anything. Her fingers fumbled but finally she got it open and found the broom and a dustpan hung inside. She hurried back to her mother's room.

Rose had managed to guide Helen away from the mess and Emily started to carefully sweep. Her vision blurred as she looked at the jumble of metal and glass. She bent down and picked up the photo, thankful it wasn't the real one. A deep scratch cut across her father's cheek.

"No," Helen cried again and hurried over to Emily. She snatched the picture from Emily's hands and hastily backed away. Helen hugged the picture to her thin chest as she sat on the edge of the bed. Slowly, she lowered the photo and softly ran her hand, almost like a caress, over John Ivers's image.

Emily's heart hurt and she suddenly realized Rose had taken the broom and disposed of the broken frame without her even knowing it.

"Come on." Rose put a hand softly under Emily's elbow. "Let's give her some time to rest."

Only once they were out in the hallway did Emily remember to breathe. She sagged against the wall and closed her eyes. Rose stood beside her, keeping watch on the open door of Mom's room.

"I'm sorry." Emily didn't know why she wasn't crying like a baby. She definitely felt the tears bottled up behind her eyes.

"It's not your fault. That's what's called a catastrophic reaction. It's part of the disease. She doesn't know how to deal with what she's feeling and the dementia steals her rational thought. What did you give her?"

"A picture of my dad." How stupid. "The other day she talked about him. I thought…"

"It was a good thought. Look."

Hesitantly, Emily peered around the corner. Mom was sitting on the bed, staring at the picture, smiling. She remembered that smile from when she was a girl. "Oh, Mom," she whispered.

"I don't think it was the picture that upset her." Rose glanced back to the janitor's closet. "Maybe it was the frame."

The frame?

She'd found it in that box that Mom had hidden in the wall. She'd thought Helen had hidden it from Earl. Suddenly, she wondered what else was in that box.

CHAPTER THIRTEEN

EMILY DROVE SLOWLY to her townhouse. She tried to think of it as home, but who was she kidding? It wasn't home. Never had been really, but the past few days combined with the time at the ranch made it all too clear. Yet she ignored her heart and body urging her to go to Wyatt's house, to have him soothe away the confusion.

Getting lost in his arms would solve nothing.

Emily was exhausted, despite having slept through most of yesterday. Emotional turmoil, not physical labor, drained her now. Somehow she'd have to prepare for the busy workweek ahead.

Once inside her bedroom, she opened the dresser drawer where she'd put the old box from Mom's closet. Dad's photo sat on top in the plastic sleeve she'd put it in for protection until she could get a new frame. Emily moved that aside and lifted the box out.

She frowned. It felt almost empty. Why would Mom hide an empty box? She set it on top of the dresser and opened the latch.

A thick stack of papers was held together by a stiff rubber band that fell apart as soon as she picked up the bundle. She unrolled the papers and stared.

Divorce papers? Mom had divorced Earl? When? No, wait. The fact that there were no signatures told Emily that Mom hadn't gone through with it. Emily looked at the date. The papers were dated two days before Earl died.

Emily set the papers aside to reveal only a blue cloth bag and some curled photographs at the bottom. She uncurled the faded pictures. One showed Mom and Dad in a steamy kiss. Emily smiled, blushed and vaguely wondered who'd taken the picture. She could ask her mom, but after the reaction with the frame, that might not be a good idea. She set it next to Dad's picture.

The other two photos made Emily's stomach churn. One was of Earl, just standing there in front of the trailer. The other was taken from a long way off, but she recognized Earl and another man shaking hands. Emily didn't recognize the man and doubted she'd ever know who he was now.

She wasn't asking Mom. The only other person who might know was Drew, and she wasn't asking him anything.

Finally, she pulled open the blue drawstring bag. Three gold coins spilled into Emily's palm. She could only stare. They were heavy and old. What were they? When were they minted? She didn't know much about coins, but to her they looked like real gold.

Emily thought of all the times they'd gone without. All the times they'd barely had enough to eat. And Mom had these? They had to be worth several hundred dollars.

Emily's head hurt. She put everything except the picture of her parents back in the box. She hadn't found any answers, at least none that made sense. Had Mom associated the frame with the divorce papers? The coins?

She wouldn't get answers tonight. Maybe never. And then a thought struck her. What else was hidden in that trailer? Was this what Drew had been looking for? Or was there something else she didn't know about?

NEARLY A WEEK had passed since Wyatt had seen Emily. It wasn't as if she wasn't on his mind. He'd be working and all of a sudden, an image or a sound would bring her full force into his thoughts. Half a dozen times he'd pulled out his phone to call her.

But he hadn't a clue what to say to her. The case was closed. They'd had one hell of a night together, and he wanted a lot more. Wyatt also wanted answers that Emily couldn't, or wouldn't, give.

Now Wyatt sat in the saddle and stared across the landscape. He'd lived here for years, and even as a kid, he'd come out here and dreamed of living this life. But everything looked different today. Drastically.

Sitting there, letting Prism nibble at the grass around his hooves, Wyatt realized it wasn't the land that had changed. He'd changed.

Emily had changed everything. She'd shaken up his world in so many ways. But what ate away at his gut was what she'd shared with him. Her past. A past she'd seemingly overcome, yet it still haunted her. He had difficulty grasping the reality of that.

He remembered his own past. That same summer, he'd been out here visiting with Granddad, working this ranch as a hand. Much like Chet was doing with Tyler, Granddad had befriended Wyatt, and they'd spent hours together in the stalls and barn.

He'd pretended he actually lived here. Not that his home life was bad. It was just city life. He smiled at the memory of some of the trouble he'd gotten into. His first beer. His first girl. His first lots of things.

While he'd been discovering who he was, Emily had been living just down the road. He'd never met her. Never even known she'd existed. If he had, he'd have probably torn that SOB stepfather of hers limb from limb. How had she not gone insane from the abuse? Wyatt's admiration of her soared.

He reached down and rubbed the beautiful horse's shiny coat. She'd loved her horse so much as a girl, the one she'd thought of when she'd first seen Prism. It wasn't her fault that jerk had destroyed the animal. And yet she carried, and suffered from, the burden.

Something about her story nagged at the back of Wyatt's brain as if maybe he'd heard about it. This was a small community. Surely that type of abuse hadn't gone unnoticed. He'd been a kid, but what about the adults around?

"How could he do that?" Wyatt asked Prism, who looked up, and with a mouth full of sweet grass, seemed to shake his head in equal bemusement. "Come on. Guess we'd better get back. Tyler will be home from school soon."

EMILY HID IN her work. The mountain of files on the conference table was visibly smaller. Almost. Dianne was probably adding files at nearly the same rate as Emily finished.

Good. Job security and distraction. Just what she was hoping for, and it was working…mostly. She forced herself to look at the next file as she rubbed her stiff neck. She should take a break, but stopping gave her time to think of Wyatt, and she wasn't quite ready to go there.

The phone rang, giving her a perfect excuse to stretch and move. She hadn't been taking any calls, but she recognized the internal ring. She'd let Dianne know she could hold off on the files for a while.

"Hello."

"Hey." Wyatt's voice shivered through the phone line and down her spine to tingle all over her body.

"How did you get through on this line?"

"Promised Dianne chocolate as a bribe." He sounded so pleased with himself, she had to laugh.

"You'd better make it Godiva or Ghirardelli or the price will skyrocket next time."

His laughter sounded good, and Emily took a deep breath to try to still the rapid beat of her heart.

The line was silent for a long minute. Then he spoke softly. "Have dinner with me."

"Now?" She looked up at the clock and, as if on cue, her stomach growled. It was after five and she couldn't recall eating lunch.

"Of course, now." He laughed again, though it wasn't quite as warm as before. "This way you don't have time to think of an excuse to get out of it."

"I don't do that."

"Oh, no. Never." His sarcasm was mild but still there.

"Okay. Give me—" She looked at the file in her hand and then her reflection in the window. She looked like she'd been buried in work all day. *And* she seriously needed a haircut. "Half an hour?" She couldn't let him see her like this.

"Half an hour, that's it. After that, I'm coming in and getting you." He hung up, his laughter echoing in her ear. It took half a second before panic set in. What was she thinking?

"Put that file down and get moving," Dianne said from the doorway. "You've got a date to get ready for."

"Were you eavesdropping? And it's not a date."

Dianne rolled her eyes and walked into the room. "Of course I was eavesdropping. How do you think I know what's going on around here? And *yes,* it is a date."

"No, it's not. It can't be. He's part of a case," she reminded her clerk.

"You closed that file."

"But I'm technically still the judge of record." The distinction was small, but real.

Dianne sighed. "You're hopeless. Get moving." Dianne hustled Emily to the small ladies' room down the hall. "You have lipstick in your purse?"

"Yes—"

"Be right back."

Emily stared at the rumpled, wan woman in the mirror and sighed. It would take more than a little lipstick to fix her up. Still, the flutter in her stomach at the idea of seeing Wyatt sent a thrill through her.

"Where's he taking you?" Dianne seemed more excited than Emily.

"I didn't ask."

Dianne gave her a look that said, "Really?" and, "You're an idiot," all in one glance. "Then we need to think middle of the road. Nice, but not too nice."

Thankfully, today had been a no-hearing day, so Emily had dressed down—a little. The business suit was still too formal for a dinner date, though.

"The jacket's got to go," Dianne proclaimed and threw the jacket out the door. "And open at least one more button…if not two."

"Dianne!"

Dianne just laughed and pulled toiletries out of her bag. Ten minutes and a lot of patience later, Dianne stepped back to admire her handiwork. "There. You look lovely."

They both stared into the mirror. There were curls where Emily had never had curls before. Her hair framed her face, softened the edges and set off her eyes.

Self-conscious, Emily grabbed the lipstick and finished outlining her lips. "So chocolate's the going rate these days, huh?" she teased.

"Yep." Dianne repacked her suitcase of a purse. "I've got grandkids to feed. Speaking of grandkids, I have to pick up Rachel at day care. It's her parents' anniversary and I agreed to babysit. It's Disney and popcorn for me."

"Go." Emily pushed Dianne toward the front door and anticipation made them both laugh.

"Promise you won't chicken out." Dianne was serious and refused to leave until Emily swore she'd go to dinner—with Wyatt. The woman knew her too well.

Once Dianne was gone, the office fell quiet. Emily went back to her desk to straighten up and pace. The clock seemed to have stopped.

Finally, she heard footsteps. She turned off her office light and went to meet Wyatt in the reception area.

"I was just—" She froze in the doorway. It wasn't Wyatt standing there. It was Drew.

Even from where she stood, Emily could smell the alcohol. Her stomach turned, and she fought back the panic and bile that rose in her throat. "I'm just on my way out, Drew."

"You can take a minute to talk." He leaned against the door frame, blocking her exit.

"I don't—" Where was Wyatt? She glanced at the clock. He should be here any minute…. She shouldn't rely on him. What if it was a normal night and she wasn't going to dinner? She'd be on her own. She *needed* to handle this.

"What do you want to talk about?" If she just stayed calm, everything would be fine. She didn't put her purse or jacket down, however, sending the signal that this would be a short discussion.

"My—stuff." He slurred the last word.

"I'll gladly help you, but what *stuff* are you talking about? You're welcome to anything out there. Maybe if you *tell me* what it is," she said, trying to push him to explain, "I can let you know if I've seen it."

He moved closer, still blocking her way. She took a step back before realizing what she was doing and forced herself to stop and stand her ground.

"You and that gold-diggin' mother of yours know exactly what you took." His voice was a low growl.

"Honestly, Drew, I don't." Arguing with him only seemed to increase his anger. She needed to get around him and out the door.

"Don't you?" He moved fast, his hand clamping like a vise on her wrist. "That old bastard assumed I took those coins and he beat the shit out of me when they went missing."

"Coins?" The image of the bag at home in her dresser flashed through her mind and must have shown in her eyes.

Emily remembered the horrible beating Earl had given Drew just before he'd gone back to live with his mom. Was that what he referred to? No intervention by Helen had helped. Part of Emily had felt sorry for Drew, but she'd been glad when he'd left since he usually doled out some measure of abuse himself when Earl abused him.

"I want the coins." He leaned in close and the odor and menace made her gag.

"I know *I* didn't take them." He shoved her against the door frame. "So if I didn't take them, you two must have."

"Drew," she said through clenched teeth. "Let me go."

"Or what?" He sounded like a little kid. "Your mom's not coming to your rescue. Your watchdog secretary isn't around. I saw her leave. So who's going to help you now, huh?"

"I'm thinking that would be me." Wyatt's voice came from the doorway. Emily sagged in relief.

"Back off, man. We got unfinished business," Drew whispered as he reluctantly released her.

"No, *you* have unfinished business." Emily hastily stepped away.

"You don't have to air our family business to the world," he snapped, tilting his head toward Wyatt.

"We are *not* family."

A slow grin spread over Drew's face. "Well, darlin', we can fix that." He had the audacity to wink at her.

Wyatt lunged but Emily stepped between them.

"Shut up, Drew," she bit out.

"Stay out of this." Drew faced Wyatt. "It's none of your business. She's trying to steal what's mine." His voice rose and Wyatt took another step forward, his hands fisted. Before any of them could blink, Emily moved just inches away from Drew. Something inside her snapped. "Here's the deal, Drew." She poked the big man in the chest. "Your father abused all of us—you, me, my mother. He stole from everyone he knew. So I understand your animosity…what with him being your father." She poked him again. "But I'm nothing like my mother. I am *not* a pushover. And if you think that hell-hole of a house was anything to covet, you're dumber than you look." She stepped back. "You will not intimidate me, or hurt my mother. Do you understand?"

"He owed me," Drew ground out, his voice low. His eyes darted to Wyatt, but he opened his mouth, anyway. "I want what's mine. You won't get in my way."

"Don't push me, Drew."

"You ain't seen nothin' yet, darlin'." Drew turned and swayed his way to the door.

Wyatt wanted to stop him. Emily could see it in his eyes, but he held back. Barely. He'd clenched his jaw tight and something hard filled his eyes. As Drew passed Wyatt, Wyatt's shoulder bump was far from accidental and pure masculine posturing.

Finally, Drew's footsteps faded into the growing darkness. Emily closed her eyes and knew Wyatt was still standing there, watching her. He was probably in his favorite pose, leaning on the door frame, hands wedged into his jean pockets. A nonchalant lean that she'd bet everyone else believed. She knew better.

Confronting Drew had not been the smartest thing she'd done. Wyatt's presence had given her courage. Though she was shaking, she didn't want Wyatt to know. She moved back into her office, pretending to look for something.

"You hiding from me or him?" Wyatt was just inches behind her.

Emily barely had time to wonder how he'd moved so quietly in those danged cowboy boots before her anger flared. She spun around, her hair flying across her face. Frustrated, she shoved the curls out of her eyes. "Don't you dare pass judgment on me," she snapped.

"So which is it?"

She didn't take the time to realize there was anger in his eyes until it was too late. It flared bright and blue.

"You can't fix everything." She wanted to shove him out the door, do something to burn off all this energy flying through her, but feared touching him would be a mistake. "I can take care of myself."

"So you *wanted* to sit down and have a nice little chat with Drew?" Wyatt's sarcasm was thick.

"No, of course not." She grabbed the back of the nearest chair. "But it's my choice how I handle my life."

Wyatt stood so close she could hear his breath moving in and out. He didn't touch her, but for an instant, a brief instant that was too strong, too painful to ignore, she feared he would. That fear was what was wrong with her and she hated it.

The fact that Earl still interfered with her life ticked her off. Most of her anger was aimed at him. It always had been, but the red haze creeping in didn't care who she was angry at. It just fed off the emotion.

Wyatt leaned in closer, and while he didn't touch her, the warmth of his body reached out and teased her. "Emily, I don't care how you handle your life. Drew's a bully, and no one, I repeat, *no one* gets away with being a bully in front of me. I won't just stand by and watch."

She spun around and stared at him, remembering similar words in his explanation to Tyler about what it meant to be one of the Hawkins men. At that time, she'd appreciated his words, appreciated the sentiment of taking care of what was his. It had warmed her.

Now it scared the hell out of her—but why? She backed away from Wyatt, knowing that by doing so, she denied her place in his world.

Emily headed for the door. Angrily, she looked up at him, ready to tell him to get the hell out of her way. His glare met hers and that was when it hit her. She was afraid of Wyatt's caring because she wanted it so much.

He looked at her, an eyebrow arched in doubt. She flung the door open and tilted her head for him to leave.

He stopped just inches away. "I'm not chasing you anymore, Emily," he said softly, but she heard the banked anger in his voice. With that, he stepped outside and she heard his boots on the pavement.

Emily didn't know how long she stood there staring at the closed door. Well, she wasn't chasing him, either. She'd find her own dinner, damn it. She was halfway across the parking garage before her temper cooled and her brain kicked into gear.

He was right.

She *was* doing exactly what he kept accusing her of, and what she kept telling him she wasn't doing. She was running away.

Hadn't she just spent the past five days convincing herself she was finished with running? Last weekend, she'd bared her soul to him, shared details of her life that she'd never told anyone. She'd let him touch, taste and see every inch of her.

She'd already let him in, already trusted him.

And what had he done?

He'd comforted her. He'd taken her up to his bed—to sleep. He'd tried to protect her from her memories, and today, from Drew.

Dianne was right. She was an idiot, but she was also smart enough to admit her mistakes.

Angry with herself, she flung her purse and jacket into the passenger seat.

Two red lights later she stopped and stared. Her eyes burned and an ache grew in the center of her chest. Why did she keep screwing things up? It was a simple dinner invitation interrupted by an idiot named Drew. It wasn't Wyatt's fault. And yet she'd made it his.

And dang it, he'd taken it. He'd let her take her frustrations out on him and he just absorbed it. The red light turned green but it didn't register that she had to move until the SUV behind her laid on its horn. Shaking her head, Emily shot through the intersection, pulling a U-turn at the next block.

IT WAS LATE. Too late for dinner, Emily figured. The ranch house was quiet and for a minute, she wondered if anyone was home. The lone light in the living room wasn't much evidence.

But the big black truck in the yard told her all she needed to know.

She approached the veranda slowly, her mind spinning with all the things she needed to say.

The lamplight spilled out onto the porch where Wyatt stood, a cup of coffee in his hand. Lord, he looked good. The light T-shirt he wore clung to all the muscles of his shoulders and arms. His jeans were worn nearly white in places and fit tight across his powerful thighs.

Heat pooled low in Emily's belly and her breasts ached at the memory of how good he felt and tasted.

"Wyatt?" Her voice trembled, though she tried to control it. She sounded afraid, but fear wasn't the emotion racing through her right now.

He turned and faced her, leaning against the support post at the top of the steps. He set the cup down, crossing his arms over his chest. If it weren't for the movement of his throat as he swallowed, and the heat in his eyes, she might think he was immune to her.

"I screwed up, didn't I?" she asked.

Silence settled over the yard, but she never broke eye contact with him. She took a few steps toward him, tilting her head back to look up at him.

He suddenly laughed, the sound rich and warm. "I'm not falling into the trap of answering that loaded question." He took a step down, closer to her. His gaze slowly moved up, then down over her.

He came down the remaining steps. "I like your red nail polish, Emily," he whispered.

She fought back the smile. He'd noticed. "I came out here to apologize."

"Uh-huh." Carefully, Wyatt reached out and pushed a wayward curl from her forehead. "I like the jeans, too."

This time her smile refused to hide.

"But you know what I like best?" He stood just inches away and the sincerity in his voice surprised her. She simply shook her head, not trusting her voice to work.

"Your backbone." Wyatt slid an arm around her, his fingers gliding sensually along her spine. "You're sexy as hell when you're pissed."

"I...gather that dinner invitation has expired," she whispered. As if on cue, her stomach rumbled.

He laughed again. "I'm thinking we can figure something out."

"Good. 'Cause Dianne made me swear I'd have dinner with you."

"I knew I liked that woman." Wyatt's kiss obliterated any remaining coherent thoughts she might have had.

CHAPTER FOURTEEN

"Yum." Emily sighed, the last of the peanut-butter sand-
wich Wyatt had made her disappearing into her mouth.
She smiled at him as he sat beside her on the porch
swing. He'd refilled his coffee cup while they'd been
inside. Now he set the empty mug aside.

"I'm glad you came out here tonight."

She turned to him, setting the swing in motion back
and forth, the slight breeze stirring her hair. "Me, too."

Their eyes met. Wyatt reached up, and she leaned
into the palm of his rough hand. She let her eyes drift
closed, anticipating his kiss.

A loud crash interrupted what would have come next.

"What the hell was that?" Wyatt shot to his feet and
threw open the screen door.

She followed him but by the time she reached the living room, he was out of sight. She heard Wyatt's voice,
soft, muffled, in the kitchen. Then a pained little voice
tore at her heart. She ran toward the kitchen.

"Stop!" Wyatt commanded when she reached the
doorway to the kitchen.

She stared at the scene before her. Wyatt had picked
up Tyler and set him on the counter. Bright red blood
soaked through the dish towel Wyatt had wrapped
around Tyler's hand. "He dropped a glass. It's everywhere," he explained, never taking his focus off the boy.

Tyler cried and squirmed. "I'm sorry," he whined.

"Can you get the first-aid kit from the bathroom?" Wyatt asked over his shoulder, then turned back to Tyler. "It's okay, buddy."

"I'm sorry." Tyler sobbed now.

Emily hurried up to the bathroom and found the white box with the red cross on it.

She nearly stopped dead in her tracks when she returned to the kitchen. Tyler's head was buried against Wyatt's shoulder, his little body trembling as he cried. A trail of red blood slid down Wyatt's arm from where Tyler held on to him.

Wyatt looked over the boy's head at her and the helplessness in his eyes surprised her.

"Here, let's get you fixed up." She broke out of her shock and reached for Tyler's little hand and turned it over. The cut was deep, and even in the dim kitchen light, she could tell there was still a piece of glass inside. "I think he might need stitches."

"No!" Tyler screamed and kicked his feet, trying to get down and away.

Quieting Tyler took way too long, but finally they had him settled in the cab of the truck. Once they hit the road to the emergency room, Wyatt practically flew down the highway, his truck eating up the road with its big tires and monstrous engine.

To Emily, it still didn't seem fast enough. Tyler's sobs had settled down to hiccuping breaths. He leaned against Emily as she tried to apply pressure to his still-bleeding hand without hurting him more. The butterfly bandages, the cotton gauze and the towel helped a little.

In the glow of the green dash lights, she saw the tightness of Wyatt's features. She knew he was debating about going even faster. The ten miles to the emergency room seemed like a million.

"How are you doing?" He didn't take his eyes off the road, but she knew he was talking to her.

"We're okay." She took a deep breath. "He'll be fine." She tried to reassure them all. The single, stiff nod gave her little reassurance that he believed her.

The edge of town loomed, the lights of the suburbs emerging out of the desert, and finally, streetlights flashed across the cab. They were close.

"It hurts," Tyler whispered.

"I know." She rubbed his shoulders. "We're almost there."

"I don't want no stitches." The panic was back in his voice. "I want my mom," he whispered and hiccuped against Emily's shoulder.

She knew that pain, that loss. Tyler opened his eyes then, and in the instant of illumination from the streetlight they passed, she saw his panic. "Have you had stitches before?"

Tyler nodded. Something told her not to let this pass. "What happened?"

He resisted. She saw the wheels turning in his head. "Dom wasn't being nice," he finally said.

"Your mom's boyfriend?"

Tyler nodded.

Emily looked over Tyler's head to meet Wyatt's gaze in the shadows. He shook his head slightly, and though they weren't finished, he wanted her to wait. She gave Tyler a hug instead of more questions.

Finally, Wyatt pulled up to the emergency entrance. Wyatt slammed the truck into Park and ran around the front of the vehicle, yanked open the passenger door and grabbed Tyler. They were inside before Emily could catch her breath.

For an instant, she stared after them, feeling left out, forgotten. She shook her head. She was being stupid again. She slid across the bench seat and grabbed the wheel. Wyatt probably didn't realize he'd left the keys in the ignition and the engine running. She parked the truck in the nearest space, then entered the E.R. through the sliding glass doors.

Despite the late hour, the E.R. was busy. Emily rushed in, but Wyatt and Tyler were nowhere in sight. She hurried to the admissions desk. The woman behind the counter looked as harried as Emily felt, but she smiled, anyway. "Can I help you?"

"Hello. I'm Emily Ivers." She tried to sound calm, straightening her spine, hoping the subliminal message worked. "A man just brought in a little boy with a cut hand? Hawkins? Where are they?"

"Yes, ma'am." She glanced to her side. "Third cubicle on the left."

Not waiting in the hard vinyl chairs? Oh, yeah, blood tended to move you up the food chain. Following Wyatt's voice, she found the pair easily.

Wyatt stood beside the gurney, holding Tyler's arm, a look of determination on his face.

"Hey." She stepped inside and saw the relief on Wyatt's face. "Have you seen anyone?" Wyatt shook his head.

As if on cue, a doctor came through the dividing curtain. She vaguely recognized him, but she saw so many docs in her courtroom, providing expert testimony. He looked at her and vaguely smiled, as if he recognized her, too.

"Evenin', folks. What do we have here?"

Wyatt reluctantly stepped away and let the doctor take over.

"I was getting a drink and dropped the glass. Ouch!" Tyler protested as the doctor gently pulled the bloodied towel away.

Emily and Wyatt each moved closer, creating a co-coon around Tyler. "He has to look at it, buddy," she explained.

"I don't want him to."

Tyler started to protest and squirm, but when he looked up at Wyatt, the little boy quieted. Emily frowned, wondering about the look that passed between them.

"I'm being tough, aren't I, Uncle Wyatt?" Tyler's voice shook.

"Yes, you are. I'm proud of you."

She could have hugged Wyatt. He was good at this.

Within a few minutes, the doctor had removed the bandages and probed the wound. "Yeah, he'll need stitches," he confirmed.

Moments later, a nurse came in, and after much dis-cussion, Wyatt and Emily were ushered out of the cubi-cle. They might be allowed to comfort Tyler, but when it came time to actually stitch up his tiny hand, no ci-vilians allowed. Wyatt was sure he could handle it and said so, but the doc wasn't taking any chances having freaked-out parents in the room.

And so they sat. Well, Emily sat. Wyatt paced.

"I can't stand this." She joined his pacing. They ended up stopping in front of a bank of vending machines.

"You want anything?" she asked Wyatt.

He looked at her as if she'd lost her mind, then raked his fingers through his hair in frustration. She watched him. He cursed and she half expected him to kick something. The judge in her returned as she tried to analyze him.

"Want to talk?" She leaned against the wall, crossing her arms over her chest. "What's bothering you, besides the fact that Tyler's hurt?"

"I… I… Hell, Emily. I'm no good at this. He was so frightened. I could *kill* that jerk boyfriend of his mother's." He stopped and looked at her. "I don't suppose admitting that to the judge on our custody case is a good idea, huh?"

Emily laughed, just a little. "You are *great* with Tyler." She stepped in close, enjoying for once being in the comforting, supporting role. "Believe me, I've seen some doozies." She shuddered just thinking about them.

Wyatt automatically wrapped his arms around her, switching places once again. This time she let him.

Wyatt smiled and leaned closer. "Thank you," he whispered as his lips met hers.

"Judge Ivers?"

Emily jumped back, nearly stumbling and Wyatt caught her elbow. He looked at someone behind her and she turned around to look.

"Randy?"

The young bailiff from the courthouse stood just a few feet away. He looked very different in worn sweats instead of his usually pristine uniform.

As they both stared at him, his cheeks flamed. "Sorry, I…didn't mean to interrupt… I mean…"

"Shut up, Randy." A very pregnant woman seated in a wheelchair smacked his arm. "And get moving."

"Yes, dear. Sorry. See you later, Judge. Sir." The couple hurried down the hall without a backward glance.

Wyatt chuckled softly and Emily turned to glare at him. "This isn't funny, not at all."

Emily closed her eyes and rubbed her forehead. Thankfully, the nurse came out just then to tell them Tyler was ready to go. Wyatt led the way to a very groggy boy bandaged up and waiting.

Tear tracks stained his cheeks, and his hand was wrapped in white gauze. Someone, probably the nurse, had put a superhero bandage on the bundle. At least Tyler wasn't sobbing anymore.

"That's the pain medication I gave him." The doctor explained his sleepiness. "He'll be up to no good in no time, won't you, kiddo?" The man smiled at Tyler before leaving them. Tyler giggled and closed his eyes, already fighting sleep.

"Come on, buddy." Wyatt carried Tyler to the truck and settled him in with Emily before climbing in himself.

His eyes closed, Emily thought Tyler had fallen asleep, but he hadn't.

"That was lots better than last time."

She looked over at Wyatt and saw his jaw tighten. He didn't shake his head or stop her this time. He wanted to know more, as well.

"You said earlier you got hurt because your mom's boyfriend wasn't being nice." She took a deep breath. "How was he not being nice?" Tyler's reluctance filled the air. She wouldn't ask him another question if he chose not to say any more.

"Dom said he was going to spank me with his belt."

"Why?" Wyatt's voice was soft, strained.

"I was playing with Mama's bead stuff. She makes necklaces sometimes. She'd told me not to, but she was at work. I didn't like it when he spanked me. So I ran." His voice trailed off.

"Where'd you go?"

"Not far. I fell down on the sidewalk." Another sob broke the air.

She didn't want to ask, the images of the little boy running from a grown man with a temper and a belt in his hand were too vivid. "Did he—"

"Mama took me to the emergency room when she got home."

That didn't explain what had happened when the man had caught him. And Emily didn't ask. She doubted her heart could take the details right now.

Silence filled the cab as they drove home and soon Tyler's even breathing provided background noise.

Emily turned to Wyatt. The dashboard lights illuminated his features, the reflection of his strength, but also his exhaustion.

He surprised her when he whispered, "If I ever see that guy—"

Emily smiled into the darkness, moved by the strength of Wyatt's devotion.

"Are you worried about that Randy guy seeing us together?" he asked, surprising her again. "He was in the courtroom the day of the hearing, wasn't he?"

Emily nodded then realized it was too dark for him to see the movement. "Yeah. He's the bailiff."

"What are the chances he'll keep his mouth shut?"

Emily thought for a minute then realized it didn't matter. "I haven't done anything wrong, but—"

"But someone could misunderstand."

"Yeah."

The silence returned and neither of them tried to

break it. She might not have done anything wrong, technically, but she knew that she'd lost her objectivity a long time ago. Emily didn't know what she would do, but she knew what she should do.

Someone else needed to handle this case from here. She was okay with that, except the only two options—her boss Warren and the other magistrates—were swamped. They couldn't pay attention or... She stopped herself. Or give the special treatment she was thinking about giving. She stared out the window the rest of the trip.

Once they reached the ranch house and settled Tyler, Emily grabbed her things and headed to the door.

"Where are you going?" Wyatt's arm slid around her waist and pulled her close.

"Home." She leaned into his embrace. She had things to resolve in her mind, and she couldn't do that with him around. She let herself linger a minute longer than she should, relishing the feel of him.

"I do have to go to work tomorrow," she reminded him.

"Play hooky." He nuzzled her neck, sending wishful desires all the way down her spine.

Oh, how she ached to give in.

Determinedly, Emily stepped back and hastily moved to the door before she buckled under her heart's pressure. "Really, I have to go." She hustled out into the predawn, hoping that distance and time would clear her thoughts and make it easier to live with what she'd done.

THE BUILDING WAS QUIET. Of course, few people came to the courthouse at 4:30 a.m. Emily let herself into her office, flipping light switches as she went. No matter how many times she told herself she was independent, she hated being alone, especially in the middle of the night.

It wasn't as if she didn't have piles of work to do. The stacks of court files still teetered on the conference table. She walked past them and sat down at her desk. She booted up her computer. And while it hummed and blinked, setting up all its paraphernalia, she put her purse away and hung up her jacket.

Her desk phone blinked. Not really a surprise. There were always messages on her phone from caseworkers, attorneys, coworkers. Usually, Dianne sorted through them.

But Dianne wasn't in yet, and glancing at her desk calendar, Emily grimaced. She wouldn't be in later, either—Dianne was off today. So Emily killed time sorting the calls, stalling.

The decision she'd made was right. She just didn't know how Warren would react. Heck, she wasn't sure how Wyatt would react. She hadn't told him what she was doing. What if…? She tried to swallow her insecurity and stood to pace, hoping to cut the nervous energy threatening to engulf her.

Determined to get this done, she forced herself to sit down. The computer screen glowed at her, and she opened her email and pulled up the senior magistrate's email address. The words were difficult at first, but as her fingers moved over the keys, they flowed.

She recused herself.

She admitted to her inability to remain impartial. She didn't need to fill in all the blanks, but she did have to explain.

The bailiff's presence in the E.R. had made her realize the risks she'd taken. The mistakes she'd made. The line she'd crossed.

She hesitated only an instant before she hit the send button. The little hourglass on the screen made her hold her breath. And then it was gone. Now it was a whole new ballgame…if there was anything at all.

What if Wyatt didn't feel the same way about her as she did him? What if… She turned to look out the window, trying to break her mind from the path it had gotten stuck on.

The sun was just coming up. A few golden-red rays slipped in through the windowpanes, caressing the edges of her desk. Emily sat there for a long time. Out at the ranch, the hands would be getting the horses ready for their day out in the pastures. Chet had told her they planned to round up the last of the new calves for branding this week. It would be long hours of hard painful work for everyone.

She pictured Wyatt on Prism's back. He'd be there at his men's sides, in the thick of everything he loved—the animals, his ranch. He'd even talked about letting Tyler go along for a bit. She'd wanted to argue, to say he was too young, but she knew she was being ridiculous. He was probably going to grow up on a ranch. He needed to know what went on. She wondered if he'd grow up to follow in Wyatt's footsteps and take over the ranch or if his parents would come back and everything would change.

She might never know.

Pain cut through her. She'd done the right thing. Half a second passed before she grabbed her purse and coat and headed to the door, slamming it behind her. The office would be closed today.

One mental health day coming up.

Emily went home and slept. Vague images of her parents, of Wyatt and the courtroom still floated disjointedly in her mind when she awoke late in the morning.

Her gaze fell on the dresser where she'd put the box from the trailer. She lay there for several long minutes staring at it. What was she going to do with it? It might turn into a disaster, but she had to take the chance and ask Mom.

She'd focus on that instead of the turmoil with Wyatt.

Mornings were busy at Sunset Haven, getting the residents up and about, plus the whole breakfast rush. Afternoons weren't as crazy.

It was, however, a tougher time for her mother, but Emily walked through the front doors, anyway.

Staff greeted Emily as she walked to her mother's room. She peeked in and saw her mom lying on the bed. Her eyes were open, but she was definitely someplace else. "Mom?"

"Oh, hello." Helen didn't sit up or even move.

"Can I come in?"

"Yes."

Emily was having second thoughts. "Are you okay?"

"Yes." Helen's voice was monotone and she didn't meet Emily's gaze.

At a loss, Emily pulled a chair next to the bed and sat down. She gave her mom time to adjust to her being there, gave herself time to figure out how to begin.

Emily figured starting with the picture of the kiss, rather than the coins, was the safest thing and so she slowly pulled it out. "I brought you something."

Helen looked at her, surprising Emily with the dullness in her eyes. "What is it?"

"This." She extended the old picture.

"Oh, my." Helen sighed, pushed herself up on an elbow and stared at the photo. "He's so handsome." She ran her finger softly over the picture. "John," she whispered.

Emily's throat tightened. She was glad she'd brought the picture.

"Do you remember that?"

"Of course I do," Helen snapped angrily. "I'd never forget something that important." She stared at it for a long time. "That's the day I got pregnant with my daughter."

Helen turned the picture over and read the date printed on the back aloud.

Emily did a double take, and a little quick math. "Wait, you were pregnant when you got married?"

"Don't tell my father. He'll kill me." Helen looked up, panicked.

"I won't tell," Emily reassured her, doing as the staff had trained her, following her mother's thought journey instead of redirecting her. "Your secret's safe with me."

Helen looked relieved.

Emily let her enjoy the picture for a while. "I have something else," she said softly.

"Oh? What?" Her mom sounded so excited, Emily hated to disappoint her and almost didn't pull out the bag. Firming her resolve, she reached into her purse.

Helen gasped as soon as she saw the blue velvet. She just stared at it.

Emily swallowed her apprehension and opened the bag, dumping the coins into her palm. "Where did these come from?"

"He stole them," Helen whispered.

Confused, Emily thought of Drew. Had he lied when he said he hadn't taken them? "Who stole them?"

"My husband." Helen didn't give a name, but Emily assumed she was talking about Earl.

"Who'd he steal them from?"

Helen fidgeted with the bedspread. "His boss."

Earl had had dozens of bosses. "Who?"

"One of the guys who put stuff on his truck." The picking increased and Emily stopped questioning.

Helen stared at the coins before quickly plucking one from Emily's hand and stuffing it into her pocket.

"What are you going to do with that?"

"What I always do. Take it to the pawn shop."

"What?"

"Put the others back. He can't see them." Helen stood and started frantically looking around the room. "Hurry. He's never gone long. It's all I have to take care of Emily."

"I can't."

"Then give them to me." Helen snatched the bag and the remaining coins. She glared at Emily, shaking a finger in her face. "And don't you dare tell my Emily, you hear?"

Emily's heart sank. Mom didn't even recognize her. She blinked back the tears. "I won't."

"She can't ever know about this. It would be too hard on her."

"Why?"

"You silly girl." Helen frowned. "She'd know what I did. She'd be heartbroken." Helen took the coin from her pocket and struggled to put all three back in the bag. "She'd have starved to death rather than give up that horse. It's all we have."

Emily fought the urge to shoot to her feet.

"What happened to the horse?" Emily's voice shook as she almost said Sugar's name.

"That idiot tried to sell him." Helen's eyes grew blank and Emily knew she was back in time.

She let her go there, though she wasn't sure if her mother was going to say anything more. "After that awful night, everyone thought the horse died." Helen shook her head. "Sugar came back the next morning while Emily was at school," Helen whispered.

Emily gasped and fought to catch her breath.

"I called John's friend," Helen continued as Emily tried to figure out which one it could be.

"Without the money from selling Sugar, we'd have never survived." Helen spoke softly. She picked up the picture from the bedspread again. "I put that money with the coins I'd hidden from Earl."

Then pieces started to fall into place. Her mother had never worked and yet, after Earl left, they'd managed to squeak by. There hadn't been much money, but there'd been just enough.

Helen had taken the coins, letting Drew take the blame. She'd sold Sugar and let Emily think he'd died.

Emily knew desperate people did desperate things, but this was too painful.

She left Helen with the picture and the bag of coins. She didn't ever want to see the damned things again.

Fifteen years. Sugar had been five years old. Where had he gone? What had happened to him? Her mind raced with questions, questions to distract her from the one emotion she was trying to avoid—betrayal.

CHAPTER FIFTEEN

WYATT'S CELL PHONE rang just as he reached the farthest corner of the south pasture. After Dancer's injuries, he'd had his crew closely watch the fence line between here and Haymaker's place. It was Wyatt's turn to ride this afternoon.

He could've pulled rank and made one of the men do it. But after a hectic week, everyone was exhausted, so Wyatt let them get some rest. Except now he had too much time alone, too much time to think.

Emily wasn't answering his calls. When she'd left abruptly the other night, something was on her mind, but he'd been too tired and focused on Tyler to ask. He hoped the tinny ring that echoed across the pasture was her, yet the number on the screen said otherwise. He considered not answering but too many people, personal and business, used this number.

"Hello?"

"Wyatt Hawkins?" A man's voice, deep and solemn came through the airwaves.

"Yeah?"

"This is Major Dixon." The man paused. "I'm your brother's commanding officer."

Wyatt froze. Prism sensed the change and froze, too.

"DJ?" Of course, DJ. "I—" Wyatt didn't even want to hear what came next. "Is he…" Wyatt whispered a curse.

"Your brother's been injured. Apparently, changes to his next of kin notification didn't make it in before he headed overseas. I apologize for the delay in contacting you."

Distorted relief forced the air from Wyatt's lungs. DJ was alive. "How bad?" Some injuries weren't much better than the alternative.

"He sustained broken bones and some severe burns." There was another long pause, and Wyatt heard papers shuffling in the background.

"What…happened?" Wyatt asked, even though he knew the drill. He'd never get that answer. Special forces didn't do things that anyone could ever really know about. DJ had warned him, but Wyatt had only half believed him, thinking this day would never come.

"Mission went bad. I can't release the details, but there was an explosion. He was on guard duty when the device went off. Two other good men died." The commander's voice cracked. "Captain Hawkins is the only survivor."

"Is he coming home?"

"He's at Landstuhl in Germany right now." The commander spoke again. "They've kept him in a drug-induced coma for a few days, but as soon as he's stable, we'll be transferring him to San Antonio. I know that's near you. I'll be in touch about the details as they're made."

"Th-thank you for calling." Wyatt's throat threatened to close. "Major Dixon? Is he going to make it?"

The major's silence was loaded with unspoken warnings. "The bones are healing nicely, but burns are trickier. We're hopeful."

After a few more pleasantries the call ended. All Wyatt heard was the wind whispering through the prairie grasses. And his own heart's pounding. Hard. Fast. Painful.

When DJ had been home after Mom was diagnosed, they'd talked about this. DJ had asked Wyatt to be his next of kin contact. Mom was too sick, and DJ hadn't wanted her to be the first one to hear bad news if something happened. DJ'd wanted Wyatt to be the strong one, the one who took care of everyone else, just like always.

Tears burned Wyatt's eyes. He jumped off Prism's back, needing to move and escape the pain. Unfortunately, the pain followed him.

He stared at the phone, wanting to hurl the damned thing clear across the plains. But responsibility weighed on him. He needed to call the others and relay what little he knew. His fingers hovered over the keypad. He just stared. And then he watched as his fingers moved, not even certain of what they were doing.

The phone rang. And rang. Before Emily's voice mail picked up, he ended the call.

No, she had enough to deal with. This was his job.

Swinging back up into the saddle, Wyatt kicked Prism into a run. He let the wind tear through the horse's mane and dry the damp on his cheeks. By the time he reached the house, the tears were gone and he'd left all his pain out in that pasture.

Wyatt didn't have time to feel. He had work to do.

EMILY FIGURED WARREN LITCHFIELD had been head of the Civil Court Division since the invention of dirt. He was a staple in the county. Everyone knew him and most people respected him. Right now, as Emily sat in his office, staring at the empty chair across his desk, she wished she was anywhere else.

"Your email made me curious." Warren walked into the room, an open file in his hand, the glasses he always wore perched on the end of his nose. As he sat down, the look he gave her over those glasses reminded her of Dianne. Not reassuring her at all.

"I assumed that's why you summoned me here."

A single eyebrow lifted. "What's the situation with this family? In a nutshell."

Warren always wanted things *in a nutshell* so he could beat it to death with a hammer and dig around in it for a while. "Boy's mother abandoned him and the uncle has provisional custody."

"Provisional? Interesting decision."

"It was the boy's request. He believes one, or both, of his parents are coming back."

"And what do you think?"

It wasn't unusual to discuss cases like this with Warren or the other magistrates. She was just wondering how it connected to her email. "I think at some point, the dad will. He's deployed overseas. He's a marine. The mother, I'm not so sure about. For what it's worth, the father doesn't even know he has a child."

Warren gave her that look again.

"Never dull, is it?" he asked, referring to their job. "So who is it you know that makes you think you should disqualify yourself?"

Emily paused to take a breath as images of Wyatt filled her mind and threatened to steal her concentration. "The uncle." She went on to explain, "The caseworker for this one is out on maternity leave and after the Dean case, I couldn't let it go unmonitored." A smidgen of relief swept through her as Warren nodded. "I took on the caseworker role. I've gotten to know him, and the boy, quite well."

Warren leaned back in his chair, the old leather squealing in protest until he stilled. "You do realize part of the reason we *have* caseworkers is to preserve our impartiality? They get to have opinions."

"I do."

"The Dean case was rough." Warren sat staring at her for a long time. "And I understand your reasoning." Another long, uncomfortable pause as he looked at the file. Her chest tightened—it was Tyler's case file. "Did this relationship with the uncle in any way interfere with your decision here?"

"To award custody? No." Emily paused and took a breath. "I didn't develop the relationship with the uncle until after that was complete. But as I got to see him and Tyler together more, it did make me cancel the court visits, though."

"Because you saw the good he did for the boy or because the uncle influenced you?"

She had to think about how to answer. "I don't think I can honestly say," she finally admitted. "He didn't *try* to influence me, if that's what you're asking."

Warren nodded and read a bit more in the file. "Three months of weekly visits? That's a bit excessive, even for you." He looked at her again.

She smiled. "I admit to being a bit paranoid, but I *was* impartial at that point."

He didn't smile back. Not that that surprised her. She wasn't sure she'd ever seen him smile.

"Fortunately, we're in a good place." He ran a finger down the page. "Doesn't matter what we do at this point. It stands as is until one of those parents shows up and requests custody. But while canceling the visits seems appropriate, it's a matter of public record that they were ordered."

Emily nodded.

"Good decision." Warren sat for a while, his fingers steepled at his chin. "And I can't transfer it until they file a request. However..."

Here came the part she'd been dreading.

"This is a court of law, Ms. Ivers. There can't be even a *hint* of impropriety. You've managed to straddle a fence here, and you've gotten lucky. If either of those parents thinks you weren't totally impartial, they could have a case against you."

"I understand."

"Disbarment will end your career. You have a bright future, but you're dangerously close to screwing it up."

"That's why I sent the email." His support was vital here. This wasn't a big city where she could recover from a reprimand more easily. This was a small town, with only four judges and a long memory. "My career is important to me. I can't lose it. But I'm also human, and I feel it's worse to remain silent."

Every tick of the clock seemed to get louder as he sat thinking. He was not a judge known for speedy decisions, so while it drove her crazy it didn't surprise her.

"Continue the visits," he finally said.

"What?"

Warren leaned forward. "They're ordered. The only way to change that order is to open the case. Frankly, I don't have the time right now. It's a matter of public record and I won't give any attorney fuel if those parents do return."

"But—"

He held up a hand to silence her. "You created this. See it through. At some point you saw a need for it, and whatever that was, it's probably still here. I appreciate your honesty."

Emily stood to leave. "Very well."

She'd taken just one step before he spoke her name.

"I trust you. You have integrity. I know you'll still do your job and protect the child no matter how well you know the uncle. If I didn't believe that, you wouldn't be working my court." He extended the file folder to her. "If either of the parents comes back, bring this to me. I'll oversee it."

Emily nodded, unsure if she was relieved or scared to death by that proclamation.

THE FIRST PERSON Wyatt contacted was Addie. As the oldest, it had always been the two of them, together, holding each other up and helping with their younger brothers and sisters.

After Mom, the shock of Tyler's and now DJ's injuries, Wyatt wished someone else would take the reins for a while.

Wyatt didn't want to tell Addie over the phone. He timed his arrival at her house to be just a few minutes before she got home from work.

He parked across the street. She'd see the truck, recognize it and assume the worst. He had a key to her place but decided to stay out on her front porch. It was screened in and nice this time of day.

It helped that she'd put the chair she'd brought from Mom's kitchen next to the small wicker love seat and the table she'd always had here. The familiar chair was comforting. He leaned back and propped his boots up on the rail, just to ruffle Addie's feathers and knock the tension down a bit.

As he'd expected, she drove into her drive and her eyes widened. She came running up the steps and didn't even chastise him for having his boots on the rail.

"What happened?"

He stood and met her. "Sit down. Let's talk."

"Is Tyler okay?" She edged down to the love seat.

"Tyler's fine. For now. I'm here about DJ." He paused a moment to catch his breath. "His commanding officer called this afternoon. A Major Dixon." He rushed to reassure her when she gasped. "DJ's hurt, but he's alive."

"Oh, thank God. Where is he?"

"Germany. But he's coming to Brooke Army Medical Center at some point."

"What…happened? From the look on your face, I don't even want to know, do I?"

"I don't know." Wyatt shrugged, ignoring the lump in his throat. "There was an explosion. He's burned and has broken bones. I don't know anything else." Saying it out loud didn't sound as bad as the images that had filled his head since Major Dixon's call.

Addie leaned forward, covering her face with her hands. "This year just sucks!" Then with a deep breath, she straightened her shoulders and looked up. "Have you told Tyler?"

He shook his head and stood at the rail. "He's been through so much. Poor kid." He filled her in on the details of the E.R. trip, minus Emily's presence there.

"You have to tell him."

"I know that," Wyatt snapped. His stress level was through the roof and he fought to bring it down. "But we need to figure out what's going on first."

"How are you going to do that?"

"I don't know." Sitting and waiting was not something he'd ever been good at. The afternoon stretched out long and quiet.

Addie finally broke the silence. "Wyatt, damn it. Focus on you. On Tyler. When DJ gets home, we'll deal with it together. You can't keep planning everyone's lives for them."

"That's not what I'm doing."

She actually laughed. "Yeah, it is. It's what you do. Sit down and listen to me."

Lord, she sounded just like Mom. He sat down before realizing why.

"None of the others remember the boy you were before Dad died." She looked him in the eye. "I do."

"That has nothing to do with this."

"Yes, it does." She glared. "I've spent a lot of time thinking about it lately. So sit back and listen. That boy was as determined to raise hell as any of us. The day Dad died, the hell-raiser part of you died, too."

The silence of the afternoon was suddenly too quiet. He knew what she meant but he denied it, at least to her.

She persisted. "Remember that summer just before Dad died?"

How could he forget? It was the same summer he'd thought about recently and compared to the one Emily had lived. "Yeah."

"You had a blast. You just about drove Dad and Mom crazy."

"Yeah, I regret that."

"No, don't you see? You drove them crazy, but they were proud of you, too. Mom said Dad had a hard time disciplining you for things that reminded him of himself. She said he used to have to go into the other room to hide his laughter."

"When did she tell you that?"

"In those last couple months."

Sisters really were a pain.

"Go home and talk to Tyler. He needs to know and he needs you. I'll call the others."

"Now who's making plans for everyone?"

"Oh, I am. I know it. But I'm not the one who has a nephew—and a judge—to worry about."

"Judge?" Wyatt's head whipped up. Addie's eyes twinkled with mischief. "What are you talking about?"

"Ha." She laughed. "You do know I talk to Tyler?"

He did. She called a couple times a week and chatted with Tyler. Wyatt groaned as reality sank in.

"Pumping a kid for information is low."

"Fishing trips? Sleepovers?" She waggled her eyebrows. "Do you really think that's a good idea with an eight-year-old? You actually think he can keep a secret?"

She enjoyed this too much, but at least it helped take her focus off DJ's problems. Helped him, too.

"Go home, Wyatt. Better yet, go see your girl." Addie winked and pushed him toward his truck. "Let me know what else you hear." The levity in her voice faded. "We'll get through this."

Wyatt was a couple miles down the road before he even realized what his sister had done. "Damn, Addie, you're good."

The sun was setting when Wyatt drove into the yard. He'd made better time than he'd intended, and now that it was time to talk, he wished he'd driven slower.

"Take that." Even from the doorway, Wyatt could hear Tyler as he blasted monsters on the television screen.

Wyatt stood watching him. This was one of the hardest moments in his life. Even worse than calling his siblings when Mom had passed away.

Tyler had barreled into his life, and somehow stolen a place in his heart. He took a deep breath and moved into the room. "Hey, I need to talk with you, buddy."

Wyatt settled on the couch, and Tyler looked up with a smile from where he sat on the floor. He'd come so far from the sad, sullen boy Wyatt had first brought home.

"Yeah?" Tyler climbed up on the edge of the couch, his feet dangling several inches above the rug.

"I—I got a call. About your dad."

Wyatt watched, amazed, as Tyler deflated and morphed back into the little boy he'd first met. The one torn between defending the mother who'd abandoned him and yearning for the father he'd never met. In that instant, Wyatt saw the strong resemblance to DJ as the light faded from the boy's eyes.

"Is he coming home soon?"

"I…don't know." Wyatt wasn't sure if Tyler was disappointed or relieved. "He's hurt pretty bad. There was an explosion." How did you tell an eight-year-old that his dad could die?

"A big explosion?" A kid's innocent fascination covered Tyler's face.

"I don't know. Probably." The brief report he'd gotten from DJ's commanding officer hadn't been that detailed.

"When can I see him?"

"He's still in the hospital in Germany."

"But when he gets here, I get to see him, right?"

Wyatt wouldn't be the one standing in Tyler's way, but he wasn't so sure about anyone or anything else.

Like hospital policies. "They don't always let kids into hospitals."

"But I went there when I hurt my hand."

"That was different. It was the emergency room and you were the one they were taking care of." Wyatt's head started to hurt.

"That's not fair." Tyler shot to his feet. "He's *my* dad."

"And he's my brother, kiddo. I know how you feel—"

"No, you don't." Tyler's voice rose an octave. "Why do grown-ups always say that?"

"Watch your attitude," Wyatt automatically corrected him.

"I don't have to. You're not my dad." Tyler ran from the room, his tennis shoes slamming against the wooden stairs. The bedroom door at the top slammed shut. Wyatt sat stunned, lost. He cursed.

He vaguely wondered if Tyler was nervous about meeting DJ. He shook his head. They'd already gone over that.

He was in over his head and sinking fast.

Feeling as if he were a hundred years old, Wyatt climbed the stairs. He swallowed the dryness in his throat when he reached the top and tapped on the bedroom door. "Tyler." No answer. No sounds at all.

None of the bedroom doors in the old house locked, yet Wyatt hesitated to open the door. "Tyler?" Before he could give in to his own uncertainties, he turned the knob and shoved the door open.

The room was empty. The window wide-open.

Wyatt cursed. The last thing he needed was to have to hunt for the kid. He frowned and went over to the window. The old cottonwood bumped up against the house here. Wyatt had forgotten about that. A memory came out of nowhere. DJ used to sneak out this way, that one and only summer he'd come out and worked for Granddad. They'd all learned real quick that DJ was *not* the ranching type.

A movement in the distance caught Wyatt's eye. Tyler was heading to the barn, and Wyatt breathed a sigh of relief. Maybe Dancer was the best medicine.

Wyatt closed the window and turned around to leave. At the door, his brain caught up with his vision. He spun back around. The chair in the corner was empty. Panic ate through him. He rushed to the dresser and yanked open the drawers—and breathed a heavy sigh of relief. All Tyler's clothes were neatly folded and put away.

The card and the plastic animals he'd shown Emily in court were carefully tucked in the corner.

Wyatt closed his eyes and whispered a soft prayer of thanks. Looked like Tyler was planning to stay after all. Somehow, that helped. For now.

EVERY TIME THE office phone rang, the palms of Emily's hands grew damp, both dreading and hoping that it was Wyatt. But it never was. She wasn't ready to explain things to him, anyway. With a deep breath she picked up the receiver. "Family Court," she answered.

"Judge Ivers?"

She recognized Tyler's voice immediately. The wobble of uncertainty in it, however, she didn't. "Tyler? What's wrong?"

He hiccuped. "My dad. He got hurt."

"Oh, dear." What should she ask? What did Tyler even know? "I'm sorry, sweetie. How can I help?"

"Are you comin' with us?"

"Uh…where are you going?"

"Santonio."

Ah, Brooke Army Medical Center. "San Antonio?"

"Uh-huh."

Emily frowned. She'd never lived in the military world, but she'd seen plenty of news stories about the hospital that worked with some of the most severe war injuries. Amputations. Burns.

"Is your uncle there?" She focused on the situation at hand. Her heart beat a mile a minute at the idea of hearing Wyatt's voice.

"No. He's down at the barn. The vet's checking Dancer." Talking about the horse seemed to perk Tyler up.

"How's he doing?" She was talking about the horse... or so she told herself.

"Better. They let him out in the pasture a little while yesterday."

That sounded good. "Can you have Wy—your uncle call me?" She wanted to know what was going on. This wasn't her case anymore, since Warren had agreed to take it in the future, but this could change everything. If DJ was back and wanted custody and questioned her earlier impartiality, Warren's warnings would become all too real.

"Does that mean you're coming?"

"I don't think so."

"But you have to." Tyler's voice sounded near panic.

"Okay, calm down," she soothed. "Why do you think I should go?"

"To make sure my dad's okay to be a dad."

Emily closed her eyes and pictured Tyler's face. Poor kid. He'd had so much change lately. Too much. "I'll make you a deal. I'll talk to your uncle and we'll figure out a plan. It will all be okay."

The line went silent, but she knew he was still there. "Tyler? Do you have another question?"

"Yeah."

She waited a beat before nudging him. "What is it?"

A long pause followed, then he whispered, "What if he—my dad—doesn't like me?"

"Oh, Tyler. How could he not like you?" Emily wouldn't make empty promises. She ached to reassure him, but this time she couldn't. She didn't know DJ.

But she knew her job. And this go around, Tyler would be her only consideration.

CHAPTER SIXTEEN

DJ Hawkins drifted in and out of consciousness. Strange and familiar voices penetrated the fog. He recognized his brother's voice. *Wyatt*. A voice he'd heard all his life, bossing him, berating him and too often cussing him. *Must be back in the States*. He tried to smile but hadn't a clue if his lips responded. He felt completely disconnected from his body.

Except for the pain. That part even the fog couldn't eliminate. His back and legs felt like they were on fire. Images of flames. Loud explosions. Searing pain rushed back. Was it real? Part of him knew it was.

A child's voice he didn't recognize broke through everything. Inquisitive and soft. High pitched. It wasn't any of his siblings, but strangely enough it belonged.

He struggled to open his eyes, fighting the weights holding them closed. He ached to see light again. Suddenly, panic swept over him. What if it wasn't his eyelids that he was staring at the back of? What if the flames had stolen his eyesight? Struggling, he strained.

Slowly, his eyelids moved. White light, stabbing agony, poured into his eyes. He slammed them closed. *Answered that question. Enough of that.*

Okay, how much of the pain in his legs was real? Did he want to try that trick again? *Sure, what the hell.* He nearly cried aloud at that bit of evidence. Okay, no more opening his eyes and no more moving his legs.

"He moved!" The boy's voice cut like glass through his brain. DJ didn't think that had a thing to do with his injuries.

"Shh, Tyler," Wyatt commanded, as usual.

Tyler! DJ's voice screamed in his mind. His son. Dear God. The son Tammie had never told him about. *Open eyes, damn it. Open.* His eyelids, remembering the recent shattering pain, refused to cooperate. *Please,* DJ pleaded to whoever or whatever might be listening. *Let me see. Let me look at my son. Please.*

The darkness remained solidly in place.

Maybe he could touch. He tried to move his fingers and felt something cool on the back of his hand. IV? Commanding the muscles of his arm to move, he waited for the response. The rough texture of the blanket brushed his palm. *Yes. Movement.*

"See!" The boy's voice, quieter now, still cut through DJ's brain.

Soft, small fingers touched his hand. Gentle. Warm. Then they were gone. No, DJ tried to scream, but he knew the only person who heard it was him, "Don't go." Suddenly, his ears heard the words. Not just his mind.

"DJ?" Wyatt's voice broke.

DJ had finally managed to get the better of his big brother. This was not what he'd had in mind all those years as a kid, but it would do.

WYATT ENTERED DJ's hospital room and stopped beside the bed while Addie waited outside with Tyler. A week had passed since DJ had arrived. Three days since they'd brought him out of the drug-induced coma.

Except for the cast on his left forearm, DJ looked fairly normal from this angle. There were still cuts on his face; one on his chin had been stitched and was healing.

The doctor had told Wyatt that DJ's helmet and the pack he'd had on his back had protected most of his upper body. His lower back and legs hadn't been so lucky.

The puckered, red skin running shoulder to foot on the right and hip to ankle on his left only hinted at the open wounds they had been. Healing well, the doctor called it. Painful, Wyatt knew. DJ said nothing.

His little brother looked exhausted, weak and in a lot of pain, but he was awake and on his way to recovery. That was all they could ask at this point. The doctor had cut DJ's pain medications so he was more alert and aware of what was going on. He'd asked so many questions. Questions Wyatt had avoided. Until now. Today he'd brought Tyler back with him.

There were common rooms downstairs, but DJ wasn't cleared to get up and go down there yet. "You ready for visitors?"

"Hell, yeah." DJ opened his eyes. "This is as bad as a jail cell."

Wyatt grinned. "And you've been behind bars how many times?" Wyatt stopped at the side of the bed. "You ready to officially meet Tyler?"

DJ's whole demeanor changed. His eyes widened and he straightened his shoulders as he took a deep breath. "Sure." The apprehension was in his voice, but didn't show anywhere else.

Wyatt stuck his head out the door. "Addie?" Shuffling feet and the click of Addie's heels on the tile were the only sounds for a long minute.

Wyatt watched silently as Tyler stepped through the door. The boy's gaze went straight to the man in the hospital bed, then he met Wyatt's. "Go on. It's okay." Wyatt tilted his head to encourage Tyler to move closer.

"Don't let all this junk scare you," DJ said, waving at the monitors and machines that surrounded his bed.

"I'm not scared." Tyler lifted his chin, and with another brief glance at Wyatt, stalked over to the side of the bed. He stuck his hand out. "I'm Tyler."

They all got the hint. This wouldn't be one of those sappy meetings. DJ took the boy's hand as if they were in a business meeting. "Glad to meet you, Tyler."

Wyatt waited for DJ to say more, but he didn't. He didn't say, "I'm your dad." He didn't say, "I'm DJ." He simply returned Tyler's handshake.

Tyler didn't move away, but he didn't move closer, either.

"You doing okay out at Wyatt's place?" DJ asked.

"Yeah." Tyler looked everywhere but at DJ. "I like the horses."

"Good to know."

The silence in the room was definitely uncomfortable. "Well." Addie moved over to the side of the bed. "Tyler has lots of questions." She pinned DJ with a glare. "We all have."

DJ looked at Wyatt. "She's going for the third degree, isn't she?"

Wyatt simply nodded and leaned against the wall. You couldn't pay him enough to get in Addie's way when she had a bone to pick. Wyatt settled back to watch the show.

"You going to let her abuse me?" DJ asked Tyler.

"That's Aunt Addie." Tyler smiled at DJ then stepped back to stand beside Wyatt, mimicking his lean against the wall. Wyatt saw the disappointment in DJ's eyes. He wanted to reassure his brother that Tyler needed time.

"Why don't you and Addie visit with your dad a while?" Wyatt moved away from the wall and headed to the door. "I'll be back."

He'd gone only a few feet into the hall before Tyler called his name. Wyatt turned to the boy. "What's up, buddy?"

Tyler looked around, taking in the nurses at the station and a couple walking down the hall, as if reluctant to say anything with so many people around.

Wyatt retraced his steps and hunkered down in front of the boy. "Talk to me." The uncertainty in Tyler's eyes nearly tore Wyatt apart.

"You're comin' back, right?"

Wyatt nodded. "I said I was." But Wyatt knew that for Tyler, an adult saying something didn't always mean they followed through.

"And I'm going home with you, right?"

Wyatt smiled at Tyler. "Oh, yeah. We're going back to the ranch tonight. You've got stalls to muck out."

Tyler visibly relaxed before his eyes.

"Look, I know you don't know your dad very well, but get to know him. I think you'll like him. And he needs you."

"Okay." Tyler stood taller.

"And, Tyler?" Wyatt reached out and put his hand on Tyler's thin shoulder. "I want you to know, I'm always here for you. Always, okay? Even when you're all grown up, I'll be your uncle. Got it?"

Tyler beamed. "Okay." Without another word, Tyler turned back into DJ's room. His voice joined Addie's, his laughter following Wyatt all the way down the hall to the elevators.

FOR THE HUNDREDTH TIME, Emily wondered how things were going in San Antonio. And for the hundred and first time, she told herself to stop thinking about it.

Staring at the now half-empty conference table in her office, she should feel a sense of accomplishment. Why didn't she? Maybe when it was totally empty. She bent over the next file and focused on reading.

"Emily?" Dianne touched her shoulder and Emily yelped as papers scattered. "Sorry. I called but you didn't hear me."

Emily shook her head and took several breaths to calm her racing heart.

"There's a call. From the facility." Dianne's voice was soft and sympathetic. She knew Emily hadn't gone to see her mother in a few weeks. Emily hadn't told her, or anyone for that matter, what her mother had admitted. She couldn't bear to think about it, much less talk about it.

"I'll take it."

Rose was the voice on the other end of the line. "We've missed seeing you, Emily," she said.

"I've been busy. H-how's Mom?" Did she really want to know?

"She's physically fine. She doesn't say much, but I think she realizes you haven't been by."

Thanks for the guilt trip. Emily shook her head. It wasn't Rose's fault. "Is there something wrong?"

"Actually, yes. I wanted to let you know we took those coins out of your mom's room. The charge nurse has them locked in the med room if you want to come get them."

Emily sat for a second before speaking. She had to know. "What happened?"

This time Rose was the one silent for a minute. "She

wouldn't let go of them. She kept trying to find hiding places, going into other people's rooms at all hours. Getting very upset when they asked her to leave."

"I'm sorry."

"Oh, don't be. It's part of dementia. She's so confused, and I can see her fear. They're a trigger. Hal was able to sneak them away from her. Since then, she's been much calmer."

"Good." Emily breathed a sigh of relief.

"Emily, she tried to break a hole in the wall of her room."

"That sort of makes sense. She had them hidden in the wall at the trailer. What could she possibly be remembering?" Emily wondered aloud.

"She's been mumbling a name."

Emily braced herself to hear her father's or Earl's name.

"Jackson."

"Jackson?" It had been years since Emily had heard that name. Jackson Wright, one of her dad's friends, had been a frequent visitor before Mom had married Earl. He'd been sweet on Mom. Even as a kid, Emily had seen it. She remembered going to his shop a couple times.

His pawn shop.

Emily froze. "I'll come get the coins. Thanks, Rose." She hung up and grabbed her purse. Did he still own the shop? Was it still in business? Heck, was he even alive?

"Dianne?" She entered Dianne's office. "Can you look up and see if there's a Wright Pawn in town? Downtown on Thirteenth, I think?"

"Sure." Dianne tapped the keyboard and in an instant had a picture up on the screen. "Here it is. On the corner of Thirteenth and Grant." She leaned closer to the screen. "Wow. Big place. I might need to go shopping."

Emily laughed and left Dianne to peruse the online listings.

Once Emily reached the facility and had the nurse retrieve the coins, she decided to stop and see her mother. Helen was in the activity room, painting with watercolors. Emily stood watching for several minutes. She was relaxed and smiling. Slowly, Emily retreated, not yet ready to face her. Not until she knew if it was the dementia or the sense of betrayal that stood between them.

Outside, summer had taken hold, and thankfully the drive to Wright's Pawn wasn't long. The building was in the older part of town and took up almost half the block. Suddenly, the bag of coins felt heavy in her purse.

The pawn shop looked different than she remembered, yet as she walked over to the counter, she saw flashes of the past.

Now, just as when she'd come with her mom, a man came out of a doorway in the back. Disappointed, Emily realized it wasn't Jackson. This man was much younger.

"Afternoon. What can I do for you?"

Emily shook herself out of the stupor the place had cast over her. "I'm sorry. I was remembering being here when I was a kid."

He smiled. "Don't get too many people in here just for nostalgia. I was here when I was a kid, too, except I didn't have much choice. My dad owned the place."

"Oh. Is Jackson your father?"

"Sure is. Though you'd think at seventy, he'd think about retiring. I'm Jack, Jr."

Emily's heart picked up the pace. "I'm glad to hear…

that he's still active. I'm Emily Ivers. Our dads were friends once."

"Ah, you're John's daughter." The man grinned. "Wait here. Dad's gonna want to see you."

He disappeared in back and a moment later an elderly man came through the doorway. "Emily? Emily Ivers?"

He grinned just like his son and she recognized him immediately.

"Goodness, you certainly have the look of John. See it, Jack? Her eyes."

"Thank you." It felt good to hear about her dad. She'd make a point to come here again, maybe take Jackson to dinner. She recalled why she was here. "I was wondering if you could help me." Emily pulled the cloth bag out of her purse and laid it on the glass counter.

She didn't have to explain what was inside. She saw the recognition on his face and her hopes rose. Maybe some of the mysteries of her mother's life would be explained.

"Where…did you get this? Is your mom—?"

"She's still alive, though she's got dementia. She lives over at Sunset Haven."

He nodded. "I'm sorry. Did she give you these?"

"No. I found them in her closet in the trailer."

He nodded again, and with arthritic fingers, he opened the bag and took out the coins. "Is this all that's left?"

"There were more?"

This time his nod was slow as he looked around the shop. Jackson waved her around the counter. "Let's talk privately."

He moved slowly, carefully, as if watching and measuring each step. He led her to a small, cluttered office in the back and offered her the worn wooden chair beside the desk. Leaning on the desk, he crossed his arms over his chest and looked at her. Jack, Jr. stood in the doorway, keeping an eye on the store and on them.

She caught a glimpse of a memory and remembered the younger man Jackson had been. He reminded her of another cowboy as Wyatt's image came to mind.

"In that bottom left drawer. Go ahead. Open it," he instructed.

Frowning in confusion, Emily pulled the drawer open. An old wooden cigar box, about the size of the one Mom had hidden in the wall, sat in the bottom.

"Take it out."

She set the box on the desk and Jackson lifted the lid. There were several dozen coins, just like the three she'd brought with her. "I don't understand."

Jack, Jr. stepped forward. "Holy crap, Dad. Are those what I think they are?"

Jackson nodded.

"What?" Emily was more confused now.

"Close the door, son."

Jack Jr. had to leave to watch the shop. Once he closed the door, they were alone. Jackson pinned Emily with a piercing stare. "I'm talking to my good friend's daughter, right? If I'm talking to the judge, I'm not going any further."

There was definitely a bit of fear in his eyes. "Your secret's safe with me."

"Earl Walker was the biggest fool I ever met. And I'm not just saying that because your mom picked him over me. I dunno, he had a kind of magic. The ladies loved him." Jackson laughed. "I'm guessing from your look that you didn't."

Emily didn't feel like telling Jackson, or anyone, how much she didn't like Earl. Or why.

"You know he drove a truck. He didn't much care what was in the back of his rig as long as he got paid." Jackson's eyes grew stormy and distant. "There were always rumors he stole from some of the loads. After he died, your mom came in here. She didn't have much. She'd never worked and couldn't support you. But she had those coins."

"You can't accept stolen property in a pawn shop—"

The old man held up a finger. "Ah, ah, ah."

She calmed and resolved to stay quiet until he was done telling her the story.

"They were never reported stolen. I checked with the cops. Which told me Earl either ripped off another crook, or the crook wasn't smart enough to figure out who took them. Heck, he might not even have known they were gone. Either way, your mom needed the money and I had it to give. So I kept quiet. I didn't want anyone coming after her."

Emily looked from the old man to the full box to the three remaining coins. "You took care of us."

"Damned right I did. Your father was my best friend." His eyes grew distant. "I could always count on him. When I was laid up a couple times, he and your mom watched out for my wife and kids." Shaking his head as if to scatter the memories, he refocused his gaze on Emily. "I owed John that, at least. Your mom didn't deserve the pain that asshole, Earl, 'scuse my language, put her through."

Jackson was a different breed of man. Like her father. Caretaker. Emily's throat tightened as the word filled her mind and she gained a new memory of her father. Good men. Jackson and her father were both good men.

And so was Wyatt. Suddenly, she understood him a little better.

"What are you going to do with those?" She pointed to the box.

"Don't know. If the guy Earl stole them from is still around, he could cause some trouble."

"I'm guessing you don't like trouble."

"No, ma'am. I don't."

That was why Emily knew the coins would stay in that drawer until a day long after Jackson was gone. She added her mother's bag and coins to the box, as well. "Let your grandkids find a treasure someday." She closed the lid and put it back in the drawer.

She stood to leave and stopped beside Jackson. "Thank you for sharing about my dad."

"Glad to. Anytime you want to know more, just give me a call."

She smiled. "I will." Despite not knowing him well, she gave the man a brief hug, then remembered something else she wanted to ask. "Did my mom ever call you about selling a horse?"

Jackson shook his head. "No. Just the coins. Why?"

Disappointment joined them in the small office. Instead of answering, she simply shook her head. She walked to the door and stepped out into the shop.

"Emily?" Jackson called her name when she was halfway across the store.

"Yeah?"

"Do you think your mom would like a visitor?"

Emily paused and smiled. "I can't promise she'll recognize you. But that would be nice. *I'd* like that."

WHY DID THE women always show up first? Wyatt wondered as he sat in the hospital's conference room listening to all three of his sisters chattering away. Technically, DJ was here, but he was still down in his room so that didn't count as male backup. Wyatt looked over at Tyler, playing with his Game Boy. He wasn't much help, either. Where the hell was Jason?

The door opened and Jason came in sporting a suit in this god-awful heat. Was he nuts?

"Whoa!" Jason stopped dead in his tracks when he came face-to-face with Mandy—or *Amanda* as she'd informed Wyatt last night she preferred being called. Amanda was several months pregnant.

Just as she'd done with Wyatt last night, she met Jason's curious gaze with a glare. "Ask and you die," was all she said.

Even Tara and Addie shared a confused look, telling Wyatt they didn't know anything, either.

Wyatt bit back the urge to demand she tell them who the father of the child was. The instinct to pound the guy into the ground, whoever he was, was strong. DJ would help, as would Jason, too, and he was pretty sure he could count on Tyler, too. But Mandy—uh, Amanda—was tough. In this mood, she could probably take them all.

From across the room, Addie shot him a look that said, "Stop—I know what you're thinking." He shrugged and greeted Jason with a handshake and a hug.

The small conference room was already full, and DJ hadn't yet arrived. Wyatt doubted they'd planned for his family when they'd created it.

"What the heck?" DJ's voice came from the now open door as his gaze took in the full room and finally landed on Tyler. The nurse held the door open as DJ wheeled himself in. "What are you all doing here?"

Wyatt saw the sheen of pain and something else, some indefinable emotion in DJ's eyes. He knew DJ had been limiting his medications, and since this meeting was about the plans for him to go home, Wyatt understood his desire to be clearheaded. He felt for him, though, as DJ winced.

"You're all nuts," DJ mumbled as he wheeled himself to the table. He stopped next to Wyatt and looked at him. "You invite everyone?"

"Didn't know we needed an official invite, brother dear." Amanda leaned across the table and DJ's eyes widened.

"What the... How..."

"Shut up. I'll smack even you. This isn't about me right now. And all of you stop looking back and forth at each other." She sighed and leaned back without another word.

Tyler stepped into the space between Wyatt and DJ, staking his place. He didn't say anything, but his presence shut the group up.

Wyatt knew this meeting would be quick, as DJ could only sit for a short period of time before the pain and discomfort got to him. Not that he'd admit it, but Wyatt could tell.

When an older woman came into the room, Wyatt was surprised. Her salt-and-pepper hair and business suit gave her a motherly air. Wyatt hadn't expected the social worker to be a civilian, either. He saw warm compassion in her eyes, and a bit of surprise at the size of the group. It was only a brief flash before she smiled broadly at them all.

"I'm Anne Davidson." She introduced herself and took the only empty seat in the room. She made a point of acknowledging Tyler, which gained her points with Wyatt, but also told Wyatt she'd temper what she said.

Everyone who entered this room seemed to get a surprise, which Wyatt found oddly amusing. Luckily, no one else was expected. When the door opened, this time Wyatt was the one in for the surprise.

Emily stepped inside, stopping right beside the door where she leaned back against the wall.

"Emily?" Wyatt stood. "What are you doing here?" Stupid question. It was probably about Tyler's custody now that DJ was coming home.

"I called her," Tyler said softly.

Either ignoring the underlying tension, or oblivious to it, the social worker opened a thick folder and pulled out several sheets of paper. She spread them on the table in front of DJ, talking directly to him.

Wyatt reluctantly sat, his mind on the woman at the door instead of on the meeting.

After Anne outlined the treatments and therapies that would be required over the foreseeable future, all outpatient, she leaned back and waited for DJ's reaction. There was none.

Everyone else in the room, however, seemed to have no qualms about speaking up.

"We can make arrangements for an apartment here in San Antonio," Jason suggested.

"Austin's eighty miles, but we can get you back and forth," Addie said.

Tyler's voice joined the fray. "I thought you were coming home with us?"

After that, Wyatt struggled to distinguish the separate

voices as they all blended. Or maybe it was the humming in his brain.

He couldn't keep his gaze from wandering to Emily. She looked great. Her jacket neatly folded over her arm, she wore her dark blue suit—she'd obviously come straight from the courthouse. Her hair was pulled back, neat and tight, and she was wearing that pink blouse—the one she'd worn that first day they'd met.

DJ's fist hit the wooden conference table hard. The soldier's strength came through loud and clear as the myriad of voices fell silent. Tyler scooted behind Wyatt's chair and Wyatt wondered at his brother's actions. Scaring the boy wasn't the way to make friends. But Wyatt understood why he'd done it. His respect for his younger brother grew.

Wyatt looked over at Emily. She'd scooted to the door's edge. Her skin had paled and her fingers gripped her purse strap until her knuckles were white.

She wasn't looking at him. Her gaze latched on to DJ and the storm in her eyes worried Wyatt.

What was she thinking? She might talk a good game, saying she'd closed the case, but Wyatt knew she'd do whatever was necessary if she didn't think DJ was fit to be Tyler's guardian.

No one spoke. All eyes were on DJ.

"This is my life I'm losing here," he said softly, belying the slamming fist. "I'll decide where I go, and I'll let you all know when I make up my mind."

With his muscular arms, DJ spun the wheelchair around and rolled to the door. He pulled it open, glaring at Emily when she tried to hold it open for him. He used the foot of the wheelchair to do it instead. He stopped but didn't turn around. "I appreciate all of your concern," he said to the hall, then with a brief glance over his shoulder he met Wyatt's gaze. "But you can't fix everything. You can't fix this."

For an instant, the soldier vanished, and Wyatt saw the little boy DJ had once been. It was but a flash of memory between them, but it was enough to make DJ's point. Wyatt nodded. *Message received. Don't interfere.*

CHAPTER SEVENTEEN

WYATT WAS EXHAUSTED. The past two weeks had taken their toll. Driving here to the hospital nearly every day, going back to the ranch at night, keeping track of everyone, worrying about DJ and Amanda and Tyler and Emily and…the ranch. Thank God for reliable foremen.

At the other end of the waiting room couch, Tyler drove his toy cars, accenting the movements with his impression of an engine.

"Hey, buddy, keep it down, okay?" Wyatt's head pounded. Even though the room was done up in a neutral black-and-tan combination, he was sick of looking at it. He leaned back on the stiff couch and closed his eyes. There in the shadows of his mind he saw her face.

Emily.

She'd slipped out of the conference room right behind DJ today, and Wyatt hadn't seen her since. Had she left? What was she doing? His siblings had scattered, too, and he wasn't in the mood to hunt for them, either.

He just wanted to go home. And sleep for about a month.

"Mr. Hawkins?"

Wyatt opened his eyes to find the social worker, Anne, standing beside him. She smiled. He felt himself smile in response. "Call me Wyatt. There're too many Hawkinses around here today."

"Can we talk for a minute?" At his nod, she took a seat across from him.

"I just met with your brother and the doctor," she said. "I wanted to give you a heads-up. Dr. Simpson is recommending discharge at the end of next week."

"That's great." DJ still hadn't told Wyatt if he was coming to the ranch, though Wyatt was sure that was what he'd decide. He glanced over at Tyler.

"I'm not going to sugarcoat things. Your brother's made wonderful progress, but he's been through a lot, and he still has a long road ahead. Even after he goes home, he'll be here several times a week for therapy."

"How long does it really take for injuries, burns like that, to heal?"

"Quite a while, months, if not longer, and even once he's healed on the surface, the damaged muscles and bone are still rebuilding. But it's not the physical healing I'm concerned about." She pulled several pages from the clipboard and handed them to him.

Wyatt took them and glanced down. He recognized them as part of the packet she'd put out in front of DJ.

"Post-traumatic stress disorder?" He met the woman's stare with a frown.

"I'm not saying Captain Hawkins has been diagnosed. Please hear me out. With so many of our military experiencing such horrific events, we know it's an issue." She took a deep breath. "I don't let any of my guys go home without someone being informed of what symptoms to watch for."

"Like what?" The words blurred in front of Wyatt's tired eyes, and he blinked to focus.

"Here's a checklist. I want you to take it with you." She pointed to specific items. "For example, not sleeping well. Being easily startled. High anxiety or depression. Withdrawal. Those are some of the more obvious symptoms."

Nodding, Wyatt cataloged the words, making a note to keep an eye on his brother.

"Mom's like that. She's kinda like Ms. Ivers," Tyler piped up from the other side of the room. At first Wyatt thought Tyler was making up dialogue for his imaginary race-car drivers, but he wasn't moving the cars. He stood a few feet away, watching him and the social worker with wide eyes.

"What?" Wyatt looked closer at the pages. Then he went back to the top of the list and read it again, mentally checking off nearly each one as he compared it to Emily.

What the— "It says women are at higher risk than men." Wyatt looked over at Anne.

She nodded slowly, a confused frown on her brow. "Women are more likely to be in traumatic situations that trigger PTSD. Domestic violence, rape, abuse…" The last was spoken softly, but thankfully Tyler was focused on his cars again. "Do you know someone else who—?"

"Maybe." Wyatt mentally cursed. Emily's stories about her stepfather, and her mother's situation, leaped into his mind. Watching her stepfather abuse those she loved had definitely left a lasting mark. Several pieces fell into place, including her jumpy reaction to DJ's outburst back in the conference room.

The nurse who'd escorted DJ earlier stuck her head around the corner. "We're done with his treatments, Anne. Captain Hawkins is pretty tired, so if you want to chat, now might be a good time, before he falls asleep."

"Thanks, Liz." Anne stood.

"Before you go." Wyatt stood as well, towering over the smaller woman. "How do you cure it?"

Anne hesitated. "Cure isn't the right word. Treat would be better." She paused to look at him, considering him for a long minute. "Early detection is key. If you're asking what kind of treatment is effective, it's different for each person. Group therapy. Drug treatments. Even immersion therapy can work."

"What if the events were years ago?"

"Your friend?"

"Yeah." Wyatt nodded. There was so much information to take in. "What can *I* do?"

"Be supportive. Be there for them. They'll *both* need that." Several long minutes passed as Wyatt let the information sink in. "If you do notice anything, let me or the doctor know."

She was referring to DJ, but who did he contact regarding Emily? He'd have to think about this when he was more awake.

"Can we go see my dad now?" Tyler interrupted.

"Yeah, let's go." He turned back to Anne. "Thank you."

As they headed to the hall, she reached out a hand and touched his arm. "Keep an eye out. If you have questions regarding your friend or your brother, please don't hesitate to give me a call." She extended a utilitarian white business card. The look of sadness in her eyes jolted him.

Wyatt took the card and slipped it into his shirt pocket. He took two steps, then turned back. "I get the impression this is personal."

She nodded one simple time. "My son. We missed the signs. He committed suicide two years ago."

"I'm sorry."

"Thank you. So please don't ignore the signs. Not with your brother. Not with your friend."

"I won't," he assured her.

"Come on." Tyler bounced from foot to foot at Wyatt's side.

Anne laughed. "You're just like my grandson. So impatient." She patted his shoulder, then escorted them back to the ward, leaving them when she got to the nurses' station. She settled at a computer, probably to add notes to DJ's file.

Wyatt liked her, but the information she'd given him left him feeling unsettled.

His thoughts kept flipping back and forth between DJ and then Emily. What the hell was he supposed to do? They stopped at the open door of DJ's room.

For now, he shelved the images and concerns. He had to focus on DJ and Tyler and plan for the future at home. But once that was done? All bets were off. He and Emily needed to talk.

THE HOSPITAL DOORS behind Emily swished open and she hurried to move out of the way. The last thing she needed was for someone to mow her over. Then she'd be the one in the E.R. Several wooden benches lined the walk and she scooted over and sat down on one with a thud. Her legs shook and she tried to catch her breath.

What was she supposed to do now? DJ's anger worried her, but she couldn't tell if it was because of her concern for Tyler or her own discomfort.

She pulled out her phone...and stared at it. She should call Warren. She'd told him she was coming down here today just to visit. He'd glared at her over his glasses in a silent warning.

He knew she was too invested in this case.

But if she called him, she knew he'd tell her to walk directly to her car and drive home. He'd handle it. The fact that he was her boss meant she should probably do exactly that. There'd be consequences if she didn't.

Sighing, Emily shoved her phone back into her purse just as a shadow fell over her. She hastily looked up, expecting Wyatt, but was surprised when it wasn't him. She blinked a couple times at his brother Jason, who stood there.

"You're the judge, right?" He extended a hand. "Jason Hawkins."

She hesitated before taking his hand, afraid he'd notice hers trembling. She nodded. "Emily Ivers."

His hands were big, but not rough like Wyatt's. He didn't say anything immediately. The silent type…like Wyatt.

He had the same body build, several of the same mannerisms and the same dark hair and blue eyes as Wyatt. So why wasn't she attracted to him the same way?

"Did you need something?" She stood. She didn't let attorneys intimidate her in the courtroom; she wasn't going to let this one do it here, either.

"Not really. Just a word."

"Pleading your brother's case?"

"Trying to. Will it do any good?"

"Maybe." She smiled, more relaxed and comfortable now.

"I hope you can give DJ time. He's always been a hothead, but he's got a good heart."

Good hearts weren't what put food on the table or kept parents from hurting their kids, intentionally or unintentionally.

"Was that display in there his norm?"

He didn't answer at first. She was curious if this was his courtroom style. He intrigued her as a fellow litigator. She'd like to see him in action.

"No. That's why I'm out here now. If I thought he'd ever hurt Tyler, or wasn't capable of being a parent, I'd be the first to call him on it."

She nodded. "I appreciate the input."

"I hope you realize Mr. Control in there is the one who's going to need help."

Mr. Control? He was talking about Wyatt, not DJ. "What do you mean?"

Jason leaned back against the brick wall and gazed out over the parking lot. "Here's what'll happen. DJ will go home with Wyatt. He can say all he wants that he's still making up his mind, but that's what he'll do."

Jason laughed and shook his head. "I give 'em a couple weeks before Wyatt tries to tell DJ what to do, which won't work, by the way. So Addie'll jump in and try to make them see eye to eye." His gaze was distant as if he was actually watching it happen, or had seen it before.

Emily marveled at how well these siblings knew one another. She hadn't a clue what that felt like. She'd always lived in isolation, as a child and now as an adult.

Jason turned to head back inside, then looked back. "You're a good match for him, you know."

"What?"

He laughed. "You're tough, not needy. Needy would suck him dry. He couldn't help it. Just remember he'll never ask for help." The doors swished open again, and Jason walked back into the hospital.

An attorney, a cowboy and a soldier. Brothers. Nothing alike and yet so similar.

And that was only the male half of the family. Inside the shadowed interior of the hospital lobby, Emily saw the three sisters gather around Jason. They all turned in unison to look at her. Her stomach twisted and her heart sank.

She hadn't a clue how to be part of a normal family.

With a shake of her head to dispel her thoughts, Emily headed to the parking lot. Her heels echoed hollowly in the deserted garage. What a lonely sound. She had to get out of here before that thought went any further and she did something stupid, like turn around and run to find Wyatt.

She'd parked on the top level, and from here all of San Antonio spread like glitter at her feet. She vaguely wondered why the parking garage got one of the best views. Rather than climb into the sweltering vehicle, she walked over to the railing to get a better peek.

"Were you even going to say hello?" Wyatt's voice was hard and cold.

She shook her head. She wasn't surprised to hear him. "No. This is an official visit." Her voice cracked and she cleared her throat. "Warren Litchfield is taking over Tyler's case from here on out."

"So how is this an official visit if you're not on the case anymore?" Wyatt stopped a few feet away. She saw him from the corner of her eye. His feet wide, his arms across his chest, the brim of his hat shadowing his eyes, he looked imposing and sexy as hell.

She couldn't, however, tell what he was thinking. Maybe that was a good thing. "Tyler told the truth in the conference room. He did call me. Right after DJ was hurt." She paused, not quite sure how he'd react to what Tyler had told her. "He was afraid DJ wouldn't like him."

Wyatt cursed softly.

"As a result, Warren instructed me to continue the weekly visits. As the court visitor, not the judge." She clarified. "So here I am."

The pause was long, but finally Wyatt spoke. "Does he really feel that's necessary?"

Should she tell him it was as much to protect her as it was Tyler? She looked over her shoulder at him. "Yes, he does."

"What do you think?"

She shrugged. "Tyler's expressed concerns and fears. I can't discount that."

"That was before he met DJ, right?"

She nodded. "It's still best to address it. Get it in the record and let Warren make a clean decision."

Unlike what she'd done by muddying everything with her emotions and hang-ups.

She turned around to look at Wyatt, drinking him in. She could no longer deny it—she'd fallen in love with him. Fallen hard and irrevocably.

The damned tears were stronger than she was. She laughed, surprising herself *and* Wyatt, as they trickled down her cheeks. She hastily dashed them away.

"Emily?" His voice was soft. Close.

She took a step away. "Please, don't." She tried to re-focus on the view.

"What's wrong?" he asked, moving closer.

"Nothing," she whispered. The silence of the parking structure settled around them. Emily could tell something was on Wyatt's mind.

"What are you thinking?"

When she looked at him, she was surprised to see he

wasn't looking at her, but at the view. "Anne, the social worker, gave me some information today."

"About?"

He hesitated before finally turning to look at her. "Post-traumatic stress disorder." His eyes were filled with worry and questions. "Do you know much about it?"

"Just what I've seen in the media and some of the reports that have crossed my desk."

He nodded. "She gave me a list of the symptoms to watch for, just in case."

"Does she think DJ has it?"

He didn't answer right away. "She just said I need to know what to watch for."

This was crazy, this whole stilted conversation was wrong. Why was she so hesitant? Why was he?

"Emily? Don't take this wrong, but…have you ever considered that you have some of the symptoms?"

That was *not* what she'd expected him to say. She stared. "What? No. That's ridiculous."

"Is it?" He turned back toward her.

"Yes, it is."

Wyatt slowly walked back to her. "From what you told me about your stepfather, the abuse, it's not ridiculous."

She shook her head, ignoring the nagging pain she felt. "That was years ago. I'm fine. You don't need to worry about me. Besides, even if it were a problem, you can't fix it. You can't change anything." Was that ragged voice hers?

His anger flared. "Everyone keeps saying that. What is so damned wrong with wanting to take care of the people you love?" He glared at her, but she didn't flinch or look away. She met him glare for glare.

"There's nothing *wrong* with it," she whispered. "It just doesn't always work."

She didn't remember moving. She couldn't recall him moving. But the strength of his arms was suddenly there. Warm. Tight.

His lips found hers, and no matter how many little voices in the back of her mind told her to stop, she didn't. She couldn't.

This was the man who'd made love to her only days ago. He was everything she wanted. A home, a family, a friend. He'd taken her heart, loved her body and cared for her soul when she'd hurt. What more could she ask for?

Her sigh escaped. She clung to him, sliding her arms over his broad shoulders and letting him hold her up as her knees went weak.

Wyatt's big, strong hands moved up and down her back, seducing and soothing. Holding her to him.

Moments later, Wyatt abruptly stepped away, dragging the breath into his lungs. "Damn, Emily." He clenched and unclenched his fists. "You're killing me."

She didn't move. When she could finally speak, her voice was a strained whisper. "I can't think straight."

"That makes two of us," he mumbled.

"What the hell are we supposed to do now?"

He paced, curling his hands around the railing and tearing his gaze away from her. "You tell me."

He was looking to her for answers? She almost laughed. There weren't any answers. "Talk? You want to talk?" she asked incredulously, her brain still on passion overload.

"Hell, no. But if I do what I want…" He let that trail off as he moved several feet away, thankfully out of temptation's range.

She took a couple steps of her own, straightening her blouse, erasing the evidence of his touch. Deep breaths didn't help a bit.

Wyatt walked back to her slowly, carefully, stopping just out of reach. He shoved his hands into his jean pockets. "This is insane. Not until all of this is settled—" He turned away and stared over the rail again.

"Until it's settled, what?" She didn't move.

He looked at her, his eyes dark and unreadable. "Until this is over, let's just keep our distance."

"What do you mean?"

"You know exactly what I mean." Anger made his voice rise. "I want you, as a woman, but all this hot-cold, gotta-toe-the-line crap is impossible."

He walked past her toward the elevators.

He was right. It was what she should've said. She opened the driver's door and paused to stare at him over the frame. "Maybe if things were different." Maybe if she were different. She climbed in and started the engine.

Emily nearly hit the concrete wall on the first turn out of the parking lot. She slammed on the brakes, struggling to tear her gaze away from the rearview mirror where Wyatt stood perfectly framed, still waiting for the elevator. She forced herself to focus on the ramp.

If this was so damned right, why did his walking away hurt so much?

Jason had pegged it. Needy would suck Wyatt dry. He'd never be able to resist his own nature to fix things... to fix her. But he couldn't.

She was just too broken.

CHAPTER EIGHTEEN

AFTER DJ SETTLED into the house, life developed a familiar routine. Tyler got up each day to go to school. DJ got up and one of the hands took him into San Antonio. Wyatt took his rotation, too, hoping the time would help him get to know his brother again.

Two weeks in, DJ's doctor cleared him to drive. Wyatt clapped him on the back in congratulations. Maybe now DJ would have more of a sense of freedom and the stress on the household would go down.

That night as they were all seated around the dinner table, Wyatt wanted to take that congratulations back. "You want to what?" Every voice stopped and half a dozen pair of eyes, including Tyler's, looked back and forth between the brothers.

"You heard me." DJ glared across the table at Wyatt. "I'm going to Dallas this weekend to get my bike." He'd left it in Amanda's garage when he'd gone overseas. "Either you can loan me the truck and I'll haul the bike home, or someone can drive me down and I'll ride it back. I'd prefer to haul it so I can check the engine before I ride it that far." DJ continued eating as if Wyatt weren't staring at him. "Your choice," he said with a full mouth.

"Seems sufficiently stupid to me, to go overseas and nearly get blown up only to come home and splatter yourself all over the road," Wyatt said.

"You *would* think that."

The brothers stared at each other and the tension in the room grew with each passing second.

Wyatt broke the silence. "I'll let you know what I decide."

DJ cursed and levered up from his seat. He was using Dad's captain's chair as it was the only chair in the house strong enough and with arms to take the pressure he applied when lifting up. Wyatt watched, worried. DJ struggled to stand—how the hell was he going to handle a huge Harley out on the open road?

But the determination on DJ's face told Wyatt that his brother had made up his mind and there was no changing it. He stared down at his half-empty plate as DJ limped out of the room.

DJ's plate was nearly full. "Yolanda, will you save that for him?"

Yolanda wrapped the plate and put it in the refrigerator without a word. No one said a word. Even Tyler remained quiet, pushing his beans around his plate. The silence was nearly deafening.

The next day, DJ went to San Antonio for therapy before they had a chance to talk. It wasn't as if Wyatt knew what he'd say. He hated that they were at odds, though. Now he stood at the corral fence, not sure about anything anymore.

Dancer looked good, healthy, as he galloped around. He was itching to get out of his pen, and Wyatt totally understood how he felt.

Over the past couple weeks, Emily had stuck to her plan to visit each Friday. Wyatt had made sure he was out in the barn or the pastures whenever she drove up.

He wasn't sure he could stop himself from giving

in and grabbing her and hauling her caveman-style upstairs. He figured that wouldn't look good in her report.

"You thinking about letting him loose?" Chet stepped up to lean beside Wyatt.

"Think Haymaker's gonna try to get at him again?"

"Probably." That was why Wyatt had been dragging his feet about letting the horse loose. He didn't want to put him at risk. Haymaker probably already knew what they were thinking and was chomping at the bit to get Dancer in his sights again. "He knows too damned much," Wyatt grumbled, then froze as he realized something he should've known before.

Son of a... If Earl Walker had sold Sugar, Palace— Pal—Haymaker, the next-door neighbor from hell, would've known about it. He knew everything and everyone who dealt in horses. Wyatt hated dealing with the old coot. He was a scoundrel and Wyatt was pretty sure he'd put his boys up to tempting Dancer to go over that fence. Wyatt would just as soon punch the guy as talk to him.

But Wyatt had something the old guy wanted. A pretty big bargaining chip. Dancer came over to the fence to say hello, and Wyatt rubbed his nose. "If this works, your love life, and mine, are about to get a whole lot better."

Wyatt wasn't calling Haymaker. The old guy hated phones. This was better done face-to-face. So he drove over. As he entered the yard, he noticed that a lot had changed since the last time Wyatt was there. Several of the old buildings had been replaced with new and shiny ones.

Either business was good or Haymaker was up to his eyeballs in debt.

A tiny Hispanic woman met him at the door and led Wyatt through the empty house. Pal Jr. lived in town, and Wyatt knew there was no way Pal would have anyone else in the house. The fact that the maid was still here so late in the day made Wyatt wonder....

"Evenin', Wyatt." Pal's big booming voice came from the front room and Wyatt found him sitting in a recliner. A TV tray sat next to the chair and Pal grabbed a remote to mute the TV. His shit-eating grin grated on Wyatt's nerves.

"Evenin', Pal." He sat down on the end of the couch.

"What can I do for you?"

"I have an offer for you."

"Go ahead. I'm listening." Pal leaned back in the recliner, the leather groaning.

"I need some information. I thought you'd probably know where I can get it."

"And if I tell you?"

"*If.*" Wyatt leaned back. "If I get it, I'm willing to negotiate a reduced price for Dancer's stud fees." The fact that they both knew Pal had been trying to get them free of charge hung unspoken in the air.

Pal rubbed his jaw, the rasp of his whiskers loud against his gnarled hand. "Hmm, seems like a fair bargain depending on what info you might need."

It was more than fair and they both knew it.

"Might be tough to get." Wyatt let the challenge set a minute. "Fifteen, twenty years ago a man named Earl Walker tried to sell a horse named Sugar. White."

"Hell, boy. That could be hundreds of horses."

"I thought maybe you'd recognize the name."

Pal shook his head. "What's special about this

horse? Why haven't you checked sales records with the county?"

"I did. Didn't find anything." He'd found the original record when John Ivers purchased the horse for his daughter and put it in her name. Nothing else.

Pal stared at him a long minute. "Don't see where I can help you." And Wyatt could tell that ate at Pal. He wanted what Wyatt had—bad.

"Well. The sale might not have been totally legal." Wyatt didn't say any more. "The horse was badly injured. Beaten. A pitchfork probably left scars."

Pal sat back in his chair. He met Wyatt's hard gaze with a glare of his own. He obviously didn't like Wyatt's insinuation, but knowledge flashed in the old man's face.

"If I know, how much you gonna charge for the stud?"

"If you give me the info *and* I can verify it, for you the fee is half. On my territory, though. Dancer doesn't leave my ranch." Wyatt didn't break Pal's stare.

Time ticked by as the old man searched around in his head, a calculator clicking behind those shrewd eyes. "There an expiration date on this deal?"

"I'd like the info soon, but nope." Wyatt was taking a risk, but it was worth it. He needed to do this for Emily, but he wasn't going to put Dancer at risk, either. He didn't like Pal Haymaker, but he did respect him as a horseman. The foal that would come out of this would be top of the line. Pal owned nothing less.

The old man stuck out his hand. "Sounds fair to me. I'll make a couple calls and get back to you."

Wyatt shook the man's hand and headed to the door. He stopped before stepping outside. "I'll look forward to your call. You can make the other arrangements through my foreman."

"Still employing that good for nothin' Chet Larson?"

"Chet's still the best foreman in the county, and you know it." Pal had tried to hire Chet away often enough.

"Ah, I'll be the judge of that." Pal turned the television back on as Wyatt headed to his truck.

Anticipation rode close on Wyatt's heels. He'd have answers. But were they answers he and Emily could live with?

IT TOOK TWO DAYS for Wyatt and DJ to speak again. Wyatt walked into the den. DJ lay on the floor.

At first, Wyatt panicked, then as DJ remained there, staring up at the ceiling, Wyatt realized his brother wasn't even trying to get up. Wyatt walked over to him, and his brother looked up at him. "You need help?" Wyatt finally asked.

"Have faith, brother." DJ pushed up so that he leaned back against the recliner, his damaged legs stretched out in front of him. He rose slowly, using the old chair as support. "If I don't learn to do this myself, I'll be on the floor forever."

It nearly killed Wyatt to stand there and watch DJ struggle. But he did it because DJ had made it very clear since he'd arrived home that he did not want anyone's help. Finally, after what seemed like hours, DJ reached back and, with the arms that had been honed to thick muscular appendages, hauled himself up to sit on the edge of the chair. The damage to DJ's legs had left them weak, and while therapy helped, he still had a long way to go before he could stand easily.

"After that, I need a drink." DJ's voice was thready as he struggled to stand and walk to the liquor cabinet.

Wyatt looked over at the other man with both admiration and concern. "What meds you take today?"

"You're not my mother," DJ snapped. "I can have a damned drink."

Wyatt walked over to the bar and poured himself a drink, as well. "It's your funeral. But before you die, try explaining to your son what a jerk you can be so I don't have to."

DJ sent Wyatt a withering glare and Wyatt turned away, catching a glance out the window at the corral across the yard. Chet was exercising Dancer in a hearty trot around the arena. With Pal's threat diminished, they'd decided to let the horse loose this afternoon.

Wyatt almost laughed. Dancer was a lot like DJ, determined but headstrong sometimes. The downtime hadn't done a thing to keep Dancer from trying to escape the corral. But until Wyatt had gotten control over him and Haymaker, he hadn't been able to let him loose.

He quickly glanced at his brother. Was that what he was trying to do with DJ? Control him? Break him? Wyatt cursed himself and turned back to face his brother. "So you wanna talk about it? The fall?"

"Just going too fast." DJ leaned back in the seat, his legs up, balancing his half-finished drink on his T-shirt-clad stomach. "It sucks being so limited. I just want to get up and go without having to think about how to make my legs work."

The sadness in DJ's voice tore at Wyatt. He missed the free-spirited boy who'd gone off to war. But there was no sense in wallowing. They had agreed when he'd come here to look forward, not back.

"You'll get there."

DJ laughed but it was a mirthless sound. "Not like

before." He tore his gaze from Wyatt and stared into his drink. "Never like before."

The silence grew heavy around them.

"I can take you to Dallas on Saturday," Wyatt whispered. For all that DJ had lost and had sacrificed, Wyatt couldn't deny him his bike or his freedom. No matter how much he disagreed with his brother's intentions.

"You mean it?"

"Yeah."

Before they could discuss it further, the front door opened and a draft cut through the room. Tyler was home. Wyatt didn't want Tyler coming in here to see them both drinking in the middle of the afternoon.

"Uncle Wyatt? DJ?" Tyler called.

DJ winced. Would Tyler ever call DJ Dad? Wyatt hoped so.

"Perfect," DJ mumbled. Yet he actually sat up straighter in his chair and settled the glass on the side table instead of in his hand.

Maybe there was hope for him, after all.

"Mr. Hawkins is here to see you." Dianne's voice broke into Emily's concentration, what there was of it. Dianne stood in the doorway, having given up on Emily answering the phone.

Emily's heart skipped a beat, which must have shone on her face as Dianne shook her head. "Sorry. *DJ* Hawkins."

Despite her disappointment, Emily's curiosity spiked. What could DJ want? "Send him in."

The man who walked slowly into her office a few moments later was not the same man she'd met at the hospital, or each week at Wyatt's house. The soldier was back, and not just because of the uniform he wore. His whole body language said warrior.

"Hello." She stood and walked around her desk.

"Hi, Emily." His smile was appealing, though stiff as if he were ignoring the pain she knew he never really escaped.

"What can I do for you?" She gestured to the two wing-backed chairs. He walked carefully across the room and sat down facing her. If she hadn't known about his injuries, she wouldn't have noticed the slow hesitance of his gait.

Once they were settled, he met her gaze. "I need your help." He laughed. "Don't look so surprised. One thing the military taught me is to speak up when you need help, and everyone needs help sometimes."

"Is everything okay with Tyler?"

He nodded. "This isn't really about Tyler. It's Wyatt."

"Oh." Emily's heart pounded in her chest.

DJ leaned forward, his weight on his left side. The look on his face changed again. It softened. His voice came out low and controlled. "Here's my situation. I'm recovering, but not fast enough, or well enough for the military. I understand the requirements, and the decision my superiors are going to most likely make is to medically discharge me."

Emily saw a flash of pain go through his eyes, but it was quickly shut down.

"I've never wanted to do or be anything else but a soldier. So I have few other skills."

She understood. "You're concerned about supporting Tyler."

"Yes, ma'am." He took a deep breath and smiled. "Tyler's amazing. Though he does talk a little too much.

He gets that from his mother." His voice softened. "She was something else, too. At some point, I have to go find Tammie."

That surprised Emily. She wanted to ask about the woman, but wasn't sure how much he wanted to share. She was surprised when he actually relaxed.

"Tammie was one of those…ethereal moments in my life. She came through, changing everything and leaving next to nothing of herself behind. I was—" he paused as if trying to find the right word "—overwhelmed."

"Do you know how to find her?"

"That *is* my one skill. I have Uncle Sam to thank for that. Finding her won't be the hard part. Catching her will."

Emily frowned. "Can I ask you something?" What she was thinking went against everything she'd believed in her role as a magistrate.

"Sure."

"Do you have to find her?"

He thought about it for a minute, then nodded. "Yeah. Tyler needs closure. He deserves that."

Emily agreed. "What does this have to do with Wyatt? What can I do to help?"

"Be ready." DJ shifted in his seat, and Emily sensed he wished he could get up and pace with his old ease. None of the Hawkins men seemed able to stay put when they were thinking.

"For what?"

"For when I tell Wyatt that until I can support my son, I'm not going to petition for custody. Hear me out." He held up a hand when she started to speak. "Wyatt and Tyler love it out on the ranch. But I can't figure out my future there." He looked down. "I can't stay out there and not kill Wyatt. Plain and simple."

Emily tried not to smile. She didn't want DJ to think she was belittling his predicament. "Jason was close," she said. "He gave you guys two weeks. You made it to almost three."

DJ looked up, shocked, then he laughed. "Okay, I guess we are a bit predictable. But do you understand?" He sobered.

"I do." She needed time to think, but she agreed with his decision, if for no other reason than to see Wyatt again.

DJ stood, slowly levering himself up with his arms on the edge of the chair. "Thank you."

After DJ left her office, Emily sat behind her desk and stared out the window. *What a mess.* If DJ didn't ask to open the case to take custody of Tyler, it sat as is with her name as the judge of record, though the case was closed. There'd be no questions about whether she was impartial or not. Time would only strengthen her situation.

She should feel good about that.

But Wyatt had been so sure DJ would come back and take Tyler. To be fair, DJ wanted that, but was trying to make a good decision, one based on Tyler's needs and welfare. Yet that left Wyatt with the responsibility, and most likely a sense that DJ hadn't followed through as Wyatt expected.

A few moments later, Emily heard the throaty rumble of a motorcycle and looked out her office window. DJ sat on a large, loud motorcycle. The uniform and the machine seemed at odds, yet both fit him—perfectly.

CHAPTER NINETEEN

EMILY HADN'T SEEN her mother in nearly a month. Guilt had almost pushed her here several times, but she'd resisted. Knew she wasn't ready. She wasn't sure if she was ready now, but it was time.

Helen Walker was fading. Emily might not have noticed if she'd visited her mother each day. But now, with the time away, she saw it. In her thinning frame. In the ashy tone of her skin. In the lack of animation in her movements, especially her hands. Hands that were, for the first time in Emily's memory, idle.

"Hi, Mom." Emily wasn't sure if her mother would recognize her today. But for the first time, it didn't matter so much. Jackson's explanation had helped ease some of Emily's doubts and concerns. She had just needed time to process it all.

"Hello, Emily."

Pleasantly surprised that her mother recognized her, Emily sat beside her on the love seat. The silence didn't feel so heavy today.

"Mom?"

"Yes, dear?"

"Thanks." She leaned her head on her mother's shoulder, ignoring the hard edges, relishing the love she realized had driven her mother to do the things she'd done.

"What'd I do?"

"You're a good mom." Emily leaned back so she could look into her mother's face. "I met Jackson a few days ago. He told me about the coins."

When the fear crept into Helen's eyes, Emily curled her hand around her mother's. "Don't worry, Mom. No one else knows." Helen visibly relaxed.

"It's a secret," Helen whispered.

"I know, Mom."

Helen's eyes grew distant, and Emily feared the confusion was creeping back in. Emily wished she could have more times like this, but even if Mom was alert all the time, life didn't work that way.

"Can I ask a question?" Emily whispered.

"Of course."

"Do you know who Earl stole the coins from?" Emily was pretty sure that Jackson had figured it out. Drew knew. He wouldn't want them so badly if he didn't. She wasn't about to ask him. And Jackson refused to tell her anything more. The elderly man was as protective as Wyatt. She had to appreciate the old-fashioned chivalry even as it irritated the hell out of her.

"I think so," Helen said.

"Will you tell me?"

"I— It's too dangerous." Helen picked at the hem of her blouse. Emily backed off. Curiosity was the only thing driving Emily to ask, and she acknowledged that it wasn't worth upsetting her mother. Maybe she was better off not knowing.

Helen looked at Emily then, her eyes clear, though the fatigue in them was thick. "I tried to do my best. I love you, Emily."

"I know, Mom."

Helen leaned her head back and closed her eyes. "This

is nice," she whispered and smiled. Emily got up slowly, not wanting to disturb her mother. For the first time in years, Mom looked relaxed and at peace.

She looked… "Mom?" Emily's voice trembled. Helen didn't respond. Her eyes didn't flicker. The breath didn't move in and out. "Mom?"

Helen was gone. She should call someone. Why now? It was time. She'd known this would come, known it wasn't far off the last time she'd been here. Tears blurred her eyes, but she refused to look away, drinking in the last images. She trembled, fighting every instinct to scream and cry. "Goodbye, Mom," she whispered and folded her arms around the woman she'd never before lived without.

THUNDERCLOUDS SETTLED ON the horizon, blanketing the hills to the west. Wyatt pulled his collar up tighter around his neck. He'd be out here at least another half hour since Prism had thrown a shoe in the last canyon.

The West Texas desert, especially with an impending storm, was no place to be walking, but he had no choice. He couldn't risk Prism.

They topped the next rise and Wyatt stopped. The big horse seemed to sense his mood and nudged his shoulder. He'd specifically taken this path today. He'd needed it. From here he could see the entire spread. The hills, the valleys, the outbuildings and, farther in the distance, the ranch house. Home. Every inch of it screamed out to him.

Empty home, it whispered.

Despite everyone who lived there, everyone who came through the doors each day, there was one face missing. Emily. He ached to see her, touch her again.

Maybe if—and that seemed like a big if at this point, from the looks of the clouds—DJ got home early enough tonight, he'd head into town.

Knowing that was unlikely, Wyatt cursed and gave Prism's reins a tug. "Come on, boy. Let's get moving. That storm's coming in fast." Besides, Tyler would be home from school soon and Wyatt didn't like him coming home to an empty house.

Wyatt didn't beat the rain. By the time he and Prism reached the barn, sheets of water were falling over them. Puddles, lakes actually, grew in the yard. Standing at the open barn door once Prism was settled, Wyatt watched it come down. He could barely see across the yard. He was already soaked—what was a little more? The kitchen light was on, which meant Tyler was home and probably fixing himself an after-school snack. Who knew what the kid would find in the cupboards. Addie's addictive cookies were long gone.

He dashed out into the downpour.

"Hope you beat the rain, kiddo," he called as he stepped into the mudroom. Tyler didn't answer, but that wasn't so strange, either. Wyatt hung up his hat and soaked duster. His boots and jeans would just have to dry on their own. The kitchen was warm. His footsteps were loud against the ancient linoleum.

"Uncle Wyatt, look." Tyler sat at the kitchen table, in Dad's big captain's chair that DJ normally sat in these days.

"What am I looking at?" He grinned at the boy who was munching on a cookie. He must have missed a batch Addie had left.

"Her." Tyler pointed toward the stove the same instant he rolled his eyes.

Wyatt looked over his shoulder then spun around. "What the—"

"Hello," Emily whispered. She leaned against the stove, a steaming cup, probably full of tea, gripped between her hands. Steam wafted up into her face, drawing his eyes to the damp curls falling around her face. She was wearing a dress. He'd seen her in business suits and jeans, but never in a frilly summer dress like this one. The soft, thin fabric was vaguely transparent and clung to her skin. Even soaking wet, she looked better than he remembered.

Words failed him and he cleared his throat to loosen them. "Uh... Is there more of that?" He pointed at the cup.

"You don't like tea." She tried to smile and took a healthy sip of her drink. "What about this?" She moved away from the stove, revealing the full pot of coffee. She headed toward the table, but he stopped her as she went to pass him.

Her skin felt cool and so soft against his palm. "Why are you here?" It wasn't a day for a court visit. He was glad to see her, but something in her body language told him he might have to rethink that.

She didn't look at him, she simply stood there, staring into her cup for what seemed like an eternity. Finally, she lifted her gaze and he felt the sucker punch in his gut.

"What happened?" he whispered. She simply shook her head and looked over at Tyler.

He understood and his heart dropped. He knew that later, without Tyler's ears in range, she'd most likely break his heart.

Slowly, Wyatt poured himself a cup of coffee, gathering his thoughts and the shreds of his emotions before turning back around to watch Emily settle in the chair next to Tyler. She smiled at the boy. Her shoulders hunched, her eyes shone with unshed tears and she held the cup in a death grip. Something had happened. Something bad. And he didn't have a clue if it had anything to do with Tyler or not.

Panic came out of nowhere and attacked. What if she was here to take Tyler? He knew it didn't really work that way, but in such a short time, Tyler had found his way into Wyatt's heart. He couldn't imagine not having him in his life.

He forced himself to lean back against the counter and shut out such thoughts. He was being a selfish jerk, thinking it had to do with him, something Addie repeatedly told him he was good at it. What if something was wrong with Emily?

Tyler finished two cookies and half a glass of milk before he jumped down from his chair. Sitting still for him was a limited activity. "I'm done. Can I go watch TV?" he asked as he bounded toward the living room.

"Do you have homework?"

"Only math. Can you help me with it after supper?"

Wyatt fought the smile. He was thrilled to have Tyler ask for help, but he knew a stall when he saw one. In this case, it worked in his favor. "Sure. Don't turn it up too loud, though."

"'Kay." Tyler ran out of the room, all the energy leaving with him.

The silence that followed was thick. Heavy. Wyatt slowly finished his coffee. Emily barely moved. She looked suddenly stiff. As if the very idea of breathing would shatter her into a million pieces.

"You okay?" he whispered, afraid to say too much.

She did that staring-into-the-tea thing again. Only this time the cup was empty. "I…" She tried to talk, but her voice faded. "I need…" She stopped again, chewing her bottom lip. Finally, she looked up at him. "What do I do?" The movement spilled the tears over the rims of her eyes.

Wyatt couldn't stand it anymore. He couldn't watch her hurt like this. Two steps brought him to her, where he hunkered down. "Emily, tell me. I can't help if you don't tell me."

She sobbed, but swallowed it deep into her chest. Finally, the words broke from her throat. "Mom. I… We were visiting. She just closed her eyes." Her voice wavered. "She…she…d-died today."

Emily crumbled. Wyatt grabbed her cup at the same instant he pulled her close. He was shocked at how hard she was trembling. It shook them both.

The linoleum was cool beneath him. She curled in on herself and he settled her close in his lap. "I'm here," he whispered, knowing she didn't hear him, but hoping that somewhere she felt him there, holding her, protecting her. He understood her hurt. Though he'd had months to prepare for his mom's death, nothing prepared you for that initial pain of losing the one person who'd always been there, always shown you love.

He didn't wish that pain on anyone. He wanted to take hers away, but was hopeless to do anything but hold her. It was all he could do and prayed it was enough.

For a long time, he just held her. His hands moved slowly up and down her back, soothing.

The rain beat against the roof and windows as lightning cracked outside. A loud boom of thunder shook the house.

"Hey," he whispered against Emily's ear. She'd cried until there couldn't possibly be any tears left. She was still soaked, which only intensified her shivers. He would stay here, holding her, as long as she needed, but the best thing for her was to get up and get warm.

"Come on," he said a little louder and leaned back.

The sound of footsteps at the back door startled her out of the lethargy and she climbed slowly to her feet.

Standing, she tilted her head back and met his gaze. He saw the instant her mood shifted.

"Thank you," she whispered, rising up on her tiptoes to kiss him.

EMILY WAS DONE playing by the rules. She'd always been a good girl, yet Earl had still abused her. She'd taken care of her mom, found her a safe place to live. But she'd died, anyway. She'd backed away from the one man who'd been willing to take her on and where had all that gotten her?

She was alone. She had no one.

She didn't want to be alone anymore.

Emily couldn't differentiate between the shivers from the cold rain and the trembling that had started as soon as Rose had moved her away from her mother.

Wyatt's arms eased them, either way.

"Uncle Wyatt?" Tyler's voice came from the doorway. "Are you okay, Ms. Ivers?" The fear in his voice stilled them both. Wyatt placed a soft kiss on Emily's forehead before stepping away.

Her shivers returned, making her teeth chatter. She wrapped her arms around her waist, finding no warmth. "I'm fine, Tyler," she lied, understanding too clearly why her mother had protected her with lies. "I j-just got too c-cold."

"Oh." Tyler perked up immediately. Footsteps at the door grew louder and Yolanda, with a huge umbrella, stepped inside.

"Can you behave for Ms. Yolanda while I help Emily?" Wyatt asked.

Tyler was being very stoic, and even in the haze of her mind, Emily saw what he was doing. He was turning into Wyatt. "Th-thank you, Tyler," she whispered to the young boy.

"Don't worry." Tyler walked over to her. "Uncle Wyatt knows how to take care of damsels in distress." His words were so earnest and sweet. Emily's eyes burned again, but these tears didn't hurt her heart so much.

"Let's get you a hot shower and some dry clothes." Wyatt led her to the stairs, his hand firmly curled around hers. He didn't take her into his room, though, as she'd hoped. Instead, he led her to the huge bathroom.

The old-fashioned claw-foot tub looked original, but a huge glass shower had been added sometime later. Wyatt reached into the shower and turned on the hot water. "Let's get you warmed up."

So he had noticed her trembling.

"I'm not that cold." They were whispering, which seemed silly and yet intimate. He moved to the door and a gasp escaped her. He looked over his shoulder at her.

This was it. This was her chance. There was no turning back. "Don't go," she said.

"Emily." His voice came out strained. "You're vulnerable now. I can't."

"I hurt. But I know what I want." She met his gaze

and held it. Her heart sank as he walked to the door. Until he stopped, closed and locked it.

He was there beside her, before she could blink, cupping her chin with his warm hands. "Be sure. Be very, very sure," he whispered as his lips found her. The splash of the water on the tile was the only sound for a long while.

Slowly, Wyatt's fingers trembled against her skin as he reached out and opened the first button of her dress. The still-damp fabric clung to her, and she knew he could see every curve beneath.

Another button opened. The fabric slid apart and Wyatt leaned forward, his lips burning hot against her cool skin. When he leaned away again, she curled her fingers in the front of his shirt and tried to pull him back. He didn't budge, just continued to undress her. Slowly. Carefully. Reverently.

Steam wafted around them with a warm kind of calm. When all her clothes had slipped away and were neatly hung to dry, Wyatt's hands, now warm, curled around her shoulders and nudged her toward the hot spray.

"Are you going to join me?" Her voice shook, and she couldn't put it off to the cold this time. She was more than warm now.

"Your choice. I won't push you, Emily."

She turned to face him and watched him follow the path of the water spilling down over her. "Love me, Wyatt."

Wyatt didn't wait to be asked again. His shirt, jeans and boots disappeared not nearly as neatly as hers had. Emily shoved the water from her eyes, needing to watch him for fear he'd disappear. His well-toned body was proof of all the hours of hard work he put in, as well as his desire for her.

He walked slowly toward her, letting her look. At the edge of the shower he paused, and she held her breath waiting. "You're sure?"

She nodded, not sure which she wanted to see more, the caring in his eyes, or the hard evidence of his desire. He took that decision away from her and stepped inside. The latch sounded loud and—blessedly—final.

Wyatt pulled her into his arms and the lingering shivers stopped. "Let me take care of you," he whispered as he pulled her close and kissed her again.

His words, the words that were the very heart of Wyatt Hawkins, vibrated through her, bringing her into him, into his world. It was all she'd ever really wanted from him. All she needed.

His care. His love.

She answered by leaning into him and returning his kiss, hoping he understood. She had no words left. She closed her eyes and let him take care of her.

The soap in Wyatt's shower was nothing frilly, nothing sweet. It was a simple soap that lathered well in his hands. Those big, work-roughened hands moved leisurely over her shoulders, down her arms, back up her belly to cup her breasts. The water rinsed away the soap suds and Wyatt's fingers slipped lower, between her thighs, to the tender spot he'd found all those nights ago.

Slowly, oh, so slowly, he stroked her, winding her up so that her breath came in heavy pants. "Wyatt." She called his name softly, and yet it echoed off the tiles.

As he brought her closer to the edge, his head descended and his lips matched hers. She was ready to explode and when he finally slid his finger inside her, she flew apart. He caught her cries of completion with his lips, his touch slow, making it last and last, making her body his.

She snuggled against his strong chest, trying to catch her breath as he soothed her with simple touches and short, sweet kisses on her face and neck.

"What about you?" she whispered.

"Oh, honey. I've waited this long." He leaned back and smiled down at her. "If I start now…there might be dinner *and* a show downstairs." His smile was wicked and warm and made her laugh. "Later…" The promise in his eyes had her blushing. "You warm now?" He smiled down at her, his forehead against hers.

She nodded and actually felt like she could almost smile back.

"Good. 'Cause half a dozen cowboys will be here for dinner soon. Let's get dressed." He stepped out of the shower and grabbed a fluffy white towel from the shelf. He unfolded it and held it out for her to step into.

Briskly, he rubbed the fabric all over her, drying and caressing. She alternately laughed and melted so that when he was done, she drifted into his arms again. The resulting kiss was magical.

Once dressed and ready to open the door again, Emily froze. In here, in this small, cozy room with Wyatt, she felt alive, safe, sheltered from reality. Out there—

"I'm right here. I'm not going anywhere," he said as if reading her mind. Before she could stop him, he reached past her to turn the handle and open the door. Cool air washed over her, but the shivers didn't return.

She didn't feel alone anymore.

CHAPTER TWENTY

THE NEXT MORNING Emily awoke in Wyatt's bed, alone. Sunlight poured in the big windows. The sound of people moving around, of life going on around her, felt safe and right. And sad.

Mom was gone. And finally at peace.

Emily dressed quickly, determined to meet the day with the same strength and determination she'd found yesterday. She had a lot to get done but right now she was doing well enough just finding the will to breathe. She needed to find Wyatt. Wanted to find him.

Last night he'd been so kind and caring. A gentle yet insistent lover. Just thinking of his touches and kisses made her pause and her knees go weak. Smiling, she stepped out into the hall the same instant Tyler ran out of the bathroom, leaving a trail of water behind him.

He might have a towel around his skinny little waist, but she knew the rest of him was totally bare. "What are you doing?" Emily asked.

"Forgot my shirt."

"You couldn't dry off first?" She walked closer to Tyler. The boy wasn't just wet, he was dripping wet, from head to toe. His hair was plastered to his head and a river of water trickled from there down his bare shoulders.

He turned to face her then and she felt as if a mighty

fist had slammed into her. On his left shoulder three purple marks stood out against his skin. She hurried over to him, carefully turning him to face her. "What happened?" Her voice trembled.

He looked up at her, his eyes widening. He glanced down at his shoulder. "N-nothing." He tried to scoot away, the banked fear thick in his eyes.

She followed him slowly, not wanting to scare him. "Tyler. You're safe with me."

"I know," he said softly.

The sound of the dripping water from the towel to the floor was loud. She didn't want to push him, but the churning in her gut wouldn't let up. Her worst fears were rearing their ugly heads. Pushing her. She took several deep breaths.

"You can tell me." She knelt down beside him. Not threatening. Trembling, but not threatening.

Tyler simply shook his head and backed away. He bumped into the door frame and hastily ducked into his room. What should she do? She knew that mark on Tyler's shoulder. It was a handprint. Fingers. Big, wide fingers.

Her throat tightened and she fought to breathe. Images of her own past tried to crowd in, but she shoved them away. This was about Tyler. Not her.

Wyatt? No, she'd have noticed before, wouldn't she? Or was she blinded by her attraction to him? Slow, struggling footsteps came to her ears, and she glanced over her shoulder to see DJ coming up the stairs.

She spun around and, with her hands fisted at her sides, faced the injured soldier. As he reached the landing, he looked up and their gazes clashed. She bit back her anger, holding still by sheer forced will. She clenched her jaw, trying to keep back the accusation, but failing. "There's a handprint on Tyler's shoulder," she whispered.

He froze, much as she had. He didn't deny nor confirm it. He simply shut down, turned off any sign of emotion or humanity in his face. She shivered. This was a man the government had paid to kill people. A man Wyatt had let come into his house.

"How dare you," she growled and headed for him. She didn't get far. Strong, hard arms grabbed her from behind. Despite the fact that she recognized those arms, she fought and screamed.

"Emily, stop." Wyatt's voice was close to her ear. It did nothing to calm her. If anything, it heightened her hurt and anger. She tried to kick back, her heel connecting hard against Wyatt's shin. He cursed but didn't let her go.

"Stop it!" Tyler's voice cut through the insanity and she looked over to see the boy, wrapped in his soggy towel, in the doorway. Tears filled his eyes. She stilled, anger fading as sharp pain and disillusionment took its place. How dare they!

Emily gathered her breath and strength and ripped out of Wyatt's arms. She looked back and forth between the two men, her anger nearly blinding. She strode over to Tyler and knelt beside him again. "Don't worry, Tyler."

"You wanted to hurt my dad."

"No, I'm just angry. I'm okay now. Can you go into your room for me and get dressed?"

He looked at her, his eyes full of distrust and questions. "You won't hurt them while I'm gone, will you?"

Emily doubted she could hurt either of these men. DJ might be injured but his years in the military had honed him into a strong warrior. Wyatt worked hard each day on the ranch. She knew intimately the extent of his muscle and strength. She couldn't look at him now. DJ she glared at.

Tyler hesitated only a minute before trudging back to his room. He didn't close the door, as if not fully trusting her. She reached out and closed it for him. And then she spun back around.

"Emily—" Wyatt started.

"No." She held up her hands. "I'm not asking for an explanation because there's nothing, *nothing* that justifies hurting a child." Her anger returned, but this time she was able to keep it under control, barely.

"There's an explanation." Wyatt turned expectantly to his brother, who leaned against the wall, his arms crossed over his chest. DJ remained silent.

"We're leaving." Emily curled her hand around the doorknob of Tyler's room.

"Emily, don't," Wyatt said.

Despite her anger she managed to see the frustration in Wyatt's face, but she chose to ignore it. "He either goes with me, or I call social services now." She pulled her cell out of her pocket.

"Then take him."

DJ chose that moment to speak? She stared at the man, incredulous. And sad. Sad for Tyler. He so wanted DJ to step up and be his dad. She didn't look at Wyatt, she simply turned the knob and went into Tyler's room.

The boy had managed to pull on his jeans and a T-shirt that looked old and well-worn. He sat on the edge of the bed, his head down, his fingers curled tight around something metal. What was she going to tell him?

"You're going to take me away, aren't you?" His voice cracked.

She had to choose her words carefully. "I think it's best right now."

"He didn't mean to. I know he didn't."

Emily closed her eyes, taking a deep breath. How many times had she heard that? How many times did the victim defend their abuser?

"Give him another chance, please," Tyler pleaded.

She couldn't do it. All her nightmares had come true. She was a fool. Her shivers returned. She could not stay here and condone this. And she sure as hell couldn't leave him here. Opening her eyes, she met Tyler's gaze through blurry tears. "I'm sorry, sweetie. I can't do that. I'm the one who let you stay here. You can come to my place and we'll sort it out, but you can't stay here."

He nodded slowly, his fingers tightening around what he held in his hand.

"What's that?"

"Mama gave it to me," he whispered. Slowly, he opened his hand. An old locket, almost as big as Tyler's palm, gleamed in the dim light.

"Can I see it?" she asked carefully. Tyler extended his hand and nodded. Emily carefully took it, popping the latch.

"Oh," he said. "I couldn't remember how she showed me to do that."

"Here." She closed it again with a soft *snick*. "Push this button here."

He followed her instructions and the locket popped open again. "There's Mama." Wonder filled his voice. "She said she was comin' back." He looked up at Emily. "Where is she? Why isn't she back yet? You think she got lost?"

"I don't know." Emily looked at the pictures in the

locket. She recognized a much younger DJ. His smile bright, his hair long and thick. So different from the coldhearted man she'd just left. The woman's image intrigued her. Long brown hair framed a face that was oddly familiar. Tyler had her eyes.

"She's pretty." Emily settled down on the bed. "I don't think she'd want you with someone who would hurt you."

Tyler pondered that. "Dom hurt me so she sent me away. Guess you're doing the same thing, huh?"

She didn't even know what to say to that.

WYATT GLARED AT his brother, wishing he could strangle DJ himself.

DJ simply walked to the door across the hall and closed it behind him with a soft click. Wyatt stood in the hall, alone. *What the hell?* This was his house, damn it. Tyler was his responsibility and here he stood in the hall alone?

He wanted to kill his brother. He slammed open the door of DJ's room. "What the hell was that?"

"You heard her. She's taking Tyler. Let her. He's better off with her than a foster home." DJ pulled the duffel bag out of the closet and threw it onto the bed. "Or with me," he whispered. He hobbled over to the dresser and yanked open the drawers. Clothing flew.

"What are you doing?"

"What does it look like? You're not stupid, Wyatt. Well, not usually. I'm packing." He slammed rumpled jeans and shirts onto the bed.

Wyatt rubbed his forehead. So much for taking his frustrations out on DJ. Life had been much simpler when they'd been kids and could just beat the crap out of each other and let Mom patch them up. "Where are you going?"

"Back to San Antonio. The only reason I came out here was because Tyler was here. He's leaving now." DJ shrugged and turned his focus back to his packing.

Wyatt almost wanted him to go. This bullheaded, angry man was not the brother he knew. But that would be a mistake, for all of them.

"So that's what they teach you in the marines? To give up?"

DJ spun around, belying his injuries, and seized the front of Wyatt's shirt. "Don't try that crap on me. You know that's pure B.S."

Wyatt had had enough. He shoved DJ, hard, watching as he stumbled back and nearly fell. "Don't what? Let you know that I've had it up to here?" He sliced a hand through the air near his throat. "I've put my life on hold." Wyatt didn't let images of Emily enter his mind. Not now. "Tyler is *your* son. *Your* responsibility. I took him in, swearing in court that you'd come home and want him. Did I lie?"

DJ was silent, dropping to the edge of the sagging mattress. He leaned forward, his forearms on his knees, his head hanging down. "No," he whispered. And then he looked up. It was impossible to look into the tear-filled eyes of a U.S. marine, even if he was your little brother, and not ache for him. Wyatt cursed.

A sound in the doorway made both men look back. And freeze. Tyler stood there, watching. Emily was behind him, her arms full of clothing and bags. They both stared, and Wyatt wondered how much they'd heard.

Emily, judging from the anger on her face, had heard plenty. "Come on, Tyler. We're leaving," she said.

"Just a sec." The boy stepped into the room. He looked up at Wyatt first, then moved farther into the room, coming to a stop in front of DJ. "D-dad?"

Wyatt wished he were sitting down like DJ. It was the first time he'd called him that, and something DJ had been waiting for.

"Yeah?" DJ did the whole manly thing of trying to pretend he wasn't wiping his eyes on the shoulder of his shirt.

"I'll be back. I promise."

"I don't think that's up to you, bud." DJ looked over Tyler's head at Emily, the emotions on his face carefully controlled. "Is it?"

She didn't answer and Wyatt was proud of her. "Don't take it out on her." He stepped over to Emily's side.

"He's right," she finally spoke. "It's up to Warren. It's his case now. Come on, Tyler."

Tyler didn't move. Instead, he reached into the pocket of his jeans, the pocket that was always stuffed to capacity. Wyatt was surprised to see him pull a chain out of his pocket, a locket dangling from the last end. "This was Mama's." He looked at it. "I didn't know how to open it. Ms. Ivers just showed me how. See?" He held out the locket and popped it open like a pro.

DJ stared at his son and then at the locket. "Yeah," DJ whispered. "I gave it to your mom."

Wyatt saw two pictures inside the locket. A girl and an old one of DJ. Of the boy he'd been.

"She said she'd come back and gave me this to prove it." Tyler set the open locket on DJ's knee. "I'll be back, too."

Tyler turned and ran out of the room, shoving his way between Emily and Wyatt, his footsteps loud on the stairs. The screen door smacked before anyone spoke.

Oddly enough, it was Emily who went first. "Someone from the court will contact you."

"Where are you taking him?" Wyatt asked. DJ remained ominously silent.

"My place." She turned and descended the stairs.

Wyatt stood at the top, watching her go. "I'll call you."

She halted at the bottom. "Don't." She looked over her shoulder at him. He thought for an instant that she was going to say something. She didn't. She adjusted the load in her arms then followed Tyler out the door.

The second slam of the screen door sounded too final.

Wyatt caught up to Emily just as she closed her car trunk. "What do you mean, *don't?*" he yelled.

"I…" Instead of talking, Emily stalked around the car and yanked opened the door.

Before she could climb in and close it, Wyatt grabbed the frame's edge and saw her wince. He immediately felt guilty, hearing the social worker's words in his head. *Easily startled. Withdrawal.*

Damn it.

He didn't want to cause her to have an anxiety attack, but he refused to pussyfoot around anymore. She'd been hurt in the past, but if she didn't know by now that he wouldn't do that to her, when would she?

Their whole future rested on her trusting him. "*This* whole situation is *not* about you and me. We are separate from DJ and Tyler."

"Really? You could have fooled me." She whirled on him. "We met because of Tyler. The visits were all for Tyler." Her voice cracked. "The only time *we* connect is when *I* need you. Thank you for all your assistance, Mr. Hawkins. I'm perfectly fine now. You've fixed everything." She threw her hands up in the air in defeat.

Turning, Emily climbed into the car and slammed the door. Somewhere in the midst of everything, Tyler had settled himself in the car. Emily breathed a sigh of relief at that. If she'd had to get out and help him, she might have lost it and given in.

Her eyes burned, and she blinked furiously as she floored the gas pedal and left a cloud of dust in the yard.

Once the tires hit the pavement, she took a deep breath and lifted her foot. Tyler sat still and silent in the seat beside her. She took her eyes off the road for an instant to look at him. "I'm sorry, Tyler." She wasn't sure what she was apologizing for. Her crying? Arguing in front of him? Letting Wyatt have custody?

"That's okay." He looked over at her. "My mom's good at getting mad, too."

"Is she?"

"Yeah." The silence grew thick. "Ms. Ivers?"

"Yes?"

"Do you think she's comin' back?"

"I hope so." She wasn't sure that was totally true at all. But otherwise, Emily hadn't a clue where Tyler was going to end up. This was all her fears coming to life. She'd made a huge mistake. She'd believed all the lies. A soft sob broke her throat. She felt like an idiot.

"Don't cry, Ms. Ivers. Mama always says it'll get better. It has to."

Emily smiled through the ache in her throat. Tyler was trying to comfort her and she wondered how many times he'd done the same for his mom. "You're going to be a good man someday."

"Yep. Just like Uncle Wyatt."

Emily would have banged her head on the steer-

ing wheel if it wouldn't impair her driving. She wished
Tyler weren't right. Wyatt *was* a good man, just not good
enough.

"YOU DID WHAT?" Warren's voice came over the phone
line.

Emily knew he didn't want her to repeat what she
said. He was just trying to wrap his brain around the
day's events that she'd just relayed to him. So she remained silent. Waiting.

He didn't disappoint her. "So you didn't call social
services because…?"

"I did what I judged to be the right thing at the moment." She knew Tyler hadn't been in any imminent
danger. DJ was actually telling her to take him. She'd
had time to wait for someone impartial to come out to
the ranch. But what she hadn't had was the trust or patience. She'd escaped because of her emotions and she
knew that.

"Where is the boy now?" Warren sounded weary.

"Here with me." She heard him shuffling papers in
the background.

"Where the hell is his file?" he grumbled.

"Are you at the office?"

"Of course I'm at work," he growled. "I'm always
at work."

"The file's in my office, on the conference table."

"With probably about fifty other files."

She wasn't sure he was talking to her. But he hadn't
hung up, and she wasn't going to be the first one who did.

"Wasn't there an aunt, or someone else involved?"

Addie. Emily had completely forgotten about Addie.
How, she didn't know. "Yes. She's in Austin."

"Get in touch with her." He was walking, she could tell. More pages flipped. "Why didn't we consider her as the guardian?"

"She didn't apply."

"Well, call her, anyway. Maybe she'll step in until I can clear this up."

"Yes, sir."

"And, Emily?" His voice was heavy as it came through the phone.

"Yes?"

"My office. Eight o'clock tomorrow morning. Don't be late." He ended the call without saying goodbye.

Emily swallowed her apprehension. "Yes, sir," she whispered to the now-dead phone. Warren had been relatively nice the last time he'd summoned her to his office. This time would be different. She looked back at Tyler, who was sitting on the couch watching TV, and knew she'd do the exact same thing again.

Part of what made her a good magistrate was her ability to fit together all the pieces and formulate clear answers. This case had been muddied from the beginning, by the hastiness of her involvement, by the shadows of the Dean case and, she hated to admit, by her own prejudices. She just needed time and space to see more clearly.

But even in the few hours since leaving the ranch she'd had enough time and distance to realize there were vital pieces of this situation that she was missing.

"Tyler?" She sat down beside him on the couch. "Can I talk to you a minute?"

"Yeah." He muted the TV with the remote.

Emily reached over and turned the TV off, knowing that even if there was no sound, the pictures would distract him. "I probably should have asked you sooner, but I was upset."

"Asked me what?"

"To tell me exactly what happened with your dad that gave you those bruises."

"Oh." Tyler looked distressed and rubbed his hand through his hair. He was already picking up Wyatt's habits. She dismissed the realization.

"I'm listening, Tyler. Just tell me the truth," she prompted.

"You won't get mad again, will you?"

"At you, no."

"No, at my dad."

"I can't promise that. But I'll try, okay?"

"Okay."

He seemed to be thinking over what to say. She hoped he wasn't trying to come up with a story.

"I was being a pest. Asking lots of questions."

"Where were you?"

"In his room. He was trying to get dressed. He was really frustrated."

"I see. Go on."

"Mama says I'm a chatterbox too much of the time. Guess she's right." He looked sad at the mention of his mother. Emily didn't push him. She waited patiently for him to continue.

"He told me to leave, to go to my room until he was done gettin' dressed."

"And did you?"

Tyler slowly shook his head and looked down. Emily could understand DJ being self-conscious and not wanting his son to see him falter—she'd give him that.

"I kept askin' questions. He tried to make me leave. He turned me around and told me to go."

"Did you?"

"Yeah. I started to, but he lost his balance and fell. He didn't mean to grab so hard, really, he didn't."

Emily closed her eyes, picturing the scene. She knew Tyler well enough to know he was telling the truth.

Dread ripped through her. She'd overreacted.

Warren was going to kill her. She was pretty sure DJ already thought she was an uptight bitch....

And Wyatt? She refused to think about that now. She couldn't. It hurt too much. Looking down at Tyler, who stared up at her, his eyes wide and confused, reassured her. She'd rather overreact than leave him at risk.

"How about we call your aunt Addie? Maybe she can come up to visit for a few days."

"So you're not mad at my dad anymore?" His eyes filled with hope.

"Maybe." She was still irritated that he'd told her to take Tyler and hadn't tried to fight for his son. *Not as if she'd have listened,* a voice whispered in the back of her mind.

"I hope she makes cookies." Tyler smiled. "Can I watch TV now?"

"Sure." Emily handed him the remote and went into the other room to make the call.

CHAPTER TWENTY-ONE

THREE FILES WERE all that remained on the conference table. Emily looked at the polished surface that she hadn't seen in months. She should feel a sense of accomplishment and relief that all the work was done. She didn't. All she felt was a sadness that she couldn't shake.

There wasn't anyone she could share her success with. No one to encourage her, like Mom. No one to smile at her, like Wyatt. She blinked away the stupid tears that kept ambushing her. *Enough.*

The phone rang, saving her from falling apart. Emily grabbed it on the third ring. She'd barely had time to say hello before Drew's voice slithered through the line. "I found your little hidey hole."

Emily cringed. She'd recognize his voice anywhere. It lived too frequently in her nightmares.

"Wh-what are you talking about?" She tried to sound calm.

"Oh, don't play innocent with me. You know what I'm talking about."

Unfortunately, she did. He must have gone out to the trailer house. If he had, all he had to do was walk into the bedroom and he'd see the pile of clothes she'd left on the bed, the open closet doors, the hole cut in the wall. She hadn't tried to hide it. She hadn't cared. Still didn't.

She heard him moving around. Where was he? What

was he doing? Was he out at the trailer now? She closed her eyes. Of course, he was.

"Shut up!" Emily heard him speak away from the phone—someone was with him. A high-pitched, indistinct voice came through the line.

"Who are you talking to?"

Drew laughed, and it wasn't a cheerful sound. "I don't owe you an explanation. We're not family, remember?" His anger was all too loud and clear across the airwaves.

Emily sat back in her desk chair and rubbed her eyes. She was so tired of dealing with him. So tired of *this*. It was time to tell him the truth. Maybe then he'd go away.

"Drew. I don't have the coins. I never did. I didn't know they even existed until a few weeks ago." She sighed, trying to figure out how to tell him what happened.

"Liar."

"Think what you want. But I'm telling you the truth." She curled her hand into a fist, focusing her anger. "Yeah, I think Mom took them from Earl, but Earl himself stole them from someone." Neither was a decent excuse. "They're all gone, Drew. Long gone."

"What the hell does that mean?" She heard him hit something. A wall? A desk?

"She pawned them. That money was what we lived on after Earl left."

The air was silent and thick with his anger. Emily expected him to explode, but this silence was far worse. She shivered, thankful they were having this conversation over the phone.

Her relief was short-lived, though, as she heard him talking to someone in the background. "Drew?"

"You took what's mine." The anger in his tone was beyond anything she'd ever heard. "Now it's my turn."

"Drew. Don't do anything stupid."

"Oh, this is far from stupid. I'm a lot smarter than you think I am, Emily. You'll see."

"Drew?"

He didn't answer. But the line wasn't disconnected. She heard something. A whimper? A cry?

"No!" A voice, a familiar voice, came over the line, just before the call ended.

She stared at the phone. *I know that voice.* Tyler!

Dianne rushed into the office, her glasses bouncing off her nose as she hurried to Emily's desk. "Addie Hawkins just called. Tyler wasn't at the school when she went to pick him up. The school told her he wasn't there all day."

"But I dropped him off," Emily whispered, then louder, "Why didn't someone call? Oh, my God. Oh, no." She stood. Whatever she remembered doing, whatever someone else didn't do, only one thing mattered now—*Drew* had Tyler.

WYATT WATCHED FROM the doorway as DJ shoved his clothes into the duffel bag, this time with more organization and determination. It was the same green bag he'd brought home from the hospital. The same bag he'd taken to boot camp. And overseas.

"Don't do this, Deej," Wyatt said softly, not sure what DJ would say or do. This man wasn't the same one Wyatt had grown up with.

Heck, who was he kidding? He barely recognized his brother these days.

The time DJ had spent in the military had taken the skinny teenager Wyatt remembered and turned him into a tough, muscle-bound man. The burns had caused DJ's legs to thin down, but his arms were as thick as his thighs had ever been and his broad shoulders almost made Wyatt feel inadequate. Almost.

"Don't do what? Get on with my life?" DJ took a moment to glower over his shoulder at Wyatt.

"That's not what I meant and you know it."

"What did you mean, brother?" DJ zipped the bag closed and slung it over his shoulder. "I appreciate the hospitality, but it's time to get out of here." His voice lacked even a drop of sincerity.

Wyatt waited until DJ reached the top of the stairs before he spoke. He didn't raise his voice. "What about Tyler?"

DJ paused. Wyatt saw him take a deep breath before he spun on his boot heel. "You know what your problem is, Wyatt? You can't fix a damned thing. You've always taken care of everything, everyone. You learned to cope, to make do. But you can't *fix* shit. Not this time." The former soldier headed down the flight of stairs.

Wyatt followed to the top step. "I asked you a question."

DJ barely paused at the front door. "Keep him." The door seemed to explode open, the wood slamming against the wall with a crash. The hot Texas sun and wind blew in, carrying a flurry of dust and dried leaves onto the polished wood floor.

Wyatt didn't remember going down the stairs, but found himself on the front porch, his big hand curled around the wooden rail. Wyatt didn't move, couldn't seem to let go of the rail. He didn't know what to do— not having an answer was foreign to him. DJ's words echoed accusingly around the yard, bouncing off the corral and barn to whip across Wyatt's ego.

First Emily, now DJ. What other failures lay ahead?

When the phone rang, he was thankful for the interruption. All that changed as soon as he heard the voice on the other end of the line. "Dianne?"

"Wyatt, you have to go after Emily. She's headed out to her mom's place. I'm sure that's where she's going."

"Slow down." He could hear the panic in the woman's voice. "What happened?"

"Emily's stepbrother called. Again." Wyatt heard her take a deep breath.

Wyatt cursed. He'd seen firsthand what a jerk the guy could be. He should have— No, she was the one who'd made it clear they were done. Still…

"I don't know what he said to her, but she was upset. Hysterical, almost. She raced out of here right after I told her Tyler didn't make it to school today."

"What?" Wyatt pulled the phone away. "DJ," he yelled as his brother climbed onto his bike, the urgency in his voice cutting through the anger of their argument. DJ stared back at him, then slowly climbed off the bike.

"Explain," Wyatt spoke to Dianne.

"I'm sorry. I'm upset." The woman was clearly distraught. "Emily said she dropped Tyler off at school this morning. But when Addie went to pick him up they told her he wasn't there today. Emily thinks Drew took Tyler." Dianne's voice shook.

"What?" Wyatt cursed, ignoring his curiosity about Addie's arrival. He looked over at DJ, who had moved close enough to hear the other side of the conversation. "Where the hell did she go?"

"The trailer. It's out on Bircham's Road somewhere. I don't know where out there. It's abandoned. I don't know if it even has an address."

"Bircham's Road?" He'd heard of it, but couldn't remember where the hell it was. Wyatt looked over at DJ,
who was nodding. "You know where that is?"

"No, I don't." Dianne answered, obviously thinking
he was talking to her.

"Sorry, Dianne. My brother knows where it is. How
long ago did she leave?"

"Just a few minutes." Dianne's voice broke. Wyatt
wished he could help her.

"Have you called the police?"

"No. I called you first since you're closer. I don't
know what to tell them."

DJ waved, indicating Wyatt hand him the phone.
Wyatt gave it up.

"Dianne, this is DJ Hawkins."

DJ's voice was so calm, Wyatt felt himself relax. Then
shook his head as he realized the little brother he'd just
been arguing with was gone—this was the soldier in DJ
taking over now.

"We're going to head over there. Dial 9-1-1 and you'll
get the county sheriff. Tell them just what you told us.
They'll know what to do. Do you understand?"

"Yes. The sheriff."

Wyatt could hear her voice clearly as it was only
slightly softer than the shrill yelling she'd been doing
before.

"Tell them the name of the road. They'll be able to
find it. If they don't know where it's at, tell them it's
west of Pal Haymaker's property about a mile. They'll
understand."

"Thank you, thank you." Dianne sobbed into the
phone, then hung up.

"You know where this place is?" Wyatt turned to

face DJ, who nodded again. The look in DJ's eyes was something Wyatt had never seen before. It reflected the anger and pain that Wyatt was feeling right now, and something else. Resolve? "I'll drive." Wyatt grabbed his truck keys.

"We'll be faster going across land."

Wyatt froze, frowning at DJ.

"Bircham's Road is a dead end that doesn't go far, but getting there will take at least half an hour going around Haymaker's spread. Across it'll take fifteen, tops."

Wyatt headed to the barn at a dead run. "Later you can tell me how you know that."

They reached the barn just as Chet was closing Dancer's stall door. "What the hell's with you two?" the old man asked.

Any concerns that Wyatt might have had about DJ forgetting his horse skills were quickly put to rest as DJ pulled out tack and saddles. Prism was obviously ready to run, as he stamped his feet when DJ started saddling Lightning first.

Wyatt grabbed his own gear. As they saddled the horses, Wyatt filled in the old man, all the while his anxiety ratcheting up. *Emily. Tyler. Emily.*

"Right behind you." Chet headed for his own equipment. Dancer wasn't ready for a ride yet, but there were plenty of other horses to choose from.

The commotion brought the rest of the men in from the bunkhouse. Once saddled up, the whole crew tore through the night with Wyatt in the lead, barely a nose ahead of DJ.

THE TRAILER WAS EMPTY. Quiet. Abandoned just like the last time Emily had been here. She climbed out of her car, waiting, looking, listening. There was no indication anyone was here or had been here. Was she wrong? Where else could they be?

Stay calm, she told herself. Go look. "Tyler?" she called out, the wind carrying her voice away. "Drew?" No one answered. Despite the day's heat, she shivered.

Part of her knew Drew had the potential to hurt people. But he was more of an abuser than psychotic. Comforting thoughts there, she admitted.

The screen door whacked against the metal frame with the wind, and Emily headed toward the trailer. She felt herself changing, shifting with each step. The sheer panic that had driven her to race out here froze inside her. All the emotions she'd begun to experience over the past few years, since moving away from here, evaporated. She withdrew into the shell she'd built growing up. She felt nothing.

The desert southwest had never been so cold.

Emily trudged into the house, leaving the door open behind her. The heat inside smelled old and sick.

She didn't get far. The mess stopped her. If Drew wasn't here now, he had been. And he'd left nothing unturned in his wake. The evidence of his anger showed in the cabinet doors torn off their hinges and the curtain rods ripped from the walls.

Emily stilled. Where was Tyler? Was he okay? Her emotions threatened to break through. No, she refused to give in.

The hallway, while shadowed, was broken by the light coming through the open bedroom doors. Both doors. Emily rushed to her mom's room, the mess as bad as in the living room. The hole where she'd found the box was now a huge gaping void. Sheet rock and clothing lay in clumps on the closet floor.

She backed away. She saw no hint of Tyler in here. She was wasting precious time. The logical part of her brain struggled to control the emotional overload.

This time she couldn't avoid seeing inside her old room. The door stood wide-open, barely on its hinges in a macabre invitation.

This room had once been her haven, until Earl had violated it with his abuse. Now Drew had delivered the final blow by tearing it apart. Huge holes in the walls told Emily he'd looked for more hiding places.

She had to get out of here. Turning, she nearly tripped over a pile of torn bedding and landed on her knees. Struggling to get up, she saw the carnage behind the door.

The collection of horse figurines she'd left, that Earl had never managed to touch, lay shattered on the floor. Broken porcelain sparkled in the dim light.

Emily reached out and found two figures left intact. Tiny ones, probably too small to be noticed. She slipped them into her pocket as the shell inside her cracked.

"Damn him." She stomped through the mess to the front door.

Tyler wasn't here. There was *nothing* here.

Except a closed front door.

She fought back the panic and let her anger take control. When the faint scent of smoke wafted past her nose, she struggled to remain clearheaded.

"Drew!" she screamed, yanking on the front door that was wedged tightly shut.

Fine. She stalked into the kitchen. Drew underestimated who she and her mother were. *Please, please let it still be there.* She knelt down, reaching into the narrow space between the refrigerator and wall. Cobwebs brushed her hand, sticky and soft. She cringed, but didn't stop until her fingers curled around the neck of her dad's old Louisville Slugger.

She remembered the night Mom had put the bat there, the night she'd brought Emily home from foster care. They'd both sworn Earl wouldn't hurt either of them again.

Smoke grew thick around her. She didn't see flames, but she felt the heat beneath her feet. It didn't stop her. She went to the front window, and in a stance her father would have been proud of, she swung. And bashed out the entire front window.

Hot, scorching air washed over her. The flames must be under the skirting of this end of the trailer. Not outside the window yet, though. She climbed out, glass scraping against her arms and legs. She didn't care.

There was no way she was dying in this hellhole. She landed with a thud on the hard-packed ground of what had been her mother's garden. She was out.

She saw smoke on the back side of the trailer, and in the flame's light she spotted the silhouette of an old pickup truck parked a few yards away.

Luckily, half the skirting on that end had blown away over the years, so she could see there wasn't anyone underneath. Relief was short-lived as she didn't have a clue where Drew and Tyler were.

She backed away, her fingers curled tight around the baseball bat. Drew had better run. But not until she'd found Tyler.

She looked around. Night was falling quick. She'd have to thank old Drew for providing the light from the fire once she found him.

There were few places they could be. The old stable had fallen over a couple years ago. There weren't even any trees to break up the flat landscape. The only real hiding place was the storm cellar.

Emily ran toward it. She'd better find Tyler there, safe and sound, or Drew would be permanently wearing the baseball bat upside his head.

She yanked open the weather-worn doors. The hinges squealed loudly in protest. Emily stared at the cobwebs and weeds that covered the stone steps. The daylight barely reached halfway down, but the growing flames' light helped.

She started down. This was supposed to be a safe haven, protection from Mother Nature's wrath.

It wasn't. Never had been.

Tornadoes weren't unheard of in this part of the world, though she'd only lived through one. She remembered it with frightening clarity. She'd been fifteen....

"Get yerself down there," Earl had barked from behind her, practically throwing Emily down the steps. She'd banged both of her knees when she fell, and blood dripped down her leg as she stood.

"Don't push her, Earl," Mom had cried.

"She's movin' too slow. She'll get us all killed by that twister." He'd slammed the heavy wooden doors closed, tightening the lock and sealing them all in the heavy darkness. She'd heard him fumbling around in the dark corner.

She could picture the cellar clearly; she'd been down there plenty. Mom had kept all the canned goods back in the cool part behind the bench and had sent Emily after jars for supper sometimes.

Light flared from the back corner. The flames of

the lantern danced eerily off the planes and crevices of Earl's face and sparkled off the jars lined up neatly behind him. Instinctively, Emily had backed up, almost preferring the rage of the storm to the rage of this horrid man her mother had somehow married.

"Just sit down," he'd commanded.

"I need to check on Sugar...." Emily tried to rise, once again driven by the need to make sure her beloved horse was safe. Not that he could be truly safe in the barn, but unless she could convince Earl and Mom to let her bring him down here, the horse had to stay there.

"Stupid girl. He's an animal. Animals know how to take care of themselves."

"Come over here, hon." Mom patted the bench next to her. Suddenly, the roar of what sounded like a freight train drowned out anything they might have said to each other. She didn't even think as her mother slipped her arms around her and she snuggled in like a little girl.

She'd forever miss her mother's calmness.

Dank, musty air filled Emily's sinuses and lungs. She fought the urge to cough, afraid that if she did she'd have to breathe in again. She had to find Tyler and get out of here.

It only took a minute, but it felt like hours for her to make sure the cellar was empty. She turned to leave, her shoulder brushing the old shelves just enough to cause the brittle brackets to give. Like dominoes, they fell. Glass jars rained down on her, tumbling and shattering on the hard packed dirt. Something hard and furry bounced off her hand. She screamed and ran away.

She tried to breathe, but the dust only caked her lungs and floated around her. Great. Just great.

Resentment at Earl and Drew—and at herself for being so careless to come here alone—shivered through her.

She stomped to the steps, still holding the bat. She climbed out into the approaching night, the flames growing bigger and brighter by the minute.

The foul odor of the long shut-up cellar followed her. She coughed, trying to clear her lungs.

"Hey, is anybody up there?" Tyler's voice came out of the prairie. It seemed so far away, yet so close.

"Tyler!" she yelled. "Keep talking. I'll find you. Where are you?"

"Over here, Ms. Ivers. In the well."

Emily almost wilted. She'd forgotten about the well. It sat clear up on the hill and her dad had filled it with cement when it had dried up. Or so she'd thought. Dear Lord, how was she going to get him out of there?

The farther she moved from the burning trailer, the less visibility she had, but the flames provided enough light for her to navigate. *There.*

The hole couldn't be much bigger than Tyler. She wished she had a flashlight, but wouldn't trade it for the bat.

"I'm coming." Tyler's voice echoed up the hole.

"What?"

"There's a pipe. I'm climbin' it. It's just like gym class."

As she knelt beside the hole, she heard Tyler struggling to climb but she couldn't see him. "I'm here," she told the void.

"I'll be tough enough for boot camp, like my dad, won't I?" His breath came in short puffs. Emily tried not to think about what could happen if he fell. *Don't go there.*

Finally, in the dim light, Tyler's head emerged from the shadows. He looked up and grinned at her. "I made it!"

"Almost." Emily reached out a hand and grabbed his arm. Only then did her panic think to recede.

She pulled as he reached the top and they both fell backward with the momentum. She closed her arms around him and held on. "Oh, thank God," she whispered. Her heart pounded from her fear. His pounded as much from exertion as the adrenaline.

She didn't ever want to let him go.

"That was almost too easy." Drew's voice gloated from the darkness. "Set the trap and the mice come play."

Emily scrambled around. Curling her fingers around the neck of the bat, she struggled to her feet. Tyler was still on the ground and she stood over him to protect him. "Drew." She glared at him. "This is below even you."

"Careful, sweetheart. I might not take too kindly to any more of your insults."

"Just let us go and we'll forget this ever happened." Tyler was on his feet now, and Emily put her arm around him, pulling him to her side.

"Now, Emily, I know you better than that." He laughed and stepped in front of them.

"Then you know I'll use this." She lifted the bat, remembering the window she'd obliterated.

"You might get in one good swing, but I've tangled with tougher than you and won."

"Then I guess I'd better make it damned good."

He laughed, but didn't move away. He was too close for her to get in a proper swing, but she wasn't giving up.

"All you gotta do is hand over the coins. All of them."

"Drew, I told you. I don't have them."

"Maybe. But I bet you know where they are."

"Don't you understand? Mom sold all of them. They're gone."

"Then get them back!" Anger flared in his eyes, and Tyler screamed as Drew lunged for her. She reared back with the bat and aimed. He lifted his arm, expecting her to go for his head.

She aimed much lower.

If she would have been able to swing full force, she'd have killed him. As it was, Drew doubled over and fell to his knees. "I thought you learned your lesson when we were kids," she shouted. "Run, Tyler!" she yelled, knowing Drew was down, but not necessarily out.

Thunder rumbled in the distance. A storm? Or was it the fire's roar? She looked back at the trailer. The propane tank out back hadn't been filled, but it probably wasn't empty.... Her car, their only escape, was parked right next to it.

"Wait! Emily!" Tyler tugged on her arm. "Look."

He wasn't moving, but instead pointed in the opposite direction, behind Drew.

A cloud of dust glowed on the hill. The thunder grew louder from that direction. And then she saw them. First one, then two, then half a dozen men on horses crested the ridge.

Wyatt and DJ were side by side. She saw Chet and Manny and Paulo, then Josh, all riding straight at them.

Wyatt pulled up first, bringing Prism to an abrupt halt a few feet away from Drew. He looked from Drew to Emily, then at the bat in her hand.

"Holy crap!" Tyler blurted out. "My dad and Uncle Wyatt are in the cavalry." He ran toward DJ, who swung out of the saddle and caught Tyler in a deep hug.

Wyatt was more cautious. "Emily?" he said softly as

he dismounted, while Chet and Manny walked over to Drew, kneeling beside the injured man.

"You okay?" Wyatt asked.

She froze as reality set in. As all the events replayed in her mind, she started to tremble. Tyler was fine. She was fine.

The sound of the bat falling to the ground with a dull thud seemed loud. Emily felt the world tilt sideways. She looked back at the trailer, now fully engulfed in flames. Blue-and-red lights strobed across the landscape as the sheriff arrived.

Help had come. And was still coming.

Help she no longer needed. She'd won.

Emily broke into a run and launched herself into Wyatt's arms.

And he caught her.

CHAPTER TWENTY-TWO

IT TOOK GOING back to court to put the last of Emily's ghosts to rest. The trailer was nothing more than a pile of ash. Drew awaited trial for a laundry list of charges, including kidnapping and arson. Emily had thrown just about everything she could think of at him. She had said a tearful goodbye to her mother, who now rested close to her father. The only hurdle left, Warren solved with a resounding whack of his gavel and his booming voice announcing, "And we're dismissed."

Emily watched DJ smile down at his son, the son he now had full custody of. Wyatt had agreed to remain a secondary guardian in case DJ needed him.

They all knew DJ planned to go find Tammie, but no one talked about that now. There was plenty of therapy and time before then, and Tyler didn't need to know about those plans right now.

"About damned time," Wyatt said as he pulled Emily into his arms once they were back in the truck. Finally. Alone.

She moved easily into his arms these days. It felt right. And so very, very good. Several long, quiet minutes passed before Wyatt pulled back and looked at her.

"I have a surprise for you," he whispered.

She frowned at the seriousness in his eyes. Shouldn't a surprise involve happiness? "What is it?"

"If I told you, it wouldn't be a surprise, now, would it?" He started the truck and they were soon driving toward the city limits, in the opposite direction of the ranch.

She pouted but no amount of questioning made him give her even a hint. She gave up and leaned back to watch the scenery fly by.

Half an hour later, Wyatt drove the big truck into the yard of the Therapeutic Riding Center and killed the engine. He sat for a long minute staring out the windshield. Finally, he turned to look at her.

She gazed at the huge horse barn. "What are we doing here?" she croaked out. He'd been concerned about her emotional well-being, but why would he think it was important for her to interact with the horses? She'd settled into life at the ranch just fine. She slowly shook her head.

Wyatt faced her and cleared his throat before speaking. "You're going in there. You can call me every name in the book, but you're going to face this."

"Why?" she whispered, looking at him with tear-filled eyes.

"I asked Pal Haymaker to do some checking." He stared out the windshield and swallowed hard. "Sugar's in there," he whispered back.

As if a gun had gone off, she jerked. It wasn't possible. Was this some type of cruel twist? *Oh, God.* She trembled.

Wyatt climbed out of the truck and walked around the front and opened her door. "Come with me?" He extended his hand.

Just then, a woman stepped out of the large, open barn door. She looked vaguely familiar, as if Emily had seen her long ago, when they were both younger. A name came out of the past. "Bonnie?" Emily whispered, and slowly climbed out of the truck.

"I didn't know if you'd remember me." The woman moved closer.

"I... Vaguely." A neighbor? One of Mom's friends? Fleeting memories of her sitting at the kitchen table having coffee with Mom surfaced. But that was all that came to her.

Wyatt's hand was warm and reassuring under her elbow, but he didn't say anything. Just followed, a wary look on his face. She swallowed, wishing... Wishing what? That he'd talk? That he'd explain? That she could express what she was feeling? She couldn't. Instead, she focused on Bonnie, following the woman inside.

"Sugar is old and retired now. But today we brought him up from the pasture where he spends his days now," Bonnie explained as she led them into the dark confines of the barn structure.

It was a huge facility. Stalls, dozens of them, lined each side of a large riding area. Even now, a group of kids was mounted on horses in the arena. Laughter and horse noises filled the cavernous building.

Bonnie led them to the last stall, away from the others, where it was quieter.

Outside the stall hung a blanket and a wooden sign with the name Sugar burned into it. On the table outside, a photo album of pictures lay open. Emily stared in wonder at the dozens of pictures of Sugar and all the kids and caretakers alike who had loved him over the years in place of Emily.

"Sugar," Bonnie called into the stall. "You have a visitor." The big horse turned, ambling up to the half door that closed the stall.

Emily could only stare, her eyes awash with tears. He was really and truly alive. He looked older, but so beautifully familiar.

Slowly, Emily reached out a tentative hand, remembering the day her father had given him to her. She'd promptly named the big beast Sugar for the pure white color of his coat. Her father's laughter echoed over time back to her. He hadn't thought much of the name, thinking a male horse should have a more masculine moniker, but he hadn't argued.

All these years later, the aged horse was still as white and as beautiful as he'd ever been.

She blinked, trying to clear the emotions from her eyes. He nuzzled her hand with his broad face and her knees grew weak. She sighed at the warm softness of his nose.

"You can go in," Bonnie said from behind her.

"I'm afraid I'm dreaming." Emily couldn't move. "Tell me how… Mom couldn't really give details." Her throat ached at the memory.

Bonnie cleared her throat. "After Earl tried to kill him—" Her voice wavered and Emily saw the old anger in the woman's eyes. "After that night, Sugar came back to your house the next day."

Memories flooded Emily's mind. She closed her eyes, seeing, feeling it all again. She shivered and Wyatt stepped closer, slipping his arms around her. She leaned against him.

"You were at school," Bonnie said, breaking into her painful memories. "Your mom was afraid Earl would finish what he'd started, so she called me. My husband, Tom, and I brought Sugar here and the people here saved him. Barely."

Emily's heart broke. She had lived with the belief that she'd sent Sugar to a certain death in the wilds of East Texas. Thank God for kind people like Bonnie and those who worked here.

"He's lived a good life." Emily could see that clearly, even while knowing that time with her hadn't been part of that, thanks to Earl.

Bonnie opened the stall door and waved her inside. Dried grasses and dirt crackled under her feet.

"Take all the time you need," Wyatt said, backing away and giving them space.

Emily had been a teenager when she'd driven Sugar away. Despite the years in between, she felt like she was a teenager all over again and her heart ached for all the hurt she knew lay between here and then.

"I'm sorry," she whispered to Sugar, knowing he didn't understand her, but needing to say it nonetheless. "I'm so sorry."

He neighed softly and shook his head. She wanted to laugh at his timing. Did he sense she needed an answer? She grabbed his brush from the battered tin bucket at the edge of the stall. She'd loved to brush him, listening to his even breathing, taking in the warmth of his big body and the unconditional love he exuded. He'd been her refuge from her abusive stepfather and her beaten-down mother.

And she'd failed him. All these years, others had loved and cared for him. She hadn't been able to do anything for him. She lifted the brush and set to work offering what little she could now.

The motion of brushing him soothed them both, and she swore she heard him sigh in contentment. She started at his big shoulders and across his back, talking softly to him. Telling him about her life, about her job, about the kids and families she'd worked with. If he'd been a human, they might have had that in common. She as a judge in the family courts, he as a therapeutic riding horse.

She passed where the saddles would rub, spots that were no longer there. Bonnie had said he was retired now and spent his days in the far pasture. But still Emily worked on them as diligently as if she'd just unsaddled him.

And then she reached the ridges across his back.

Her heart stopped. Her hands trembled.

The scars were deep and wide. *Dear God.* What had Bonnie said? They'd struggled to save him. She trembled in the wake of the memory of her stepfather's hand lifted, the pitchfork in his meaty fist. She heard again the screams and this time she knew they weren't going to be banished. This time, she knew she couldn't ignore what she'd been unable to stop.

But this time the pain wasn't as harsh.

Emily walked around to face Sugar. She rubbed his ears, just the way he'd always liked. Then carefully slipped her arms around his neck and buried her face in his mane. "We beat them all, Sugar," she whispered to the horse. "We survived."

Sugar nudged her shoulder then, and she laughed, the sound filling the stall. She stepped away, putting the brush back and turning back to the door. "You need to get your rest, old man." He followed her and stuck his head out over the door. He nudged her again. "Okay, okay." She laughed, then looked back at him one more time. "I'll come back again. I promise."

She heard footsteps behind her and hoped it was Wyatt. It was. She looked over her shoulder at him.

What was she going to say to him? Not a single word came to her.

She wished the ancient horse could give her advice. He'd heard all the wishes and desires of her heart when she'd been a girl. He knew her better than anyone else.

Wyatt leaned against the stall door just inches from where she stood, watching Sugar just as she was. He didn't say a thing.

He'd brought her here, forced her to face her past. He'd risked her anger, her hate and losing her.

She couldn't move. Could she take such a risk for him? Was she able to? Was she that strong? Looking over at Sugar, she didn't find any answers.

"Thank you," she whispered.

Wyatt seemed to freeze, then slowly he moved away from the stall door and faced her. "You're welcome. I wasn't sure if you'd want to do this or not, so I didn't ask."

Emily moved closer to him, gently putting her hands against his chest, hoping he'd slip his arms around her. He didn't disappoint.

"Emily, I know I can't always fix everything. But I promise you, I will always fix the things I can."

"Always?" Her voice shook, hoping, wishing.

"I love you, Emily," Wyatt whispered.

"I…" Sugar nudged her shoulder, and Emily stumbled into Wyatt's arms. She threw her head back, and with a laugh, put her lips right up to his. "I love you, too. More than I can ever show you."

Applause erupted around them, and Sugar whinnied loudly in approval as Emily kissed Wyatt, long and sweet.

* * * * *

Books by Kathleen Eagle

Harlequin Special Edition

Visit the Author Profile page at
Harlequin.com for more titles.

THE PRODIGAL
COWBOY

KATHLEEN EAGLE

For All My Relatives

CHAPTER ONE

"Looks like he ain't coming."

Bella Primeaux glanced up from the news report on her smartphone display. The cowboy claiming the next bar stool was half-shot and full-ugly. She didn't know him, wasn't interested in knowing him, and there was no point in sparing him more than a glance. She pressed her elbows against the bar and swiveled two inches to the right, turning a cold left shoulder.

"What's that you're drinkin'?"

Bella glanced right. Another one was moving in. She was book-ended by Crude and Rude. Experience told her that if they got no satisfaction, their type would go away.

"What does that look like to you, Loop?" the one on the right asked the one on the left. "Seven and seven?"

Loop? Bella swallowed the urge to laugh. She'd interviewed a rodeo cowboy named Rope who'd given a shout out to his brother Cash and his friend Spur. But *Loop?*

"Looks like tea." Loop was perceptive.

"Is that some of that Long Island iced tea? You wanna try some, Loop?" Rude signaled the bartender. "Bring us three more of these."

"Lemme try hers first," Loop said as he reached for Bella's glass from the left.

She slipped her phone into the woolen sack that hung

over her shoulder on a braided cord. He could have her drink. She was leaving anyway.

"Is it whiskey and tea?" Loop sniffed, slurped and slammed the glass on the bar. "It's just tea."

"And it's yours now, Loopy," said a newcomer to the growing group.

Bella turned to her left, and her glance traveled quickly over the glass in the one called Loopy's grubby hand, past the full-ugly face to a faintly familiar one that loomed in the shadows above Loopy's cowboy hat. Familiar, fine looking, and frankly unsettling. It had been years since she'd seen the man, but he wore the years as well as his own straw cowboy hat. Surprising, considering where he'd spent the last couple of those years. His hat was battered, and his jeans and T-shirt had seen better days, but he made them look camera ready. She'd lost what little touch she'd had with high school friends, and Ethan Wolf Track was no exception, but she'd never quite shaken her interest in what he was up to. Generally it was no good.

But his smile was as disarming as ever.

"Sorry I'm late, Bella."

Loopy peeked over his shoulder and then turned back to Bella with a whole new brand of interest in his glazed eyes. "Why didn't you just say you were with Ethan Wolf Track? Hell, man, we were just—"

"Long Island iced tea all around. Loopy's buying." Ethan's hand appeared on Loopy's shoulder. "Right, man?"

"It's just tea. There's no whiskey," Loop said.

"Long Island iced tea isn't made with whiskey or tea." Ethan jiggled his hand rest. "You been living under a rock, Loopy?"

"Same as you."

"Nah, look at the difference." Ethan laid his hand on the bar beside Loopy's. "You need to get yourself some sun, boy."

Bella glanced between the two faces. The "boy" couldn't have been any younger than the man, but he didn't take exception. Ethan was still *the man*. The memory of a younger but no less commanding Ethan letting the boys know who was boss flashed through her mind.

"Iced tea for two," the bartender announced, landing the glasses on the bar with a thunk. "As for the other two, you want another beer? It's the same price as tea."

"No beer for these horses, Willie," Ethan said as he claimed both glasses. "Tricky, ain't it, Loopy? Pullin' the wagon and riding it, too?"

"You got your parole officer, I got mine. Far as I'm concerned, beer don't count," Loopy grumbled. "And it's *Toby*. That's a Toby Keith song, 'Beer For My Horses.'"

"Not without Willie," Ethan said as he glanced at Bella and gave a nod toward a corner booth. "Not on my wagon."

Bella was off the bar stool, but she wasn't looking for a booth, and the man and his boys could do what they pleased with their wagon. She wouldn't be vying for a parking spot at the Hitching Post. She'd already crossed the place off her list of possible sites for her report on Rapid City's hottest singles' hangouts.

"Would you rather go someplace else?" Ethan asked her quietly.

She looked up, taken by the change in his tone. He was speaking for her benefit alone, and he sounded sincere, even hopeful. Tension drained from her shoulders as she shook her head. "We can catch up right here."

As she neared the high-backed booth, she saw a big book lying open on the far side of the table beside a cup half-filled with black coffee. She slid into the near side, her back to the room.

"Looks like he ain't comin'," she drawled as she checked her watch.

"Maybe he's still working on his story." He set his glass on the table and dropped his hand over the book, which he closed, swept off the table and deposited on the seat beside him in one quick motion. His eyes danced. "Better be a good one, huh?"

She shrugged, subtly acknowledging that he was playing along. "You were here all along. All I saw was the hat."

"It serves many purposes." He pulled down on the brim, shadowing all but the generous lips and their slight smile.

"I'm surprised you remember me."

"I watch TV."

"So…you don't actually *remember* me."

"Really took me back when I saw you sitting on that bar stool. You sat in front of me in—what class was it? English?"

"History."

"History. Don't remember any names or dates, but I never forget a woman's back. You have a small—" he hooked his hand over his shoulder and touched a spot near the base of his neck "—beauty mark right here."

"*Beauty* mark?" She laughed. "It's called a mole."

"Not in my book."

"Which book is that?" She wondered about the one he was sharing his seat with.

"History. My favorite class. Liked it so much, I took

it twice." He dropped his hand to the seat as he leaned back, grinning. She imagined him patting that book as though he wanted to keep a pet quiet. "You were there the second time around."

"No wonder you had all the answers. You'd already heard the questions."

"I didn't hear anything the first time." He leaned closer, getting into the reminiscence. "We did a project together. Remember?"

"I wasn't going to mention it. You still owe me."

"I do?"

"I bought all the materials. Actually, I did all the work. You were going to come to my house the night before it was due, but you never showed up."

"Forgot about that part." He arched an eyebrow and cast a pointed glance at her watch. "How do you keep getting mixed up with guys like that?"

"I'm not meeting anyone," she confessed.

"Then what the hell are you doing here?" He pulled a dramatic grimace as he glanced past her.

She shrugged. "Checking the place out."

"For what? This ain't no singles' bar, woman. This is a hole in the wall."

"Maybe I'm not single. Maybe I'm here doing my job." She gave herself a second to rein in her rising tone. "And maybe I didn't need to be rescued."

"In the old days, you wouldn't've said *maybe*. Once you got to talkin', you were as sure and self-determined as any girl I ever met." He gave her the no-bull eye. "I don't know about the rest, but you're not married."

"That doesn't mean I'm single."

"I think it does." He took a drink of his tea, then

looked at her again. "So how much do I owe you for labor and materials?"

"Since it was a required class, I think you owe me your diploma."

"I showed up for the report. I had all the facts and figures. Hell, we got an A, didn't we? Can't do any better than that." He shook his head. "We'll have to come up with something else. You sure don't need my diploma."

"And you sure have a better memory than you first let on." She gave a tight smile. "I guess we can call it even. Being Ethan Wolf Track's history project partner raised my lowly underclass social status a notch."

"What were you, a sophomore?"

She shook her head.

"Freshman?"

She smiled and nodded.

"How did you get into that class as a freshman, for God's sake?"

"I took a test. Actually, I took several. They had a hard time coming up with a schedule for me." She lifted one shoulder. He had his muscles, she had her brain. "And you were a senior and the captain of everything."

"You were smart. It didn't take a test to figure that out. You were goin' places." He glanced around the room. "Better places than this."

"I go where the story is. Or where we think it might be." She tested out a coy look as she sipped her tea. "Stay tuned."

"Do me a favor. Give me a heads-up if this place is gonna be raided. I try to stay out of trouble these days."

"By doing what?"

"I guess you could say I'm a cowboy."

"Like your brother?"

"Not a rodeo cowboy like Trace. A working cowboy. A ranch hand. I work for the Square One Ranch."

She had no idea where that was, but he seemed to think the name of the place spoke for itself, so she made her usual mental note. *Find out. It could lead to something.*

"So you're one of a dying breed," she said. "I did a story on a guy who calls himself a cowboy for hire. He says he has more work than he can handle. Do you ride a horse or an ATV?"

"What's an ATV?"

"All terrain…" She caught the smile in his eyes. "You know, vehicle."

"Those kid toys? Couldn't call myself a cowboy if I rode one of those things. Hell, I was raised by Logan Wolf Track."

"He trains horses, doesn't he?"

"He does, and so do I. I'm training a mustang right now. Entered up in a contest." He winked at her. "Gonna win it, too."

Déjà vu on the Wolf Track wink. She'd been on the receiving end of one or two of those babies years back, and the experience had given her the same tummy tickle that was *not* going to get a smile out of her now.

"You're talking about the competition they're running at the new Wild Horse Sanctuary near Sinte?"

"The wild horse program is pretty new, but the Double D Ranch has been there forever," he reminded her. "I hired on for a couple of summers when I was a kid, back when old man Drexler was running it. Now it's his daughters."

"I know. I've been reading up on the place." She took a breath, a moment's pause. They'd been playing a circuitous game, and she'd just landed at the foot of a ladder. One person's connections could be another person's rungs. They could be fragile, but as a journalist, she was weightless. Most sources had no idea she'd gotten anything from them.

But Ethan Wolf Track wasn't most sources. Sure, he'd been a source of adolescent anxiety and disappointment, but hadn't that been his job back then? It was up to the captain of everything to teach the princess of nothing not to expect too much. Bella had always been a quick study.

Still, he owed her.

"I think it's wonderful, the way the Drexlers have worked out a deal with the Tribe to set aside some of that remote reservation land for more sanctuary."

The Tribe being her people and Ethan's adoptive father's people. Logan Wolf Track was a Lakota Sioux Tribal councilman. Ethan looked Indian, too, but she'd never asked him about his background. Everyone knew that his mother had left Logan to raise her two boys, whom he'd legally adopted—just up and left and never came back—but nobody asked too many questions. It wasn't their way. Ethan and his older brother, Trace, were Wolf Tracks.

"Are you working on a news story?" he asked.

"I've been digging around." She folded her hands around her glass and studied the two shrinking chunks of ice. "There's definitely a story there—one that goes back a ways—but I'm looking for the details on my own. It's not the kind of assignment I'm likely to get from KOZY-TV."

"Why not? They don't like mustangs?"

"They're fine with mustangs. They don't like digging around."

"Isn't that how you come up with news? Dirt sells."

"But sleeping dogs don't bite, and the suits at the station—such as they are here in good ol' Rapid City, South Dakota, you know, not exactly coat and tie—they don't want to get their business-casual clothes torn." She ignored his quizzical look. "Let's just say they don't pay me to dig." She smiled. "But it's fun, isn't it? You dig?"

He chuckled. "Postholes, yeah."

"When you were hiring out as a kid, did you ever work for Dan Tutan?" The change in his eyes—quizzical to cold—was barely discernible, but it was there. "You know, the Drexlers' neighbor."

Oh, yeah. He knew.

But he shook his head. *Interesting.*

"There's a story there," she said with a smile. "Big-time rivalry. Maybe some political back-scratching going on that could affect Indian Country. And that's where I come in. Like I said, strictly on my own." Was he ready for the kicker? Timing the kicker was Bella's journalistic specialty. "Tutan wants the leases that went to the Double D for the sanctuary, and he's got a friend in D.C.—Senator Perry Garth."

He stared at her. Or *through* her.

Perfect timing.

"South Dakota's beloved Senator Garth. Tutan and Garth go way back. And Garth is on the Indian Affairs Committee, as well as the Subcommittee on Public Lands and Forests."

"Politics." He shook his head. "You just cruised past my point of interest. My story's in the training competition. My interest is in the horses." He drank half of what was left in his glass in one deep pull.

"I just thought…because Logan is on the Tribal Council…"

"That's *his* story." He set the glass down and smiled as he slid to the end of the booth. "You wanna talk politics, you're followin' the wrong Wolf Track." He glanced toward the bar and its deserted stools. Remote control in hand, the bearded bartender was surfing channels on the screen above the Bud Light sign. "Looks like your fans have moved on."

"I doubt that pair watches much news. They know *you,* though."

"Yeah. You need a name to drop in low places, you're welcome to use mine." He gave her his signature wink again. Damn if it didn't give her the same deep-down shiver. "You decide to do a story on wild horses, look me up."

And *damn* if he didn't walk out first, taking the book she hadn't been able to identify.

ETHAN SAT BEHIND the steering wheel of his pickup, parked in the shadows across the street from what had once been the Hitching Post. The neon had given up the ghost on the letter *H,* so it was now the *itching Post.* The sign had called out to him the first time he'd seen it. He'd finally had his freedom back—most of it, anyway—and it had some weight to it. He was itching to do something different with his life, but damned if he knew what. So he'd answered the blinking call of the itching Post. He'd claimed a bar stool, wet his whistle after a long dry spell and gotten himself wasted. *Stupid* drunk.

The next morning he'd looked at himself in the mirror and scratched his face. He'd scratched his neck, his shoulder, dug all his fingers into his hair, looked in the mirror again and nearly busted a gut laughing.

The sign said itching post, you idiot. Not scratching post.

If he'd learned one thing from spending two years behind bars, it was that the word *freedom* pretty much summed up everything a man had to lose. Freedom was living. Two years without it and you had a foot in the grave. Deadwood. Reviving that foot meant getting a leg up somehow. He hadn't been quite ready for South Dakota. He still had some growing up to do.

He'd gone to Colorado—as good a place as any that wasn't South Dakota—and taken up his parole officer's suggestion that he continue on the path he'd taken with the Wild Horse Inmate Program. Ethan had answered correctly—*yeah, I like that idea*—but mentally he'd added that the prison program couldn't claim credit for anything except maybe backing him into the right corner, the one that gave him a clear view of where he'd come from and where he might go. He'd spent most of his life within earshot of a horse barn, which might have been why he'd taken horses for granted, along with every other promising path he could have taken instead of the one that had cut off his slack.

Before the horses—before Logan Wolf Track—his life was hazy. He'd been Trace's little brother. They'd had a mother, but she was part of the haze. Even after she'd married Logan, her part of the family equation was hazy. *Muddy,* more like. He remembered the sound of her voice and the way she'd drawn out certain words so that South Dakotans looked at each other and shrugged. An accent, they'd called it, but to him it was the sound that settled an unsettled mind. *Mom's here.* He couldn't picture her face, but he still felt an odd sense of relief when he heard her voice, even though it was only in his head. He was up to his neck in hot water, hot *muddy* water, shrouded in early-morning haze, but he wasn't alone. He could hear her. She hadn't gone away.

And neither had that stupid kid. God, how he hated that quivering, shivering little boy who still clung to the soft tissue of his innards. He was pitiful, that kid. He had to get tough or get dead, that kid, and he'd damn sure better not show his face. Keeping that kid quiet had been a full-time job. Ethan needed all the help he could get, and he'd assigned roles. Whether they knew it or not, every person, place or thing within spitting distance had a part to play, and he'd taken it all for granted.

Including the friendship he might have had with the woman who'd just stepped into the spotlight under the itching Post sign. Of course he remembered her. Straight-A student with a straight body and a straightforward approach. She would go places and do things, and she wasn't letting anyone get in her way. Not that his charm was lost on her, or that he wouldn't pass up the chance to use that to his advantage, but there was an air of dignity about her that gave her some protection from guys like him.

But not from guys who had no use for dignity.

Tom "Loopy" Lupien and his forgettable sidekick were back in play, following Bella out the door. Two colorless figures casting long shadows across the dimly lit sidewalk. He'd thought they were gone. Must have been hiding out in the can.

"Hey, did the Wolf make tracks?" one of them called after her.

"You need a ride?" the other asked. In this light it was hard to tell one from the other, but it didn't matter. Any friend of Loopy's had been scraped from the mold underneath the empty barrel.

A remote-control lock chirped, headlights flashed, car door opened and shut, engine roared. Bella was safe. Ethan smiled to himself. No-nonsense Bella.

No sooner had she turned onto the street when another engine fired up. An old Ford pickup—even older than Ethan's rattletrap Chevy—emerged from the lot behind the building and followed her car.

Damn. Loopy wouldn't be able to bring any prey down himself. He was a scavenger. The other one must've been driving. Between the two of them, they could do some damage.

Ethan joined the parade. When they reached a one-way residential street, Bella parked her little white Honda on the curb near the front entrance to a modest two-story apartment building. Ethan peeled away from Loopy's tailgate, pulled over to the opposite curb, and watched Loopy and his pal roll past Bella's parked car. They'd taken the hint. Ethan chuckled. *My job here is done.*

Bella hopped out of her car, slammed the door and turned toward Ethan's pickup, gripping some kind of bag made out of blanket material with a string handle—was it a purse, or a grocery sack?—under her arm.

"Hey! I carry a .38 Smith & Wesson, and I know how to use it!" she shouted across the street. "So whatever you're thinking, think again."

Her face was hidden in the shadows, but her hands were steady, her shoulders squared and her long black hair shone blue-white under the streetlight. He didn't know who she thought she was talking to, but she wasn't bluffing.

And he loved it.

He was thinking, *I've got your back.* Not that she needed him, but he was there, just in case.

Hell of a woman, he told himself as he watched her stand her ground. She was on TV, but that was just a job. It wasn't her life. Pretty cool. Cool enough to get the message without some big explanation to go with it. Whatever her interest was in Senator Perry Garth—the man who'd helped put Ethan away for two years—it was of no interest to *him*. Neither was any rivalry between neighbors, nor tribal politics. Ethan was looking for a new life. He wanted the kind of freedom Bella had—the opportunity to chart her own course, to do a job and then some, and that some could be more than what somebody else was willing to pay for.

The last time he'd seen her, she'd been a sweet young girl with a big brain. He'd assigned her brain a role, but the girl was sweet and young, and she'd had that straight body and those big ideas. Sure, she'd had the hots for him, but back then she'd been more appealing walking away from him in a huff than looking up at him all wide-eyed and innocent. She'd had some growing up to do.

She turned and mounted the steps to the front door.

I've still got your back, Bella, but I can appreciate your front now, too. Turn around. Let me see those pretty eyes.

No such luck. She pushed the door open and disappeared.

Ethan grinned as he shifted out of neutral. Yes, sir, little Bella Primeaux had grown up just fine.

CHAPTER TWO

THE TINY RESERVATION TOWN of Sinte, South Dakota, hadn't changed much, but the house Bella had grown up in looked different. In only five years weeds had taken over Ladonna Primeaux's flower beds. A swing set occupied what had been the vegetable garden, and an old Jeep had muscled in on the shrub roses that still more or less lined the driveway. Mom had fussed over that yard the way some women gravitated toward babies. With her gone, it looked like most of the other yards in the neighborhood—a cottonwood tree or two, a bunch of kids' toys, maybe a deck and some struggling grass.

Bella could hear her mother now. *Don't ever let your yard go, Bella. All it takes is a little interest. People who take an interest, those are the interesting people. They're the ones you always want to talk to.*

Ladonna Primeaux was an interesting person. Everyone thought so. Bella had been certain of it. Her mother was as knowledgeable as she was opinionated, which was fine by Bella. Nothing wrong with having opinions if you had the knowledge to back them up. Mom was also dependable, practical and psychic. It wasn't always easy being the only child of a woman who was constantly one step ahead of the one Bella was about to take. But she'd followed the deep imprints of her mother's foot-steps until there were no more.

The home they'd shared wasn't there anymore, and the house alone gave no comfort. No point in lingering, hoping for more than memories. Bella didn't need guidance or approval anymore—she knew who she was and where she was going—but with her mother's death she'd been cut off at the roots. She was growing as a journalist, but every time she looked at her résumé, she felt like a fraud. Maybe not on the outside—she had the look, totally—but deep down she was missing something.

Her KOZY-TV News assignments rarely touched on Indian issues, so she'd started blogging as Warrior Woman, and her site was gaining followers. But the comments from people who claimed to be Native were few and far between. Maybe they were out there but just weren't saying so. Or maybe they weren't even there. Maybe what was missing was new growth. Her interest in Lakota issues was real, but what about Lakota life? What about the home she'd left as quickly as she could and the mother who'd encouraged her daughter to fly while she'd remained in the nest? What about the remnants of those severed roots? Deep down they were still there, like shorn whiskers creating an itch that needed attention.

Guess what, Bella, you're not a kid anymore. You need to touch up your roots or grow some new ones.

A stop sign and two right-hand turns took her to Agency Avenue. The old Bureau of Indian Affairs building with its spacious offices had been turned over to the Tribal government, and the BIA had moved into the building once occupied by the Tribe. Sign of the times,

Bella thought as she took in all the changes. There were more windows, fewer walls, and the colors of the four directions—red, white, black and yellow—had replaced BIA green and tan. There were new names on the directory. Indian names. But there were no office numbers, and so she asked the receptionist whether Councilman Logan Wolf Track was in the house. *He's around here somewhere* was the old familiar answer. Monday-through-Friday casual.

"Of course I remember you." Logan greeted her with a handshake when he came out to greet her. He was lankier than his son but not as tall, not quite as handsome. "Full scholarship to a fine college on the East Coast, right?"

"University of California at Berkley."

"I meant West Coast." He smiled easily. "I remembered the important stuff. Full scholarship, terrific college and Bella Primeaux. Your mother was so proud of you we could hardly stand it."

She lifted one shoulder. "Sorry about that."

"Hey, just kidding. We're all proud of you." He glanced through the plate glass that separated the sparsely furnished lounge from a small parking lot. "And we sure miss your mother. She was something else, wasn't she?" He turned back to Bella, assuring her with a nod. "In a good way."

"She was the best nurse Indian Health ever had."

"She sure was."

"She could have been a doctor." It was something she'd always thought, but she couldn't remember saying it out loud before, giving due credit, open admiration. She'd felt it, but she hadn't said it within range of her mother's ear. What kind of range did Ladonna Primeaux's hearing have now?

"She was a damn good nurse."

"Yes, she was." *But she could have been a doctor.* She'd said so herself, many times. What she'd never said was that she'd had a child to feed. "I ran into Ethan the other night."

"Where?"

"In a bar," Bella said, an answer that clearly surprised Logan. "Rapid City. I live there now."

"I watch you all the time on TV." He lifted one shoulder. "Well, not every day, but whenever I watch the news."

She smiled. It was good to be watched and even better to be acknowledged. She owed him something in return. "Ethan's following in your footsteps."

"How's that?"

"Training horses. He mentioned the wild horse training competition. He says he's going to win the big prize."

"I hope he does. Help him make a fresh start. Hope he's not spending too much time in the bars." He glanced away. "I haven't seen much of Ethan since, uh…"

"Since he went to prison?"

"He told you about that?"

"He didn't have to," she said quietly.

Logan gave a mirthless chuckle. "Made the news all the way out to California, did it?"

"The news is what the media makes it, and I'm part of the media now. I know these things." She smiled. "All we talked about was high school and what we're doing these days. He gives you credit for raising him to be a cowboy."

"A cowboy? That's down to his older brother, Trace.

Although outside the rodeo, I'd say Ethan's the better hand when he's of a mind to be. They're both good, mind you, but Trace goes in for a wild ride, and Ethan…well, he's wild enough on his own."

"He was drinking iced tea."

"In a *bar?*" Apparently even more surprising.

Bella nodded. "Straight iced tea."

"I saw him at the Double D earlier this summer," Logan recalled. "First time in two years. Said he was entering the training competition. Said he was working for a rehab program."

"He told me he was a ranch hand. Square One Ranch. Something like that."

"Square One?" His tone put the news on par with tea in a bar. "That's a program for kids in trouble. Hell, that's right outside Rapid City. I didn't know he was living that close by. He didn't, uh…" Logan's wan smile spoke of a father's discomfort with being the last to know. "He didn't say."

"I thought it was a cattle ranch. That's interesting." What was left out was always more interesting than what was said. Bella added it to her mental file marked *Ethan*. Also interesting was the way she'd filed him under his first name.

Maybe because it was an old file. She was just realizing how far back it went and how carefully she'd kept it up. No surprise that he'd joined the army after he graduated. No surprise that he'd been gone awhile and come back home. No word of his military experiences, which was also no surprise. The return to Indian Country was never questioned. But he hadn't stayed around long, and the next Ethan Wolf Track news flash had been surprising. *Dirt sells,* he'd said, and if she'd been a little further along in her career, she might have tried to track him down. Not because he was in trouble—no surprise there, either. Not because the story involved a woman—most of Ethan's stories undoubtedly involved women. But there was an odd political connection.

Ethan Wolf Track and a senator's daughter? Now that was interesting. And Bella would have bet her new mobile phone that what was left out was far more interesting than what was reported.

"He's pretty sensitive about Senator Garth, isn't he?" she asked.

"Couldn't say." Staring out the window at a young couple getting into a pickup with a washing machine in the bed, Logan didn't blink. No sensitivity there. "Ethan spent two years in prison for taking Garth's car. His daughter was the one who took it, but she wouldn't stand up for him. I'd say he was sensitive about *her,* but I'd just be guessing." He turned to give Bella a what're-you-gonna-do look. "Too damn stubborn for his own good."

"He said he worked over at the Double D when he was a kid."

"Couple of summers, yeah. Like I say, Ethan's a good worker. I'll bet he's real good with those kids in the Square One program."

Bella wondered why Logan seemed so clueless about his son. If she were still alive, Ladonna Primeaux wouldn't be betting or guessing, she would be asking. On the other hand, Bella herself wasn't exactly being subtle about fishing for clues about the man's family, and he was trusting her with what few he had.

A twinge of guilt pushed her to switch tracks.

"The Double D took some grazing land away from a neighboring rancher, didn't they? I know some of it was public land, but wasn't there a Tribal lease, too?"

"Yep." Logan smiled. He liked this topic. "We decided the Wild Horse Sanctuary took precedence. The Lakota are horse people."

"But Senator Garth has a longstanding friendship with Dan Tutan, who is—"

"My wife's father." His smile broadened. "We just got married. Haven't told Ethan yet."

"So, uh…"

"Whose side am I on? The horses' side. So's my wife. I haven't heard any objections from the senator. What's he gonna do? The Tribal Council determines how the land will be used nowadays. It's called self-determination."

"That term is so twentieth century," Bella teased.

"Yeah, well, some of us go back that far."

"All of us do. The whole relocation program and termination of reservations policy in the 1950s, and then the switch to Indian self-determination in the 1970s, seems like it was only yesterday." She smiled. "We studied it in our high school history class. Ethan sat behind me."

He laughed. "Now that must've been interesting."

"It was unsettling." She folded her arms beneath her breasts and held on tight as she glanced away. "What was interesting was twentieth-century American Indian history and how we're supposed to finally have a say over what we do with our lives. And our land." And the fact that Ethan remembered the mole on the back of her shoulder.

Bella shifted her stance, cleared her throat and her thoughts, and turned back to the Lakota leader. "So you don't think the senator can interfere with the Wild Horse Sanctuary? He sits on a couple of key committees."

"Let him sit."

"I was thinking of doing a story." He gave her a look that that reinforced his suggestion. If the story had to do with Garth, she was wasting her time. She gave a diffident shrug. "Maybe a series on the Tribe's involvement with the Wild Horse Sanctuary."

"Involvement?"

"In a good way," she added hastily.

"Kind of a *feel-good* story about Indians and horses? That always works. Sally'll take all the TV spots she can get. You know Sally Drexler—I mean Sally Night Horse—is the woman behind the whole program. You talk about a white tornado..." He chuckled. "That's from an old TV commercial. White tornado."

"Must've been before my time."

"Mine, too. Even before self-determination, but around here some things are as timeless as Indians on horses. Especially now that you've got YouTube." He grinned. "So I say go for it. If you need me, I'm in."

"Thank you." She smiled. "Actually, it wouldn't be for KOZY-TV News. My suggestions there fall on deaf ears. They hand me an assignment, and I make it happen. Whether it means anything to anyone..." She glanced away, gave her head a little shake and turned back to a man who was known for having good ears. "That's what I was doing at the bar the other night. I was looking for different types of singles' hangouts. The place is called the Hitching Post. Doesn't that sound like a place to connect?"

"Depends on your idea of hitching, I guess. Never

really got the hang of hangin' out. But Ethan…" He shrugged. "I don't know, Bella. If you're asking me about—"

"I'm not," she said quickly. But she *had* asked, and she shouldn't have. "I only meant to say that I'd run into him. You know, just saying."

"Not telling." He smiled indulgently. "Just saying."

"Do you know anything about Square One? Is it a good program?"

"It's pretty new, but they're building a good reputation. We've had some kids placed there through Tribal Court."

"Why don't we go out there and take a look? You haven't seen much of Ethan lately, and I'm looking for connections."

"I'm not much of a connection, Bella. I don't think Square One qualifies as a singles' hangout, and I don't qualify as a single. My wife's coming home for good pretty soon. The army's letting her go."

"Her choice?"

"Yeah." Again he grinned, but this time it was purely for personal pleasure. "I'm gonna be a father again."

"Congratulations. Wow." Apparently he'd wasted no time. "So how about it? Do you have some time today?"

"I do, but if Ethan's there, I'm not gonna show up un-invited. He only let me visit him once when he was in prison. Took me off his visitors list after that."

"Why would he do that?"

Logan shook his head. "I married his mother, and he took to me right away. After she left, he was different. For a while we thought sure she'd come back. His brother and I did, anyway, but Ethan never asked about her. Never jumped for the phone the way Trace did, never expected any more from her. He kinda became his own little man, you know? He got a little older, he tried to find his father. We didn't have much to go on, so it didn't pan out. Far as I know."

"You helped him?"

"Did what I could. He had a picture and the little bit his mother told him. The guy was part Indian. Don't know where he was from, though. Ethan looks a lot like the guy in the picture. I don't know what would've happened if we'd found him."

"Ethan didn't seem like one to dwell on the past. History didn't interest him all that much."

Logan smiled wistfully. "Don't let him fool you. He's as smart as they come." He punctuated a cocked finger with the cluck of his tongue. "Ethan's your connection to Square One."

WITHOUT A GPS Bella would have missed the turnoff to Square One Ranch. The sign stood so low to the ground that the dancing heads of the tall crested wheat grass obscured the small print. *Rebuilding Our Lives From the Ground Up.* The two visible roofs turned out to be a hulking old barn and a spanking-new two-story box. It wasn't until the access road took a dip that she saw the small ranch-style house that had to be a good place to start searching for someone in charge of the operation.

An attractive young blonde opened the front door before Bella mounted the steps. Bella knew the routine. Country dwellers saw visitors coming a mile off. At half a mile they had the vehicle categorized—known or unknown, in- or out-of-state, on target or gone astray.

In good weather they met you outside. In bad weather they opened the door just enough to check you out with eyes that challenged your motivation, not to mention your common sense.

But Bella had an advantage. "I've seen you on TV." The woman offered a handshake. "Shelly Jamison."

"Bella—"

"Primeaux, right? You're even prettier in person."

"Thank you. I'm aiming for professional."

"You've hit that target, too, but my observation stands." Shelly tucked her hands into the back pockets of her jeans. "What can I do for you?"

"Show me around and tell me about your program."

"You think we might be newsworthy?"

"I met with a councilman from my reservation. He suggested I come out and take a look."

"Tribal Courts have sent us a few kids since we started the program." The hands came out of the back pockets and the arms were quickly folded up front. "We haven't had any complaints."

"And you still don't." Bella shaded her eyes with one hand so she could offer an unsquinty smile. "Councilman Wolf Track said you were doing a good job here."

"Wolf Track? We've got a Wolf Track on the payroll here." Shelly glanced toward the weathered barn as her shoulders relaxed and dropped a full two inches. "Hell of a good worker."

"Ethan," Bella supplied. "I went to school with him."

"He can't be on the Tribal Council, can he? He hasn't been... I mean, he keeps busy around here, like, 24/7."

"His father's the councilman."

"He never mentioned that. You don't think that's why we get… I mean, we didn't hire Ethan as a favor to any—"

"His father didn't know he was working here. Really, I'm not here to, um, dig up any dirt." Recalling Ethan's words, Bella almost smiled. "KOZY loves a feel-good story, and I thought we might find one here. Ethan has been—"

"I know where he's been." Shelly grabbed a chunk of hair that had strayed from her low ponytail and hooked it behind her unadorned ear. "You tell anyone who asks, Ethan Wolf Track is doing just fine. The boys really look up to him. Tell the truth, he's quickly becoming indispensable around here."

"I'm not here on any kind of assignment. I've heard only good things." Bella followed the direction of Shelly's gaze toward the hulking barn. Noisy swallows darted in and out the tiny doors of the clay row houses tucked under the edge of the gambrel roof. "I'm interested in the wild horse part of your program, and I thought maybe I could take a tour." She lifted her shoulder. "And if Ethan's around, I'd like to say hello."

"Oh, he's around. Dependable as they come, that guy."

Bella smiled. "If anyone asks, I'll relay the message."

"I don't know anything about Ethan's family." Shelly stepped down to ground level, putting them on par, height-wise. "It's just that good help is hard to find when you're paying in hot dogs and beans."

"There must be other rewards," Bella prompted.

"You get to be around wild things. Wild kids, wild horses and what's left of wild country." Shelly moved into the shade of a tall cottonwood, and Bella followed suit. "Wild hearts attract each other."

"How's yours?"

Shelly grinned. "I'm the maypole they all get to dance around. I have to crunch the numbers and find the wherewithal."

"I like that image. This could be a good story, and KOZY isn't the only media outlet I can access." Bella smiled. She didn't mind throwing her TV connection into her pitch. Most people—local people, anyway—were dazzled by it. If they had nothing to hide they eventually opened their doors. Sometimes they couldn't resist even if they *did* have something to hide. Besides, everything she was saying was true. "Do you have time to show me around?"

Of course Shelly did.

She led the way with a "follow me," and they started toward the barn. "The bunkhouse is new." She pointed toward what might have passed for a truncated no-name roadside motel—plain white, no-frills. "Kitchen and commons area downstairs, bunks upstairs. You wanna see inside? Nobody's there now except the cook."

Bella shook her head. "Another time. Who paid for the improvements?"

"We qualified for a government grant and scored some private funding, as well. We get community support, too. People come in and teach whatever skills they have to offer." Shelly glanced over her shoulder. "TV reporting must require all kinds of skills."

"You mean, besides talking to the camera?"

"Are you kidding? You're talking to thousands of people."

"I don't think of it that way," Bella said absently as

they rounded the corner of the bunkhouse and headed toward the barn.

"I'd be shaking in my boots and tripping over my tongue," Shelly said.

"You get used to it. The scary part can be trying to get information out of people who don't want to talk or pictures of things they don't want you to see."

"We tell the kids, once you find out what a relief it is to come clean, you'll never want to—" They turned another corner and ran into an old flatbed farm truck with its hood up, one guy standing and another guy squatting next to the front tire, and one pair of boots sticking out from under the orange cab.

"Did you guys run over somebody?" Shelly called out. She glanced back at Bella and nodded toward the two faces now turned their way. "There's your man." She raised her voice. "You've got a visitor, Wolf Track."

"You patted her down, didn't you?" Ethan wiped his hands on a rag as he rose to his feet. "Was she packin'?"

"Packing what?" Shelly asked.

"A .38." Grinning at Bella, he touched the brim of his straw cowboy hat in salutation. "Smith & Wesson, right?"

Bella's eyes widened as she and Shelly approached the truck. "That was you?"

"You saw the pickup that cruised past? That was trouble."

"You followed me?"

"Trouble followed you. I followed *them*." Beneath the bent brim of his hat a smile danced in his dark eyes. "You don't wanna tip your hand out on the street like that, Bella. Some people might find a Smith & Wesson even more tempting than a Bella Primeaux."

She returned a level stare. "Neither one was there for the taking. As I said, I know how to use it."

"If you really knew how to use it, you wouldn't be giving away your advantage by broadcasting it."

"This sounds like an interesting reunion," Shelly injected, amused. "I'm guessing high school sweethearts."

"No. Never." Bella laughed. "I was a lowly underclassman when Ethan was the cock of the walk."

"The *what?*" Ethan said.

"You were the captain of everything except the cheerleading squad."

"And our little two-man history team." He winked at her, and she wondered whether the gesture had become pure reflex. "I dropped the ball on that one. It was your leadership that got us on the A list."

"Well played, captain. Credit your teammates. We'd love to hear a play-by-play. Sounds like the makings of an excellent lesson in humility." Shelly slipped an arm around Bella's waist. "Please stay for supper so the boys can watch their hero recover whatever he's fumbled."

"Thank you, I will." Bella gave Ethan a sweet smile. "I'm interested in seeing how a cock walks the straight and narrow walk. We already know how he talks the talk."

"You *do* know a cock is a rooster, right?" Ethan said.

"Of course. My mother had one. Beautiful plumage. But the hens got tired of him, and the neighbors complained about the crowing." She shrugged. "So we ate him. I made a tiny dance bustle out of his tail for my little cousin."

It took a moment, but Ethan burst out laughing. The

boy standing near the truck joined in, and the one underneath called out, "Whoa!"

"Are you watching what you're doing there?" Still chuckling, Ethan returned to his duty. "Has the oil finished draining from the filter?"

"How am I supposed to tell?"

"Use your eyes, Dempsey. See anything dripping?"

"Out of the *filter*, Dempsey, not your face," the other boy jeered as Dempsey scooted out from under the cab.

Ethan tapped the scoffer's barrel chest. "You're not gonna make it as a comedian, so you'd better learn to make yourself useful for something else." He reached through the cab window and drew out a box. "Step two."

"I gotta get back under there?" Dempsey whined.

"What do you say, Bongo?" Ethan laid a hand on the big boy. "You wanna do the oil filter?"

Bongo chuckled as he glanced under the hood. "Does it go on top?"

"No, you gotta get down and dirty."

Dempsey laughed. "Good luck gettin' him back out."

"So that was our automotive program," Shelly said to Bella as she turned her toward the barn. "The next stop on our press tour will be the henhouse. One of the few centers of serious, steady, no-bull productivity on the place. Besides the kitchen, where we have another woman in charge. I swear, Bella, the testosterone…" With a smug smile she glanced back. "Carry on, boys."

Ethan looked up at Bella as he sank down, butt to boot heels. "You stay for supper, me and the boys'll show off our table manners. We just learned that passing is our first option."

"Yeah, but Bongo still wants to run with the bowl."

"Shut up, Dempsey," Bongo called out from under the orange cab.

"Count me in, Shelly," Bella said, amused, hesitant to move on. "I'm really interested in your program." To be honest, she felt favored, much the way she had the day Ethan had tapped her on the shoulder in history class and pointed his finger in her direction and then his own. *You're with me on this one.*

"I'm interested in her .38," Dempsey said, loud enough to be heard.

"Jeez, Dempsey, what's wrong with you?" Bongo asked. "You *do* know a .38 is a gun."

"Sure, I do. And I figure she can read the No Firearms sign out at the gate. You're just rude, Dempsey. Ahh!" Bongo kicked both legs in the air. "Something's dripping on me!"

Ethan tipped his head and leaned to one side. "Is it hot?"

"No, but it don't taste too good."

Dempsey leaned back against the truck and howled.

"Maybe you'd better keep your mouth shut and get done, Bongo," Ethan said. "I gotta get cleaned up for supper."

FOLDING DINING TABLES flanked a large pass-through window that separated the kitchen from the commons area. Two worn sofas, a card table, a TV and a few chairs furnished the opposite end of the great room. The setup was a small version of the commons at the Indian boarding school Bella had attended before her mother decided she should come back home and go to little Sinte High School. It was not Bella's choice—the South Dakota mission school had a good reputation for preparing kids for college—and she remembered questioning her mother's judgment, even accusing her of being selfish, which had turned out to be true. Her mother jealously guarded those years, claimed them as *her* time. But what she really meant was *their* time, and Bella had had no idea how short the time would be.

She wondered how many of the two-dozen boys who lined up at the window and came away with plates loaded with meat and potatoes would be taken home by their parents if and when the state stepped aside. They behaved like the boys she'd gone to school with, jostling for position, be it in suckling, pecking or batting order. Dying to get noticed, an expression a few of them would take literally if they found no other way. But here they were allowed to be boys while they learned to be men. If they could, and if they would. She'd reported on more than a few who did not.

"You really are their hero," Bella noted after Bongo and Dempsey had taken the long way around the tables to congratulate Ethan for "scoring."

"Yeah, they think I'm bad," he said with a smile.

"Which is good."

"In their eyes, maybe. Should I leave it at bad, or should I admit to a generous helping of stupid?" He shook his head as he cast a glance at the fluorescent fixture overhead. "I don't know, Bella. I'm new at this job, and I'm kinda wingin' it. You never know what's gonna work with these gangsters."

"They don't seem like gangsters."

"A couple of them are here because they won't go to school. They'd rather sit in a hole and smoke weed." He scanned the tables behind her. "Some have done worse."

"What's worse than throwing away your best chance to climb out of a weedy hole?"

"How long have you been reporting the news? You tell me."

She drew a deep breath as she ran down her mental list. She'd interviewed hardheads in all shapes and sizes. "Throwing away your next best chance on top of the first."

"Which is why they're back to Square One. It's a good option for kids who are open to this kind of rural life."

"Is it good for you?"

"It's perfect for me. Tailor-made." She gave him an incredulous look, and he laughed. "No, I'm serious. I've got a place to stay, but I'm free go. I get to eat and sleep and shower whenever I feel like it. I'm doing something useful, and they pay me for it. Plus, they let me keep a horse here." He winked at her. "I'm makin' progress."

She poked at her mashed potatoes with her fork. "I went to Sinte this morning to do a little research."

"Research?"

She nodded without looking up. "I spoke with your father."

"If you're interested in horse training, Logan's your man."

"I'm interested in the story *behind* the horses."

"How much time you got?" He gave her a sly grin. "Some 'tails' are longer than others."

It wasn't much of a joke, but the way his eyes sparkled, she had to reward him with a laugh.

"And some kicks are harder on the gut than others," he added, the sparkle fading. "So watch yourself, okay?"

The smile fell from her face. "Are you talking about Logan?"

"I'm talking about poking around behind the horse. I'm talking about being in the wrong place at the wrong time with the wrong questions." He sipped his coffee, studying her over the rim of the cup. He set it down slowly. "With all this interest in sleeping dogs and horses' asses, have you thought about doing something useful?"

"Like what?"

He frowned briefly. "Maybe go back to school for veterinary medicine."

She laughed. "You know, I never had a dog, and I've never really ridden a horse."

"No lie?"

"I try not to do that, either. So I bet you're thinking, an Indian girl who's never had a dog? No way."

"I'm thinking, a girl who's never been on a horse? That is heartbreaking."

"I didn't say I'd never been *on* one. I got on, got scared, had a very short ride."

"End of story?"

"Well, I've always loved horse stories, but you get up there, and the horse raises his head right away and starts prancing around, and you're so high off the ground..." She could almost feel the prickly tummy-to-toes *whoosh* just thinking about it. "I was six years old. That was my one chance, and I blew it."

"Stick with me, Indian girl." He cocked a forefinger at her. "I'm all about second chances." He smiled. "You want one?"

She stared at him. She knew that come-on look, the

charismatic smile, the reflexive wink—she'd seen it all, generally directed at someone else. But she'd only been favored a time or two, and her adolescent self had yearned for *once more, Ethan. Look at me that way again, and I'll follow you anywhere.*

Thank God he hadn't. She would be in a fine mess now, wouldn't she?

"Tomorrow's my day off," he said. "Come back in the afternoon and let me take you riding."

"Today was *my* day off."

"That's right," he recalled. "They don't pay you to dig."

"They do, but only in certain places. They're called *assignments*. I'm very good about getting my assignments done before I go back to digging in more fertile—" she demonstrated, sinking splayed fingers into air serving as ground "—loamy ground, dark and loaded with secrets. In my business, there is no right or wrong question, only true or false answers."

"Ask me no questions, I'll tell you no…" His smile was slight, almost sad. "Truth is, I've got no answers. I'm still looking."

"My mother told me once that she was taught not to ask questions, but eventually she decided it was no good to hang back." She sat back in her chair, listening in her mind's ear, reciting word for word. "'We live in a world full of people who love to give answers. They might not be generous with anything else, but they have answers to spare. If you don't ask, they think you're not interested. And if you're not interested…'"

"I'm interested. I'm asking." His smile turned inviting. "Would you like to go out with me sometime?"

"What time tomorrow afternoon?"

"Whenever you get off work."

"I have some flexibility in my schedule. I could try to move some things around." She pulled her woolen shoulder bag into her lap and fished out her phone. "What's your cell number?"

"I don't have one."

"So you don't have a phone number?"

"No numbers." Ethan looked straight into her eyes and gave the two words—*true* words—a moment to sink in. They were heavy enough to crush her *no wrong questions* theory. And then he smiled. "I'll be here all afternoon. Come when you can." He smiled slowly. "Just call out my name."

CHAPTER THREE

BELLA'S INTERVIEW WITH the chairman of the Rapid City Autumn Art Festival had gone well. Carson Watts described the juried competition and made a point of mentioning several of the Native artists by name. The city was gaining a reputation for galleries and shops specializing in American Indian art, and the annual festival in the fall rivaled the one that marked the beginning of tourist season in early June.

Of course, holding the art show the same weekend as Pumpkin Fest didn't hurt, Watts admitted. You had your pumpkin catapult and your beer garden with the oompah band going full tilt downtown, while the east end of Main Street hosted the more "genteel" residents and visitors. What he hadn't said—but she knew—was that his brother-in-law was the head honcho of the pumpkin party, and his own wife had chosen chairmanship of her brother's quilt show committee over her regular fundraising assignment for the art festival. Bella had interviewed the Pumpkin Fest planners earlier in the week. They'd had her cameraman sampling German beer and opining on brands of bratwurst. She had laughed off the offer of beer for breakfast and thought better of telling the friendly group how much she hated bratwurst.

With the community celebrations covered, Bella had convinced her producer to let her take a look at the Double D Wild Horse Sanctuary for a possible story about the training competition, which would come to an end in another few weeks with some kind of performance. She was reminded that a story about the competition had been aired and that it would make sense for the same reporter to do a follow-up.

Or maybe it didn't really matter.

Go ahead, Bella. And since the wild horse place isn't too far from the reservation, why don't you check with your sources there? See if there's anything interesting going on.

She would take that as an assignment.

Her car rumbled over the cattle guard at the gate to the Double D Wild Horse Sanctuary. It had once been a cattle ranch, and she passed a few Herefords grazing alongside their white-faced black calves as she sped down the gravel access road toward an imposing white house. Upon closer inspection the place became less imposing. It was big, but the white paint needed refurbishing. The Office sign told her the house was more than a home, and the wiry old cowboy standing on the porch looked like a fixture worth investigating.

He rattled down the front porch steps on bowed legs, pumping his elbows like a flightless chicken as Bella approached. She read *Where have I seen you?* in his eyes and cheerfully introduced herself. She enjoyed being recognized.

"I'm looking for one of the *D*'s—whichever Drexler sister is in charge today."

"No more Drexlers. We got Night Horse and Beaudry, but no Drexler. Both girls are married now."

Bella smiled. "Are you Night Horse or Beaudry?"

"Me? No. Gosh, no, not me." Blushing, the little man

adjusted his straw cowboy hat and did a little boot scoot in the dirt. "Them girls are like my own kin. Hooli-han's the name." He stuck out his hand. "Everybody calls me Hoolie. The girls are around here somewhere. Pretty sure Sally's over by..." He nodded toward the barn. "Here, let me show you."

Bella followed the old cowboy, whose friendly chat-ter reached the ears of a lovely blonde, who appeared in the open doorway leaning heavily on a sturdy cane with a tripod base. The woman shaded her eyes with her free hand and then flashed a huge smile.

"Well, I'll be damned. The paparazzi have finally tracked me down."

Bella recognized the former Sally Drexler from the original KOZY interview. The new last names would come naturally soon enough.

"Where's your camera, Miss Primeaux?" Sally laugh-ingly demanded as she emerged from the barn. "I'm ready for my close-up."

"What've you done now, girl?" Hoolie chided. "I told you, my film star days are over, so don't be signing me up for any more of them promotional videos."

"You're our most authentic-looking relic of the Old West, Hoolie." Sally turned to Bella as she pulled off her work gloves. "You do a story on the Double D, you get Hoolie in the picture for free. For a donation, he comes with woolly chaps." She offered a handshake. "Sally Night Horse." She glanced at Hoolie, grinning. "I love saying that. *Sally Night Horse.*" To Bella she added, "We're newlyweds."

"Not me," said Hoolie.

"Hoolie turned me down years ago," Sally said. "You

KOZY people sure are quick. I just sent the email this morning."

"What email?"

"You know, where it says *Got news? Contact us.* I told them they oughta be setting something up for the grand finale of our training competition." Sally patted Bella's shoulder. "And here you are. My favorite reporter, too."

Bella frowned. "My producer didn't say anything about an email."

"Thought of it on her own, did she? I'm sure glad she didn't give it to the guy who came out here before. He didn't know a mustang from a unicorn. Have a seat." Sally gestured toward a wooden bench on the shady side of the barn and then proceeded to beat Bella to the far end of it.

Bella hesitated. Whatever physical strength the woman lacked, she more than made up for in vitality and sheer will. She seemed to fill up more than physical space. She had considerable personal presence.

"Come on, take a load off. Mine's heavier than yours, so humor me." Sally patted the empty space beside her. "Sit down and tell me what you need. We've got pictures, we've got stories, we've got facts and figures. It's been one hell of a ride, and we haven't even gotten to the best part yet. I mean, *I* have, but that's because I've met my soul mate. And I've only nibbled around the edges of that discovery. The ride gets better and better. There's so much more we can do here."

"I'd better get to haulin' that hay," the old cowboy muttered, edging away.

"Are you blushing, Hoolie?"

"It's my farmer tan." He lifted his cowboy hat. He was ruddy below the eyebrows, pale and polished on top. "It ends right here. See? Don't you be signing me up for any stories with pictures, Big Sister." He replaced his hat and tugged at the brim in deference to their visitor as he backpedaled a step or two. "Never know what you're gonna say."

"I'm just sayin' it's all good." Eyes dancing, Sally glanced at Bella. *Between girls.* "And I'm still looking forward to handing over that twenty-thousand dollars to the winning trainer. Thank God I'm not judging. I've been getting pictures from the trainers. You should see some of the riders they've lined up to show the horses. You wanna show us a gentle horse, you put a kid in the saddle, right?" Sally took a deep breath and glanced heavenward. "I need more prizes."

"Maybe I could help you get some. Show me some of your pictures and I can find a way to use them. We do community support spots all the time."

"We'll take some of those." Sally nodded. "But what I really want you to cover is the competition. Show off the horses and the people coming from all over. If I had to make a choice…"

"Maybe we can do both. It doesn't hurt to try."

"I wanna show you around." Sally balanced her weight on the cane and levered herself off the bench. "The best view is from the back of a horse, but I need to rest up first for that."

"Start with the pictures," Bella suggested as she sprang to her feet. She wouldn't offer help unless she was asked, but she was ready. And, yes, she was also ready to ask a little and offer to listen a lot. "Tell me more about your program," she said as they headed for the house. "How you got started, what it takes to create a sanctuary. Talk to me about how you get the land you need and cooperation from all the bureaucrats that would have to be involved with something like this. And your neighbors. You must have some helpful neighbors. Not everyone wants a wildlife sanctuary butting up against their pasture."

Sally moved like a woman living in a body that couldn't keep up with her mind. Bella had seen the same frustration in her mother, and it scared her a little. Not the hint of impatience—she understood that—but the reality. It was a feeling she tucked away, to be studied later.

"Come on inside," Sally told Bella when they reach the top of the porch steps. She nodded toward a wheelchair parked beside a porch swing. "On days when the saddle's out of reach, that's my ride. MS." She reached for the screen door. "You know, multiple sclerosis. The last guy KOZY sent out was here for about ten minutes. One look at me, and he was after a whole different story. He wanted to put me in my wheelchair out in the corral, gather some horses around me and then mike me up. That's what he said. And you know what I said?"

"I know what *I* would have said."

Sally laughed. "And that's what I said, too. Not to mention, that chair is camera shy." She led the way through an old-fashioned foyer and nodded toward the first door past the foot of the staircase. "But I know a slacker from a doer. Glad they decided not to send a boy to do a woman's job this time."

The door led to an office whose walls were covered with pictures of horses—all sizes, colors, attitudes and settings. The heart of the matter. Sally probably spent more time in this room than she wanted to, so she brought her outdoor world inside. This was the Double

D's hub. Her regular desk chair was probably the one sitting on the porch, but there were a couple of padded folding chairs and a daybed, lots of room to roll around, a desktop computer, file drawers and desk trays galore, and an array of framed family photographs standing on shelves above.

Sally took a shot of a foursome down from the shelf. "This is Hank and me with my sister, Ann, and her new husband, Zach. This was taken at their wedding. Hank was the soloist, and I was the maid of honor. That was just last spring." She flashed Bella a smile as she reached for another shot of four smiling faces. "And here's *my* wedding picture. We work fast here. You know this guy." She pointed to Logan Wolf Track. "He married my BFF Mary Tutan just a little over a month ago. Double wedding." She looked up, eyes dancing. "Me and Hank figured what the hell? Everyone else is doing it."

"It doesn't look like that's what anybody in this picture was thinking," Bella said of the four glowing faces. She glanced into a frame on the shelf above the wedding pictures.

"That's Trace Wolf Track," Sally said, indicating the man on the bucking horse. "Logan's adopted son." She took the picture down from the shelf. "You know him? Rodeo cowboy."

"I went to school with his brother."

"You know Ethan? He's one of our contestants. He's even better looking than this guy, if you can believe that. Have you seen him lately? He's like—"

"I met with Logan recently over at the Tribal Office," Bella said, sparing the shot of Trace Wolf Track in action little more than a glance. She knew how to learn a lot by asking only a little, but it wasn't a two-way street.

Seeing Ethan would not enter into this conversation. She was keeping that close. "Indian Country is one of my beats whenever my producer thinks there might be something newsworthy going on."

"Logan's been a big help to the sanctuary," Sally said. "Backed us on leasing some Tribal land, which gave us a leg up on getting a big tract of public land adjacent to the reservation. We'll be able to take on a lot more horses."

Bella set Logan's older son back on the metaphorical shelf. Now she was getting somewhere. "Your neighbor was running cattle on that land, wasn't he? Dan Tutan?"

"Damn tootin' he was. Poor guy's losin' it." Sally laughed. "In more ways than one."

"What do you mean?"

"I don't know, he's just..." Sally snapped a lever on her cane and telescoped it closed. "To all intents and purposes he lost his daughter, Mary, a long time ago, but now that she's married to Logan, the plot thickens."

"How so?"

"Let's just say ol' Dan better start tootin' a sweeter tune or he won't be bouncing that first grandbaby on his knee. Of course, if I get to be godmother—which I'm counting on—he'll have to go through me no matter what."

Sally hadn't told Bella anything she didn't already know, but a baby brother or sister for Ethan seemed like a pretty big deal. Since Logan and Mary had just gotten married and Logan had said he hadn't seen much of Ethan, she wondered if he knew. Or cared.

And why did she wonder or care whether Ethan cared? She was looking for a story about Indian land and Dan Tutan's good friend Senator Garth. Ethan Wolf Track figured in somewhere out on the fringe at best.

"Is everything signed and sealed on the leases?" Bella asked. "I mean, I've heard you might have some opposition."

"Just Tutan, but the Tribal Council already shot him down."

"Tutan has influential friends in Washington. One, anyway."

"Who?"

"Senator Perry Garth. I just wondered if you'd actually gotten anything on paper."

Bella read the message in Sally's eyes. *Of course I'm dotting the* i*'s.*

"The leases turn over in November," Sally said. "I don't care who Tutan's cozy with. D.C.'s a world away. The people I deal with at the regional Bureau of Land Management office, the ones who handle wild horse issues, they tell me renewal's in the bag. They need this sanctuary. They've got no place to put the horses they consider unadoptable. That's what we do. We give them a home where they can roam." Sally's grin was infectious. "You know, with the deer and the antelope. No buffalo. Wish I had some. Hank would love that. I don't suppose you've met my husband, Hank?"

"I don't think so."

"He's not from this reservation, but he has connections here. In fact, I think his father worked for Tutan some years ago, but I don't know much about that. We haven't talked much about… Did I tell you we got married at the Tribal building? In the judge's chambers. It was so cool. No fuss at all, just *bam*." Sally slapped the back of her hand into her palm. "Man and wife. Love it." She smiled. "I don't think Tutan's gonna give us any trouble. I think he's afraid of Hank."

Fear. Could be something... "Why?"

"They've had words. I don't know exactly what those words were, but they weren't friendly." Sally took another picture down from the shelf. Two young women— Sally and someone in an academic robe. "It wasn't so long ago that it was just my sister, Ann, and me running the place. We had Hoolie and a few high school kids working for us, some volunteers helping out. Then Zach Beaudry came along. Another rodeo cowboy. Have you heard of him?"

Bella shook her head. Rodeo itself held no interest for her, but she knew better than to show it. Listening—her strong suit—had always served her well. Talkers like Sally tended to ramble, dropping crumbs of information along the way. With any luck Sally would wander back and pick up the tidbit about Hank's father working for Tutan. Even if she didn't, Bella had sniffed the crumb and made a mental note of the scent.

"My husband works the rodeo circuit as a medic, so that's how he knew Zach." Sally perched on the edge of the big desk. "Life's funny, isn't it?" she went on. "Not much happens for the longest time, and then Zach's pickup breaks down outside our gate and the Double D family starts growing." She gave a catbird's smile. "And 'Damn Tootin' isn't very popular around these parts. So I'm not worried."

"I don't know much about rodeo. The only name I know is Trace Wolf Track." And the name was clearly a connection to the horses, which were Sally's claim to the land. "Do rodeo contractors ever get hold of your mustangs?"

"First of all, they're not mine. And the people who adopt horses could use them that way, but I doubt it happens often. Good bucking stock is hard to find. You almost have to breed for it, and those animals are valuable and well taken care of, so if you're looking for some kind of scandal…" Sally's smile had gone cool. "I was a rodeo stock contractor for a short time years ago. I took good care of my animals."

"Oh, I have no doubt," Bella said quickly. "I'm interested in the making of a sanctuary, the commitment to providing at least some animals with the space to be wild. I could really get into a story like this."

Sally's eyes lit up again. "That's what I like to hear."

"But I have to convince my producer to let me do it."

"Tell your boss that first guy flat out offended me, and I don't want him back." Sally reached for a Post-it pad. "Better yet, give me the guy's name and number."

"Let me handle it." Bella reached into her shoulder bag—her ever-present office on a string—and poked around while she spoke. "You might want to check on the public lands leases. I've heard that one of their favorite tactics is to come up with a snag when it's too late to get it straightened."

"Whose tactics?"

"Bureaucrats. My mother used to say the word as though it had been soaked in sour milk." She produced a business card from her woolen bag. "If you smell anything fishy, would you call me?"

"I was gonna offer you lunch, but now…" Cautiously Sally took the card in hand. "Dead fish and sour milk?"

Bella smiled. "Damn tootin'."

BELLA HAD CALLED AHEAD, but she didn't know whether to knock on the door of the house at Square One or walk in. She hadn't seen an office sign anywhere. Or, for that matter, any sign of an office. She remembered knocking on the door of the Wolf Track home years ago, shoring up her courage with a bit of self-talk and going in search of Ethan. She'd gone over what she would say as she stood there on the front step, grateful that the log house was far enough out of town that no one would see her. Too far to walk. Too windy, too cold. Her mother was waiting in the car, keeping it running, keeping the heat on.

How did you end up with him as a partner on this project? Why don't you just do your part and let him twist in the wind?

Because it would be incomplete. Because I'd get laughed at. Not him. Me. *Because I thought we'd do this thing together.*

She could almost feel her mother's angry stare boring into her back as she headed around the corner of the house. *So who're you gonna team up with next time? Not some football hero, I hope.*

Oh, yeah, the heat was on.

"I got your message."

Bella was snapped back to the present and whirled around to find that this time the heat was coming from Ethan's eyes. They'd always made her a little nervous, made her feel as though he knew more than she did. Not that what he thought was terribly important, but he was older, wiser, more experienced, and he knew things. He had answers to questions she hadn't thought of yet—at least back then.

"I said I'd come."

"I said I'd be here." He adjusted his battered straw hat by the brim and smiled. "A man of his word meets a woman of hers."

"I hope we're really going to ride horses." She stuck out her right leg. "I wore my boots." With riding heels. Guaranteed to keep her feet in the stirrups.

"Pretty flashy." He gave a nod toward the barn, and she lowered her boot—a step, she hoped, in a useful direction. "Did you buy those today?" he asked.

"Last night."

"First pair?"

"First pair of cowboy boots, yes. They're not very comfortable." She picked up her pace. One step behind was not her way.

"You gotta break 'em in."

Her boots squeaked on cue. She glanced up at him, and they both laughed.

"I paid a visit to the Double D this morning," she told him as they approached a rail fence. "I'm going to ask if I can to do a feature on the competition. I want to tie it into land use and can't-we-all-just-get-along and stuff like that." She braced her arm over the chest-high fence and turned to him. "You say you're going to win?"

"Get along with who?" he asked, ignoring her question.

"Oh, you know, the farmers and the cattlemen, the cowboys and the Indians. How can you be sure you'll win?"

He gave her an incredulous look. "Damn, woman, let it go. That is *so* past history." He bumped her arm with his elbow. "To boot, we both already passed history." He tipped his head back and laughed. "Ah, funny stuff, Bella. Wait till you see my horse. He can go from zero to sixty and stop on a dime."

She smiled. "Turning your thrill gauge upside down is he?"

"My thrill gauge?" He laughed again. "It's pretty easy to thrill me these days. I get a kick out of simply turning a knob and pushing the door open." He demonstrated with a handful of air. "All by myself."

"No hands tied behind your back?"

"That was always my brother's favorite boast." He squared his shoulders and pitched his voice down low. *"Hell, I can do that with one hand tied behind my back.* So I always wanted to go him one better."

"I'll bet *that* was some competition." Bella rested her elbows on the rail and surveyed the pasture beyond. No horses. No cattle. Just grassy hills, clear blue sky. "I read about your conviction," she said quietly. "And, no, it wasn't *big* news out where I was, but it wouldn't have been news at all if it hadn't involved a senator."

"His daughter," Ethan amended. "Politics and sex, right? The only thing missing was money."

"Money's always somewhere in the mix."

"Don't look at me." He turned his back to the fence, which positioned him for a challenging look at her. "I stole a car and a girl. No money."

"There was money somewhere, Ethan. That's where the power comes from."

"I did the crime, I did the time, and now I'm done with it."

She frowned. "You pled not guilty."

"Against the advice of my attorney. Turned out I *was* guilty." Leaning back, he glanced past her, tucked his lower lip under his front teeth and gave a deafening whistle.

Bella turned toward the sound of pounding hooves. A stout buckskin galloped toward them, his mane flapping like a black flag.

"Impressive," Bella said.

"Damn straight." Ethan betrayed his secret, opening his hand to let the horse snuffle up a tiny brown treat. "Big Boy, meet Bella. She's a reporter. She's got a ton of questions. Help me show her some answers."

"I haven't asked you anything."

"I noticed." He slid her a subtle wink. "You're good."

"Yes, I am. Are you going to show me the dime-stopping routine?"

"Nope. I'm gonna take you out riding. Watch this." Ethan climbed the fence, lured the horse into position with another treat and a little sweet talk, grabbed a fistful of mane and mounted. He grinned at Bella. "How do you like my wild mustang?"

"Amazing. How long since he was wild?"

"How long since I whistled? A minute or two?"

"He's not wild. You've tamed him."

"If I turn him out of this pasture, he'll head for the hills and his band of brothers. He won't give me another thought until I go out there and run him back in."

She nodded at the unfettered horse. "Will he do that for anyone else?"

"No one else has tried. You want to?"

She shook her head. "I want a kid horse."

"The kids are out in the field. Meet me at the gate by the barn and we'll steal their horse for an hour or so."

She watched him ride away, loping the buckskin along the fence line. Quite a picture, she thought. Both magnificent looking, neither quite tame. Together they made a story, and she could stand aside and watch and listen and make notes. She could find that story and tell it in a good way, so that people would find it and feel it and value the lives they lived at the back of beyond. She had a role to play.

And she'd said she would do the horseback-riding scene, hadn't she?

Well, at least she looked the part. She opened the appointed gate and watched Ethan swing his leg high over the buckskin's head and slide to the ground.

He grinned. *Did you see that?* And she nodded, suitably impressed. The mustang had earned another treat.

"He took to this apple-flavored stuff right away, which is kinda surprising. It's generally an acquired taste." He scratched the horse's withers. "Ain't it, Big Boy?" He glanced over the buckskin's back and peered at the bright blue horizon. "So you've really never had a look at this country of yours from the back of a horse?"

"Country of mine?"

"Isn't this part of the land Warrior Woman blogs about? The Great Sioux Nation, she says." He flashed a knowing smile. "That's you, isn't it? Warrior Woman?"

It was her blogging handle. "How did you know?"

"I'm an Indian, too, Bella. I'm not sure what tribe, but it's in my blood," he told her. And then he disappeared into the barn with the horse following him as far as the open door. Within seconds Ethan reappeared carrying a saddle on his shoulder. "I know how to read sign."

"What sign?"

"The sign that somebody wants to be waited on. Saddle rack's in here."

"I don't have a horse."

"I'll get the horse. You get the saddle." He grinned at her as she walked past him. "Together, we're gonna ride."

Half a dozen saddles were shelved on wall pegs just inside the door. "Any saddle?"

"Any saddle," was the response from outside.

She eyed the hanging array of horse headgear. "What about the other stuff?"

He appeared in the doorway.

She turned and quickly pulled down the nearest saddle. "Got one."

She thought he might take it from her—the damn thing was heavy—but he walked around her and selected two sets of headstalls with reins.

"So you use your tracking skills on the internet?" She followed him into the corral and dropped the saddle beside the one he'd brought out. "That's interesting. That's a topic worth exploring. Are you a hunter?"

"No. Never hunted. Never will. Lost my right to bear arms." He gripped the handful of tack and did a quick biceps curl. "Except these. These can go bare."

"They're quite impressive." He was wearing a gray T-shirt, and for the first time she noticed some ink peeking out from under his sleeve. On impulse she pushed his sleeve up and discovered a pair of hawks fighting in flight. "The artwork seems a little amateurish."

"You don't like that?" He glanced at it and shrugged. "Neither do I, but I'm stuck with it. Don't know what I was thinking." He offered a sheepish grin. "Literally. Nothing like a three-day bender for blowing the mind."

"Was that the first thing you did after your release from prison?"

"Hell, no. First thing I did was go around turning knobs and pushing doors open. Hold this." He handed her one of the headstalls. "Getting drunk was the first thing I did after I got discharged from the army." He spoke quietly as he approached the mustang. "And the second thing. Maybe the third thing. I lost count."

"But the army was *before*…"

"Yeah, before. But I did some stuff *between*. Check it out, Big Boy." The buckskin lowered his head and snuffled the proffered headstall. "I did road construction, worked for Logan, followed Trace around a little bit. Even took a few college classes."

"Where you met Senator Garth's daughter."

"And the rest is history." He turned to the horse. "The woman is a history freak, boy." Ethan lifted the simple, handmade-looking piece of tack over the horse's head. There was no bit to coax into his mouth. "What's past is present, they say. How're we gonna live with that, huh? You and me?" He glanced over his shoulder at her as he rubbed the horse's face. "So come on, tell me the truth. Have you really never ridden?"

"I just need a gentle, well-broke mount," she said, sidestepping the question. "Nothing fancy. No stopping on a dime or going on a tear." The closer the moment of getting on a horse came, the less she wanted to think about her long-ago but never forgotten experience.

He smiled. "I'll go wake your horse up."

"But first…" She shoved her hand in the front pocket of her jeans, pulled up the contents and flipped a glinting dime, which he caught midair. She nodded. "Prove it."

He laughed. "Yes, ma'am."

He flipped the reins over the mustang's withers, vaulted onto his bare back and put on a quick show for her. The horse leaped into action, skidded to a stop and reversed directions like a swinging door.

Bella knew little about training horses, but she was impressed. "How long have you been working with him?"

"Little over two months."

"And he was completely wild?"

"Came straight out of the hills." Ethan swung his leg over the horse's withers and slid to the ground. "Course he'd had a couple of human encounters. For one, he's a gelding. But I had no part in that, did I, Big Boy?" He patted the horse's shoulder.

"Who *did?*" she asked.

"Any doctoring these horses get is done by a vet. They try not to interfere too much when the horse is in the wild, but you need geldings for the adoption program."

Bella felt the urge to pat Big Boy, too, but she stayed put. "Did he come with the name, or did you give it to him?"

"That's just what I call him. There's gonna be an auction after the competition to benefit the sanctuary, and this guy will bring in big bucks. I figure naming rights go with him."

"And if you named him, you'd be hard-pressed to let him go."

"There's always another horse." He entreated her with a nod. "Come hold him for me."

"I don't…"

"Sure you do. You two have a lot in common. You're both observers."

She took one cautious step, then another. Ethan reached for her hand, uncurled her fingers with his thumb and drew her palm to the horse's big, soft nostril. It widened as Big Boy took her measure and found her acceptable. Ethan placed the ends of the reins in her hand.

The thing about animals smelling fear must have

been an old wives' tale, Bella thought as Ethan walked away. Or maybe that was just predators. Animals driven to knock you down, step all over you and eat you alive.

"You wouldn't do that, would you, Big Boy?" she whispered. "We have that in common, too. We're gentle creatures. We eat plants."

Ethan emerged from the barn leading a small black horse. "This one's for you." He dropped the lead rope, and the horse stood patiently while he straightened the saddle pad and set the saddle.

"Does he have a name?"

"This is Sister Sara."

"She." Bella looked up and found Big Boy staring back at her. "A mare. We like mares. They're usually gentle, aren't they?"

"This one is." Ethan brought the mare over and traded reins. He watched Bella take quiet stock of the mare's response to her. One female sizing up the other.

"Would you rather do something else?" Ethan asked.

"No. Oh, no, I've been looking forward to this. Obviously." She dug one heel into the dirt and tipped her toe toward the sky, showing off her new boots again.

"One step at a time, then. Step one is to mount up."

No problem—as long as Sister Sara didn't move. Ethan spoke to her while Bella got herself lined up, put mind over matter and pushed off. One smooth move. Victory.

"How's that feel?" Ethan asked.

She looked down at him. "So far, so good." Nobody was moving yet.

"Yeah?" He smiled. "You look good up there. You feel okay?"

"I do." Bella nodded quickly. "I do. We're steady. Nobody's nervous. This is a good start."

"Take the reins easy and find your contact point."

She felt a little jittery as she slid the leather straps through her fingers. Where was it, this contact point? Would it show the horse that she was in charge?

"Easy," he said softly, laying his hand over hers. "This isn't a lifeline. You don't hang on with these." He moved his hand to her thigh. Now she *really* felt jittery. "You hang on with these."

"I know. I know that."

He looked up and considered her face for a moment. She wasn't sure how much the hand resting on her thigh had to do with it, but her insides were all abuzz.

"Okay, just how bad was your experience?"

She lifted one shoulder. "I got dumped. Hard."

One corner of his mouth twitched. "I mean, with a horse."

"I've never been dumped by anything else." A little fake indignation calmed her nerves, and she smiled. "I got left in the lurch on a history project once, but since I landed on my feet, it doesn't qualify."

"How long is it gonna take you to forgive me for that one?" He turned to Big Boy, whispered something and reached for the top of his headstall.

"Forgiving is no problem. It's the forgetting. It just seems to jump out there when I need a good comeback. And what are you doing?"

"Turning my horse loose. I'm going with you." He slid her boot out of the stirrup, put his hand under her knee and lifted it toward the saddle swell. With a light touch on the saddle horn and a toe in the stirrup he swung up effortlessly and settled behind her. "Our Sister Sara's gonna take us both."

"She doesn't mind?"

"Doesn't seem to. Do you?" Bella shook her head. "We're just gonna amble along so you can get the feel of being safe on a horse. How's that?"

Bella nodded, and Ethan guided her foot back into the stirrup, then took the reins in his left hand and urged the horse through the gate and into a pasture that had been grazed down to crisp nubs.

"I remember sitting across from you in the library," he said, "working out the plans and looking stuff up. You were so damn serious, thought you knew it all, and if you'd been a little less bossy, maybe a little older…"

"What?" she coaxed.

"You mighta been in trouble. I remember going along for the fun of it, thinking you were way too smart, too cute, too mouthy and too young. What I don't remember is why I didn't show up that night."

She laughed uneasily. She could almost feel the inked wings of the birds on his arm fluttering against her shoulder. "*You* were serious about other things."

"I was living in the moment." He laid his free hand on her shoulder. "You know what? You need to relax. How bad were you hurt?"

"I wasn't hurt. I was mad."

"At the horse?"

"Oh, that. I broke my butt."

He laughed.

She didn't. "Hairline fracture of the coccyx."

"Oh, yeah, that hurts. Sorry. No wonder you're tense." Slowly he began kneading her right shoulder. "Let's try to loosen you up some. Let me untie this knot so you can let your arms down." He rested his chin on her left shoulder and rocked it side to side. "This side, too. Stop thinking. You don't need a comeback."

No kidding. Tight loops began opening up, raised parts lowering, hung-up pieces sinking, and, oh, it all felt good in concert.

But she wasn't about to start singing.

"Shouldn't you pay attention to the road?"

"You've got the front seat." He chuckled soft and low, his breath warm in her ear. "Lean back and take the reins. Then you'll really be in charge."

"You're making me nervous."

"Take the reins in your left hand. You can still hang on to the swells with your right. Not the horn." He touched the high pommel that anchored the saddle horn. "The swells."

"I don't want to make the horse nervous," she muttered, but she accepted the assignment.

"She's a kids horse," he whispered as he drew his hand back and slid it around her waist.

She quickly sucked in her belly and then half expected somebody to laugh at her. Who cared whether she had a waist? She was fine. She was healthy and fit. Her jeans rode her hipbones, and his hand had no business hovering around there. But it was warm and comforting, and she was pretty far out of her comfort zone. Still, with all the square inches of surface her body possessed, the only patch she felt at the moment was underneath his hand.

And then he moved it. "Lean back," he said, and he pressed her to him. "Relax and get into the flow with us." His fingers stirred. "Sister Sara ain't the nervous type, and she's got the sweetest rockin' horse lope. You wanna try it out?"

"Not yet."

"Is it me or the horse?"

She laughed a little. "It's me. I don't want to be afraid. Horses are *beautiful*."

"What about me?"

"You're beautiful, too."

"Do you want to stop being afraid of me?"

She turned her head quickly and found herself shaded by the brim of his hat and basking in the warmth of his gaze. "I'm not…"

He stopped her answer with a soft, sure kiss. Her words would have been meaningless, anyway. A hollow denial would be a waste of breath. Words stood no chance against a kiss, and his was pure and promising. She drew in the feel and the scent of him, meeting his kiss in kind.

Yes, I do.

He lifted his head and smiled down at her. "Give me time. I'll show you how."

She glanced at the horizon. Time was easy. There was nothing to it. Being together was something else.

"Talk to me," he said. He nudged the mare, and she picked up her pace. "Tell me about your college days. What was it like for you? Was it hard?"

"Very hard, and very good for me, thanks for asking."

He rested his chin on the top of her head, staking a claim. "You always talk cute when you're nervous?"

"I rarely do things that make me nervous. This is out of character for me."

"You go on TV. Most people would be shaking in their boots."

"Would you?"

"Hell, yeah. God knows what I'd say. But you never miss a beat. First time I saw you, I said, *hey, I know her.*" He chuckled. "But I didn't, did I?"

"What did you *think* you knew about me?"

"You were always one to speak your mind, but only when you had something to say. I thought down deep you were pretty shy." His hand stirred against her midriff. "Pretty. And shy."

"It's not down that deep."

"When you read about me going to prison, did you say, *hey, I know him?*" A beat passed, and then another. "If that's what makes you nervous—"

"It's not," she assured him. "I didn't say anything. I just kept reading. One thing about not speaking up until you have something to say is that you get to hear more, maybe see more, than you would otherwise. That's how I knew you, not from something I read."

"And you liked me."

"No, I didn't. I had a crush on you, but that's not really the same thing. I was beneath your notice until you needed me to get you through a required class."

"Needed you?" He snorted. "I could've done that thing myself."

"But you didn't have to."

"And you know damn well I noticed you."

"You teased me."

"Of course I did. I was a cocky eighteen-year-old. And you were, what, fifteen? Believe it or not, I don't go around lookin' for trouble."

"That's my job."

He laughed. "You're doing just fine, Bella. Whatever hurt I caused, you rose above it. And now I'm the one who gets to polish up his image when he says, *hey, I know her*."

"No apology for calling me Bella the Fella when one of your buddies said I needed to grow a pair?"

"Aw, jeez," he groaned. "I said that?"

"I was fifteen and flat as a board."

"What did you do? I know you didn't go home and cry."

"I threw a pencil at you, but I missed. And then I went home and grew a pair."

"A very nice pair. I noticed, Bella. I definitely noticed." He laid his free hand on her shoulder again, then rubbed it down over her arm. "You've relaxed. You notice the difference in Sister Sara? No resistance."

"I'm doing better?" She smiled. "And I'm not freaking out inside. I'd like to try it on my own." She glanced up at him. "Next time."

"We're havin' a next time?"

"I was thinking of blogging on you."

"I don't think I've ever been blogged on. I notice you're pretty good at it."

"You won't find better."

"Why don't we pull over to the side of the road and you can start now. Does it hurt the first time?"

"I'm betting you're pretty thick-skinned."

"Only in some places."

"I'll make a deal with you," she said. "Come over to the studio when you have a little time. If I'm on a story, you can tag along if you want to. And then I'll start doing you. Blog style."

"You make it sound real tempting, but I've been out of circulation for a while now. I'm what you'd call fresh fish. You throw the net over me, I'll be taking you for one crazy ride."

"Throw the net over you," she mused. "I like that. It's quotable. Where's a pencil when you need one?"

"You're still using pencils? Don't they get hung up in the net?"

"Still funny after all these years." She turned to look up at him. "With your looks and my brain, we might actually be a team this time."

"You've got looks, lady. Good looks. *Great* looks."

She flashed him a smile.

"Hey. You're supposed to say something back."

"*Of course* you have a brain, Ethan. It's all in the application."

CHAPTER FOUR

ETHAN HAD NEVER been to a television studio, and he didn't know what he was expecting, but it was something a little grander than the building KOZY-TV shared with a veterinary clinic and a real estate office. The station occupied the lion's share of the space, and it was flanked by an impressive tower, but the news desk was smaller than it looked on TV, and the weatherman stood in front of a solid green backdrop instead of a map. Bella called it magic. Ethan added the word *tricks*.

There were wires and cables hanging from the high ceiling and strung across the dark floor, lots of equipment on wheels, messages and images dancing on big and small screens, and two monster cameras. The cameras looked cool. Everything else was disappointing, like shaking hands with the actor who played Ironman and realizing his hand was half the size of yours.

Bella introduced two behind-the-scenes people who showed him how their gadgets worked. It was one computer, two computer, three computer, four. "More machines, fewer bodies," the young engineer said. "The station manager says if I can grow an extra ear and another hand, I'll have a job for at least five more years." He nodded at a pretty young woman hurrying past with an armload of file folders. "But she won't."

The woman skidded to a stop, neck arched. "Won't what?"

"Marry me," the young man said.

"In your dreams, Richard."

Richard grinned as they watched her disappear bit by lovely bit down a flight of stairs. "What I could do with another hand," he said under his breath.

Bella was already moving Ethan on to the next tour stop, but he tapped the man's shoulder in passing. "Machines can't replace a man's hands, no matter what anyone on TV says."

He left Richard laughing his headphones off.

"I'll show you how we switch over from news to weather," Bella was saying as they stepped into a den of rubber snakes on the dark news set. "Hey, Paul, is Darryl here?" she asked an older man who was monkeying around with a big camera. "I want him to meet Ethan Wolf Track." She turned to Ethan. "Darryl Brugmann is the—"

"Sports guy." A bright-eyed fellow with a spiky haircut appeared with a firm handshake at the ready. "Any relation to…"

"His brother." Sports guy was a short guy. Ethan grinned. "I caught Trace's interview with you a few months ago."

"Your brother's a hell of a bronc rider. What's your event? Rodeo usually runs in the family, and you look like a bulldogger to me."

"Nope. I got no interest in wrestling a steer to the ground just to let him up again. The rodeo genes went to my brother. I got the hand-me-down overalls." Ethan shoved his hands in the back pockets of his jeans. "I'm a workin' man. A cowboy, at least for now."

The sportscaster looked up at Bella. "Interesting. Are you doing something on cowboys? Or overalls?"

"I'm showing a friend around the studio before I go out on assignment."

"How far do you have to go? I'm covering a game tonight, and I need the new Betacam with the good tripod."

"I'll use the old camera," Bella said cheerfully. "I don't need a tripod."

"And I get John."

"I don't need John. I have a workin' man right here." She threaded her arm though Ethan's and around his back, smiling up at him. "Right?"

"Right. You don't need John." In the face of all the fancy equipment, he felt damn good about edging John out of the picture.

"What they say about working cowboys must be true," Darryl said. "Kinda like a Swiss Army Knife." He looked Ethan up and down, checking to see whether he was the deluxe model. "Your brother sure can ride."

"He sure can." Ethan smiled. He was standing there with Bella Primeaux's arm around his waist.

Brugmann gave a snappy salute and turned on his heel. "Have fun, kids."

"You think you like somebody," Ethan mused as he watched the little man make his swaggering exit. "And then you meet him in person."

Bella smiled. "Darryl thinks he's a big fish in a small pond. The only part he's got right is the size of the pond."

"Maybe you need to stop messin' with fish and find yourself a real man." Before she could slip away, Ethan slipped his arm around Bella's shoulders and gave her an affectionate squeeze. "Not a John, though. You don't want a John." He frowned. "What does John do, anyway?"

"He's our cameraman. We're down to one. The way the station's been cutting the budget, I'm surprised *I* still have a job." She patted his midsection. "Are you any good with a camera, cowboy?"

"I can point and shoot."

"That's all I need. Otherwise I have to shoot myself."

She was walking him toward a set of stairs. He hoped they led to the great outdoors. "Sounds like your job is harder than it looks."

"It depends on the assignment, and this one could get weird. We're going to talk to a dog breeder."

Ethan stepped back and let Bella take the stairs first. "We're talkin' puppies?"

"Puppies by the cageful. An affiliate in Boston got this lead on what they think is a mill shipping puppies out east. Apparently the owner agreed to let us take a look, so maybe it's a legitimate breeder." She turned when she reached the top of the stairs. "South Dakota doesn't require a license, so legitimacy is in the eye of the beholder."

"I can't shoot puppies," he teased as he stepped onto the landing. "Sorry. That's just wrong."

"I doubt we'll get to see many puppies. If these people are the kind we think they are, I'll give you a nice reward for full-face shots of any of the people. What would you like?"

"Like a prize at the fair?" He smiled hungrily. "Something from your top shelf."

She gave him a quick lesson on the handheld video camera and loaded the necessary equipment into her car. Ethan offered to drive so that she could use the GPS on her phone to find the place, which was pretty far out in the sticks. When they got there, the gate across the access road was locked.

Bella was back on the phone. "Hello, this is Bella Primeaux from KOZY News. I have an appointment for an interview with Mrs. Mosher. The gate's locked." She lowered the phone almost instantly. "They said to wait."

"Somebody's coming." Ethan appraised the approaching vehicle. It was a Hummer, for God's sake, bearing down on Bella's angelic white Honda. A South Dakota farmer with a Hummer? "I've got a bad feeling about this, Bella."

"Welcome to my world. You never know when something interesting might turn up"

"No, this is a feeling I've had before. Many times. Same world, different neighborhoods." The Hummer pulled over on the side of the rutted road inside the gate, and Ethan positioned the Honda for a quick return to the highway.

Whap. Whap. The Hummer's two front doors slapped shut.

"Good thing I'm not alone." Bella took the camera out of its case and presented it to him like a newborn baby. "Remember to hold steady and keep rolling. Don't shut it off unless we're getting back in the car. I'll keep them talking, so they'll forget about you."

Ethan glanced toward the gate at the sound of somebody rattling chains. The way the creeps were crawling up his back, they might have been jerking on his. The smaller of the two gatekeepers emerged first, while the other one took care of the chain, lock and gate. Neither one was in a hurry to welcome anybody.

"What do you want me to do if it gets weird?" Ethan asked quietly as they got out of the car.

"Keep rolling."

The face of the younger man working the gate was partially obscured by a sweatshirt hood. The smaller guy—billiard-ball bald and bearded—strolled ahead two paces as though he was in charge. Ethan stepped back and turned the camera on.

"Mr. Mosher is unavailable," the bald guy said.

"*Mrs.* Mosher booked the appointment," Bella said, her tone friendly. "She said she welcomes the opportunity to show off her dogs."

The droopy hood shielded the younger man's eyes, and his lips barely moved. "Mr. Mosher likes his privacy, and he has the final word."

"Which is *no trespassing.* And no—" Baldy's hands shot out and snatched the camera "—pictures."

"Give that back!" Bella shouted.

Hoodie grabbed for Bella, but Ethan shoved him to the ground before he could get a firm hold on her. She staggered, caught her balance and went for the camera again. Baldy threw it down on the blacktop and raised a booted foot over it.

"No!" she screamed.

"Bella, leave it!" Ethan shouted. Hoodie was trying to get up. Ethan was forced to give him a swift kick in the ass before he could prevent Baldy from booting the camera. "Stay down or I'll break something," Ethan warned.

"You and me both." Big words spoken in a wary tone as the older man glanced at his prone partner and took a step back from the camera, giving the lie to his own statement. He pointed his finger at Bella. "No pictures."

"Elaine Mosher agreed to an interview with KOZY," she repeated with commendable calm.

"Well, her husband musta disagreed," Baldy said. "He's trying to make a living here, and you news people just wanna make trouble. That's what you do."

Ethan stood between Bella and the two flunkies. "Where's your phone, Bella?"

"In the car."

"Get in the car," he told her gently.

"That camera's checked out to me, and I'm not going anywhere—" trusting Ethan's upper hand, she leaned over to pick it up "—without it."

"You'd better hand it over, or I'll have to take it," the bald man said.

Ethan laughed. "You and what army?"

Baldy glanced at Hoodie, who was picking himself up off the ground. "You're the one threw it down," Hoodie muttered. "It's busted anyway."

"Get in the car, Bella."

"We gotta get the camera," Baldy said. But he didn't move, and Hoodie's hesitant step was unconvincing.

"Come on, punk." Ethan offered a cold smile. "Try me again."

Hoodie took a moment to consider. He turned his eyes from Ethan's, glanced at the camera and rubbed his carbuncled jaw with an oily hand. "You didn't get nuthin', and that thing's busted anyway."

Baldy pointed to the cattle guard that stretched between the gateposts. "Cross this line and you're on private property."

"Is that a fact?" Ethan eyed each man in turn. "I don't see anything that's gonna stop me from taking the lady wherever she wants to go. Bella?"

"I'm done with this for now," Bella called out from the car.

"How 'bout you two?" Ethan asked. "You done?"

Baldy glared at Hoodie, who shrugged as he backed off. "We'll just tell him they didn't have one," Hoodie said. "Or tell him it's busted. That's the truth."

The two men turned and started walking back toward their mighty Hummer. "You're about to get more than a kick in the ass," the older one said.

Ethan returned to the car, smiling. "I got mine in first." He closed the door and glanced toward the camera. "Sorry. I didn't see that coming. You didn't tell me this was hazardous duty."

"I didn't know it would be hazardous."

He glanced at the camera she was cradling in her lap. "Is it busted?"

"I don't know. I turned it off, but now I'm afraid to turn it back on. I'll leave it to the techs."

Ethan had never been so glad to pull a car away from a driveway. If it had been just him, he would have stood his ground, no problem. But he was no brawler, and Bella was no brawler's broad. "You shouldn't be going out alone on something like this."

"It sounded like just another assignment." She tugged at a wisp of hair escaped from the clip at the back of her neck. "It wasn't supposed to be like this. We arranged for an interview. We were surprised they agreed, but that seemed like a clue that there wasn't anything going on. But I think there was." She turned in her seat. "I think we got something, Ethan."

"You need a bodyguard more than a cameraman."

"I'm sorry. I really didn't—"

"Hey, nothing to be sorry about except the camera,

which was my fault. They ever send you out to that place again, give me a call." He chuckled. "Hell, who'da thought reporting the local news could be that much of a rush?"

"There's obviously a story there. The Boston affiliate might even send somebody out."

"Is that good? Would you get to stay on it?"

"We'll see." She lifted a shoulder. "Commercial dog breeding isn't regulated as strictly here as it is in, say, Massachusetts. But cruelty is cruelty."

"They're not gonna blame you for the camera, are they?"

"I hope we got some pictures. If we did..." She studied the camera for a moment and then looked up. "Would you like to come over for supper tonight?"

"What, *you* owe *me* now?" He laughed. "If we got pictures, let's call it even."

"Okay," she said quietly.

"And start over. I gotta be somewhere at six, but after that, let me take you out for supper."

"You don't think I can cook?" She gave his shoulder a light jab. "Smart girls can't cook? Is that what you think?"

"Course not. Why would I...?"

"Is it true that smart girls can't dance?"

The line rang a bell right away, but he let her wait a moment for his guilty glance. "That's no way to ask a girl to dance," she chided with a smile.

He lifted his shoulder. "Did you dance with me?"

"Should I walk away and let him wonder, or dance with him and remove all doubt? Hmm." Squinting, she tapped her chin and then looked skyward. "Walk away,

I told myself. Blow his mind. Nobody's ever done that to him before."

He smiled. "And?"

"I wasn't much of a dancer, was I? You would've remembered if I'd walked away."

"It was my turn to lead. I think that's what threw you off your game."

"I had no game," she admitted. "I was there because it was my cousin's birthday, and that was the only reason my mother agreed to let me go. That and the chance to take a picture of me in a dress."

"It was blue, wasn't it? The material felt real soft, but underneath you felt like you'd taken a bath in starch."

"Guess I was scared stiff."

He glanced, grinned, and they groaned in unison.

"Not anymore, though," she said gleefully. "Stood up to those two thugs today. Got the camera back. Asked you over for supper. I'm not even afraid of being turned down."

"I can be there by seven-thirty."

"Two-twelve."

"Can't stay that late. I'm a workin' man."

"*Apartment* two-twelve."

He grinned. "Just sayin'."

HE WAS ALSO a student. Ethan had done well in the correspondence courses he'd been allowed to take before his release from prison, and he'd been able to transfer a few of his credits toward a college degree, but now he sat uneasily in the back row of his first real class in nearly ten years. He wasn't the oldest guy in the group, and he sure as hell wasn't the dimmest bulb in the string. When they'd gone around the room introducing themselves, he'd simply given his name, mentioned his job, said he was training a mustang in his spare time. Nobody had asked him where he'd been for the past two years. He wasn't sure what his problem was, but he was uneasy with feeling uneasy. Come hell or high water, he could save himself as long as he took it easy. He was far from feeling any heat in this class, far from being in over his head.

So what was his problem?

If he was back to square one, if he was nothing unless he was easy, then where was he? *Who* was he?

That's what you're here to learn, Wolf Track.

It was going to be an interesting class. He'd tested out of all the bonehead stuff, so he was able to take a course that counted for something. An American lit class was a good bet for a guy who'd spent two years reading books like a fiend. He'd gotten the reading list ahead of time, and he'd already read everything on it, then started in on the list again. Take nothing for granted this time around, he told himself, even though his parole officer's advice was to take it easy, easy does it, *go easy on yourself.*

Hell, he'd never had any trouble going easy. Easy was no challenge at all.

It was time to try something different.

"Yeah, this is my second time with this one," he said in answer to the teacher's question about the assignment at the top of the list. "But I'm noticing some things I didn't see the first time."

"SOMETHING SURE SMELLS GOOD."

It was the right thing to say when a guy walked into the apartment of a woman who'd just cooked supper for him, but it was also true. He wanted to tell her how pretty she looked with her sleek black hair falling loose behind her shoulders, but he decided to play it safe.

He handed her a bottle in a brown paper sack and grinned when she pulled it up by the neck. "I almost went for the box, but then it takes a while if you like it cold."

She read the label. "Pre-sweetened, and with lemon. Excellent choice."

"The clerk said it was the best they had."

They shared a polite laugh. He glanced from window to window—the big one with the sofa in front, the smaller one over the table with the white cloth, two plates, one candle—and back to Bella, who was watching him, waiting for something. Not a kiss, that wasn't it. "You've fixed your place up real nice. It makes you feel good when you walk in."

"Thank you. It's California thrift shop. I love color, and I want to be comfortable."

Colors. Right. He took another look. "Earth, water and sky. You brought it all inside."

She smiled. "I hope you like chicken."

"I'm lovin' this one already."

She gave a sweeping gesture toward the table. "Sit down. It's all ready. I'll fix the tea."

"Can I help with—"

"I want you to sit." She disappeared around the corner of a partition, but she kept talking. "I was just going to have water, so this is perfect."

Ethan sat down at the pretty little table and listened to the sound of cupboard doors gently opening and closing, kitchen tools softly clinking. Home kitchen sounds, not institutional. It sounded almost musical. He wanted to be part of it. If he hadn't quit smoking he would at least have been able to light the candle.

"Guess what?" she said as she set glasses of tea on the table. "No, I won't tell you. I'll let you see for yourself later." And she was gone again.

She returned with serving dishes, one steaming, one piled with chunks of crusty bread. He was salivating.

"I hope you like cacciatore."

"Is that chicken?"

"With vegetables and sauce. Do you like sauce?"

He was ready to jump into the dish. "I'm a sauce fanatic."

She turned on her bare heel. "I forgot the—"

He caught her hand. "We're gonna ride double in this chair if you don't sit down pretty soon."

She gave him a funny look, and then she laughed, lowering her shoulders by several inches. "Matches. They're right over here."

He let her go, but he held out his hand when she came back. She laid the matches in his palm, her fingertips lingering, inviting him to curl his around them briefly, just to say thanks.

He lit the candle, and she served him his supper, candlelight dancing in her eyes. The food tasted so good he didn't want to talk. She looked so good smiling back at him across the table that he didn't want to eat. He wanted to look and taste and smell, and just be right where he was with this woman sitting across from him.

"Where'd you learn to cook like this?" he asked when they had finished their food and she finally allowed him to follow her into her neat little kitchen. "Your mom?"

"She gave me the basics. Meat, roots, corn, season with salt and pepper. In California I discovered variety."

She nodded toward the serving dish as he set it on the counter. "Sauces. Lots of fruits and vegetables. I had a roommate who showed me what to do with it all. He'd grown up with all that fresh produce. Who knew herbs and spices started out as little plants?"

"You had a guy for a roommate?"

"Two. Two girls and two guys." Bella rolled her eyes and laughed. "My mother hit the roof when she found out, but it was already a done deal. I wanted to live off campus my senior year, and rent is really crazy out there. I was carrying a full course load and waiting tables as many hours as I could get."

"Sounds like you learned how to party."

"Did you hear the part about full course load and waiting tables?" So pretty, the way she lifted one shoulder as she turned on the faucet. "It was worth it. I loved having a lot on my plate. I lapped it up."

"It shows. You've filled out nicely."

"Thank you." She slid the dinner plates under a growing mound of bubbles as she slid him a second-thought glance. "I think."

"That's what I mean. You were always thinking, but now you look pretty while you're doing it. No matter what you have to say, it's a real pleasure for me to listen."

She laughed. "Why, Ethan, that's the nicest thing you've ever said to me. Also the screwiest."

"That's what happens when I shoot straight. It sounds screwy." He reached for the serving dish. Not much left. "What should I do with this? Toss it?"

"Oh, no. That'll be soup." She took the dish and scooped the contents into a plastic bowl. "That's the Ladonna coming out in me. Don't let anything go to waste."

"You called your mother Ladonna?"

"Only when she wasn't around. Which—" she gave a tight smile "—she isn't."

"You miss her?"

"More all the time. Don't you?"

He held up his right hand and wiggled a crooked middle finger. "I broke this playing football. She helped the doctor set it. I coulda sworn she was the doctor and he was the assistant."

She nodded, gave him a funny look as though he'd said something wrong. Or screwy. But all she said was, "Doesn't look like they did a very good job."

"I took the splint off too soon. Didn't wanna miss another game."

"Were you able to play?"

"Hell, yeah. I can always play."

The smile she offered struck him as sympathetic. He was open to all kinds of feelings from her, but sympathy wasn't one of them. He'd done the damage all by himself.

"Actually, I meant do you miss *your* mom? You must've been pretty young when she left."

He looked down at his bent finger. It had angered him a time or two, that finger. Jumped out there and made him look stupid. Caused him some trouble he could have done without. "I was five when she married Logan. Seven when she left."

"Left? I thought… I guess I assumed she died."

"She was just gone one day. I don't know what happened to her after that. I hardly remember her."

"If you were seven, you must remember—"

"I was seven, and I hardly remember her. Nothing else to report. End of story." He backed up to the counter and braced his butt against it, bracing for more even though he'd said there wasn't any. So far he didn't mind the questions, partly because he didn't have many answers. And partly because this was Bella. He felt good about her, didn't mind admitting, "I guess I thought everyone knew she walked out on us."

"Let's see, if you were seven, I would've been four or five. Ladonna would've been finishing up her nurse's training. We would've been living in Grand Forks, North Dakota." She raised her brow. "Either the news didn't travel that far, or it didn't make an impression on me."

"Damn. All this time I was embarrassed for nothing." He smiled. "Been tryin' like hell not to let it show."

"And you succeeded."

"Until now." He folded his arms. "Tell you what, though, I had a fine dad."

"Have."

"Have," he acknowledged quietly.

"So, do you want to talk dads now? That's where I missed out."

Good, he thought. *Over to you.* "What happened to him?"

"Killed in a car wreck. It wasn't until I was in high school that I heard he was drunk, *and* he was with another woman. Ladonna never told me that part. I had to hear it from one of the other woman's relatives." Her eyes challenged his. *See? So?*

"Maybe it wasn't true."

"I was a baby when it happened." She reached for his arm. "Let's go sit in the living room. Show-and-tell time. What's in your wallet?" She smiled. "Do you have pictures?"

"Of what?"

"Family? Friends? We're swapping stories. Time to look at pictures." She directed him to the sofa while she rustled around with some stuff on a bookshelf. "I'll bet you haven't seen a school yearbook in a while."

"You win, darlin'. Man, this is a comfortable sofa." He looked up, smiling as she sat down with an armload of books. "California thrift shop?"

"Rapid City furniture store. My one big splurge."

"Good choice." He rubbed his hand over the butter-soft leather. A school yearbook landed on his knees. "Do me one solid. Don't quote me on that blog of yours, okay?" He grinned. "Unless I said something intelligent."

They turned pages and revisited faces, and his own warm feelings surprised him. No regrets. No desire for do-overs. They'd walked the same halls, shared some of the same friends, or relatives of friends. Each had memories the other enjoyed hearing about, because there were shared ties to a place they were beginning to enjoy being from. Sinte was part of them.

The scrapbook Bella pulled out afterward was more personal. Memories mixed in with pictures of people and places—a nice little history book. It was something he didn't have, something he'd never missed, never thought about. Saving bits of the past made no sense to him. He decided it was a female thing, and he suddenly realized his life hadn't included females in ways that might make sense to one of them.

He looked down at the picture of a little headstone sitting in the middle of the big prairie.

"We always took care of my father's grave on Memorial Day," Bella recalled. "Ladonna never said anything bad about him. Never said much about him at all unless I asked, and then it was always kind of vague, some little tidbit she plucked out of nowhere. Like she was saying, I don't have anything to say about that, but here's something you'll like."

She brightened. "He named me. My father named me Bella. I found out what it meant. Beautiful. That made me happy for a long time. And then I put it together with my mother's name, and it made me so mad that they were both dead, and I couldn't ask them whether it was an accident or some kind of comment or curse. Or maybe it's a joke." She gave him a perfunctory smile. "What do you think?"

"I think you lost me. Had me at *beautiful,* lost me at—"

Her eyes widened. "Belladonna? *Deadly poison?*"

"Oh, yeah. Interesting." He slid his hand over hers. "Anyone ever suggest you might have a tendency to *over*think?"

"No. No one ever has. But, then, these are things I've never told anyone else." She squinted a little, second-guessing him. "Are you suggesting…?"

"No." He surrendered, both hands up. Whatever it was, he wasn't. "Not at all. I'm just catchin' up here."

"You have to wonder, right? Your parents are gone, and they took so many answers with them. So you think about what you have from them, you turn it over in your mind, and you wonder what more they would have given if they'd had more time. Don't you?" She didn't seem to notice him shaking his head. "Like when I asked—you know, the way we all do—where babies come from, my mother said they come from the seed a man plants inside the woman he loves. I liked the sound of that. It took me quite a while to come up with the next question."

"How does he do that?"

"Why does she let him?" She turned her palms up, empty. He didn't dare drop any of the words that sprang to his mind. "I mean, why doesn't she just plant it herself?"

He offered a lopsided smile. "I'm gonna say *because it's man seed* was not her answer."

"You're right. It was not." Her smile was pretty indulgent. At least it was a smile. "She said the seed comes from the man a woman loves, and that love is like water and sunshine. It makes the baby grow. I liked the sound of that even better."

"It's beautiful."

"It doesn't sound screwy at all, does it? It's pure and simple, and it sounded like the straight, God's honest truth."

"Should've left it at that. I would've. I never asked." Ethan slid down and rested his head against the back of the sofa. "One day I got mad at Trace and called him a name that, you know, started with *mother,* and Logan heard me. He sat me down and told me that was about the worst thing you could call a man. Hell, I knew that. That was why I said it. But the look in Logan's eyes…"

He shook that sad look out of his head. "I never used that word again. Not around Logan. I don't remember exactly how old I was when he told me the facts, man-to-man. Simple, straightforward, but respectful, you know? It was good, coming from him."

"Your father—*biological* father—he was Indian, too, wasn't he?"

"Yeah. We had different fathers, Trace and me. She said mine was Indian. Never knew his name, but there was a picture of the two of them. I don't know where he was from, though. I kinda look like him." He chuckled. "Good-lookin' dude."

"Absolutely." Bella closed her scrapbook. "I'm glad you were with me today."

"So am I. Does that kind of stuff happen often?"

"I've been told to go away. I've had the door slammed in my face. But, no, nothing like what happened today. But that wasn't the end of the story. Did you catch me at six?"

"On TV?" He shook his head. "I was in…"

"That's right, you had to be somewhere." She glanced at the clock. "But it's just turning ten. You got pictures, Ethan. One full face and one sort of." She held her hand up to her eyebrows, shading her eyes. "But the really good part…well, you'll see for yourself," she promised as she reached for one of the remotes on the side table.

Within moments there she was on the screen, but the anchor, she said, was just teasing her story. "It'll be on at the end of this segment. It's big enough that it'll keep people in suspense for five minutes."

"You gotta be careful about going out to places like that. You know how to defend yourself?"

She lifted one shoulder as she set the remote aside. "I really do own a gun."

"You don't carry it."

"But I know how to use it." Another one of those token smiles. "And I know a few moves."

"Show me."

"Not unless I have to."

"Good move to start with. Keep your weapon a secret." He leaned closer and lowered his voice. "Wait until I make a move."

"I thought we were friends. I don't have to defend myself against friends."

"Expect the unexpected, even from friends." He took her shoulders in his hands. "A word is the only defense you'll need."

Her soft smile was a welcome sign. Her hand in his hair was a sweet surprise, its pressure drawing his head down for a meeting of smiles, mingling of breath, mixing of impressions made by moving lips and fingertips. He'd been saving this kiss for a long time, guarding it, fearing for it, thinking long and hard about the look and the mind and the heart of the woman who could take it from him. *Expect the unexpected* sounded good, but he hadn't expected Bella. He couldn't have known how good he would feel giving her an experience that had all the magic of a first kiss. He wanted to draw her closer, but he was afraid he would scare her away. Let her invite him, and let him go easy.

She lifted her arms around his neck, and he turned his head to one side, lightly taking the measure of her lush lips with his, touching and tasting, catching her breath in his mouth, tickling her mouth with his tongue. And when he felt her tremble under his hands, he drew her to him and kissed her thoroughly.

She kissed him back. She'd dreamed of this kiss long ago, made it happen a hundred ways, cooked up a thousand dreamy details—some raw, some overdone—and she'd been a believer for the very long time it had taken to become a woman. She'd held out for the hundred ways and the thousand details, and here was the first, the way of the kiss. It made her breath falter and her insides flutter. It made her reach up and lean forward, part her lips and greet his tongue. It made her a believer again.

And then, when the greeting was complete, she kept her eyes closed and licked the taste of it from her lips. "I haven't been…"

"Neither have I." He kissed her again, briefly. "Take it slow?"

"Yes," she said without thinking, and then on the other hand, "No." And that sounded almost as ridiculous as what came next. "Surprise me."

"I thought I was."

"Not yet." She'd dreamed a hundred ways times a thousand details. It would take…

He shook his head slowly, his gaze affixed to hers, and she had no idea what he was thinking as he looked at her, his hands gently kneading her shoulders. His lips came down on hers softly again, and then came the turn of his head, the touch of his tongue, the warmth of his breath and finally more kiss, good kiss, much more kiss. She opened herself up to him and welcomed the taste and the scent and the feel of him.

Then he backed off, giving her a little breathing room, thinking space. She glanced up at the clock, and broke both the kiss and the mood as she sat up straight. "Oh, no, I think we missed it!" she exclaimed, turning to the TV.

He blinked. *Damn. Who the hell cared about…?*

"No, we didn't. Here it comes."

What she was saying didn't make as much of an impression on him as the sound of her voice, the way she held her shoulders, moved her hand. Oh, he got the gist of the report. He'd been on the inside getting the scoop firsthand. Anybody could see what was going down, and hey, he *did* get a little footage. But Bella looked terrific. The two thugs looked terrible. The camera mike picked up the few words that were exchanged before the picture did a three-sixty and went to black.

"Hot damn." Ethan slapped his knee. "My first—"

"Shh, here comes the good part."

Her rich, smooth television voice was truly the good part. It was familiar but different. Even more authoritative than usual. The raid that had taken place soon after her producer called the sheriff department was good, too, but Ethan was enchanted by the sound of her voice, the way it gave weight to the words and import to the story.

"It was a puppy mill," she told him. "I don't know why the woman said we could go out there and talk to her husband. She'll probably get in more trouble with him than with the law. The sheriff was able to get a warrant and get past the gate before they could cover up all the—" She pointed to Baldy and Hoodie walking across the screen in handcuffs. "Look. Serves them right. I guess those two tried to resist. The Moshers went quietly and made bail, but the two flunkies are still guests of the county."

"Who took these pictures? They didn't send you back out there, did they?"

"No, just John Carney, the cameraman."

"The real cameraman?"

"You're the real cameraman on this one, Ethan. You got the goods."

"I was about to, but then the news came on." They exchanged warm smiles. "That's really something, Bella. You uncovered a puppy mill. Where they…manufacture a lot of puppies?"

"It's like factory farming for dogs. We're running a follow-up tomorrow with a warning that it gets graphic. People from out of state answer ads for puppies, they don't realize what they're—"

"You and John?"

She frowned. "Me and John?"

"Doing the follow-up."

She smiled. Was he jealous? "I wanted to take you, but I really wasn't supposed to let you run the camera."

"What were you supposed to do?"

"I was supposed to get an interview. I would have asked my questions from behind the camera. Budgets are tight in the news business these days. But, Ethan, this was too good. This is really going to make a difference, at least for those poor dogs. They've all been rescued by the Humane Society."

He touched her arm. "You could've gotten hurt. You shouldn't be going out on stories like that alone."

"Hey." She laid her hand over his. "It's almost never like that. It's not a dangerous job. Taming a wild horse, that's a dangerous job."

"What's in the follow-up?"

"They got some pictures of lots of skinny animals crowded into cages stacked in filthy, crumbling shacks. And that isn't the half of it, Ethan. Yes, those bitches are used as puppy factories. It'll have to be edited, but people will get the idea. And I'll be interviewing the sheriff and maybe talking with the affiliate that put us on to the story." She was glowing. "It's my story. And

I probably wouldn't've gotten any video if you hadn't been there."

"You could've gotten hurt."

"Okay, I could've gotten hurt." She squeezed his hand. "But I didn't."

He leaned in for a kiss, prefaced with a whispered, "I'm glad."

CHAPTER FIVE

ETHAN'S KISSES TOOK Bella out of her head. Her whole being rushed to be where he touched her, and there were no loose ends. His kiss went on forever, and his mouth made hers sing without sound. His hand tucked under her shirt made her skin tingle from the middle of her back to her bare toes. All she had to do was feel the all-over excitement. It didn't matter whether he felt it, too. He did—she could feel it where their bellies met—but that was just part of the process. She didn't have to figure anything out or plan the next step. This was happening. She was unfolding, stretching out and connecting up, and it felt right. Where one kiss ended another began.

Until it didn't.

But he still held her and slid his fingertips lightly over her skin, and looked into her eyes like the besotted schoolboy he never was. She wondered how she looked to him. Like she would follow him anywhere? Because she would. No words required. All he had to do was lead the way.

He pushed a strand of hair back from her face and gave a reflective smile. "I can't stay tonight."

She bit back, *No one asked you to,* in favor of a matching smile. "It's okay."

"No, it isn't. You don't know me, Bella. And the thing is…" He withdrew his hand, pulled her shirt down in back as though he'd disturbed something on a shelf. "I'm ready to jump out of my skin right now, and that's not the way I want this to go."

"This what?"

"This…you and me. I didn't expect…"

"What didn't you expect? That I could give you—" she gave him a bold below-the-belt glance "—that?"

"Honey, I've been out of circulation long enough that even the slightest smell of a woman makes me so hard it hurts." He kissed her gently and touched his forehead to hers. "But that's not what I want. Not with you. Not tonight."

She kissed him back, a quick it's-fine-with-me kiss, and then freed herself. It really *was* fine.

"Can I ask you something?" she said quickly. Because asking questions was something she knew how to do. "The woman you went to jail for… Have you seen her since you got out?"

"Last time I saw her she was on the witness stand. Man, that was…" He gave a dry chuckle and shook his head. "And I didn't go to prison for her or because of her or anything like that. It was me. I was stupid."

"She said you drove off and left her after she told you to take her home and gave you the keys to her daddy's car." She glanced up at him. "That's what I read."

"She went off with somebody else and left me with the car." He leaned back and searched for the story on the ceiling. "We went to a party at somebody's cabin up in the hills. Craziest party I've ever been to, and that's just the part I remember. I didn't know anything about her father—didn't even know who he was—but it ended up that I had the car and not the girl whose daddy owned it. And the rest was my word against everyone else's."

"She's been in the news since. Her father's still try-ing to cover for her."

"She's a live wire, that woman. If you're lookin' for trouble, she can help you find it."

"Were you?"

"I was chasin' my tail back then." He reached for the straw hat he'd set on the side table, planted his elbows on his knees and toyed with the hat brim. "Tried play-ing football for South Dakota State, but they wanted me to take classes at the same time."

"Imagine that." Bella smiled even though he wasn't looking.

"Tried the army. I was fine with that for a while, but then I, um…" He shook his head. "Like I said, I'm not much of a hunter. Not with a gun, anyway. But, yeah, I was a lone wolf."

"Caught in a trap?"

"Nope." He glanced up, gave a self-effacing smile. "Paws on the ground, nose in the air, eyes wide open, nobody can touch this lobo. I got nobody to blame but myself."

"You sound like a totally rehabbed man."

He gave a nod and a wink. "One day at a time, kiddo."

"Kiddo?" She punched his arm. "I guess that ex-plains why you can't stay."

"Hey, I don't call just anybody that." He laughed. "Okay, I don't call anybody that. I don't know where it came from."

"It goes nicely with that sexy wink."

"Now I'm totally deflated." He leaned over, took her chin in hand and kissed her, fast and firm. "I mean that, Bella. And this." He laid his hand on her cheek and kissed her again. Another kiss followed, and then another, each lingering a little longer than the last.

"Do you *want* to stay?" she whispered when he straightened, gradually separating himself from her.

"Absolutely." He clapped his hat on his head and pushed off, hands on his knees. "I need to get back to Square One."

"There's something to be said for showing up where you're expected." She stood, too. This close, this enclosed, she was keenly aware of his height and his powerful build. Ordinarily she would have stepped back, required space. But with Ethan, this close was not close enough.

"And it's not that hard," he was saying.

"Who knew?" Silly comment. Overused filler. Bella wasn't fond of filler.

"You did. Some people have to learn these things the hard way." He took a piece of her hair between two fingers and let it slide through until his hand reached her shoulder. "Believe it or not, what's happening between us is new for me." Gently he squeezed her shoulder. "Like I picked up an egg, and something soft and sweet hatched in my hand. I don't know what it is, but I damn sure want the chance to find out."

"You didn't have a female judge, did you?" She smiled. "Of course not. A line like that would've gotten you off with time served."

He laughed. "Time to reel in my lines and hit the road." He took a step in that direction, and then had a second thought. "If I can get the day off, can I take you out on Saturday?"

"This Saturday?"

He nodded, his eyes bright with promise. "You like rodeo?"

Not particularly. "Is your brother riding?"

"Yeah, and it's been a while since I've seen him ride. He's doin' real good. Heard from him last week. He has a new girlfriend." He smiled. "Sounds pretty serious."

"The marrying kind of serious?"

"I wouldn't be surprised." He shoved his hands in the front pockets of his jeans. "So how 'bout it? You date real cowboys?"

"Not so far." She looked at him quizzically. "Funny. I never thought of you as a cowboy."

"How *did* you think of me?"

"I tried not to. You made no sense to me. Or *for* me. But look at you now. You've got the boots, the Wrangler jeans, the hat." She jerked her chin, pursed her lips in the general upward direction. "That hat looks as though it could tell some campfire stories."

Ethan snatched it off his head and turned it over in his hands, as though he hadn't seen it in a while. "Logan gave me this hat, long time ago. Thought of switching to outlaw black, but I'm pretty attached to this hat."

"I never thought of you as an outlaw, either." She folded her arms. "What time Saturday?"

"We'd have to leave before daylight, drive down to Nebraska. It's a midday show."

"If you can get time off."

"I'll get the time off if I get back on time tonight. Part of my retraining program." He tapped her arm with his hat. "You're keeping me in suspense here, woman. My ego ain't what it used to be. But I'll tell you what, I know how to get the most out of a twenty-four-hour pass. After the rodeo, I'll take you dancing."

"Oh, that's a real incentive. You know how long I've avoided dancing?" He cocked an eyebrow, and she nodded. "Yes. That long."

"The wait is finally over, baby. Wolf Track is back."

She laughed. "So much for a bruised ego."

IT TOOK A little over seven hours to get to the rodeo on Saturday. Seven short hours. The road was empty, the sun rose in a clear sky, and the conversation was packed with upbeat memories and down-home anecdotes. Bella had the local history, and Ethan's curiosity knew no bounds. She didn't mind letting him steer. It was his pickup after all. His party. He'd trusted her with enough truth to test her acceptance, and she'd passed. It was the kind of test a good reporter handled well. She was glad he wasn't in this thing—*what's happening between us,* he'd called it—for anything more than dinner and a show. No bed-and-breakfast. That was a good thing, and she owed him props for good sense. She really did.

They met Trace and his beautiful blonde lady behind the stock pens when they got to the rodeo grounds. The first moments were all about the brothers, all back-slapping and inside joking. No matter where the years had taken them, they were close at the roots. Bella and the blonde exchanged smiles as the camaraderie spilled over.

"You remember Bella Primeaux?" Ethan asked Trace.

Trace offered an eager handshake. "I remember Ladonna Primeaux. The nurse?"

"My mother. I take it you broke some bones."

"Nothing major. Got carried out of the Sinte rodeo arena once or twice as a kid."

"He's got a hard head," Ethan said.

"Runs in the family. But don't tell my—" Trace reached for the stunning beauty he'd brought with him "—special lady." He introduced Skyler Quinn, who asked Bella the inevitable question about having met before.

"You get Rapid City TV stations on the other side of the Hills?" Ethan asked. He turned to Bella. "Easy for me to keep a low profile around you. I'm just the guy with that TV reporter."

"I know what you mean. I'm the guy with the Dairy Princess." Trace laughed at Skyler for groaning. "It's true," he said. "It's a woman's world. Guys were put on earth to carry the water."

"Well, break out the canteen, honey. The special ladies need to rinse off all that soft soap." Skyler winked at Bella before turning to Ethan. "Trace tells me you're training a horse for the Mustang Sally competition."

"I am." Ethan adjusted his hat. "Hear you and Trace are entered up, too."

"Just Skyler," Trace said. "I'm the coach. The only horse I'm entered on is that little black." He gave an over-the-shoulder nod toward the pen at his back. Bella glanced politely toward the fence. "Tomcat, he's called. Good match for me. High roller. He can get a little snaky, but we'll rack up the points." Trace tapped Ethan's arm with a loose fist. "Your big brother's headed for the finals again. Mark your calendar."

"I won't miss it this time," Ethan said.

"Damn straight you won't." Trace reached *up* to plant his hand on his *little* brother's shoulder. "So, you like your job? Start your classes yet?"

"Yeah, I do and I did." Ethan clapped his hands and

rubbed them together, clearly eager to move on. "Let's get something to eat."

"Nothing for me until after I ride." Trace turned to Skyler. "You hungry?"

"You know me. I can eat anytime," she said.

"Right." The two of them exchanged an intimate glance. Yes, he knew her. "But my little brother needs food now, and I think I know just the place."

Ethan stepped back. "You can just point us in the right direction. Then we'll meet you somewhere later."

"Not so fast," Skyler said as she reached for Bella's hand. "We've got some getting acquainted to do." She met Ethan's gaze. "And some catching up."

Ethan tipped his hat, offering Skyler a cowboy salute. "Thank you, ma'am."

"You've had a long drive," Skyler told him.

"Not quite as long as yours," he said. "Did you come down from Newcastle?"

"I live closer to Gilette," Skyler said. Wyoming was big territory, small town, which meant that mileage was not an issue. "Trace has been helping me out with the ranch, and I've been helping him ride like nobody's watching." She caught Trace's eye and smiled lovingly. "Except me."

"Why don't Bella and I go get something to eat while you two get a room?" Ethan teased.

"Mind your manners, kid." Trace gave Ethan a backhanded slap on the chest. "She's determined to keep me off crutches."

"Good luck with that, Skyler. My brother enjoys the agony of victory."

"It sounds as though you've both been to the nurse's office," Bella said.

"Emergency services only. The mark of a real cow-boy," Ethan assured her.

Trace tapped his brother's arm. "Let's ride. I'm on a tight schedule here."

"I parked my pickup—"

"Way the hell on the other side of the arena. Come on, kids."

Trace loaded the foursome into his shiny white club cab pickup, drove a few blocks and pulled up in front of a restaurant called Better Than Your Mama's Spaghetti. He glanced at each of his passengers in turn. "What do you all think?"

Both women approved, Bella saying that her mother never made spaghetti and Skyler that her mother wouldn't let her eat it.

"Works for me," Ethan said.

"I know how to fill up that hollow leg of yours," Trace told him. "I've eaten here a few times. The spaghetti can't hold a candle to mine, but it's pretty damn good."

"Wait a minute," Skyler said. "Didn't you tell me you were a lousy cook?"

"I forgot to mention the three exceptions." Trace ticked them off, starting on his thumb. "Enhanced pea-nut butter sandwiches, everything-goes-into-it soup, and excellent spaghetti."

"He's right," Ethan said as he followed Bella out of the cramped backseat of the pickup and onto the side-walk. "Trace perfected all three—when he wasn't keep-ing me in line. Logan's right-hand man. Riding herd on me was a two-man job."

"Two men and a bottomless pot of spaghetti," Trace said. "Took a little time to get Logan on board the spa-ghetti train. Devoted to his macaroni, that guy."

"That's the way he is. Loyal to the end and then some." Ethan shook his head. "Loyalty is good for filling graveyards." He glanced at his brother. "I think I read that somewhere."

"He's been there for you, Ethan."

Ethan nodded.

"And now he's found a woman who deserves his loyalty. Our mother—"

"I know all about our mother. Far as I'm concerned, a smart man doesn't put himself out there like that."

Bella took it all in. Trace was a rider; Ethan was a fighter. She wondered whether these were two more categories—*two kinds of people in this world,* Ladonna used to say—that deserved their own pages in her mental notebook. You found your niche at your first rodeo, and for the rest of your life you had it all figured out.

She slid quietly into a dark corner booth along the front wall, and Ethan slid in beside her. There were menus to be studied and water to be sipped, but the conversation was not over. Not until big brother said it was over.

"Cut Logan some slack," Trace instructed. "Every man gets one free pass on being a fool for love. Who was it that said 'Fool me once, shame on you. Fool me twice, you can't get fooled again'?"

"Somebody who got the quote wrong," Bella injected.

"Exactly." Trace cocked a finger and fired her a point. "But it's no shame to love somebody. Matter of fact, it's a shame if you don't. Maybe one quote doesn't fit all."

Ethan checked the front of the menu again. "Better than your mama's, huh?"

"She never knew what was good for her, little brother. You gotta pity her a little bit for her loss."

"I don't even like to think about her," Ethan said as he turned back to the list of entrées. "Why don't they turn a light on in here?"

Trace reached up and pulled the cord for the blinds, shedding considerable light. "I know what you mean."

He *thought* he did—Ethan would give his brother that much credit. And more. Hell, any credit to be had, Trace deserved it. He was a good man. He was Logan's true son in every way but DNA. If Trace didn't like to think about their mother, it was because of what she'd put him through, the hurt she'd put on him, the bad stuff Ethan didn't remember. Maybe he should be able to remember some of it, but he didn't. And the reason he didn't—he was just speculating here—was that he was like her, created in her image, *her* right-hand man. He shared in her faults. He—not Trace—was their mother's creature.

"So what's on the program?" Ethan asked. "Besides the next world-champion bareback rider."

"You talkin' to me?" Trace's De Niro was actually halfway credible. He drew a folded piece of paper from his breast pocket, set just below his sponsor's stitched-on logo, and tossed it on the table.

"Cowboy poker," Ethan announced as he scanned the program. "Thought they'd stopped doing that."

"You don't see it around here much. Hard to find takers after what happened down in San Angelo."

"What happened?" Skyler asked.

"What's cowboy poker?" was Bella's question.

"Some woman wasn't playing with a full deck, and she got her watermelon thumped," Trace said.

Bella and Skyler exchanged a look. "Colorful," Skyler said. "You mean she was—"

"I'm sorry, darlin'." Trace put his arm around her. "But there are some games women should not be playing."

"—*pregnant?*" Skyler's eyes widened.

"I picked the wrong fruit." Trace pulled her head to his shoulder. "Rest your worried melon right here, hon. No animals or unborn children were harmed. Some woman got kicked in the head was all." He turned to Bella. "They take four volunteers from the audience, sit them down at a card table in the middle of the arena, deal a hand and turn out one of the livelier bulls. Last player to leave his seat wins the pot. Which is what tonight?" He nodded at the paper in Ethan's hand. "Five hundred bucks?"

"That's what it says."

"You're right," Skyler said. "That's not a game for women. We're way too smart."

"How about five hundred pairs of shoes?"

She lifted one shoulder. "That might be different."

"Have you checked out the night spots?" Ethan asked Trace. "Bella's dying to go dancing with me."

"The Killer Hayseeds are playing at a place near the arena. I hear they're pretty good."

Ethan grinned at Bella. "What do you think?"

"I think Killer Hayseeds sounds like the perfect follow-up to cowboy poker."

Ethan turned his grin on his brother. "We're in."

SKYLER AND BELLA watched the Grand Entry from seats Trace had chosen for their view of the arena and the bucking chutes. His event came first, and he'd invited Ethan to help him set his rigging. Ethan seemed pleased, almost touched, or as close to touched as Bella had seen him. From her convenient perch she watched the activity behind the chutes, watched the two brothers confer over the equipment, and exchange words and handshakes with other cowboys.

The proceedings became nothing short of operating-room serious when Tomcat was loaded into the chute. Ethan took charge of setting the rigging and making sure his brother's glove was sufficiently rosined and his grip was solid. When Trace nodded for the gate to be opened, Ethan turned cheerleader. Bella half expected him to tumble into the empty bucking chute.

Trace did his fans proud. Tomcat rolled and pitched, twisted and turned, but Trace was unshakable. His score put him on top in the standings, and when he joined them in the stands, Skyler's kiss apparently put him on top of the world.

"Where's Ethan?" Bella asked.

Trace turned to look behind him, then turned back, frowning. "Snack bar, probably. Like I said, hollow leg. At least I don't have to buy his ice cream anymore." He grinned as he took his seat. "You got any chores you want done, Bella, you can pay him in spaghetti and ice cream."

"He helped me with a dangerous assignment the other day, and he didn't charge me anything."

"Oh, yeah, one other form of payment works." Trace draped his arm around Skyler's shoulders and settled in. "He can't resist an adrenaline rush. What kind of danger did you treat him to?"

"He got to hold the camera," she said, and then she related the puppy-mill story.

"Those two were lucky Ethan was in a generous…" Trace suddenly leaned forward and peered toward the far end of the arena. "What the hell?"

"What is it?" Skyler wanted to know.

"Little surprise in store," Trace said with a chuckle, and then he sat back and tugged at the front of his hat brim. "I sure hope these Killer Hayseeds turn out to be as good as they say. Sounds like something you might name a bull, huh? You like country music, Bella?"

"It's okay." She hadn't figured out what Trace was looking at, but she was working on it. Two rodeo clowns were pulling a cart loaded with a plastic patio table and four chairs into the arena. "Is it halftime already?" she wondered.

"Wrong sport," Trace said. "We don't go for a lot of downtime around here. This is what you call your—"

"Audience participation time," the announcer said. "Please welcome our four volunteer gamblers, in for a round of cowboy poker!"

It was Bella's turn to lean forward. "That's Ethan."

Trace drew a deep breath. "Yep."

"Is he helping with the… He's sitting down at the table."

"And that's the surprise."

"Not really," Skyler said. "He's your brother."

"You won't catch me messin' with bulls, darlin'."

"Has he done this before?" Bella asked.

"I doubt it."

A gate slammed, and a couple of levers clanked in the chute area below. Bella looked down and saw white horns, chocolate hide, no daylight on either side of the animal crammed into the chute. It moved, and the whole enclosure rattled.

She eyed the arena. The clowns in their droopy over-alls and red suspenders were setting up the table for the four players. A moment later Ethan started dealing cards.

"The last man to remain seated wins the pot," the announcer said. "Five hundred dollars, winner take all. You ready for Ace High, boys?"

One of the men waved.

"I hope your hard head runs in the family," Skyler said.

The gate opened, the bull stepped out, and the game was on.

"This is crazy," Bella said quietly.

"I'm getting used to it," Skyler said.

The bull seemed to have eyes only for the smaller of the two clowns, who was jumping up and down like a string puppet. "Every bull wants a piece of Jackson," Trace said. "He's the best in the business."

The big brown bull lowered his head and shoveled the bullfighter clown out of the way.

"But so is Ace High."

"He's a bull," Bella said without taking her eyes off the action. "Bulls don't do business."

With a quick about-face, Ace High took a run at the closest player's hand. Cards flew, two chairs went down, and two cowboys scrambled in two directions.

Trace laughed. Ethan was still sitting there within spearing distance of a pair of horns, and his brother was laughing. "Forget the cards, bro. Save the jewels." He grinned at Skyler. "Hell, that's what I'd do."

On his next pass the bull took out the table, along with the third cowboy. Ethan was the last man seated. He stood to claim victory just as the big beast swung around, lowered his head and flew across the arena like a cannon ball, sweeping him ass over sawed-off horns.

Skyler and Bella shot out of their seats. The rodeo

clown darted toward the bull as Ethan rolled out of its way and got to his feet. He gave his head a quick shake, recovered his hat and greeted the announcement that he'd won with a two-finger salute.

Trace laughed, slapped both his thighs and gave a victory whistle as he rose to his feet.

But then he shook his head and muttered, "Crazy kid," as he headed for the aisle. He turned and motioned to the women. "Let's go take inventory, see if he's all there."

"He's missing something upstairs," Bella said under her breath.

They met Ethan at the pay window. He'd already pocketed his winnings and was grinning to beat the band.

"Any blood?" Trace called out.

Ethan bent his arm and showed off a skinned elbow.

"Child's play." Trace turned a fake gut jab into a hearty handshake. "You coulda warned me, bro."

"And spoil my entrance?" Ethan shoved his hands into the pockets of his jeans, still grinning like a triumphant teenager. "Hey, remember when we entered the wild horse race at the Standing Rock Rodeo? This was like that. The kind of thing you do on the spur of the moment. You give it too much thought, you're gonna back out."

"You were about twelve, and I was—"

"Half as old as you are now, and what are you doing for a living?" Ethan tugged at his hat brim. "I rest my case, big brother. I know you won more than I did today, but I'm ridin' just as high as you are. Supper's on me."

"Supper? You just ate." Trace glanced at Bella as he

slapped Ethan's gut with the back of his hand. "Can't fill him up, can't put any weight on him."

"I can wait a little while," Ethan said, all innocence. "Is there any dancing anywhere this time of day? Bella made me promise to dance with her."

"He's lying," Bella told Trace with a smile. "Dancing is the last thing I'd want him to promise me."

"What, then?" Ethan slipped his arm around her. "Make a wish, darlin'. I've got a pocketful of found money and I'm ready to spend it all on you."

Bella glanced at Skyler.

"Our first date I let Trace coax me onto a Ferris wheel. I'm afraid of heights." Skyler smiled. "Sometimes a little crazy doesn't hurt."

"I know where there's an old-fashioned jukebox," Trace said. "Take my mind off the final go-round."

The little hole-in-the-wall Trace took them to was enjoying some unusual late-afternoon business, thanks to the rodeo. Riders and fans mingled at the bar, traded change for tunes, and toasted winners and losers alike. Trace and Ethan made the most of the party atmosphere. They traded taunts and dance partners, told stories on each other and reveled in the rediscovery of each other's company. It couldn't last the way it once had, but that only made the minutes count more.

At least it did for Ethan. Not that he'd ever say anything that sappy, but he could tell that Trace knew. Trace always knew how Ethan felt, even if he didn't know exactly why. Didn't matter. They might be two very different people, but they were brothers.

And Ethan knew how Trace felt about Skyler. He was glad to see that lovesick look in his brother's eyes. Trace would make a great family man—hell, he'd looked after his younger brother like some papa grizzly—and if he'd chosen Skyler, he'd chosen well. He always chose well.

Ethan nodded as Trace flashed him a thumbs-up across the dance floor. He was a mind reader, that guy. He could always tell when Ethan's head was totally in the game. The message was clear. *You're doin' good, little brother.*

Ethan leaned back and smiled at the lovely woman in his arms. "Did your mama teach you to dance?"

"Obviously nobody did," Bella said. "And my partners generally excuse themselves after one dance."

"Guess your previous partners were mostly tenderfeet. Or maybe they expected to lead."

"They should've said so." She laughed. "Okay, yes, my mother taught me to dance. 'In case you ever have to,' she said. I also know how to get out of a headlock or a moving car *if I ever have to.*"

"Relax and follow me." He drew her close and pressed his cheek against her sleek hair. "All I wanna do is hold you. I won't be giving you a score." He could feel the effort it took for her to relax, but she did. A wave of release fell slowly from her shoulders, and she was finally pliable. "There. Now we're dancing."

"We are?"

"We are."

She rested her cheek on his shoulder, and after a moment she whispered, "I like dancing."

It was a start. Ethan hated to cut it short, but now that he'd come back down to earth, he had to follow through with his plan. One day off was all he had, and he was not going to blow the trust he'd earned at Square One. He couldn't stay to watch his brother take the final round in his event, but Skyler exchanged cell phone numbers with Bella and promised to call no matter how things went.

Trace would do well. He always did.

"Why did you do that poker thing?" Bella asked Ethan after they'd been on the road awhile. He was surprised she'd waited this long. They were only a few miles from the state line.

And there was only one honest answer.

"For the hell of it."

"How many times do you get to be a fool for fun?"

"What do you mean? I came away with five hundred dollars. How does that make me a…" He glanced at her and chuckled. "Okay, but it was fun to watch, wasn't it?"

"It was not."

"I heard you yelling for me."

"I never yell."

"Ha. You called my name."

"The same way I called my dog's name when she was about to get hit by a car." She folded her arms. "The dog had sense enough to move."

"You have a dog?"

"I had one when I was a kid. She was smart about cars." She turned her face to the side window. "But men with guns, not so much. She was killed by a hunter."

Ethan felt a chill crawl down his back. "A hunter?"

"My uncle used to take her hunting. I'm the one who should have had more sense. I shouldn't have let her go." She turned to him again. "Do you hunt?"

"Never have." He stared hard into the headlight path. "Never have."

"Three men in the house and you didn't turn out to be a hunter? What kind of an Indian are you, Ethan?"

"Wish I knew." Much better topic. "Hell, I don't much

care who the guy was who, uh, planted the seed, but I wish I knew where he came from. You know, who his people are, whether they're hunters. Logan claimed me and gave me his name, but I can't claim his tribe. *Your* tribe." He flashed her a quick grin. "I want a tribe, hey."

"Hey." Bella smiled. "There's the Tribal rolls way and the Indian family way. You're in the family way."

He gave her an incredulous look, and they both laughed.

"Logan's been a good father, hasn't he?"

"The best."

"You and Logan have nothing but good to say about each other. It's none of my business, but I'll ask anyway."

"Because you're in the business of asking questions."

"Can't help myself, I guess." She cleared her throat. "Why are you keeping your distance?"

"It's not *my* distance, it's…" He lifted his shoulder. "Space. I guess."

"You've got it." She gestured toward the Welcome sign as they flew past. "South Dakota has a good supply of space."

He let the hum of the pickup motor fill theirs. She was asking him a serious question, one he knew he'd created in Logan's mind. One that troubled his own.

"He was there during the trial," Ethan said quietly. "I couldn't look at him. I didn't want him to have to hear his name, the name he'd given me…"

It was a name that had fit him well. He never had to explain it the way Trace did. Ethan looked like a Wolf Track. The first time he'd written his name on a school paper, he felt like he was somebody. A boy with a man's name.

He'd wanted to do the name justice, but so far he'd come up short.

"It all seemed pretty unreal. I didn't take it too seriously. It was a party. A big steam-blowin' three-day bash. No one cared who anyone else was. I couldn't believe I'd be found guilty, couldn't believe I'd go to prison over something so crazy." He shook his head. "I didn't believe it until I heard those doors shut and lock behind me.

"And then Logan came to see me there. He never said anything one way or the other about what I'd done. He talked about anything but that. I couldn't let him keep coming to that place, getting locked down with me. I took him off my visitors list." He spared her a glance. "It was the least I could do, you know? Spare him that."

She nodded. "How did you cope with being locked away for so long?"

"I went home in my mind."

"But you haven't gone home since you got out. You haven't told Logan any of this, have you?"

He shook his head again. "I will. Soon." He gave her a lopsided smile. "Not that it's any of your business."

"I have a confession to make."

"Careful," he warned.

"No, I do. I've read everything I could find about your case. Police reports, court transcripts, newspaper reports. Anybody else's car, there's no way you would've spent two years behind bars."

"It wasn't about the car," he reminded her. "It was about the girl."

"Who came with the car."

"The car came with her."

"And they both belonged to Senator Garth, who's known for throwing his weight around."

"He's got plenty to throw." He reached for her hand. "Listen, Bella, it's over now. I came through okay. At least I think I'm okay. If you notice any screws loose, don't try to fix me yourself. Just walk away." He squeezed her hand. "Okay?"

"Walk away from what?"

"From trouble you don't need."

CHAPTER SIX

HE WALKED BELLA upstairs to her apartment and waited without comment while she unlocked her door. But rather than turn to him, she pushed the door open and stepped inside.

From the scenes he'd watched and the pages he'd read, this wasn't the way your average, ordinary date was supposed to go.

He braced his forearm high on the door frame, just to show that he was cool right where he was. "How about a good-night kiss?"

She turned to him and gave him a not-for-prime-time look. "I'm not going anywhere. Are you?"

"It's after midnight." Which was prime time for old habits, but he'd knocked himself out to get his date home at a reasonable time.

"You don't get a full day off?" She moved in on him now. "You might be a little reckless, but I don't see any loose screws. And if you have any, well…" She touched his chest with tellingly tentative fingertips. "Look at me, Ethan. I'm not walking away."

"This is your place. Tell me to go now, and I will." His arm came away from the door frame, but it would have been unfair to touch her before he had her answer in words. "If I stay, we're going to make love."

"I know." She reached for his hand, drew him inside

and closed the door behind him. "That's the kind of kiss I want. The let's-get-it-on kind."

"That's not what I said."

He took her face in his hands and kissed her gently, the approach of an unassuming supplicant. She lifted her chin, granting more access. He took her in his arms, kissed her hungrily, the approach of a hopeful guest. She slid her arms around his back and stood on tiptoe so she could serve him fully with ample lips and searching tongue. He drew a deep breath, replete with her heady scent, and he took in the taste of her, the welcome-to-me comeback from her mouth.

It was almost too much for an appetizer, but not enough, not nearly enough, to meet his needs. He touched his forehead to hers, eyes closed, hopes high.

"I said we'd make love if I stayed. Will you do that with me?"

"You'll have to show me how," she whispered.

He lifted his head. "You're—"

"Not a virgin, no. I've had sex." No more whispering. "I've never made love. I don't *think* I have." Her smile seemed apologetic. "I hope I haven't."

"You'd know." He smiled. If he knew Bella, she'd done some reading, too. "For once, you won't have to think." He kissed her with absolute purpose. She wanted him, whatever having him would mean. And she couldn't help speculating.

He chuckled. "I know what you're doing, darlin'. I can hear it. Stop thinking."

She lifted her chin and smiled. "Make me."

He made her take him to her bed without further discussion. By the light from the hall he was able to get his bearings. The fat candle and the book of matches on her dresser beckoned. He struck a match, touched it to the blackened wick and blew out the match flame as the hall light went out.

Good. He wanted to feel her, to be felt by her, but he didn't want her to see too much. Not this time. He couldn't be sure what she would think if she put the feel of him together with the look of him in the light.

He turned and found her seated in a chair, struggling with one of her new boots. He took the heel in hand and stripped it off, followed by its mate. His own worn boots came off with an easy swipe of the hand. She stood quickly and unsnapped her jeans, as though she was afraid any dithering might bring on doubt. His doubt or hers, it didn't matter. He would banish it. He stepped in, took the bottom of her shirt in hand and peeled it over her head. Her hands were momentarily out of the picture, just the way he wanted them. For now.

He knelt before her, slid her zipper down slowly, tucked his hands into the open vee and spread the fabric wide. She wore a cotton bikini. He pressed his smile to her belly, and rubbed his lips back and forth over her soft skin. Her splayed fingers crept into his hair. He felt a slight trembling in her hands. He pushed jeans and bikini over her hips, and drew his hands down her legs. When he reached her ankles he lifted each one in turn, and she stepped out of her pants.

He skinned his shirt over his head, picked her straight up and stepped over to the bed. Then he kissed the top of each of her breasts, just because they were there, peeking over the cups of her bra.

He looked up. "You have condoms?"

"I said I've had sex. It's been quite a while, though, so...no."

"Yeah, me, too. But I have condoms." He let her slide along his body until they were face-to-face. "Hope they haven't expired."

Neither of them was in a laughing mood. He lowered her to the bed, and he hovered over her, kissing everything he could get his lips on without pouncing on her. He would go slow and take pleasure from giving her pleasure. He was almost certain he could do that. Take it slow. Give pleasure. Make love.

Her bra was fine and thin, perfect fabric for teasing nipples into tight beads while he rocked his hips against hers and coaxed her thighs apart. He took one nipple in his mouth and made the fine thin fabric wet, then pulled the strap over her shoulder, licked and suckled the tight bead until he could almost taste nourishment.

"Let me take it off," she pleaded, as though she'd outgrown the last bit of her clothing and it hurt to have it on.

He fully understood.

"Let me." He blew on her wet nipple as he reached under her and pinched the hook from the eye. She shivered.

"Is that good?"

She nodded.

He moved over her other nipple and treated it to the same mouth massaging and tongue lashing and pulling out of stops its twin had received. She called his name or, rather, moaned it, and the sound slithered into his ear and plunged straight for his groin. He propped himself on his elbows, used his hips to pry her thighs even farther apart and pressed his straining penis tight into the crevasse he'd created. Tight, but not too hard. Not too fast. No rush.

She thrust her hands into his jeans and grabbed his

cowboy ass. Tough enough to break a knife blade, tender enough to bear the marks from her fingernails for days. Damn, it hurt so good.

"Take these off," she demanded.

"When I'm ready."

He slid down and kissed her midriff, farther down and kissed her belly, still farther and kissed the juncture of her thighs, and heard her breath catch and felt her suck everything in and hold every bit of herself at bay.

"I'm not ready," she whispered.

"Better than latex," he said, but he took her at her word and traced her slippery folds with a gentle finger as he moved over her. "Take my billfold out of my back pocket whenever you *are* ready." He nuzzled her neck and suckled her earlobe as he slipped his finger inside her. She gasped. "And then you can have my pants."

With his help she did what she was told, but he would not take his hand from her until she had come to the edge of wildness and given in. She started to shudder, and he would not let her stop, not without him deep inside, taking him deeper and making the wildness grow and scream and sing and burst open and pierce the dark with a shower of sparks.

SHE LAY BESIDE him quietly for long moments, enjoying the freedom to touch him anywhere she felt like it. And she felt like touching him everywhere. He was a beautiful man, and she took pleasure in his masculine physicality. She wasn't going to ask him whether the stories about prisoners beefing themselves up were true, but clearly he had taken care of his body. One day maybe he would tell her about the time he'd spent there, and maybe there would be some things she didn't want to hear. But she wanted to be the one he confided in. She wanted him to feel free, the way she felt free with him at this moment. Was that the effect of lovemaking? Trust and a sense of belonging?

No, she hadn't made love before. But now she had.

"Trace asked whether you'd started your classes," she said as she turned to him, knowing he was awake. He'd been touching her, too. "What kind of classes?"

"College classes. Right now I'm taking American lit and History of the American West. Thought I'd stick close to home this term."

She pushed up on her elbow and propped her head on her hand. "Are you just starting out?"

"Nope. I have a few credits in my jacket."

"Your jacket?"

"My record." He laid his hand on her shoulder and rubbed it back and forth. "I've got all kinds of records. My college record is the best one. I'm like you. Straight As."

"I didn't get straight As. I got some Bs." She rolled to her back and grinned at the shadow the flickering candle threw on the ceiling. "Three."

He chuckled. "You set a pretty high bar."

"I did not. You did, with your straight As. I don't like contests. Never did."

"You don't like to lose."

"Who does?"

"Admit it. You liked it all over when I won that poker game."

"Don't be silly." She turned to him again. "Okay, I did. But mainly because the bull hadn't broken your body into a whole bunch of pitiful pieces." She laid her hand on his smooth chest. "I like your body just the way it is."

"Even with the ink?"

"It's growing on me." She dragged her hand over the contours of his chest, over his shoulder and down his arm to his tattoo. His birds must have been sensitive. Either that or they were actually mating in flight. She smiled. "You're growing on me."

"Yeah, I know. Try to ignore it and maybe it'll stop showing off."

"How long can you stay?"

"You mean time-wise?" She laughed, and he growled and nipped at her shoulder. "I could just eat you up. Are you hungry? I'm starving. Let me make you some breakfast."

"At four in the morning?"

"I've never met an Indian who was such a slave to the clock."

If he didn't want to stay in her bed, so be it. She threw her legs over the side and reached for the French terry robe she kept hanging over the footboard. "I thought you said you'd met my mother."

"La—"

"Shh." She turned quickly and pressed her fingers over his lips. "No names. This would not be a good time to wake her." Silly, she thought as she slipped into her robe. Her mother would be the first to say so. But she wasn't so sure. Sometimes she felt a familiar presence, and she wanted to do the unthinkable. She wanted to call it back rather than send it on.

"You need to brush up on your traditionalism, Wolf Track." She shook her head. "Slave to the clock."

"I said I'd do the cooking. I like to eat when I'm hungry." He gave a dry chuckle. "Whenever I can."

"Are you an eggs-and-bacon man, or do you—"

"Hey." He reached for her hand. "I'm a happy man right now. A very happy man. If I fell short, it's because I'm a little rusty. I promise to do better by you next time." He drew her hand to his lips and kissed her palm. "There's that word again." He touched the tip of his tongue to the center of her palm and made her shiver. "Time."

She didn't know what to say, so she put her arms around him and kept him there with her body instead of her words. She wanted to banish all doubt, but she wasn't sure what it would take. Words wouldn't cut it. He wasn't fearless, after all, and she might just be the only person in his world who knew it. It took him a moment to return her embrace, and she could only guess why. Maybe he was thinking too much, or remembering or yearning for something more. Maybe lingering in bed didn't appeal to him. Or maybe he was just hungry.

One thing was certain. There was nothing rusty about Ethan Wolf Track.

"You okay?" he whispered cautiously.

She nodded. She wanted a next time. She truly did. And getting all clingy might scare him away.

Keep it light, Bella.

"And I promise you…" She gave him an awkward parting pat on the arm as she slid away. "You're not short."

It was a relief to hear him laugh.

So SHE'D HAD SEX, but she'd never made love. He was beginning to wonder if he ever had. He'd sure given it his best effort tonight. It wasn't even an effort. It was more like a gift that he meant to give, to feel it taken and kept, but it kept coming back to him. Maybe that was why they call it *coming,* he told his suddenly overactive mind. It was a rush, all right, but not the kind that rolled over you and blew away. The feeling was still with him, like a new kind of hangover. The good kind, which was something he'd never had before. Something nobody in his right mind would question.

But this woman was the queen of questions.

"What made you decide to try college again?" she asked as he poured the last of the pancake batter into two spreading dollops.

"I didn't actually try college the first time." The hot skillet started the batter bubbling almost instantly. Somewhere in the back of his mind a voice told him to wait until the whole face was full of blisters. Man's voice? Woman's voice? He shook his head. "I tried sports and parties and hangin' out."

"That's the way you got through high school."

"You notice every little detail, don't you?" He scooped up the first pancake and flipped it, golden side up. "About the time I realized it wasn't working for me anymore, along came a recruiter. I signed up. I figured Logan would approve of the army because he'd done his hitch and he never complained." He flipped the second pancake. "Not that I was looking for his approval—I wanted to go my own way—but I wanted his respect."

"I'm sure you had it."

"I don't know."

"Well, you have mine. Has he seen you flip pan-cakes?"

"He's the master flipper." He slid a fresh hotcake

atop each stack on the plates in waiting. "I had one little problem with being a soldier." He handed her the two plates. "I wasn't very good at shooting at people," he said airily as he turned off the stove.

"Understandable. Is that why you don't hunt? You're not a good shot?"

He joined her at the table, where she'd already set glasses of orange juice and a platter of bacon. It was still dark outside. There was something cozy about sitting down at the breakfast table before daybreak with a woman wearing a soft white robe and a smile on her face.

Something that made it feel okay to let the stories just keep on coming.

"I shot *expert* with every weapon they gave me. That's the highest qualification you can get. They thought they had a real Sergeant York on their hands." He took a drink of juice and then gestured with the glass. "You know about Sergeant York. You shoot *expert* in history."

"World War I hero."

"I tore up those targets like a human paper shredder. They sent me over to the Middle East. Fine. I'm ready, willing and more than fit for duty." He tipped the glass and studied what was left of the orange juice. "Until the first time I had a real human being in my sights," he told her quietly without looking up. He wasn't gonna quit now. "Couldn't do it. I shot over his head." He drained the glass.

He cut into the pancakes with the side of his fork, sopped up some syrup and shoveled the food into his mouth. It had no taste. He made a project of chewing and swallowing. When he looked up, she was waiting.

No note taking, no disbelief in her eyes, no pity or judgment. She was listening.

He lifted one shoulder and tried to crack a smile.

"One time I put my weapon down and tackled a guy that needed shooting, sure as hell. I don't know why. Damn near got myself killed. Coulda gotten my whole unit blown to pieces. Went off the deep end, drinking, getting into fights. Ended up in psych. They sent me home with a general discharge." He glanced out the window. "Logan wanted me to appeal it, but I couldn't see it. Hell, stuff I did was flat out dishonorable. That's what they should have stamped on my papers."

"They must've given you some kind of treatment while you were in the psych unit," she said gently. Which was not really what he wanted. "Was there any reason why you couldn't…" He speared her with a look. *Say what you want to say.* "Other than the obvious? That the target is human."

"One doc said I wasn't crazy. Another one said I was. He didn't use the word, but that's what it boiled down to." He lifted one shoulder. "Pretty sure most of 'em thought I was fakin' it."

She didn't say anything, but she was looking at him pretty hard.

"If I was, I wasn't conscious of it. I wanted to shoot somebody. I really did."

She shook her head. "The only part that sounds crazy is you apologizing for not killing anyone."

"You can't run an army that way."

"You don't get VA benefits, then."

"I get medical. If I lose it again, they'll try to put me back together. But I don't get the GI Bill. You know, to pay for school." He poked at his pancakes. "I'd rather pay for it myself anyway. Let the real soldiers have the benefits."

"You'll earn yours like a real cowboy?"

He gave a lopsided smile. "Playing poker in the bull-pen, yeah."

"Maybe with a little more psychiatric treatment you'd unlock some sort of—"

"Childhood trauma? No, thanks. Sleeping dogs, re-member?"

"They're everywhere," she said as she reached for her orange juice. She hadn't eaten much. "We all go around stepping over our sleeping dogs."

"Which gives people like you some job security. You get to wake those dogs up and make 'em bark their fool heads off."

She smiled. "And free the puppies."

"Yeah. You do good work, Bella. You and Warrior Woman."

"How long have you been following my blog?"

"I wouldn't say I'm a follower. I don't get on the computer that much anymore. I started taking classes when I was, um…you know, in prison. I got to use a computer. Warrior Woman did a whole series on Indian gaming. Another one on water rights. I used some of that in one of my courses."

"How did you figure out it was me?"

"I'd see you on the news." He took after his break-fast in earnest, now that the focus was on her. "A couple of words here, couple of words there, you put two and two together…"

"You were taking math?"

"I was taking Research and Writing, Miss Smarty-Pants. You helped me get another A."

"You're welcome." Her smile went with the smarty-pants. Which he knew for a fact she wasn't wearing. She finally cut into her pancakes. "Have you seen any of the posts I've been doing on the latest court cases concerning payments on Indian land?"

"That wasn't one of my topics."

"Senator Perry Garth is one of my topics."

"Ah, Senator Perry Garth." He wagged a slice of bacon at her. "The senator in particular is not one of my topics."

"Why not?" She snatched his bacon. "He's trying to hold up the transfer of public land leases from the Tutan Ranch to the Double D Wild Horse Sanctuary."

"I thought that was practically a done deal."

"Practically." She took a bite of bacon, gave it a couple of chews, and then wagged it back at him. "Do you know what *practically* means in Department of the Interior terms? In Bureau of Indian Affair terms? If you get the right person pushing the buttons, you can slow a done deal down to an everlasting simmer. Just ask anybody on the Tribal Council."

"Never had much interest in politics, Tribal or otherwise. Like I said, not one of my topics."

"Water rights?" she recalled. "Tribal gaming?"

He shrugged. "Drinking and gambling."

She rolled her eyes. "Okay, what about the horses?"

"Now you're talkin'. Big Boy gets auctioned off, I want it to be part of something big. He's a hell of a horse."

"You're a hell of a trainer." She nodded at his empty plate. "Would you like more?" He flashed his palms in surrender, and she reached for his plate. "When are you going to show Big Boy off to Logan?"

"When we're ready."

"I want to be there. It's an important part of the story." She piled her nearly full plate on top of his empty one. "The Wild Horse Sanctuary story. There's so much to it, Ethan. Saving the horses is only the beginning. We're all related, you know. *Mitakuye Oyasin.*"

"Yeah, I've heard that somewhere. I believe it." He smiled as he took the last of the bacon. "We shouldn't be shooting each other."

"On that observation alone you should qualify for the GI Bill. What are you majoring in?"

"Staying out of trouble." He licked the bacon grease off his thumb. "I haven't gotten that far yet. I just started taking classes. It's gonna take some getting used to."

"History and literature. Interesting choices."

"I figured I'd better pick things that would hold my interest. You know, to start with. I've got people advising me on courses and job prospects. I'm learning how to take people's advice, or at least consider it. I've taken some swings and chalked up some strikes."

"You've had at least one unfair call against you."

"Best advice I've gotten lately is not to dwell on things. Hell, I was hanging over the edge looking for a better view. Guess I'm lucky I didn't fall any farther than I did."

"What would you *like* to do?" She tipped her head to one side and gave him what he'd come to call the counselor look. "If you had a clean slate, what would you choose?"

"If I had a clean slate, maybe I wouldn't have much to offer. Maybe I wouldn't know anything." She scowled, and he shook his head. "I'm not putting myself down, Bella. I learn the hard way." He grabbed his empty glass.

Something to study. "I think I could teach. The kids at Square One, I can relate to them. They're like Big Boy. You can't push them, but you gain their trust, you can lead them."

"Pretty obvious, those boys would follow you anywhere."

"I'd want to lead them to trust their instincts. The good ones. Like you do."

"I've never heard of bad instincts, have you?"

"Good point." He laughed. "Can I borrow it?"

"You talk to Logan and you can have it." She reached for his hand. "Just call him. Your instincts will take over, and the two of you will get past whatever's keeping you apart." She smiled. "And then I can get a few pictures of you working together for my story."

"I don't have a problem calling him."

"Yes, you do. But you'll get over it."

"Is that what your instincts tell you?" He drew his hand away and started gathering up what was left on the table. "You don't know everything, woman. As smart as you are, you've got some holes in your education."

"One less as of this morning." His eyes met hers, and she smiled. "I've finally made love."

CHAPTER SEVEN

"ALL RIGHT, WOMAN. I called him."

And this was the first time Ethan had actually called *her,* Bella realized. The very first.

"And?"

"And the party's at his place. Logan's a big believer in working horses in a round pen. You know, the sacred circle. I don't have one over here, so I said I'd haul Big Boy down to his place. You're going with us."

"Is that an invitation?"

"You want pictures, you'll have to take them this time. I can guarantee your safety. And Logan and me... all is forgiven. I guess."

"You guess?"

"I told him I wanted him to take a look at my horse, and he told me to bring him on over. That's how it's done. No hashing over who did what last year or last century. You just move on."

"Whatever it takes. I'm glad you're—"

"The deal is, he helps me come up with a routine that'll really show the horse off, and I help him paint my old bedroom. He's getting it ready for his next kid."

"When?"

"I don't know. Couple of months, I guess. That's a woman's question. Or a reporter's."

She laughed. "When are we going? That's my question."

"As soon as you can. I got to work on time last weekend, so I'm golden."

"You sure are."

Moving on had always been his way, but these days Ethan was taking it at a collected walk rather than a headlong gallop. He was getting used to the pace. He thought he would have to sign his life away in return for the use of Square One's horse trailer, but Shelly didn't even bat an eyelash. "You're in charge of the horses, and the trailer goes with them. It's your call, Ethan. As long as you bring Bella Primeaux back to visit soon."

His call. He had a call, and suddenly he wasn't averse to using it. He wasn't locked up anymore. Pick up the phone and talk. No justification necessary.

It had been too long since he'd seen Bella. Four long days. He could tell she'd been watching for him—she was out the door the instant he drove up in front of her building—and the sight of her made his heart skip a beat. Her black hair, caught up in a ponytail, gleamed in the sun. She was dressed in jeans and a sweatshirt—there was an autumn chill in the air this morning—and she carried the tools of her trade in a bag that hung from her shoulder.

She was always prepared, ever mindful of the way the bits and pieces of the world around her connected up. He admired her mindfulness. At the same time, he was fearful of it, and he wasn't sure why. Maybe she would see things in him he didn't want her to see, though he couldn't imagine what that would be. She'd read up some on his crime, and he'd told her the rest. She liked him anyway. She'd made love with him anyway.

She was something, this woman. As soon as she hopped into his pickup, he had to kiss her.

They talked a blue streak all the way to Sinte, and by the time they walked in the Wolf Track front door, Ethan was feeling just fine about seeing the man who'd raised him.

"I'm ready to paint," he announced as he shed his denim jacket and tossed it in the old brown chair near the front door where he'd always piled his stuff when he came inside.

"You want to do that first?" Logan asked. "Or hang up your jacket."

"Just testing." Ethan grinned. "You always said, get the chores done first, then you can play," he said as he reclaimed the jacket.

"That's exactly the kind of recall I need," Logan said as he offered Bella a handshake. "Glad you could come. Mary's getting out soon, and I want everything to look nice when she comes home." He turned to Ethan. "If you still remember anything I told you, it must be worth using again. Probably should write it down so I don't forget. I just got a pair of reading glasses. You believe that?"

"And you're having a kid?" Ethan laughed. He was feeling downright comfortable. "Better not be using pin-on diapers, old man."

"I wear bifocals," Bella said. She glanced at Ethan as they followed Logan and the smell of coffee. "You didn't notice, did you? I used to wear glasses. Now I wear contacts."

"*That's* what's changed. I knew there was something," Ethan teased.

"It has nothing to do with age." Bella assured Logan

as he handed her a cup of coffee. "Neither does maturity."

"Living proof right here." Ethan took a cup from the cabinet and poured his own coffee. He was home. "What color are we going with? Pink or blue?"

"White. But I've already primed it, so it won't take too long. Hasn't been painted since you moved out."

"Sure hope the primer covered everything up."

"That's what it's for." Logan led the way down the hall, bypassing a row of boxes that hugged the wall. "Couple of boxes I've been saving for you and Trace. Stuff I thought you might want. Trophies, books, pictures."

"No pictures," Ethan said. He turned to Bella. "*No* pictures." God only knew what kind of pictures of him Logan could dig up.

"Too soon, huh?" Logan laughed. "Good thing we have a basement. I guess a baby will mean a lot of stuff we've never had around here. But don't worry. I won't be throwing anything else away. Only moving it to… Remember this one?" He plucked a book from the largest of the boxes and showed the cover to Ethan first, then Bella. *Where the Wild Things Are*. "One of his favorites. He used to know it by heart."

"I still do, so you can keep it for my little brother. Or sister. Wouldn't that be cool? A little sister." He tapped his father's chest with the back of his hand. "Hey, she's gonna look a lot more like me than she does Trace."

"If she's lucky she'll look just like her mother. Mary's beautiful. Hey, remember this?" Logan dropped the book into the box and turned his hand into a living puppet with forefinger and pinkie as ears, middle fingers tapping thumb to create a menacing muzzle. "Track Man's coming after you."

Thank God Track Man didn't complete the old routine by going for his armpit, Ethan thought.

"Look at him." He jerked his chin, pointing his lips the Indian way. "Track Man has a golden eye." His glance connected with Logan's. "I'm glad you got a ring this time. That's the way it should be. It should work both ways."

Track Man fell apart as Logan laid his hand on his son's shoulder—an earnest gesture—and then playfully pulled the brim of his hat down over his face. "You're about due for a new one of these, aren't you?"

"Nope. My dad gave me this one." Ethan adjusted the battered hat. "It goes everywhere with me."

"Well, put a drop cloth over it and let's get to painting."

Logan stirred the paint while Ethan showed Bella the view from his old bedroom window. The backyard was more than hobbyhorse land. It was Logan's real home. In the horse world, Logan Wolf Track was a well-respected name. He'd developed training methods based on Lakota tradition. He'd even written a book about them. His sons had learned what they'd been willing to learn. Ethan told Bella he wished he had paid more attention as he got older, but before he'd gotten "too big for my britches" he'd followed Logan around the very pen they were looking at like a pup on the heels of its mama.

"Is too big for your britches anything like being a smarty-pants?" Bella asked.

"Nope." He slid her a flirty wink. "It took me a long time to grow into my paws, but the britches were another story. For a while there I never did have a pair that fit."

A few hours later, Bella stood on a rail on the outside of the round pen while Logan leaned back against the inside, a pile of horse gear at his feet. They were watching Ethan work Big Boy on a lunge line. Logan had expressed his approval of Ethan's progress many times over with a simple nod. He reminded Bella of her mother. Sometimes a kid wanted a few words. You might have learned not to expect the effusiveness you saw in other parents, but you still wanted to hear words. You wanted the people around to hear those words.

They weren't kids, Bella reminded herself. As Ethan said, they knew how to read sign. Their people exercised the kind of patience and subtlety that mainstream society had forever misconstrued. She and Ethan couldn't afford to do the same. They were the bridge between two worlds.

"It's good to see him like this," Logan said. "It's been a while since he's seemed comfortable in his own skin. You must have something to do with that."

"I'll let you in on a little secret. I've had a crush on Ethan just about as far back as I can remember."

Logan glanced over his shoulder, smiling. "Probably not much of a secret, huh?"

"Oh, I think I kept it to myself pretty well." She laughed. "Or not. Thought I did at the time." She watched Ethan signal the horse for a lead change. She only recognized the maneuver because he had showed it to her earlier. "You know he didn't steal that car."

"'Course he didn't. But you try going up against a United States senator. Especially one who's been a senator as long as Garth has, and *especially* in this state."

Bella nodded, still gazing at Ethan. "Big fish in a small pond."

"You got that right. I tried to talk to his daughter after it was all over, see if she'd do the right thing, but it was no go. Garth got wind of it and threatened to charge me with harassment or some kind of…" He turned his head to her sharply. "Don't say anything to Ethan. I don't want him to know. I knew I was on shaky ground, but I had to try."

"Is Garth using that against you in any way? Politically, I mean."

Logan lifted one shoulder. "I don't have much to do with him politically. Have you started working on that story you mentioned?"

"I've been nosing around. I know the Double D Wild Horse Sanctuary was granted the use of some public land that Tutan Ranch livestock has been grazing for years."

"Tutan's permits ran out," Logan said. "Sally got her application in, and with the leases the Tribe switched over to her and the backing of the BLM Wild Horse Management office, her case was ironclad. She gets the land."

"Done deal, right?" Bella shook her head. "Except Garth's committee's thrown it into bureaucratic limbo."

"Oh, jeez." Logan scowled. "That's not what I need to hear."

"As far as I can tell, it's the transfer of the public land he's trying to block right now. But can he interfere with Tribal leases?"

"He can cause delays. You know how that goes." He turned to watch his son. "You don't think it's because of Ethan?"

"I'm betting it's about your father-in-law," she said. "Dan Tutan."

"You think he wants to get at me? Because of Mary?"

"You guys all have this idea that it's personal. Sally thinks Tutan's afraid of her husband."

"Hank?" Logan shook his head. "Tutan liked to give Sally a hard time, but she doesn't take crap from anybody. She was standing up to Tutan before Hank came along."

"I'm sure she was," Bella allowed. "But in a pond as small as South Dakota, all the fish have a way of bumping into each other. You've got your brown trout, your big white lake trout, and then you've got your cutthroat trout." She shook her head. "That's a lot of competition."

Logan burst out laughing. "Ah, that is *beautiful*." Ethan was approaching with his quick buckskin as Logan called out, "You got yourself a live one, son."

Ethan grinned. "The horse or the woman?"

"Both." Logan offered his hand for the horse's inspection. "You ready to saddle him up? What are you using on him?"

"Hackamore, like you taught me."

Logan watched Ethan sort through the gear he'd left on the ground. Then he reached for an unusual-looking length of rope he'd draped over the fence rail. "I made something for you." He held it out for Ethan's inspection.

Ethan rubbed the intricately woven rope between his fingers. It was made of multicolored strands—shades of brown, gray to near black, tan to blond. Tiny ends sticking out all along its length made it looked prickly, but when Ethan shook it, it seemed to come alive.

"Snaky," he said appreciatively. "Feels like horsehair."

"It's a mecate," Logan said. "It's a rein handmade from horsehair. Got my first one from an old vaquero I

met down in New Mexico one time. He taught me how
to make them. It's all I use. You want try it out?"

"Sure."

Logan took Ethan's hackamore and started untying
the old reins from the bosal, the chunky noseband that
substituted for a bit. "There's something about the life
in this thing. You can feel it in your hands. You get a
connection with the horse you don't have with leather
or hemp."

"How come you never showed me this?" Ethan asked
when he held the newly attached reins in his hands.

"I'm pretty sure I did. Maybe you weren't watching." Ethan looked up, and Logan smiled. "Hey, I probably didn't say, *see this, Ethan?* I always figured you'd
learn when you were ready. You've always had your
own need-to-know agenda."

"I didn't realize how much I'd learned from you
until…"

"You needed to know?"

"Yeah. Until I needed to know."

Ethan exchanged the halter and lunge line for the
hackamore and saddle, all the while thinking about how
easy it had been to work alongside Logan and Bella earlier, painting a room that held good memories and an innocence he'd all but forgotten about. There was only one
wall he'd hated to run up against in that house, only one
wall he couldn't quite paint over, even though its color
wasn't quite clear, and he wasn't sure how much of it
had ever existed outside his head. An array of pictures
hung on it, and he couldn't quite make *them* out, either.
He'd been pretty young when he'd moved into the house,
but not so young that a normal kid wouldn't remember.

So, fine, he hadn't been a normal kid. He'd come

to this town, this house, this life, with a whacked-out mother, and he had a vaguely bad memory of her. He didn't know why it had to bother him now. But it did. And now that the bothering had started, it would continue until he faced it and dug down to the bottom of what was eating at him. But for now he forced those thoughts away. He had a job to do, a job he loved more every day. His four-legged partner was learning to trust and teaching Ethan a lot about adjusting to change. One day at a time was the key.

It felt good to show Logan the progress he'd made. He didn't have to do much to put Big Boy through his paces, and the mecate made it even easier. He'd decided to show the horse off in reining, and for that he would gradually switch to a bit. But it wouldn't be the bit that would coax Big Boy to stop and spin and back up as though he were making dramatic moves of his own accord. It would be the rider's body, the shifting of his weight.

Ethan dismounted on the far side of the pen and looked enquiringly over at Logan, who took the hint to cross the ring and check on the fit of his gear. He asked about the fabric of the cinch, then offered the use of a saddle he thought would be a better fit for a short-backed horse.

They both knew the conversation was superficial, but Logan played along until Ethan hit him with the question that had been bouncing in his mind for the past twenty minutes, using his father's own term.

"I guess you had your own need-to-know agenda, at least where my mother was concerned."

Logan looked at him curiously.

Ethan stared at the house. "She'd been on her way out the door five minutes after she first walked in."

He shrugged. "That's what Trace says. Seems like you should've seen it coming."

Logan smiled wistfully. "Your mother was an on-the-job learning experience. By the time she left, I knew she was gone for good."

"And that it was good she was gone?"

Logan closed his eyes and shook his head, still with that sad little smile. "I never said that."

"Maybe you should have."

"It was my need-to-know moment. I didn't think it was yours."

"I remember feeling relief that she was gone, and I knew I wasn't supposed to feel that way." Ethan ran his hand along Big Boy's warm neck. "Hell, she was my mother. But *I* knew, too. She couldn't come back."

"Why?"

"Because I didn't want her to. And I put her out of my mind for good. Can't even remember what she looks like." He looked to Logan for help with the shadowy pictures on the nonexistent wall. "It bothers me sometimes. Gives me a kind of a cold, sick feeling. Guilt, I guess."

"You have nothing to feel guilty about."

"I wanted you to…"

"Stop her? Get her back for you?" Logan laid his hand on Ethan's shoulder. "I'm sorry it went the way it did. If I could've—"

"No. That's not it." Frowning, Ethan shook his head. "I don't know what I wanted."

"Let's put it behind us." Logan gave Ethan's shoulder a parting pat. "How about we take a ride? I'll saddle up two more horses."

The suggestion was vaguely unsatisfying, but it was

a relief at the same time. Ethan embraced the relief end of the spectrum.

"You got a kid horse?"

"I've got the mustang Mary and I decided not to enter in the competition because we didn't want to show you boys up." Logan nodded toward the side of the pen where Bella stood waiting. They started walking, Logan grinning broadly. "Just kidding. We're not putting Adobe up for auction. We adopted him."

Ethan smiled. "You're on a roll."

"And I've got that great little mare." Logan nodded toward the pasture.

"How about taking a ride with us?" Ethan said as they approached Bella. "Logan's got a horse for you."

She shook her head. "You two go ahead."

"We can double up on the mare."

"No, you guys go ride your wild mustangs. I have my own gadgets to play with. I've got some good pictures." She took a small camera from her amazing bag and showed him a couple of pictures of him riding Big Boy. "Want to see the video?" He laughed and shook his head. "I want to make some notes while it's all still fresh."

"In other words, you don't ride?" Logan asked.

Bella gave a diffident smile. "It shows, huh?"

Ethan put his arm around her shoulders, a gesture that, to his surprise, felt as natural as breathing, as comfortable as the smile on his face. "She does fine with a backseat cowboy along."

"Thanks, but you two go on," Bella said. "Just let me get a picture with both horses."

"We don't have to take them out right now," Ethan told her. He turned to Logan. "You got some time this week to maybe work with me on the maneuvers we talked about?"

Logan let the buckskin snuffle him up again before scratching the horse's neck. "He's got the deepest stop I've seen."

"Yeah, we've been working on that." And Logan's appreciation was sweet icing on the cake.

"His spin is coming along. A smooth rollback would be impressive." He nodded. "When can you get back this way?"

"You call it. I'll work it out."

"Why don't you leave him here and let me get to know him a little bit? Come back as soon as you can."

Ethan grinned. "I'll see about leaving the trailer, too. Then I'll *have to* come back."

Bella felt a little guilty about spoiling the plan to go riding. She would have been fine with staying back while the two men took off on their horses, but she was just as happy to head back home.

And surprised when Ethan took the wrong turn. They were headed down a dirt road instead of the highway.

"Aren't we going back to Rapid City?"

"Taking a little detour." He nodded toward the flat-topped, cone-shaped hill up ahead. "Haven't seen Sinte from the top of Badger Butte since the last time I rode up there with Trace. How long has it been for you?"

"Forever. Literally."

He gave an incredulous glance. "You've never climbed Badger Butte?"

"Never." She was probably the only person in town over the age of ten who could say that, but that just made her special.

"I get to show you the view for the first time? You can see the whole valley from up there."

"Do you have to hang off the edge to see it?"

"Hang off…oh, yeah." He smiled. "No, that's just me. You can stand anywhere you want. It's a helluva sight. Can't wait to show it to you."

"I'm happy with an up-close-and-personal view from the valley floor."

But they were still bumping along the roller coaster of a South Dakota dirt road. Ethan didn't even slow down for washboards. He drove like every other male she'd ridden with on these country roads. She had done an accidental one-eighty on a washboard once, an experience that taught her to seek blacktop whenever possible.

"Did you tell Logan your news?"

"What news?"

"About going back to college."

"Oh, right." He shook his head. "Forgot."

"Oh. I thought when you were having that little huddle on the other side of the corral…" They hit a rut, and she quietly reached for the grab handle above the door. "Can't wait to hear what he has to say when you tell him."

"Why? So you can add that to your story?" He glanced at her. "I don't want to be part of any horse-turns-bad-boy-around fairy tale, okay?"

"I just meant…" She sighed. "Listen, I'm not climbing that hill, so why don't we just turn around?"

"It's gonna take five minutes."

"Never climbing to the top of Badger Butte for me is kind of like never going hunting for you. I can't deal with—"

"Look, Bella, I'm not afraid to hunt. I'm just not interested."

"I'm not afraid of heights. I'm just not a fan."

Ethan spared her a cold glare before slamming on the brake, spinning the pickup around and gunning the engine.

"Stop! If you don't stop, I'm jumping out." She pulled the handle just enough to make it click. He slowed the vehicle and pulled over, and she jumped out. And then he drove away. She watched him disappear over a rise in the rutted road.

What the hell was wrong with that man? She didn't like heights, okay? There were things he didn't like. There was no call to push—that was all she was saying. She wasn't trying to get him to take down a deer so she could eat meat. Not every man was a hunter.

And not every woman was a damn climber.

It wasn't a steep grade, but she was puffing as she approached the top. Like it or not, she was going to get a view from the high ground. She didn't like hiking. She certainly didn't like admitting she needed to start getting more exercise. But she didn't care about Ethan driving off and leaving her on foot. She'd asked for it. She'd *demanded* it. He'd said it himself—told her to walk away if he started acting like he had a few screws loose. She was a wise woman, a warrior woman, and she was doing just that. Walking away.

It was too bad she'd left her bag in the pickup.

The view from the top of the rise gave her a thrill. She could see herself bursting into song. She could also see herself heading down the other side and marching right past the pickup parked at the bottom and the man leaning against the driver's side door.

And she almost did.

"I'm sorry, Bella."

She stopped.

"Please ride with me."

She turned and gave him the coldest look in her arsenal—and she had some icy ones stored up.

"I didn't mean to scare you." He pushed away from the pickup, shoved his hands in his pockets and scraped his boot heel across the hardpan as he approached. "All right, I did, but I won't do it again. Ever."

Was that sincerity in those hooded eyes?

Damn, she should just keep walking.

But she didn't. She'd walked far enough. "I'm afraid of heights." She grabbed a handful of soft T-shirt and pressed her fist against hard belly. "Understand?"

"Perfectly."

"No pressure. No ifs, ands or buts. I don't do heights." She pulled back and punched this time. His gut was rock hard. "And no teasing. Got that?"

"Yes, ma'am." He was doing pretty well on the straight-face score.

She narrowed her eyes. "Because you don't want anybody trying to coax *your* monsters out from under your bed."

"You're right. That's why I don't own a bed."

"Wherever you sleep, then." She let go of his shirt. "You and Logan were having yourselves a real reunion, Ethan. You could've topped it off with your college news."

"It's no big deal." He lifted his gaze above her head and shrugged. "Because, it's not like I've graduated or anything. I'm just taking classes."

"And I read a script in front of a camera. Your father

THE PRODIGAL COWBOY

goes to meetings and listens to a rehash of the proposals that didn't get passed last month. Your brother hangs on to a bucking horse for ten seconds at a time."

"Eight seconds."

"Not *even* ten seconds at a time."

He looked her in the eyes again. The corners of his mouth started twitching, and he couldn't hold back. He had to laugh.

And she had to laugh with him.

He draped his arm around her shoulders, and she took his hand with hers, lacing their fingers together. He walked her around the front of the pickup.

"You wouldn't really have jumped out of the pickup if I hadn't stopped, would you?"

"I'll never tell." She glanced up, offering a smug smile. "I might need that one again."

"You wanna hang out tonight?"

"I don't hang out."

"I do." He opened the pickup door. "Your place?"

"Where else?"

THEIR LOVEMAKING, BREATHTAKINGLY hot and spicy, was filled with the taste of salt and the pungent scent of musk. He took her standing, and she rode him sitting. They held each other off one more moment and pushed each other one more fraction of a fraction, and called each other's names one more way and one more time.

Their lovemaking was sweet and slow, filled with whispers and warm breath, and the fine feel of smooth skin and long cool hair and short damp curls. He took her gently and she received him deeply, and they traded endearments neither had ever spoken before. And when they were sated with all the pleasure either had ever imagined, they wrapped each other in their arms and legs and moved languidly to touch and reassure.

"Ethan."

"Hmm?"

"I admire you."

He gave a self-satisfied chuckle. "You've got a crush on me."

"That's old news." She traced a circle around his flat nipple. "I've learned a lot about you since you came to my rescue at the Hitching Post."

"The itching Post. Didn't you notice the sign? The *H* is missing. That leaves you *itching*."

"You, maybe." She offered a saucy smile. "What are you going to do about it?"

"Enjoy it. It's that kind of itch. The kind you don't wanna scratch off." He closed his eyes and smiled. There was much to be enjoyed. "What do you admire?"

She pressed her lips to his chest. "The way you handle yourself. You're your own man. I like being with you. I like being my own woman while I'm with you." She pressed her lips to his chest. "I'm glad you don't want to scratch me off, but if you have an itch, a little scratching might be in order."

He kissed her forehead. "I've made some big choices in my life that didn't work for me. I don't want you to find yourself thinking of me that way." He threaded his fingers through her hair. Here in the dark it was easy to talk. There was no heaviness. It was all wrung out of them, and so he could say without hesitation, "I don't wanna be the first bad choice you've ever made."

"You're a big choice for me, I'll grant you that. And so far, so very good." She scooted up along his side and rested her chin on the kiss she'd imprinted on his skin as surely as the tattoo artist he'd visited long ago. "But you have a way of distracting me when I want to say something, especially when it's about you."

"The scratching thing? That's a pretty basic male instinct, Bella. Even if I do it better than anyone else you know, I'm still just another—"

"It's not a competition, Ethan. I admire *you*. You're not afraid to make more big choices just because you've run into some obstacles. You haven't let the detours break your stride." She slid her hand over his hip. "I love to watch you walk, by the way."

"Same here. You should've seen yourself marching down that hill."

She growled.

"Look, I know where you're goin' with this. I feel good about what I'm doing, but I'm building on a pretty fragile foundation. Let me work on it awhile. Okay?" He twirled her hair around his finger. It had life, like the mecate. "Your mom never got to see you on TV, did she?"

"No."

"She knew where you were headed, though. She knew who you were." She laid her cheek against him. "You're beautiful, Bella. You know that, don't you?" Her response—a small sound—wasn't quite an agreement. "She knew that, too. Hey, Belladonna is one of those miracle drugs, like aspirin. I looked it up. It's powerful. It helps people, but you don't wanna abuse it. Ladonna gave you her strength, and you ran with it."

"Logan's done the same for you."

"I ran the other way. But I'm back. Still, you're way ahead of me, Bella. I need time to catch up."

"The story behind the Wild Horse Sanctuary is something we can run with together. And there's more. I think there's a lot more."

"More story?"

"More *to* the story. More history."

"Is that your specialty? Digging up the past?"

"Let's see…what courses did you say *you* chose to start with?"

He groaned. "Damn, you're good."

ETHAN WOKE UP in a cold sweat. A bright horror filled his head and popped his eyes open, peeled them wide against the dark. He didn't know where he was, whether he was awake or dreaming. Part of him was in a dark place, and the rest was still somewhere else.

Somebody was dead out there in the field. He'd heard an explosion, but what flew wasn't shrapnel or body parts. It was a cloud of birds. Screeching birds, wildly flapping, desperately churning the air. A man popped up from the tall grass. And then *pop! Pop!* Firecrackers made Ethan jump and cover his ears, and the man's face went all red. And then he vanished.

Ethan rubbed his hand over his own face, hoping it was dry. It wasn't, but it didn't feel red. He knew what red felt like. Warm and watery at first, but when it went cold it felt sticky.

God help him, he was dreaming again. He'd gone months without landing in whacked-out places in his head at night, seeing things that looked like they'd been slapped together by a madman wielding a paintbrush—eyeballs popping out of birds' nests, Indians slithering through the grass like alligators, handcuffed men dressed in orange and women washing their hair in blood.

He wasn't going back for any more medical treatment. No more medication—all that did was make him groggy. He was gonna tough this thing out. It had almost faded away, and he could make that happen again. Stay busy, stay healthy, wait the devil out.

He turned to the woman lying close to his side, and he kissed her hair. She hadn't stirred, so he must not have made any noise. He must not have thrashed around. He was taking a chance of exposing himself by staying the whole night. Exposing the nature of his...little disorder.

Hell, plenty of people had nightmares. They weren't all crazy, and neither was he. Hadn't Bella just pointed out to him all the progress he was making? And it wasn't like she didn't know where he'd been.

Sometimes he wondered if *he* knew where he'd been. There was something different about this night's dream, though. There was urgency to it, the sense of a presence just below the surface.

But the surface of what?

CHAPTER EIGHT

IT HAD BEEN almost a week since Bella had seen Ethan, and she wasn't expecting to run into him at the Double D. The sight of his pickup barreling down the gravel road gave her butterflies. Here she was, doing her job, and there *he* was, parking in front of the house, and she couldn't wait to stow away the tools of her trade and turn to trading wisecracks and secret smiles with her cowboy.

Her cowboy. It sounded crazy, even within the private walls of her suddenly giddy head.

But she wasn't starry-eyed enough to start shirking her responsibilities. Final preparations were being made for the Wild Horse Makeover Horse Show, and she was finishing up her background work. That was her pretext, anyway. She was covering the big finale, but she was also getting closer to pinning down Senator Perry Garth's involvement with the allocation of the land that belonged to her people.

She'd met with the treasurer of the Cheyenne people in Montana—one of the tribes that was fighting with the Interior Department over missing payments—and she was convinced that Senator Garth's fingerprints were all over those billion-dollar bills. She knew she was working both ends against the middle on this story— and the Double D was somewhere in the middle—but that was the way investigative reporting worked sometimes. You started with one small piece out of place—a small player, a local matter—and you searched for a hole left by that piece.

And if you cared about the piece, if you couldn't abide that hole, your passion for the search intensified. The competition finale was her KOZY assignment. She was working on the Garth connection independently, and there was something a little too cozy going on with the senator. Why would he interfere with a Bureau of Land Management recommendation, stand in opposition to a determination made by the Tribal Council and essentially expend valuable political clout for a relatively small-time rancher like Tutan? Just because Tutan offered a good place to go hunting?

Suddenly there was all manner of coziness.

And more than one stimulus for passion.

Ethan waited for her to reach him and kissed her when she did.

"You don't mind showing us off publicly?" she asked.

"I don't see any public around." He glanced left and right. "Do you?"

"Not at the moment."

"I keep forgetting, you really have a public."

"I'd like to forget it. Well, most days. But the closer I get to home, the less I have to worry about it."

"It's been a while since I made the news. I don't think anybody remembers."

"I'm not worried about that." She reached up and tugged on his hat brim. "Not at all. But when you win this contest, you'll be making the news again. Is that okay with you?"

"I ain't livin' in the past, darlin'." He took her hands in his. "The present suits me better every day."

"What are you up to today?"

He nodded toward the front door. "Checkin' in with Sally on the facilities for the horse show. Logan's been working with me on a routine that'll show Big Boy off to his best advantage. I want to make sure—"

"Well, I'll be damned."

They turned to find Sally Night Horse watching them through the screen door.

"No, you won't, Sally." The deep voice came from behind her. "I did two funeral solos last month. In my heart I was singing for your salvation." A tall handsome Indian appeared in the doorway behind Sally, who was pushing the door open. "If my wife's trying to make another match, you might wanna check the fine print. Make sure she's got you registered for heaven."

"Aren't they adorable, Hank? You've met Logan Wolf Track's boy, haven't you?"

Hank Night Horse met Ethan at the top of the porch steps with a handshake, and then he extended his hand to Bella. "You've been taking more pictures today?"

"Never enough pictures. Actually, I was hoping we could talk."

"You guys can talk," Hank said. "I'm just a quiet man trying to keep up with a force of nature." He put his arm around Sally's shoulders and leaned close to her ear. "This man is not a boy. And no man wants to be called *adorable*."

"I mean as a couple. I had nothing to do with this one, but I see no reason why the Double D can't take credit." Sally waved her visitors inside. "We've got our hands full right now with the sanctuary, but in my next life I'm running one of those online dating services. I think I could make a fortune."

She gestured toward the office door. "Come on in and have a seat. We're just discussing a little hiccup we might be holding our breath over while we get this horse show on the road here. Like we need another detail to worry about right now."

Hank sat back against a counter, arms folded, while Sally took a seat in the wheelchair that served as an office chair in good times and as legs when hers weren't getting her where she wanted to go.

Bella started for a folding chair, but Sally pointed to a daybed piled with pillows. "You two take the...we'll call it the love seat. Bella, remember how you offered to help us get some community support messages on TV? You know, about donating prizes for the competition?"

Bella nodded, but her smile was for Ethan as she patted the space beside her on the daybed.

"We don't need any more donations right now. Annie— my sister—she has a generous brother-in-law who's ponying up for all that. Says he needs the tax write-off. What we need is public support. We need horse lovers."

"The news coverage should help."

"And we've got Skyler Quinn—" she glanced at Ethan "—your brother's Skyler, another Double D matchup. We've got Skyler working on a documentary.

"But here's the latest thing that worries me." She snatched a folded paper off her desk and snapped it open. "I got a letter today about the public land. Some glitch in the paperwork. I've already fired off a response. I told them to ask their assistant. She's the one who knows where the mother of all glitches is buried."

"I'm pretty sure the holdup is a few pay grades higher than assistant," Bella said. "I have some low-level friends in high-level places. Reliable sources, we call them. Your neighbor, Mr. Tutan, doesn't want to give up the land. He has one of our South Dakota senators doing his bidding." She glanced at Ethan. "I know this hits close to home in more ways than one, but—"

"I got no skin in this game," Ethan told her. He looked at Sally. "Horsehide, but no skin."

Bella felt a chill. If she wasn't mistaken, Ethan's beautiful black eyes had just gone stone-cold.

"But the decision's been made." Sally looked up at her husband and then turned to Bella. "Hasn't it? What exactly do your reliable sources say?"

"It's being reviewed. What does the letter say the holdup is?"

Sally lifted one shoulder. "That they're waiting on some signatures."

"There's a big investigation going on with the Bureau of Indian Affairs," Bella said. "Billions of dollars in lease payments on Indian trust land are missing. Completely unaccounted for. Apparently there's been a slow, steady leak that's been going on for years."

"Stolen?" Sally asked.

"They don't know," Hank put in. "Some stolen, some never paid, they can't figure it out. Probably never will. It's just gone, and who has time to track it down? You know how that goes." He glanced at Bella. "Some of us do, anyway. Most of our Indian trust land has been handed down many times over, and Tribal members don't designate heirs, so it gets chopped up among the direct descendants. Since this has been going on for generations, you maybe get a statement showing pages of parcels of land that you have pennies' worth of interest in. The Bureau's a mess, which makes it easy to rob.

You don't even have to bother to cover up your tracks. The red tape does it for you."

"That's terrible," Sally said.

Hank smiled. "Oh, yeah. It's terrible."

Bella chimed in. "Senator Garth has been sitting on relevant committees for as long as he's been in the senate—which is longer than most of us have been alive—and, of course, he says he's outraged. But there isn't much of a paper trail. There's an abundance of paper, but no trail. So he's all for offering a settlement, and then we let bygones be bygones."

"I don't see how our little public land lease would be connected."

"It probably isn't," Bella assured Sally. "Not directly. But according to my source, Garth is being questioned pretty closely. And on another front, he's suddenly particularly interested in certain parcels of public land, including Tutan's leases."

Sally frowned. "Why?"

"They're friends," Bella said. "They have been for years. According to my sources, Garth loves to hunt. He used to bring his pals out to Tutan's place every fall to go hunting. Tutan hosted quite a party back in the day. And Garth made sure Tutan had all the grazing permits and leases he could possibly want."

Hank was studying the toes of his boots. "Do you have any idea how far back this annual tradition goes?"

"Twenty years," Bella said. "Maybe more."

"My father used to work for Tutan." Hank looked up, his eyes suddenly haunted. "Seasonal laborer, but during hunting season a lotta times he'd stay on to help out with some of those parties. He disappeared. By the time they found his body…" He was talking to Bella's reporter persona now. "Well, they said he'd been drinking and he'd probably shot himself. Could've been an accident. Maybe suicide. Hard to tell, since he'd been dead for weeks."

"Was he with one of those hunting parties when he went missing?"

"The last time we heard from my father, he called to let us know he'd be staying down here for a couple more weeks, working for Tutan. But after he disappeared, Tutan said he thought my father had gone home to North Dakota after they brought the hay in. Some coyote hunter actually stumbled over my dad's body. There was an investigation. Tutan said he'd had some hunters come through, but he couldn't be sure."

"Was there a gun?"

Bella turned to Ethan. His question surprised her. He'd been so quiet that the very sound of his voice surprised her. He was staring at his hands. "Did they find a gun with his body?"

"They found a shotgun that had been reported stolen and a decomposed body full of shot. My dad didn't own a gun. He didn't hunt. His job was bird-dogging. Flushing pheasants—"

"Out of the brush. They put the gun…" Ethan cleared his throat. Bella could feel him shaking. "They probably put the gun there."

"They?" Hank said.

Ethan shook his head blindly. "Whoever."

"How long ago did it happen?" Bella asked Hank.

"Twenty-one years."

Ethan turned to her. "Is this all part of your story?"

"It could be. Hank, how much—"

"I've gotta get going." Ethan patted Bella's knee and

stood to leave. "This looks like another job for Warrior Woman."

"It's definitely..." Bella got to her feet. "Ethan, you wanted to ask about the final—"

"The show, yeah. Some of the details..." He didn't even spare her a glance. "I'm working out my routine," he told Sally. "I'll call you."

And then Ethan was gone. She hadn't imagined his reaction to Hank's story. He was trembling. She wanted to tear after him, but if she caught up, the questions would roll off her tongue, and he didn't need that right now. She was dying for answers. He was running from the questions. What a pair.

"Bella," Hank said, "what's this all about? What story?"

"I'm not sure." She turned away from watching one of her passions retreat and faced the question that could be at the heart of the other. "I'd like to know more about your father's death."

"So would I."

She needed a corner piece of the puzzle so she could start framing the problem. "What was his name?"

"John Night Horse."

ETHAN'S DREAMS WERE built on pieces of memory. He knew that now. There was a trail of crumbs locked inside his brain, and if he ever got hungry enough for the truth, all he had to do was gather those crumbs. He was in love with a woman who made her bones gathering crumbs.

And he couldn't get away from her fast enough.

Trouble was, he didn't know where to go. Truth was, he was getting hungry. Hungrier by the minute. It wasn't like he wanted to tell a story or solve a mystery or save anybody but himself. He just wanted to move on. He wanted to take what Logan called the red road—the good way—and he wanted to walk toward a dream, a good dream. He was tired of nightmares, tired of running away.

And so he ended up on his father's doorstep again.

"Did you forget something?"

He'd left Big Boy in Logan's pasture. He'd left the trailer. He'd left all of his training gear. But none of that was forgotten, and his father knew it. Logan could always tell when something needed to be said, even if half the time it never was. But that was Ethan's doing. Logan was always ready to listen.

"Yeah," Ethan said as he took a seat at the kitchen counter. The requisite coffee was being poured. "But I'm afraid it's coming back to me."

"Afraid?" Logan set the steaming cup of black coffee in front of him. *Pejuta sapa.* Brush up on your traditions, Bella kept telling him. He had grown up with Logan's traditions. Maybe more had sunk in than he'd realized.

"I won't be. If I can put it together, I think the fear will go away." He put his hands around the cup, comforted by the heat. "But you might not like it."

"Don't worry about me, Ethan. I have strong shoulders."

"I know. You're a good father. You always were." He glanced up. "You were a mother, too. You were both."

"I don't know about that. I could say I did my best, but, hell, I could've done better."

Ethan wasn't going to protest. Not now. He had to get the real stuff out before he lost his nerve.

"Did you know my mother was steppin' out on you?"

"I suspected." Logan sipped his coffee. "I should've known, but for a long time I didn't want to."

"Yeah, I know how that goes."

"You were so young," Logan said. "Did you…see something?"

"Yeah, I did. I saw lots of things that didn't seem right." Details. More than he wanted to dwell on. He had to stay on track. "I had to go with her sometimes. Got so I didn't want to, but I didn't want to make a fuss, either. I didn't want to make any trouble." He cleared an unmanly sting from his throat. "I didn't want to lose you."

"You…" Logan was beginning to struggle, too. He didn't want to show it any more than Ethan did. "She'd say she was going to Rapid or Pierre for something, and she was taking you. I didn't like it that she favored you over Trace, but you were younger than he was, so…" Logan drew a deep, unsteady breath. "And I told myself if she had you along, it had to be on the up-and-up, you know?"

Ethan nodded. They were gonna help each other out with this. Try not to look at each other too much. That would be rude.

"Where did she take you?" Logan asked.

"Hotels, sometimes. Parties at big houses. I'd sit in a room and watch TV." Ethan looked up at the ceiling and shook his head. "I couldn't tell you, but, *God,* I wanted you to make it stop."

"I'm sorry."

Ethan nodded. He took a quick drink, let the hot coffee burn his tongue and clear his throat. "I think I saw a man get killed."

"Wh-what?"

It wasn't like Logan to trip over a surprise.

Ethan nodded. "I just came from the Double D. Bella's got this whole political conspiracy theory she's trying to make a story out of, and, uh…" He gave an openhanded gesture to help pull the words out, keep the report going. "They got to talking about the Tribal leases and your father-in-law, and how he's trying to hang on to land he's been taking for granted because he's got Senator Garth on his side." He glanced at his father. "And you know I don't wanna hear nuthin' about Garth."

Logan nodded.

"Anyway, Hank lets on that his dad used to work for Tutan, and that he got killed. And he starts talking about these hunting parties Tutan used to put on for people like Garth. Political people. Powerful political people."

"What happened to Hank's father?"

"Well, Hank says his body was found on Tutan's property, all decayed and shot up. Tutan said he didn't know anything about it, so…case closed."

Logan grunted in disgust. "One of those federal murder investigations with an Indian corpse. No clues, no witnesses, no arrests."

"There *were* witnesses. And I wasn't the only one." He could feel the heat from Logan's shock, but he couldn't look up as he told him, "Mom was there, too."

He felt the familiar hand take hold of his shoulder. It gave him strength.

"I've been having dreams," he said. "I've had crazy dreams for years. Firecrackers scaring a flock of birds. A man standing up in the tall grass. Blood." He looked into his father's sympathetic eyes. "Lately the dreams have been showing me things I don't remember. But I know they happened. When Hank told us about his dad, I felt like I'd been there."

"Did you tell him?"

"No. It was just a feeling." He shook his head. "No, it's more than that, Dad. It's a fact."

A heavy moment passed.

"What do you want to do?" Logan asked quietly.

"I was just a kid. It was a long time ago. I don't think anyone'll believe me." Ethan sighed. He felt the pain of that day as keenly as he had twenty years ago.

"Where were you when all this happened?"

"I don't know exactly. She left me in the pickup. I think I got out."

"Damn. You could've been killed."

"She always told me that if I said anything about the parties, you'd send us away. She said we were just having fun." He rested his head in his hand, rubbed his forehead, trying to wipe some of the trouble away. "I was so glad when she left, I just put it out of my mind. All of it."

"I guess we all did."

"I gotta tell somebody." Ethan lifted his head. "Coming from me, it probably won't mean a hill of beans, but..."

"I'll be there."

"It ain't your story."

"But you're my son."

HE WANTED TO tell Hank first. He figured that would be the hardest, even with Logan there to stand by him, but it wasn't. Hank didn't doubt him, and he didn't hold it against him for keeping it to himself all these years. Ethan wondered how the man could take it all in without going off on somebody—or just going off.

"You weren't keeping it a secret," Hank said. "Your mind was protecting you."

"I don't know about that. Had a pretty thick head for

a while there. Nothing got through to me. But lately, the last, I don't know, ten years or so, things kept popping up. Something happens to get stuff going in my head at night."

"You've been through a lot in the past ten years," Logan said.

"The thing is, all that stuff makes me look like either a liar or a nutcase. Like I'm just trying to get back at Garth."

"That's for the law to figure out. We know what happened," Logan said.

"Yeah. The law," Ethan echoed.

"That's where the story goes next," Hank said.

"Before that, there's one more person." Ethan gave a dry chuckle. "And she's gonna want to run with the ball. I don't know how we'll prove it, but—"

"We don't have to prove anything," Hank said.

"He's right," Logan said. "We'll turn everything over to the FBI. They have to reopen the case. Get Tutan to talk. Track down everyone who was there."

"What if they find Mom?"

"One more mystery solved." Logan shrugged. "Hell, she deserted us, and we moved on. I divorced her. You grew up. We're on the Red Road." He smiled. "We've found women who know how to love us."

"You for sure. After this bombshell, I'm giving Bella some space."

"Do you want space?"

"I want…" Ethan looked his father in the eye. "I want Bella."

"My advice—and I know you haven't asked, but this is your need-to-know moment—is don't keep it to yourself. Tell her."

"So that's it," Ethan told Bella. She'd met him at Logan's place. He'd said he wanted to show her what they had done with Big Boy, and he did. There was something to be said for bringing the story full circle, bringing it home and showing her that he had done what she'd given him the confidence to do. He'd been truthful with his father. And then he'd been truthful with her. "Pretty far out there, isn't it?"

"It all fits together." She held out her cup to Logan for a refill. Kitchen, frybread, coffee. It was the traditional way. The family way. "You know I'm going to follow this thing as far as I can."

Ethan laughed. "You wouldn't be Warrior Woman if you didn't."

"And you know that if ever I was ahead of you, you just caught up."

No more laughter. Ethan saw the sincerity in her eyes, and he cherished it. He also knew it was true.

"Can I run the camera for you?" he asked. "Carry your water? Saddle your horse?"

"No horse," she said. "You're beautiful on horseback. I just want to watch you."

"Chauffeur you around, then."

"I have to be allowed to do something for *you*," she said sweetly.

"Translation," Ethan said, casting a glance his father's way. "Baby, you ain't gonna drive my car."

CHAPTER NINE

THE MAN AND the horse appeared to be having a little
tête-à-tête. Bella could see the man's lips moving as he
raked his fingers through the horse's lush mane. Ears
standing at attention, the mustang bobbed his head once.
After a few more words from the man, the regal buckskin gave his head a quick shake, and the man laughed
softly.

She slowed her pace as she approached the corral,
thinking this must be the way a woman felt when she
happened upon her man patiently sharing a teachable
moment with their child. She wanted to turn into a fly
and light on the fence post.

But she also wanted to be herself and be welcomed
with open arms.

"Are you two planning your strategy for tomorrow?"
she asked as she let herself in through the corral gate.

Ethan turned quickly, his eyes betraying his surprise.
He glanced down at her feet. "You walkin' on cat's paws,
woman?"

Bella grinned as she planted her right heel in the
dirt, toe pointed skyard to show off her blindingly white
walking tennies. "You like my new sneak-up shoes?"

"New boots, new tennies—you got a thing for shoes?"

"The boots hurt."

"They're not made for walking, honey. That ain't

the way to break 'em in." He turned his shoulder to the horse, who then followed him across the corral. "'Course, jumpin' out of my pickup on the fly was a damn good way to break me in. Learned my lesson on takin' *no* for Bella's answer." He rewarded Big Boy with his left hand as he took Bella under his arm on the right.

And she was right where she wanted to be.

"Then it was worth the blisters on my feet."

He glanced down again. "You got blisters?"

"Lessons all around." She slipped her arm around his waist. "Logan just left to pick up his wife at the airport."

"We're alone." He gave her a come-on look.

She glanced up at Big Boy. "How's your strategy coming?"

"So far, so good, now that we've got the place all to ourselves."

"How does that help you win the training competition?"

"Oh, that." He scratched the horse's neck. "We're set, aren't we, Big Boy?"

Big Boy bobbed his head, and they both laughed as the horse snorted and walked away.

"Actually, he's all set. But I need a little encouragement." Ethan turned to her, smiling. The shade from his hat brim fell over her face. "Encourage me."

The back of his neck felt warm under her hand, his hair soft between her fingers. She drew his head down and embraced the surge of female power as she kissed him.

Its effect shone in his eyes. He looked dazed for an instant, but then he took charge and pulled up another alluring smile. "You wanna go inside? Just painted my old bedroom. We could break in the new carpet."

She drew back, answering with a saucy smile of her own. "I don't want to do it in a room full of baby furniture."

"Do what?"

"Give you rug burn."

He chuckled. "No furniture yet. Mary gets to pick that out."

"Still," she said, glancing toward the barn, "I'd be imagining baby furniture. I'd prefer a nice haystack."

He groaned as he took her hand and walked her back to the gate. "Now you've got me thinking baby, nursery, 'Little Boy Blue.' Some encouragement."

"I do my best." She looked up at him. "Hank called me after he met with an FBI field agent at the Rapid City office. They're taking your story seriously."

"You call that your best?"

"They're reopening the case."

"No kidding? Actually digging up the whole thing?" He was genuinely surprised. Skeptical of the kind of reception he might get for his twenty-year-old recollection, he'd gone to the regional FBI office on his own. Sure enough, the agent he'd talked to hadn't seemed too impressed, but he'd taken down all the names Ethan could come up with, along with the dates he'd figured out since he'd put his memory together with Hank's story.

Names, dates and forensics were the facts the agent had said he could check out. A long-buried memory was a little dicey.

What about a long-buried Indian and an unsolved murder? Ethan wanted to know. But he hadn't asked. He wouldn't risk being taken for a smart-ass. Never again. Especially not by a cop.

The agent had said he would be in touch, so Ethan

bit his tongue while he offered a handshake. And since that meeting, he sure hadn't been holding his breath. He figured he'd done what he could. But it wasn't until he'd called Bella and then Hank to let them know what he'd done that he felt relieved of a burden he didn't know he'd been carrying.

"I don't know what they'll dig up besides the evidence that's been in storage all these years, but they will search for your mother," Bella said. "And they'll question Dan Tutan and Senator Garth."

"You think it's too late?"

"It's never too late. Murder will out." She gave his hand a quick squeeze. "Eventually."

"Here's one for you." He squeezed back as he opened the gate with his free hand. "'Justice is the constant and perpetual will to allot every man his due.'"

"Oh, I like that." She slid past him and through the gate he held open for her. "Who said it?"

"Some old Roman. I memorized it during my trial. It was on the wall of the courtroom." He closed the gate behind them and turned to her, smiling. "I like it, too. Put it in Warrior Woman's pipe and let her smoke it."

"I hope John Night Horse gets his due. Even if nobody goes to jail, let the truth be told. Let's get it out there."

"That's your job." He glanced past her. Between Bella and the horse standing in the corral behind her he'd found new purpose for his hard-earned freedom. "My job is to show the truth about Big Boy. Let people see what his kind can do."

"I thought your job was to win the big prize."

"That, too," he said with a wink. Keep it light, he told himself. He didn't want her to think he was counting on the money. It was more about the recognition and how he could use it—along with his education—to neutralize at least one of the strikes he had against him.

Okay, the money would help, too.

He glanced toward their two vehicles, parked side by side. The Square One horse trailer was hitched to his pickup. The boys had painted his name on it, along with a big horseshoe and something that was supposed to be a wolf's paw print but looked more like a high five. Ethan had assured them that it worked either way.

"You wanna hang around and meet my new mom, or should we do the decent thing and get out of their way?"

"I forgot to tell you. They're staying in Rapid City tonight. Logan said to tell you he'll be back in time for the show tomorrow." Bella stepped out ahead of him and turned, smiling, her hand still in his. "And so will I."

"You're not goin' anywhere. I need you with me." With a firm tug he reeled her back and drew her into his arms. "Tonight." He gave her a quick kiss. "Tomorrow."

"If we rule out hay wisps and rug burns, that leaves your father's—"

"We're getting a room."

The hotel at the tribal casino had one vacancy left. The desk clerk told Ethan that this was going be his lucky night and asked what game he would be playing.

"I didn't get lucky 'til I quit gambling," Ethan told the young man. He thought he'd sounded pretty damn clever until Bella mentioned cowboy poker while they were waiting for the elevator. As soon the doors closed he planted a kiss on that smart mouth of hers that left her breathless. He could tell by the way she was looking at him when the doors opened. She didn't seem to no-

tice the guy who gave him a thumbs-up as they stepped
off the elevator.

"You won big, huh? Slots or tables?"

"Horses," Ethan quipped.

"Bet on the buckskin," Bella added, all dreamy-eyed.

"ARE YOU NERVOUS about the competition?" she asked
gently.

They'd made love twice—once like hungry young
lovers who couldn't get enough, once like deliberate, devoted admirers who took it slow and still couldn't quite
get enough. They'd lain in each other's arms, stirring
now and then to touch and be touched, until she tried
to feign sleep in the hope that he could get some rest. It
didn't work for either of them. "I'm pumped," he said
after a while and pressed a kiss into her hair. "I don't
mean to keep you awake."

She gave a soft, pleasured sound. "I'm pretty pumped
myself."

"Win or lose, I feel good about Big Boy," he said
quietly. "He's in peak condition—nothin' prettier than
a lineback buckskin—and he handles like a precision-
tuned race car. Better, even. A car's got no heart. Big
Boy...size, color, speed, all that's a bonus. Big Boy has
heart." He drew a deep breath and blew it out quickly.
"Yep. I like our chances."

"You can't lose, Ethan. Even if someone else wins."

"I guess everyone who makes it to the show has the
right to feel that way. Sally said a couple of them brought
the horses back and dropped out." He chuckled. "And
then there's my dad, who pulled his horse from the competition so he wouldn't have to give him up. Gave him
to his wife."

"You won't mind giving up Big Boy?"

"Sure, I'll mind. But he's gonna sell high, bring in some serious money for the program."

He took her snuggling against him as his cue to slip his arm beneath her head so she could pillow it on his shoulder. She imagined his thoughts bouncing around wildly in his head, tumbling into the back of his throat and onto his tongue.

"And you can't just walk off with one of these mustangs without meeting Sally's requirements," he continued. "Actually, the BLM's requirements, but you gotta deal with Sally, and she's got her own smell test."

She smiled to herself, because it was dark and only she knew how deeply she was into him. "Could you pass it?"

"You kiddin'? Not even gonna try. I don't let just any woman get this close to my armpit, you know."

"It's your shoulder I want." An understatement.

"The armpit is like the shoulder's underbelly. Can't have one without the other. But you gotta admit, I clean up pretty good." He gave a deep chuckle. "I'm workin' on it, anyway."

"You don't have to convince me." She turned her head and kissed the closest part of him. Warm skin and hard muscle. "I have a crush on you."

"I'll see your crush and raise you…" He groaned. "Hell, I'm all in, Bella. I'm crazy about you."

"You're raising my crush with your crazy?"

"Yeah." He touched her temple, tucked her hair behind ear and whispered, "I'm crazy in love with you."

She felt light-headed, the rest of her body whooshing out from under her the way it did when she neared the edge of a high place. She didn't even have to look down. She could feel the fall coming.

Stay focused, she told herself. "Is the crazy part the underbelly?"

"Does that scare you?"

"No." She was no liar, but how could she say she wasn't scared? On the other hand, how could she say anything else?

Except maybe that she loved him right back.

"If it ever does, I want you to walk away. I mean that." He kissed the top of her head. "We need time to figure this out. I've never been in love before. Crazy, yes, but love? Uh-uh."

"I don't think I have, either. Unless it's the same as a crush that never went away."

"Maybe that's the underbelly for you, huh? The seed? Maybe we can make it grow."

She had only to lift her head, and he met her halfway for a kiss.

"I like our chances," she whispered.

MUSTANG SALLY'S WILD HORSE Makeover Horse Show was held at the Sinte rodeo grounds. It was a beautiful, warm autumn day, and the grandstand was packed. Sally Night Horse and her sister, Ann, were in charge of the program. Sally insisted on being called *Master* of Ceremonies—never *mistress*. Ann didn't need a title. She was the detail person. Their husbands were busy moving the show along. When Hank spotted Ethan saddling Big Boy on the shady side of the horse trailer, he took a quick detour, his beautiful yellow Lab, Phoebe, in tow.

"Did you see your brother's horse perform?" Hank asked.

"He looked good, didn't he?"

"Not as good as the rider. Skyler's got a nice seat."

Ethan patted the dog's silky head and grinned. "I'll tell Trace you said so."

"Just don't tell my wife."

Bella stuck her head out the pickup window. "I don't think your wife has anything to worry about."

"No, but I do," Hank said. "Sally has a nice seat, too. Plus a bottomless sleeve full of tricks. Remind me to tell you how we met sometime."

"Can I put that tidbit in my story?" Bella brandished her camera.

"Oh, no. It's not for prime time."

"Sounds like just the kind of anecdote that could help me sell the story."

"Please don't tell Sally that." He glanced up at the crow's nest next to the ring and waved. Sally waved back. "I swear, that woman's ears are better than Phoebe's."

And then the atmosphere changed. Hank shifted, turned slowly and offered Ethan a solemn handshake. "I want to thank you."

Ethan looked down at their clasped hands. "It might not come to anything. You know, legally."

"It's already come to something for us, hasn't it?" Hank laid his hand on Ethan's shoulder. "Some people call it closure. I don't see it that way. The truth opened us up. That's the way I feel."

"So do I."

Hank lifted his chin in Big Boy's direction. "You've got a winner there."

Ethan nodded.

"HEY, ETHAN!"

He turned toward the familiar voice. Big Bongo and bigmouth Demsey. Trouble and more trouble, and damned if he wasn't glad to see them. "Who turned you two loose?"

"We're all here," Dempsey said. "Shelly brought us on the bus. She told us not to bother you before the show, but we just wanted to…"

Bongo stuck out a beefy hand. "…wish you luck."

Ethan shook Bongo's hand and ruffled Dempsey's spiky hair. Out of the corner of his eye he noticed that Bella had her camera going again, but he didn't flinch. He was getting used to having her lens pointed his way.

"He needs an oil change," Bongo said.

Ethan laughed. He was up next, and a good laugh was just what he needed.

HE WAS MAGIC. Bella didn't know much about horses, but Big Boy's rider was unrivaled. As long as the judges weren't deducting points for battered cowboy hats, Ethan had first place in the bag.

"I want that horse," the man standing beside her said.

Bella spared him a quick glance. "Trace. I didn't see you there."

"Hard to take your eyes off him, isn't it?"

"Yes, it is." Ethan was putting the horse through a series of reining patterns, seemingly effortlessly.

"We're talking about the buckskin, right?"

Bella had no more glances to spare, but she did smile.

"You think he'd mind if I got in on the bidding?" he asked.

"We're talking about Ethan, right?"

Trace laughed.

"I can't think of anything that would please him more."

AFTER ALL THE riders had shown, the trainers were asked to bring the horses back into the arena and chat up prospective buyers while the judges conferred. Bella covered the activity with her camera. She was charmed by Mark Banyon, the young son of a local teacher named Celia, who had no intention of letting the horse he'd named Flyboy go to just anyone. An interview with the horse's trainer, who introduced himself simply as Cougar, served to reassure her that a disabled veteran's group would be bidding on the horse, and God help anyone who tried to run up the bidding. He and Mark would have easy access to Flyboy, who was destined to become the centerpiece of the therapy program that had enabled Cougar to "rejoin the living" after recovering from his war injuries.

"And if you want a fairytale finale for your story," Cougar told Bella as he reached for Mark's mother's hand, "you can bring your camera to our wedding."

"As long as we get copies of all the pictures," Celia said.

"As long as I can bring a date." Bella nodded toward Ethan, who was chatting up his "new mom" on the other side of the arena.

"That guy?" Cougar smiled and shook his head. "Big showboater, that guy. I don't believe that horse was ever wild. Pretty sure that's a ringer you see there."

Bella returned the smile. "I'm pretty sure Ethan's the best there is."

Cougar laughed. "For a free wedding video I won't argue."

Bella made her way across the arena, pausing here and there for a still shot before sneaking up behind her man of the hour. One thing she'd learned by making the rounds to gather her story was that Big Boy was a big hit, even among Ethan's competitors.

Logan extended his hand. "Bella, come meet my wife."

Ethan turned quickly, smiling when their eyes met. "I gotta get me some of those sneak-up shoes," he said.

"It's not the shoes," Bella assured him as she took her place in the circle. "It's the Lakota blood. Be prepared to jump out of your skin at least once a week, Mary." She offered Logan's wife a handshake, and then she automatically glanced at her emerging baby bump.

Mary's hand went to her stomach, completing the wordless acknowledgment between women.

Logan clapped a hand on Ethan's shoulder. "You were tired of being the baby, weren't you, son?"

"I'll gladly turn that role over," he agreed. "Is it too late to order up a sister?"

"I've decided to keep us all in suspense," Mary said. "I like the idea of letting the baby surprise us."

"Speaking of surprises…" Logan nodded toward the crow's nest. "Looks like our master of ceremonies has something to tell us."

SALLY STARTED OUT with an order.

"Everyone clear the arena except the trainers and their horses. I'm just as anxious as anybody else, so step lively, folks. I've got some introductions to make, and then we'll get the results from the judges."

Bella looked up at Ethan, smiled, and turned to follow everyone else who'd been excused.

"Oh, wait." Sally's voice boomed. "Everyone except the press."

Bella looked up. Sally nodded. "I don't care whose girlfriend you are, you're still the press."

It took all of about two minutes to empty out the arena. Bella took some footage of the lineup while Zach's brother, Sam, was introduced as the donor of the grand prize. He gave credit to his daughter, Star, who had inherited a winning lottery ticket after her mother's death. Sam didn't mention the source of the money, but Bella knew the story.

Next came the introduction of the judges, who were well-known in the horse world and included an Olympic champion, a man who'd trained horses for the movies, another who trained for the Royal Canadian Mounted Police and a stock show champion. The mustangs had been trained for various styles of riding and different kinds of work or sport. They would prove that mustangs made fine mounts. Their story would bring support for the Double D Wild Horse Sanctuary and for the preservation of the American wild horse.

And the auction would bring much-needed cash to the program. But the auction wouldn't start until the winner was announced, and the microphone was suddenly silent. Those in the arena pretended to ignore the crow's nest. They turned to each other, exchanged a few comments, laughed nervously.

Bella took more video, and then she sidled up to Ethan. He needed some distraction. "Have you met Cougar?" she asked. "The one with that gorgeous Paint."

"You like Paints?" He rubbed his buckskin's cheek. "Don't worry, boy. She's no judge."

"Cougar's an army vet, too. He trained Flyboy to be a service horse. You know, for therapy."

"I saw that. That's some fine work. I could get into that kind of work."

"Yes, you could."

He gave her a tight smile. "I've got a ways to go, though, haven't I?"

"Time or distance?" She slipped her hand into his and gave a quick squeeze. "Either way, I'm right beside you."

Ethan turned to her, and for a moment everything around them receded. He didn't care where he was or what else was going on. Wherever, whatever, Bella was with him. All was right with the world, and he told her so with a wink and a smile.

There was movement in the crow's nest. The Night Horses appeared first. Then the Zach Beaudrys. Then the Sam Beaudrys. And finally the judges.

"Here comes the announcement," Bella said.

"And the twenty-thousand dollar award for the best mustang trainer in the first annual Mustang Sally's Wild Horse Makeover Horse Show goes to..."

Ethan kept his cool when his name was called, but Bella did not. Her kiss would have shocked her public. The details of her whispered promise of a private celebration set his ear aflame. His sober, sensible, traditional Bella nearly knocked him off his feet.

For the second time.

And he was damn sure it wouldn't be the last.

* * * * *

She had hopes, high hopes. She wanted to hear him say
he'd taken one look at her and felt the same way she
had: here was someone he wanted to get to know better.
Someone attractive, appealing—even sexy.

But the moment passed. Then another. He studied the
darkness beyond their little pool of light. "You never
leave someone behind in battle. Never."

Not sexy. Kind of grim, actually.

"Were you in the military?" she asked.

"Yes. Were you?"

"No." But there was a compliment in there. It wasn't
sexy, but it was something. "No one's ever asked me that
before. What makes you think I might have served in the
military?"

He didn't answer her.

She wanted to see his smile again. She nudged him with her shoulder. "Come on, tell me. Was it my fabulous driving skills? Do you think I'd be good at driving a tank, or what?"

His smile returned briefly. "That wasn't your first time off-roading."

"I couldn't call myself a Texan if I'd never taken a truck off-road."

She wanted to touch him. She'd already stood in the warmth of his arms. Heck, he'd already had his hand on her rear end twice, even if both times had been during an escape.

Fortune favors the brave. Those had been the man's own words.

"You want to know why I thought you might be in the military?" She dared to reach up and touch the back of his neck, the clean skin above his collar. She let her fingers comb through the short hair at the back of his head. "It wasn't this haircut. It's short, but not as short as the soldiers from Fort Hood."

"I'm a civilian now. A regulation haircut would be too…unnecessary." He didn't shake her off or step away, but he didn't touch her in return, either, except with his gaze.

She let her hand slip over his shoulder lightly before falling away. "I'll tell you what gave it away. It was the way you ordered me to get back in the truck. Do they teach you to bark out orders in that tone of voice? It's scary as hell."

"It didn't work on you." He grumbled those words, which made her smile.

"I'm stubborn like that, and I already know it's not a good trait. I hear about it from my family all the time."

She pushed away from the door and turned to face him—which meant she stepped over his crossed ankles with one foot and stood in her minidress with her legs a little way apart, his boots between hers. The night air was cold on her inner thighs. "But I didn't bark out any orders like a military man, so what made you think I might have served? Come on, talk to me." She gestured toward the red and blue glow on the horizon. "We can't go anywhere, anyway. Was it my haircut?"

She was joking, of course, but her laughter faded at the intensity of his gaze. She couldn't look away, not even when he turned his attention from her eyes to her hair, somewhere near her temple. Her ear. Slowly, so slowly, his gaze followed the length of her hair as it lay on her shoulder, as it curved over her breast, as it disappeared in the open edge of his coat, near her hip.

She wanted him. He was leaning against his vehicle, arms crossed, ankles crossed, not moving a muscle, setting her on fire with a look.

"There's nothing military about your hair," he said quietly, and he looked back up to her eyes. "It was your head. You keep a cool head."

"A cool head." She breathed in cold air, willing herself to say something, to do something, although her thoughts weren't cool at all. "That's it?"

"That's not all that common." He pushed away from the door and stood before her, a little too close, and not nearly close enough. "You also didn't leave your ex and his friends behind, even though they didn't deserve your help."

Kiss me, kiss me.

But the man didn't move an inch closer. "They were lucky. If I hadn't wanted to dance with you so badly, I would have gotten you out of there before trouble started, and they wouldn't have had you around to bail them out."

Wait—what? To heck with her ex and the fight. "You wanted to dance with me?"

"The second that band played anything remotely resembling a slow song. I ignored the beginnings of that fight, because I wanted to see if the band would play something we could dance to. It's the only way to touch a woman you barely know without being too…"

"Handsy?" Dear God, she sounded breathless. She was breathless.

"That's the word."

He'd wanted to touch her from the start. This insane chemistry was the same for both of them.

He didn't reach for her now. Why didn't he reach for her?

"So dancing is an acceptable way to touch a woman you just met." She kept her voice low in the dark.

"Right."

"And we decided keeping someone warm when it's cold out is allowed."

"True." He didn't move.

"Graham." Emily put her palm on his chest and tilted her face up to his. "It's cold out."

Don't miss
How to Train a Cowboy *by Caro Carson,*
available now wherever
Harlequin® *Special Edition books and ebooks are sold.*

www.Harlequin.com

HARLEQUIN®

SPECIAL EDITION

Life, Love and Family

Save **$1.00**

on the purchase of ANY

Harlequin® Special Edition book.

Available whever books are sold,
including most bookstores, supermarkets,
drugstores and discount stores.

✂ - ✂

Save **$1.00**

on the purchase of any Harlequin® Special Edition book.

Coupon valid until September 30, 2018.
Redeemable at participating outlets in the U.S. and Canada only.
Limit one coupon per customer.

52615825

Canadian Retailers: Harlequin Enterprises Limited will pay the face value of this coupon plus 10.25¢ if submitted by customer for this product only. Any other use constitutes fraud. Coupon is nonassignable. Void if taxed, prohibited or restricted by law. Consumer must pay any government taxes. Void if copied. Inmar Promotional Services ("IPS") customers submit coupons and proof of sales to Harlequin Enterprises Limited, P.O. Box 31000, Scarborough, ON M1R 0E7, Canada. Non-IPS retailer—for reimbursement submit coupons and proof of sales directly to Harlequin Enterprises Limited, Retail Marketing Department, 22 Adelaide St. West, 40th Floor, Toronto, Ontario M5H 4E3, Canada.

5 65373 00076 2 (8100)0 12373

U.S. Retailers: Harlequin Enterprises Limited will pay the face value of this coupon plus 8¢ if submitted by customer for this product only. Any other use constitutes fraud. Coupon is nonassignable. Void if taxed, prohibited or restricted by law. Consumer must pay any government taxes. Void if copied. For reimbursement submit coupons and proof of sales directly to Harlequin Enterprises, Ltd 482, NCH Marketing Services, P.O. Box 880001, El Paso, TX 88588-0001, U.S.A. Cash value 1/100 cents.

® and ™ are trademarks owned and used by the trademark owner and/or its licensee.

© 2018 Harlequin Enterprises Limited

HSEHOTRCOUP0718

Looking for more satisfying love stories
with community and family at their core?

Check out **Harlequin® Special Edition**
and **Love Inspired®** books!

New books available every month!

CONNECT WITH US AT:

Facebook.com/groups/HarlequinConnection

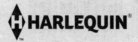 Facebook.com/HarlequinBooks

Twitter.com/HarlequinBooks

Instagram.com/HarlequinBooks

Pinterest.com/HarlequinBooks

ReaderService.com

⊞HARLEQUIN®

**ROMANCE WHEN
YOU NEED IT**

HFGENRE2018

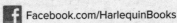

Reward the book lover in you!

Earn points on your purchase of new Harlequin books from participating retailers.

Turn your points into **FREE BOOKS** of your choice!

Join for FREE today at **www.HarlequinMyRewards.com.**

Harlequin My Rewards is a free program (no fees) without any commitments or obligations.